DEMON'S THE GRAVE

BOOK ONE

E.M. MacCallum

Printed in Canada

First Printing, 2015

Edited by Matthew Baugh, Lori Titus & Jessica Meigs

Cover Art: Amygdaladesign.net

ISBN 978-0-9947782-1-5

www.emmaccallum.com

DEDICATION

To my family. You were my beta-readers, my encouragement, and my butt-kickers. Thank you

PROLOGUE

Each syllable of her practiced incantation was perfect to her ears.

Years she had dedicated herself to those words. Being the only one of the three who could perform it, it was probably the only reason she was still alive.

Kneeling before the giant bonfire in the forest's clearing, the dark-haired woman tilted her chin up. The blood tickled her cheekbone as her eyes met the gluttonous flames, reflecting their need.

With a slow, careful hand, she wiped the blood free, fearing that any sudden movement could shatter the rising power. The little brat had cut into her eyelid but, thankfully, not her eye. The cut didn't bother her as much as the self-made one in her hand. It stung as she pressed it into the thirsty earth, inviting the otherworldly presence.

Behind her, the incessant protests from the brothers dissolved to silence. They felt it. They must have. The air was heavy, a warning. Something nefarious slithered in the dark, something they couldn't see.

She suppressed a shudder, and her voice rose above the popping flames. Her excitement bristled the hairs on her arms, making her insides shiver.

She wasn't sure if it was the adrenaline or the raw power that made her teeth want to chatter and her bones rattle against muscle and flesh. She wanted to scream, run, fuck, and kill all in the same instant, but she had to bottle it up, let it rattle her bones until she passed out. Part of her thought she could pass out in the surge.

A stifling presence swelled, snuffing out the world's influences until the night transformed into something frighteningly still.

Even the frogs and crickets ceased. They waited and listened. She could sense the anticipation.

She felt the sacred vibrations all around her. A false move, voice, or intention could shatter it. She adored it like a warm bath on a cold day or food on an empty stomach.

It had been years of waiting, yearning, and pleading with the world to see this moment unfold.

The pains her body endured were paltry compared to this—compared to him.

One of the brothers attempted to speak.

Hissing through her teeth, she glared over her shoulder.

The taller man's jaw shut with an audible click of teeth. Doubt shadowed his rigid features, and he looked to his smaller, more violent brother.

The second man with flaming orange hair clasped his knees to catch his breath and was looking up at the flames, then to her. The Devil lived in that one. He must have felt the earth speak to them. Not at the same level as she, of course, but he must have sensed it.

The more ruthless of her two tormenters remained quiet, knowing what he'd done.

His mistake earlier could have botched the entire ritual. If the ritual had failed, she knew he wouldn't pay for it; she would. She'd waited too long for this moment and suffered too much to allow that now.

Fear got the better of her, and she whispered through the silence, quivering the thickened air. "If you screwed this up because you can't catch a kid, you'll pay." The idea spawned a physical pain in her chest. Frustrated with the emotions, she twisted the heartache into something she could comprehend: anger.

The redhead smirked as if it were the most amusing thing she'd said all day. She was no match for him physically—he had demonstrated that on more than one occasion—but this time would be different.

Stillness gave way to a chill. His chill...no, his power. Despite being so near the fire, she felt like there was ice in her veins.

He was closer.

She gripped the black, leather-bound book to her chest and felt the power disturbing the air.

She hardly felt the howling wind above, though she could see it twisting the tip of the bonfire in a fiery vortex.

According to her book, the flames acted as a conduit between the two worlds.

Her partners shouted in alarm, and she smiled inwardly.

They were fools, always bossing her around, thinking her inferior. The bruises on her arms and legs would fade, and so would her memories of them. She doubted she would even think of them after tonight.

"What is this?" a mellifluous voice that might as well have pulled her into an embrace, whispered at her. He asked only her, not them, but *her*.

For a split second, she forgot to breathe.

She gasped, and the exhilaration wracking her limbs shuddered through her voice. He was here at last, he was with her, he came after all the grueling work and sacrifice. This had been a moment she feared she might only experience in her imagination. She wanted to exclaim, "*It's you!*" but knew better. This demon wouldn't want praise even if she fell to the ground weeping.

Swallowing the nervous bile in the back of her throat, she called out. "Do you like her?" The confidence ringing in her voice surprised her. Her insides were a sloshing muck in comparison.

"I wanted the other one," he answered in obvious displeasure.

She listened to his voice echo in her head and tried to memorize it, to capture it.

She searched the bonfire, wanting to see him. *Those idiots*, she thought. *There were only two. I'd told them which one to sacrifice, and what do they do? They could have ruined everything!*

Breaking from her composure, she protested. "She couldn't have gone far. I can find—"

"You're wasting my time." His abrupt tone straightened her spine.

For the first time since initiating the ritual, she felt a hint of fear. "I did not mean to. Please, what may I—"

"You sacrificed the wrong one."

"I sacrificed her for *you*," she answered, lifting her hands pleadingly. She knew running back to find the other child would take too long. The portal would close in a few minutes.

Shaking dirt off her fingertips, she cleared her throat.

This was her last gateway to a better place, she reminded herself. "I want to join you in the Demon's Grave," she blurted in painful desperation.

The air was growing thinner, less vibrant, less…magical.

Dread wriggled inside of her as the silence stretched—ached.

On the verge of panic, she hoped he hadn't abandoned her. "You can choose your Neophyte. I asked the Keeper from this realm, and he confirmed this rule." Her heart fluttered like a trapped butterfly. "I wish to leave this world and join you. Choose me!"

She heard her two partners behind her protesting, but she couldn't make out the words. She didn't care what they had to say. They were dead to her one way or the other.

"Please!" she implored the darkness. He couldn't be gone already; the heaviness of his power lingered despite the dilution around her. It was like stepping out of a pool. Air wasn't as thick as water, and this was beautiful, a hot spring of power.

"No other could have summoned you." She spoke so fast that her words melted together. "Only one with demon's blood could." She slapped her bloodied hand against her stomach, attempting to calm the chaos.

"This is true," the tenebrous tone said, smothering her anxiety. She hadn't lost him after all. Despite the comfort, she couldn't stop shaking; her entire body rippled with raw emotion.

She tried to smile, her lips twitching with the effort. "As a gift rather than a sacrifice, I present these two." She glanced over her shoulder at the brothers.

Standing side by side, several feet back, they stared, dumbfounded. She savored the realization dawning on their faces.

"What?" the taller brother snapped, anger darkening his stubbed face. "You…"

"I accept," the melodic voice interrupted.

Hearing the demon, the two went rigid.

Flushing with pride, she turned back to the lowering flames. Their time was almost up.

The brothers didn't scream. A strangled gurgle was all she heard before she knew that *he* had taken them. He had accepted her gift, heard her plea. The few powers she retained in this world would expand tenfold within the Demon's Grave, with him.

A shiver of delight rocked her as she tried to stand before the bonfire. "Take me as your Neophyte," she demanded, her knees threatening to disobey her body.

Within the darkness on the other side of the blaze, his voice had grown fainter. "No."

At first, she didn't believe what she'd heard. She hesitated, staring into the flames, masking the confused betrayal as best as she could. "You said, 'Yes.'"

"I agreed that you had demon blood in you, diluted as it may be."

Anger scorched her throat, and her fingers curled into fists. "I brought you here. I gave you gifts and a sacrifice of equal blood." At the mention of blood, she wiped the stinging cut in her eyelid again, smearing it across her cheekbone and into her hairline.

"No, your sacrifice was not of equal blood. I didn't want that child. I made it clear. The other was a better choice."

She had dedicated the last seven years of her life to this moment. She had endured pain, torture, beatings; she had murdered for him. During all of it, she had one comfort: that he would take her as his Neophyte.

All the psychic signs, meditations, and even the spirits she corralled confessed this to be true.

She shifted her weight, afraid she might collapse. His presence receded. She tasted blood the moment her teeth dislodged from the wet divots left in her lips. The sharp pain was almost a pleasant distraction.

"I killed that child for you," she called, as if this scratch in her already tarnished soul would make a difference to a demon.

"Thoughtful, but not accurate," he said, sounding amused at her pain.

Hearing his apathetic tone made her hatred boil. "What about me?!" Her voice echoed in the clearing. *Me-me-me-me.*

The gravity of the supernatural magic disappeared. In an instant, the flames were extinguished, leaving her cold and alone.

She flexed her fingers in denial, waiting for the presence to return. The pain was nothing compared to the heat that resonated from her chest, the twisted pain that brought tears to her eyes.

The leaves rippled behind her in the wind. The frogs, crickets, and any other nocturnal creatures resumed their songs as if nothing had happened.

Mental screams rang in her ears, the words

repeating themselves like a broken record. *What about me? What about me? What about me?*

Falling to her knees, Nell stared at the smoldering embers and watched smoky tendrils curl toward the moon. She pondered searching through the blackened pile of wood, hay, and ingredients for the bones of the dead child. Part of her wanted to try and summon him again, but she couldn't move. She knew he wouldn't come again.

The blood from the cut in her eyelid dribbled through her lashes, stinging her eye, and still she didn't move.

CHAPTER ONE

I hadn't written the note, but it was undoubtedly my handwriting.

Spine bowed with the weight of my backpack, I raised the torn, lined paper to my face again. My sweaty fingertips already softening the edges of the note.

The detail was uncanny. The little 'e's that looked like 'c's and the cursive mixed with print. Hell, I'd know those fat 'D's that Read described as 'butts' anywhere.

I frowned at the words: *Dismal is the Demon's Grave.*

*Dismal and dark...*I thought, unsure why.

The note had been masquerading as a bookmark in my *Writing for the Media* textbook, I knew it couldn't have been there for more than a day. With finals looming I kept all of my books close.

I sidestepped, narrowly avoiding a head-on collision with a fellow college student.

There was something familiar about those words,

nearly tangible. I'd initially ignored the note, but the words were tacky, adhering to the inside of my skull.

Ahead, a whizzing sound overrode the hallway's raucous din. I looked up in time to see the greasy-haired skateboarder bearing down on me.

Instead of looking ahead, he was distracted by a bouncy, busty girl in a tank top.

My joints locked and for a split second I forgot to move.

It seemed everyone else had moved to the side of the hallway, except me.

At the last second, I blurted a high pitched warning. He jerked his head up and our eyes locked. Arms windmilling, he leaned back on the board to stop.

Stumbling sideways, I avoided the collision by a hair. He pushed into my backpack, knocking me into a girl who screamed before hitting the locker.

"Oh crap," I sputtered, ready to apologize.

Glaring, she started to say something when the skateboarder's string of curses drew everyone's attention. Pivoting to face me, his skeletal cheeks scarlet. "Will you watch where you're going? I had the right of way, goddamn it!"

"What the…" I shrugged my backpack farther up my shoulder to stall as my mind reeled at the absurd accusation. "Where *I* was going?" I demanded. "You're skateboarding in a busy college hallway, jerkface!"

Straightening his oversized red shirt he said. "Yeah, until you jumped out in front of me; right in the *middle* of the fuckin' hallway."

If I hadn't been close to the wall, I would have staggered back into it. The jerk really thought this was all my fault.

Before I could think up a retort the skater boy tucked his board under his arm. "Next time maybe pay attention to shit outside of your preppy little world, bitch." He brushed the greased hair from his face.

"No…" I started and realized my argument would be about as useful as my kid sister saying, 'no you.'

My face burned and my fists curled the note into my palm.

Over the skater boy's shoulder, I saw Phoebe Williams' glossy, honey hair. My friend wiggled through a pair of girls, snapping. "WTF, move will you?!"

She was the familiar face I needed to see.

"Hey," Phoebe nodded to me and glanced at the greasy guy, then back to me. "What's going on?"

Two against one and the second being far taller, leaner and scarier, the skater-boy shrugged. "It's nothin'. I don't need some PMS breakdown. I'm outta here." Pivoting, he stalked off like he'd won the argument.

Phoebe shouted after him. "Come back anytime you're not afraid, Olive Oyl."

I was too busy turning to apologize to the girl I knocked into to see if he reacted, but she'd already disappeared.

Straightening, I tried to regain some composure despite hearing someone in the crowd say, "Aw man, that would have been a hilarious wipe out."

"What was that all about?" Phoebe asked again. "I was going to tell you all about a stupid nightmare I had last night and here you are starting scenes again. This cry for attention isn't healthy, you know." She smirked.

Squeezing the note in my hand so she wouldn't see, I said, "I orchestrated the perfect equation leading to a crash. Him on the skateboard plus me daydreaming equals..." I made a exploding sound with my lips and knocked my fists together.

"I don't know if being a reporter is your calling. You might be meant for the movies, Nora. Those visual effects were riveting."

"Shaadup. What are you doing at this end of the school anyway?"

Phoebe's classes were often in another building entirely.

"Waiting for Aidan. He said he'd give me a ride home."

I cringed inwardly, hoping it didn't show.

"He should be here any minute."

I shook my head and blurted, "He's nowhere close now."

"How would you know?" Phoebe scanned the crowd.

Don't tell her, it's stupid and she won't believe you. I shrugged.

Phoebe flashed pearly teeth that were almost too big for her mouth. "Almost didn't recognize you with the new hair."

"Does it look like toasted coconut to you?" I asked. I twisted the ponytail around my fist to show Phoebe.

"It looks like hair," Phoebe replied. "You look really weird as a blonde. Just sayin'."

"I needed a distraction from all this studying. Toasted coconut seemed like a good idea at the time."

Together we joined the flow of the crowd of college students. It wasn't hard to notice that people were getting ready to take off. Most classes would have ended or were about to and the hallways were growing thicker with bodies.

Phoebe had one of her sideways smirks. "We need to get you a guy so you're not prone to toasted coconut on a weekend."

"Ha!" I barked. "I have no time for guys. What I need is a nice long weekend away from all this." It wasn't like Phoebe had been on date in over six months either. Besides, there was college to think about, summer jobs, next year's tuition. Guys would just have to come later.

In her best radio DJ impression, Phoebe shoved her fist to her thin lips. "Congratulations! You are one of our lucky finalists for a long weekend getaway. Let's not forget to include some of your bestest pals and cohorts," after a pause, she added, "and of course, boys. That would be a penis, one for you and one for me. What do you say to that?" She almost knocked me in the shoulder with her fake microphone.

Leaning into her hand, I said lamely. "Read and Cody aren't my type."

Phoebe snorted and dropped her hands. "Cody has his nuts caught in Robin's nest and Read, well he's an asshole, not a guy. We can uninvite him."

"What is with you two?" I blurted, then threw my hands up fast enough to make her jerk back. "Forget I asked."

"Good idea," Phoebe said and changed the subject. "We should ask Aidan to come."

"Uh, no."

"He's cute."

"He's creepy."

Phoebe rolled her dark green eyes. "You're irrational."

"And you're pushy." I looked up at her and flashed teeth in a satisfied grin.

Phoebe sighed. "Touché. So, meet at lunch tomorrow and we'll figure it out? And, just so you know, Aidan's coming. Read's already asked him."

I faltered in my step. "Read *is* an asshole."

Phoebe grinned. "Told'ja. And we might not have to look for a place to camp."

Adjusting my backpack on my shoulder I started to slow as we reached my locker. I noticed Phoebe didn't carry anything with her. She rarely left the school with more than a few books at a time. "What do you mean? Did Robin get angry about Whitefish Lake again?"

Phoebe snorted. "Yes, but that's not it. Aidan says he has the perfect place."

Aidan Birket was coming. Something about that made my stomach drop. I never really liked Aidan and not knowing why was doubly frustrating. He wasn't mean, cruel, annoying, or any quality I can list that would stretch my dislike beyond instinct. There was something about him that was just off.

"What perfect place?" I asked, hearing the edge. I focused on the locker door instead of Phoebe.

"Wouldn't say. I guess we find out tomorrow." Phoebe leaned against the locker next to mine and stretched her arms over her head. Her olive tanned stomach was toned to perfection. I suppose wanting to get into physical education had benefits.

"You do that to make people jealous?" I asked and tugged down her white t-shirt. "You'll stop traffic."

Already there was an anonymous whistle from the crowd.

Grinning, Phoebe lowered her arms and jutted her

chin at me. "What's that?"

To my horror, she was looking at my fist. A bit of paper poked out.

So much for a temporary distraction. "Nothing."

Dismal is the Demon's Grave. It didn't even make sense. Maybe it was someone with really similar handwriting and it somehow got stuck in my book.

Unless it wasn't my book. Students scattered their stuff across the library tables like they were prepping a picnic. Marly from my media class had been across from me this afternoon.

Dropping the backpack off my shoulder, it fell with a thud against the linoleum.

"You okay, Fuller?" Phoebe quirked a thin, yellow brow.

"Yeah, yeah," I muttered and pulled the *Writing for the Media* book free.

"Are you missing something?"

Flipping the book open I saw my name scrawled at the top.

My shoulders slumped and hope whistled by. It must have been a prank. There was no point wasting time thinking about a stupid note with finals in a few weeks.

"Hey look." Phoebe's swan-like neck stretched. "It's your book, imagine that," she said flatly.

Part of me wanted to tell her what I'd found but if she mentioned any of it to my family I'd be wheeled off to the sanitarium. I wish that were a joke.

Until I could explain the note, I'd have to hide it.

Slipping the note in my jeans pocket I started stuffing the locker with books I didn't need. Slamming it shut I met Phoebe's eyes. "It's nothing," I said, hearing the darkness in my own voice. "You should go save Robin instead."

Looking past Phoebe I could see the petite former cheerleader arguing with a handsome, blonde guy from the football team. Phoebe had pointed him out once or twice. If someone was into sports, leave it to Phoebe to know who they were.

"That's weird," Phoebe said slowly, eyes narrowing.

I took advantage of Phoebe's distraction and slammed my locker shut. "I'll see you tomorrow!" Before she could speak, I bolted into the streaming crowd.

As much as I adored Phoebe, she'd never understand the note or my family.

CHAPTER TWO

During supper, Read texted me an apology about inviting Aidan.

Crap. That meant Phoebe got to him. I hated it when she did that.

Seeing me shake my head, Mom sighed. When I looked up, it was as if she'd read my mind.

"I remember when the yearly weekends were just outside the patio doors. You kids were so cute putting up those tents." The smile slipped, and she met my eyes, lowering her voice. "You guys will be safe this year, right?"

I, of course, agreed and gave her a strained smile.

It was just supposed to be the usual bunch and maybe Robin because she was Cody's girlfriend. Why Aidan, though? Whenever we were close to each other, my stomach would clench and my spine felt taut.

I guess there was always the option of not going. I could fake an illness or pretend to have other plans. On second thought, it would be more believable to fake an illness. Oh, the sad, sad life I lead.

I realized I was twirling the new blonde hair around my fingers and immediately stopped. Instead, I texted a lie to Read: *It's all good. I hope Aidan comes*! I made sure to add that exclamation mark. Maybe it would cloak the lie, and he wouldn't see through it. It was always easier to lie in a text message. If he'd seen me, I'd have never gotten away with it.

After supper, there was studying. I managed to dedicate twenty lousy minutes before my attention started wandering. I could read the words and not retain a lick of it.

Resting my forehead on the cool, open textbook, I hoped I could pass Professor Chase's essay. Every essay to date, she'd given me a solid, red C-.

I could hear my little sister, Mona arguing with our mom in the living room about going to the park with Dad on the weekend. He'd been distracted these last…oh, ten years or so and didn't have much time for us.

When one-year-old Caitlin's high-pitched wails tore through the air, I knew homework was a bust.

I stood, and it felt like sandbags had invaded my every limb. I shuffled to the stairs and forced myself to take the steps two at a time, hoping to increase blood flow.

After finals, I was going to have to treat myself.

Once I was at the top of the stairs, my eyes caught the open bathroom door. Every muscle ached. *Oh yes, a shower*, I thought. A hot, steamy, forget-your-cares shower would be perfect.

I did a zombie shuffle to my bedroom for clothes.

The idea of the shower still sent tingles down my arms. Gathering up the essentials for my shower, I thought about the weekend.

This year, I'd planned for a camping trip, one I'd hoped to share with my friends, but with Aidan butting in with some great idea…I sighed.

Whatever he had planned, it was probably something like camping. We'd play drinking games and roast marshmallows. Maybe after a few shots, I could get Phoebe to tell me what was going on with her and Read. Or maybe I'd get Read to, if he was drunk enough.

I smirked, recalling the trip two years ago when Phoebe was dared to run through the campground naked. She was so fast most folks didn't know what to make of it. Then there was the year where a simple game of "chubby bunny" ended with Read's chipmunk-cheeked victory dance to Michael Jackson's "Thriller." Needless to say, we were asked to leave, but not a single soul was sober enough to drive, and we had to wait until morning.

Locking the bathroom door behind me, I tested the door handle to be sure. With Mona's affinity for pranks, one could never have too many locks.

Starting the shower, I went through the monotonous routine of undressing and brushing my hair. My reflection left much to be desired. Weeks—no months—of my hair trapped in a ponytail made me look strange when it fell past my shoulders. The new color was foreign, and I found myself staring for several seconds.

"I don't care what Phoebe says," I told the girl in the mirror. "I think blonde looks good on you."

Large blue eyes blinked back at me, the bags beneath them seeming a little heavier today than yesterday. Sleep deprivation does that, I suppose. My grown-out bangs framed my childish, round face, almost reaching my chin. I set down the brush as steam clouded the girl in the mirror. My muscles ached to feel the warm water.

I flung open the glass shower door, then sealed myself in. Warm water beat down my hair and back, swirling my troubled thoughts down the drain. Well, at least until tomorrow, when I'd worry about the weekend, the note, and whatever else I could. With this much overanalyzed stress, I'm certain that, by thirty, I'll have to take up drinking just to make the voices go away.

"That's it," I breathed into the wall. "You're obviously irrational and insane."

I ignored the internal flinch that came with the joke and grabbed the shampoo. My thoughts kept snapping back to the note as if it were attached to an elastic band. *You didn't write that note*, I told myself.

I realized I was scrubbing the shampoo too hard. I was mad. All I wanted was peace, and I couldn't even grant myself that.

After flushing the shampoo from my hair, I reached for the conditioner. It was empty.

Groaning, I put the empty bottle back on the shelf and contemplated abandoning the warmth to get another bottle from the cabinet.

I procrastinated by piling my hair on top of my head to pass time, when a movement caught the corner of my eye.

Startled, I froze and found myself staring at the

shower door. A finger was tracing letters into the steam from the other side.

My shoulders dropped. The little bugger almost got me this time. She must have crept downstairs for a butter knife to pick the lock. If it hadn't been a fire safety issue, I'd have locked her in her room every night.

Rolling my eyes, I untangled my fingers from the mass on top of my head. A moment of privacy, that's all I asked for. This wouldn't be the first time she'd broken into the bathroom while I was in the shower. Mona liked to steal my towel, clothes, or toothpaste. When I'd come out fuming, she'd break out in raucous laughter. Mona was blessed with an infectious laugh; it probably saved her life during the dramatic height of my puberty.

Hoping to scare her, I rapped on the glass hard enough to make my knuckles sting. The door rattled over the sound of the water. "Mona! Get out of the bathroom or I'll tell Kyle you love him!"

I half expected to hear a girlish giggle or scampering for the door, but there was nothing. The letters continued to streak themselves in the glass, unhindered by my racket.

Listening, I wondered if she'd decided to change tactics.

The letters were backwards. A backward 'E' followed by a 'N'. I stared in confusion, not knowing what to say or do. Who was there? Mona was my only suspect. No one else would try something like this. But if it wasn't her, then who?

"Mona?" I demanded, my voice surprisingly in control.

There was no answer.

I felt my muscles freeze despite the hot water. I tried squinting through the clear lettering to see if I could make out a shape, a shadow or a figure. Anything to give away the intruder.

I leaned so close that my nose could follow the flat of the finger along the steamy door. Past it, I could see someone there, hunched over. It was definitely not a kid. The height didn't…I was holding my breath.

Panic exploded. The shrapnel seared hot enough that my scream came out as a squeak. The burst of fear had kidnapped my voice! I wondered if they knew that I was aware it wasn't my little sister. Every muscle in my body had stiffened as I watched the writing continue.

Where was Mona? And what would happen when the writing stopped?

Concentrating on moving my cramped muscles, I dropped.

I cracked my knee on the unyielding tiles, and tendrils of pain shot through my joints. I gritted my teeth to stifle my voice while my hands slapped out on either side to catch my balance.

The letters had stopped.

Automatically, I covered myself, unsure if the door was going to fling open. Feeling as if I had cotton stuffed down my throat, I strained for any sound to reassure myself that I could speak. I managed a whisper that not even I could hear over the shower. Taking a deep breath, I tried again, raising my voice only to hear the same wheeze.

I waited for the footsteps, for the door to open, for an attack—for *anything*.

My pulse resounded in my head. It felt like I had been kneeling there for an hour with one arm across my chest, the other pressed to my mouth, leaving teeth impressions in my lips.

Nothing was happening.

I tried to see through the door, but the room was steaming enough to fade the letters and shield the intruder.

My hand over my mouth peeled away. My shaky palm wiped the steam from the bottom of the glass door. I could make out the green bath mat but no feet.

The suspense heightened, and I realized I *needed* something to happen. Being alone with my thoughts wasn't helping. Who was here? Where was my family? I had been so worried about finals and a damn weekend; it all seemed so shallow now. I found my voice, and it cracked. "This isn't funny anymore…"

Only the splashing water answered.

My gaze shifted up to the letters. They were beginning to collapse in on themselves.

To see them clearer, I wiped a hand along them on my side.

N-I-S-D-E-N-E-K-C

I turned the water off so the silence could shriek.

I stood with the help of the walls. The imprints of the tiled floor throbbed in my bare knees.

The water dripped behind me in steady, rhythmic beats. My heartbeat easily outpaced the sound.

I swallowed the lump in my throat and searched for the shadowy figure.

I listened for a few more seconds, staring at the letters before me—no, the message. It was beginning to fade faster.

I realized all at once that I had to know what it said.

Shoving open the shower door with my shoulder, I prepared to dive for the hallway in case there was someone there to catch me.

The glass door banged against the edge of the toilet and revealed an empty bathroom.

Stunned for several seconds, I forgot that I was naked. Fumbling for the white towel hanging beside the door, I wrapped it around me. Not that I believed anyone was in the bathroom with me anymore, but my nerves were starting to fray. Someone had written those letters. *Someone* had been in here.

I slammed the glass door shut and twisted to peer at the message.

In a solid line, it read:

O-N-E-S-O-U-L-O-F-B-L-A.

I frowned, realizing that this wasn't Mona-material.

The words dropped down to another line, drooling condensation.

C-K-E-N-E-D-S-I-N.

The new line hadn't been there before. It wasn't there when I was in the shower.

ONESOU? No, Maybe Ones oul of black…

Shaking my head, I tried again, taking in the second line.

One soul of blackened sin.

This wasn't Mona.

The stinging thought lingered as my eyes darted to the door, which was still locked, to the small window over the toilet. The forest-green curtains and white mini blinds were closed. The window itself could only open a few inches anyway. It wouldn't be enough for even Mona to climb through, let alone an intruder.

Cupping my temples in my palms, I dropped my head.

On either side of my feet were two large shoe impressions in the bath mat.

Chapter Three

I decided that the impressions could have been a man's size ten or eleven dress shoe.

They definitely didn't belong to a seven-year-old girl. Even if she slipped into a pair of Dad's, I'd have heard her clomp inside. No amount of toe curling could keep them on her small feet, and it couldn't have been Dad. He wasn't home, and he's *not* that type of dad.

The impressions began to rise, blending into the plush carpet.

Dizzy from the thoughts playing bumper cars in my head, I sat down on the toilet lid. *What just happened? This wasn't normal.* I hadn't had an episode since I was five. They said I was back to normal, they said…

Looking back, I saw the letters had vanished with the steam.

Surveying my items, I counted everything. Even my underwear was left.

Nothing in the bathroom had moved, not even the

lock.

Hands before my lips, I cast one final glance around the small bathroom and attempted to clear my throat. My voice cracked, but it was there.

My mind reeled, grasping for any rational thought I could before wondering, *Ghost*? We'd lived in this house for fourteen years, and there hadn't been any signs of ghosts, plus it would have rendered my beliefs, or lack thereof, invalidated. *Ghosts aren't real.* I pushed the bathmat with my toe.

Leaning forward, I unlocked the door and took a moment. I wanted to make sure I could stand without falling. With the help of the counter, I stood and gathered my clothes in my arms.

I wasn't sure I was still alone, and I couldn't shake the feeling of being watched despite the bathroom being too small to hide even a child. Disturbed, I tried to shove the idea away. I wasn't being watched. I was being paranoid. "You're better than this, Nora. You're not a kid anymore," I whispered.

I saw something move from the corner of my eye.

Frantic, I spun around to the window. My heart hammered inside my head, making the room warp and shift.

The white venetian blinds were open, though the window remained closed. I tried to remember if they'd been closed before the shower and realized I wasn't sure.

My lips parted, and I knew I wanted to scream but didn't. Instead, I ripped open the bathroom door.

The cool air was a staggering shock.

I nearly tripped over my own feet getting out into the hall. Gripping the towel, I ran, feet thundering. I didn't bother to be quiet.

The heaviness was still on me as if those eyes were right behind me, launching me into my bedroom. I couldn't grab the door fast enough.

Pulling it shut, I didn't dare peek over my shoulder. I didn't want to see that something might be there, breathing down my neck.

As I leaned on the closed door, I heard Caitlin let out a shriek.

I took a deep breath to calm myself against the invading, smothering shadows. My hand shot up the wall until it knocked the light-switch on.

The sanctuary flooded with reassuring light, and I could breathe.

I locked the bedroom door, not that it would save me at this point. This wasn't the first time I'd felt those eyes. When I was younger, just after our move to this house, I'd felt them. It was as if someone were hovering behind me, just out of reach, watching—always watching. Back then, things around me would move. Toys wouldn't be where I'd left them; lights would flicker on and off. No one but me saw any of this.

When I told my parents *she* was still around, they couldn't handle it. Ghosts cost me three weeks in a psychiatric ward, a weekly psychiatrist, and years of pills that sometimes made me sick.

With the pajamas still pressed tight to my chest, I realized I was shaking. It wasn't cold, but the adrenaline was powering down, leaving shudders in its wake.

I peeled away from the door before diving for my bedside lamp. I turned it on before switching off the main light. I needed a light tonight. It had helped when I was little.

Curling back the covers, I ducked under them. You better believe I changed into my pajamas under the covers.

The heavy gaze had lifted, but I feared it would come back.

Clothed and protected in my blankets, I stared at the shadows on the wall. I dared them to move and prove me right while at the same time I prayed that they'd stay still. Outside, the wind shook the trees, but the shadows from my lamp didn't waver. I knew this should make me feel better, but it didn't.

Was it happening all over again? Did I trigger it somehow with stress? Was I crazy?

No, I couldn't be crazy. I was a 'successful recovery.' They'd said so. But that left me with what option? There's insanity, ghosts, or one hell of a trick by Mona. Though I wanted to believe it, I didn't think Mona's mind was capable of it.

Am I afraid of death? A little. Am I afraid of ghosts existing? Meh. The darkness between worlds? I let that question hang precariously on the edge of acknowledgement before discarding it. Am I afraid of being stamped insane? I shuddered and ignored that one too.

I felt the pressure of tears at the back of my eyes and tried to convince myself that I had overextended somehow. Finals were coming, Aidan was joining our weekend, I still didn't have a summer job…

I could hear Mona and my mother talking near the stairs, but I couldn't quite make out what they were saying. My teeth continued to chatter, and I was certain I'd drawn attention with my stampede through the hallway. I couldn't let Mom or Dad know this happened, especially Dad.

Dismal is the Demon's Grave.
One soul of blackened sin.

I convulsed with each dying burst of the shakes, pulling hard on my nightgown, twisting it in my fist. "You won't get me again," I whispered. "I didn't write that note. I didn't see that message."

It was well past midnight when I succumbed to exhaustion.

Chapter Four

Hungry spiders crawled through my dreams, just like they'd done when I was five. Though it wasn't them I had to watch out for: there was something bigger and meaner out to get me.

A shrill wail erupted just as a spider found me, and I jolted in my bed.

Despite the start, I felt as if sleep had cheated me and almost fell back asleep. I was jolted back awake by the idea of meeting spiders again.

Going through the motions, I did my routines, said what was expected, and went through classes until lunchtime.

Shuffling into the lunchroom, I hoped I'd relaxed a little. I was tired, but after a coffee and Red Bull, I was functioning—barely.

I could see a shock of honeyed hair as I made my way through the tables. Phoebe had secured our usual table in the college cafeteria alongside Read Wallace.

The two looked like a ying-and-yang symbol sitting across from each other. They were the same height and same basic build, though Read was skinny and Phoebe lean with muscle. Their coloring was also a contrast: Read with his dark hair and pasty skin and Phoebe with her blonde hair and olive complexion.

Approaching the table, I slung my overweight backpack into an empty chair and took a seat next to Phoebe.

She didn't look up at first. Her ravenous gaze was devouring her lunch before touching it. The sandwich, apple, three cookies, and a Coke were scattered about, taking up far more room than necessary. Tilting back her pointed chin, she winked at me, her shoulders hunched over her food as if she meant to protect it.

Across from her, Read rummaged through his red lunch bag. His dark brown hair—almost black—masked his eyes. "Hey, Nora." Read pulled a narrow white can covered in Japanese writing from his bag. Read had a distaste for normalcy. He wouldn't be caught dead with grilled cheese or pizza for lunch unless it was imported or some obscure variety.

"Hi, Read," I replied and ignored his double take. I knew my lack of sleep was starting to show, and I was certain my hair was only partly still in its ponytail.

"You're blonde," he said.

Oh, that. I stretched my lips in what I hoped resembled a smile.

Dismal is the Demon's Grave. One soul of blackened sin. It was like an incessant loop that I couldn't scratch out of my head. I stopped myself before I could thud my fist against my temple.

I hadn't noticed the silence, but the other two

seemed to find it disconcerting. Read broke it first, looking at me. "Are you ready for *the* weekend?"

Phoebe's teeth cracked into the stiff hide of the apple, and she said, while chewing, "Don't be stupid. Of course she is."

He brushed his hair away from his grey eyes and glared at her. "Last I checked, Nora could speak for herself."

"Absolutely," I said with over-exaggerated enthusiasm. The last thing my scrambled nerves needed was another argument between the two. Read and Phoebe used to get along better than anyone in our group. I hadn't heard a kind word between them for months. Whenever asked, neither would say why.

I opened my paper bag and tried not to glance between them. "There's that new campground by Whitefish Lake."

"I like that lake." Read waved a fork in my direction. "I think Aidan has—"

"You hated that lake," Phoebe interrupted.

Read wiped at his face with the back of his fork-holding hand. "You don't have to spit at me."

Phoebe made a childish face.

I wracked my mind for something to interrupt them when a lanky girl with pouty lips and a cherry tattoo on her bare shoulder nudged Read's shoulder with her hip. Phoebe and I might as well have been invisible the way she smiled at him. Of course, at the rate I was going today, I didn't mind.

Find me an invisibility cloak! I thought and smirked.

Read flashed a casual smile to the new girl. With his chiseled cheeks, full lips, and mysterious demeanor, women were attracted to Read like wasps to sugar.

The girl purred to him, "You should come to baseball practice tonight." She included an exaggerated hair flip halfway through her sentence.

Phoebe stifled a giggle with a snort. Read was one of the worst athletes we knew. Even worse than me, which was saying something.

The girl seemed to take notice of Phoebe for the first time and blinked in surprise. Whether she recognized Phoebe or not, I'd never know, but her lips twisted as if ready for a fight when Read said, "I'd love to, but I have a test to study for. You going to be busy around nine?"

The girl smirked without showing her teeth, mostly at Phoebe, who remained seated with her eyebrows raised.

I glanced between the three of them, unsure how to repair the thin ice that coated the conversation. "Um," was all I managed before the pretty brunette agreed to Read's terms.

"Don't keep me waiting." The throaty purr in his ear wasn't just for him. It was like watching a dog with a hydrant.

Without turning my face, I shifted my gaze to Phoebe. She was watching her knuckles as she cracked them one at a time. It was a classic nervous twitch she'd developed as a kid. *Ruh roh.*

The girl left, adding extra sway to her hips, knowing Read would be watching, and he was. The goofy smile remained when he turned back to us.

"You want me to teach you what baseball *is*?" Phoebe asked between cracks.

"Interesting," I blurted without thinking.

"That's Heather," Read said as if Heather had been the topic of conversation before.

Phoebe shrugged her narrow shoulders and bit into her sandwich.

As if cued, I looked up and saw two familiar people walking our way.

The odd couple bee-lined through the tables, gripping lunch trays. Robin Thurston was leading, but I could easily see Cody's narrow features and bleached hair behind her. The top of Robin's head reached his chest, and she wore four-inch heels just to accomplish that height.

The petite former cheerleader grinned at me. When she wasn't smiling, which was rare, her full lips almost touched her pert nose.

Returning the smile, I strained to lift the heavy backpack to the floor so Robin could sit.

"Hey, everyone," Robin announced and squeezed in on the other side of me. "I like the hair, Nora." You wouldn't expect someone her size to have such a volcanic voice. As she said *hey*, at least three tables turned to see if she was talking to them. She wore her favorite sunglasses on her head. They coupled as a hair accessory in keeping the chin-length, chestnut hair from brushing her face. This week, it was riddled with golden brown highlights. Last week, it had been deep red highlights, the week before green.

Cody plopped down on the other side of Robin and towered over everyone at the table, even while sitting.

We all managed an obscure greeting between bites.

"Cody," Phoebe prompted, "did you hear about Aidan's idea for the weekend?"

Cody's smile was brief, never showing teeth.

Robin piped up before he could answer. "I don't think either of us have."

I felt that familiar buzz. The disturbance in the air that often came just before…

Aidan Birket set his tray of cafeteria food on the table with a clatter.

His wild, roan-colored hair was spiked in all directions as if he'd just rolled out of bed. His square face was pale, leaving grey circles under his eyes most days and enhancing his shocking eyes. It was his eyes that caught most people's attention. Pale blue, electric—like they were staring straight through you. No, *into* you. It was like he saw your soul and knew things about you that you didn't. I hated that.

"Good afternoon," he said, taking a seat beside Read. Despite his wild, unkempt hair, he dressed well. New jeans and a tight t-shirt accented his lean chest and arms.

I muttered a reply that melted in with the others and stuffed my face.

He and Read had hit it off at the beginning of the year, and Aidan had come to lunch with us ever since.

"We were just discussing your idea for the weekend," Robin informed him with a bright smile.

Read started to speak, but Robin interrupted—she often did—though it wasn't out of spite; it was just Robin. "You know, I heard Claire Weatherbe was going to have a pool party on Saturday. Also, the Gregory twins were renting a cabin at the beach." Her bright green eyes glistened with ideas. She nibbled on a cracker before making a face. "We're not going camping down at Bow Valley Lake again, are we?" She followed Aidan's gaze around the table, her disapproval evident.

Aidan smiled, closed-lipped and polite. He always seemed to smile to be sociable, not because he wanted to. "No, it's not Bow Valley Lake."

Robin eagerly leaned forward in her chair, eyes bright. "You're coming this year, right? The more the merrier." Cody nodded along with her, mute as ever.

"He's already coming, guys." Phoebe turned to Robin and rolled out her tongue to show off the half-masticated food. Robin, like many times before, threatened to never sit with us—again.

Aidan's voice continued alongside Robin's, and I barely heard him say, "It'll be good to get away for a weekend before the last of finals."

"More people means more beer." Read patted Aidan's shoulder with approval.

Phoebe rolled her eyes. "Heather can't come."

"Who is Heather?" Robin was as alert as a ground squirrel.

Before chugging her Coke, Phoebe said, "Read's new girlfriend."

"She's not my girlfriend," Read protested with a hiss. "Stop being a bitch, Phoebe, or you're on toilet paper detail."

Robin's head bobbed in slow-motion as if she were trying to follow the conversation. She trailed her eyes between them before looking at me with raised eyebrows. "Read's girlfriend?"

I shrugged; I didn't want to press it. If pushed, Phoebe could get nasty. So I said, "There isn't a girl Read hasn't hit on. Of course there's a girlfriend."

Looking thoughtful, Read said, "Just ones I don't want to keep for a while. There's girls I like. I just never flirt with them."

"Like Heather?" Aidan volunteered with a smile.

"She's just one I won't keep for a while." Read half smirked and looked to Aidan as if they shared some boyish secret.

I rolled my eyes when I realized Read had never hit on me—not once. He'd flirted with Phoebe, even Robin from time to time, but never me.

Stiffening, I realized Read was watching me, and I raised my eyebrows at him in question.

All he did was smile before turning scarlet and looking away.

Well, that was new.

"Why can't Read's girlfriend come?" Robin asked. "I'd like to meet her."

I leaned back in my chair hard enough to make it jump. For some reason, I thought Phoebe might be swinging a fist.

Instead, she was tilting back the Coke to swish the liquid in her mouth before spitting it back in the can and drinking it again.

Robin actually gagged. "Phoebe!"

"Why were you arguing with Cooper Mesick the other day?"

"What?" Robin paled a little.

This brought Cody forward in his seat to speak for the first time. "The guy who's been harassing you?"

Robin waved it off, looking frightfully pallid under her tan. "It's nothing," she said.

"Didn't look like nothing," Phoebe said with a self-satisfied smirk.

Cody was glaring at Robin, and Robin was glaring at Phoebe. If Robin's eyes could shoot daggers, Phoebe would be in ribbons.

Oblivious to the exchange, Aidan pointed at Robin with his fork and asked, "Would you rather do any of the other suggestions, though? I don't want to impose."

Tearing her eyes from Phoebe, Robin glanced at Read and said, "Um, no, I'm fine with whatever. With *who*ever." She gave me another pointed look as if I could communicate telepathically.

I pretended not to notice. I was too tired to play this game.

When Aiden went to ask Cody, he was already nodding toward Robin as if to say, "Whatever she says," though his mouth had turned down in a scowl. Aidan paused before asking, "Nora?"

I bristled, feeling the hair on the back of my neck rise. I met his electric eyes and tried to keep from flinching. "I'm not sure I can go this year."

At the same time, we looked away from each other.

Sometimes, I wondered if he could hear my thoughts. It might explain why he avoided me the way I did him. I remembered one day at Read's before going out to a club and Aidan cancelled the second I walked in the door. Read thought I had done something to piss him off. It took half the night and several highballs to convince Read otherwise.

Phoebe's eyebrows pinched when she looked at me.

Aidan blew a strand of his wild roan hair away from his face with a sigh.

"I say we go to your place," Read said, slurping from the white mystery can.

Without looking up, Aidan said, "Well, I was thinking of going to a place my family owns outside of town. If you guys want to come, you can. It's kind of like camping out there."

Robin wrinkled her nose at *camping*.

"Well, there's shelter and we won't need tents," Aidan said. The hope in his voice was almost tangible. "I mean, there's no running water or sewer."

"Like a cabin? I'm listening." Phoebe set her bony elbows on the table and rested her head on her fists.

Robin groaned a protest and lowered her head, staring at her food instead. I think I was the only one who heard her mutter. "Maybe I can't go this year either." I tried to keep my face neutral.

Aidan continued, between bites of his chicken sandwich, "I can guarantee that it's one of the best places *I've* ever been to."

"Where's that?" Phoebe asked.

"Can't tell you." Aidan shook his head, quite serious.

"What do you mean?" I snapped before I could stop myself. "How will we know what to pack or how long we'll be gone if we don't know where it is?"

At first, Aidan looked ready to start an argument. Instead, he took a deep breath and forced the polite, closed-lipped smile. "The reason I say that I can't tell you is because it's a bit of a family secret."

"You want us to see your secret place?" I asked, my tone far more condescending than I intended. Surprising myself, I felt the harsh pinch of guilt and tried to cover it up with a playful smile as if I were joking. I doubt it was convincing.

Dismal is the Demon's Grave. One soul of blackened sin. My hand curled into a fist.

Aidan's smile was starting to irritate me. "It's just for kicks, Nora. Where's your sense of adventure?"

Phoebe wiggled in her seat. "This will be fun." She nudged me with her elbow. "Be spontaneous for once."

Robin straightened in her seat. "Sure, Cody and I will come." She looked at Cody for approval. Cody stopped chewing for a moment to smile at her without showing teeth, squinting his light brown eyes through blonde lashes.

Phoebe nodded. "I could use a little excitement and get out of this boring old town."

She was right, not much happened in Leland.

I glanced at Phoebe and Robin for support, finding none. I didn't want to be the only one to chicken out, but my stomach was twisting into knots.

Phoebe was nodding at me, her eyes wide with encouraging peer pressure.

Read looked over the cafeteria, perhaps searching for Heather before he said, "I'm in. But, uh—yeah, what Nora said. What should we pack? I don't want to bring swimming trunks if the place rains all the time. Do we need passports or money? I mean, Aidan's family has been everywhere."

Aidan was shaking his head. "No, no, just pack a few pairs of clothes and sleeping bags. It's not far from here, and there will be shelter," Aidan said, a muscle twitching alongside his high cheekbone. "Bring what you'd usually bring camping, except for a tent."

Robin asked, "Is this for just one night? Will it take all day to get there?"

"It's an hour drive outside of town. I was going to spend one night, but we could do more if you guys want," Aidan said.

Phoebe's rueful smile targeted me. "Fuller's coming."

I had to admit that Phoebe had a point about my blundering sense of adventure. And though Aidan gave me the creeps, I was probably being irrational.

Dropping my chin, I darted my eyes to Aidan. "If I die on this vacation, I'm coming back to haunt you."

I'm an idiot. Plain and simple.

I didn't need a skateboarder to point it out this time.

"Fair enough," Aidan replied without missing a beat.

"Is that a yes?" Excitement rippled off Robin like a personal perfume.

I gave her a reluctant nod. I was being spontaneous, right? Maybe I could figure out what it was about Aidan that disturbed me or just solidify the fact that that I was truly an idiot. So far I seemed to have a knack for that. Or maybe I could…talk to Read? I wasn't sure how I felt about that yet.

Robin began to reminisce about past weekend outings. There would be some new memories to make, and why shouldn't I join in? I couldn't duck out because Aidan Birket gave me the creeps. Hell no, I couldn't.

I looked up to see the electric blue eyes watching me. We both looked away at the same time.

CHAPTER FIVE

I gathered Caitlin from the living room and wiggled the six month old into a jacket. She didn't fuss; instead, she found this to be a rather interesting exercise and flexed her fingers over and over.

On her head I put a warm hat, just in case the spring air wasn't as warm as promised. Caitlin had a bundle of curly blonde hair; she'd been born with most of it. During her first wintery months of life, she had enough static electricity on her head to light a small home.

I shrugged on a light coat while Mona slowly put on her coat one arm at a time and took a few lazy minutes to tie up her sneakers, one loop at a time.

"Going out!" I called into the house and strapped Caitlin into the stroller. The baby batted at my wrists before slobbering on them. "You're a peach," I told her, and she looked up at me, all blue-eyed innocence and shiny drool.

"Okay, not too late!" Mom's delayed shout came

from the den. She and the housekeeper were thinking of new ways to decorate the house. Mom was a part-time interior designer, so the house was always changing.

Upon opening the front door, Mona pushed past me into the twilight ahead of us. Her long, brown hair that reached her butt fluttered like a heavy flag.

I lifted the stroller until we were down the two front steps.

Mona took the handles and pushed Caitlin beside me. She talked about her day so fast that I began to wonder if she'd ever come up for air. She had a wonderful experience in art class with macaroni, glitter, and glue. Mona was thoroughly convinced that her macaroni medley was the best in class.

The most noise Caitlin created was nonsensical jabbering that eerily resembled Mona's. After a while, Caitlin would grow bored of that and draw out a single note just to hear her voice jolt with each crack in the sidewalk.

On our third block, Mona started complaining about her feet, and I realized Caitlin had gone quiet. Peering into the stroller, I saw she'd fallen asleep.

"All right, all right, we'll head home." I patted Mona's head, and she nodded in agreement.

Mona started talking, but I wasn't paying close enough attention to her ramblings to know the context.

The lethargic sun slunk below the western mountains. The gargantuan shadows stretched themselves over the valley. The air was nippy, and houses flickered lights on inside. Evening came quicker here than anywhere else because of the mountains.

Our stretched shadows ambled ahead of us.

"Nora?" Mona asked annoyed. "Are you listening?"

"Hmm?"

Against my ear, I felt air followed by a whisper. "Pssssssssst." The sensation rippled goosebumps down my right arm and stopped me dead in my tracks.

Mona eased the stroller to a stop and squinted at me through the orange rays of light. "I said, did you see the moon?" Mona pointed to the chalky full moon opposite the sun.

I tilted my chin up to look and lost my breath. The distraction had worked.

It was beautiful. The oversized disc appeared almost fake against the fading blue sky. A few stars twinkled to life, but not many. "Wow," I breathed, feeling Mona move closer to me.

"I don't like it," she admitted in a soft voice.

"Why not?"

Air brushed my earlobe again, just before, "*Psssssst.*"

Jumping, I searched the ground and quiet houses. "Did you hear that?" I glanced down at Mona's upturned, uncertain face. She didn't answer but canted her head and pretended to listen.

"It's like a hissing noise," I explained, and we both fell silent. As much as I strained to hear it over the neighborhood noises, it wasn't there.

"A bug?" Mona asked at last.

Just block it out, I thought, my head swimming in a surreal haze. Was I making all of this up right now? Was it all in my head? From the look on Mona's face, I knew it very well could be. *She's helpless here with me,* I thought. If I turned into the monster from my own childhood, she wouldn't be safe with me.

"*Psssst.*"

Mona's lips parted, and I could have screamed in joy at her acknowledgement until she said, "Kyle said that on full moons, witches come out and eat kids. He said they like girls more than boys and it happens all over the world. That's why there's so many missing kids…"

The joy detonated, leaving hollow disappointment in its wake.

Taking a deep breath, I gathered my wits. *I am the adult*, I reminded myself. "Kyle's wrong. There's no such thing as witches."

Mona's pinched brow lowered as if she wasn't entirely convinced.

I motioned forward. "Let's keep walking. What were you saying before?"

"Can you push Caitlin?"

I obliged by taking the stroller before we set off again.

Mona walked alongside me, and her hand came up to grip my wrist. She kept glancing at the moon, her urge to talk dissipating.

The silence left me with the idea that the eyes were back. The weight of them pressed into the back of my neck.

Struggling for another topic, I realized I hated Mona's silence. "Witches are only in storybooks. Kyle was pulling your leg."

Mona's lips formed a tight line of disapproval, and she wouldn't look at me, only at the moon.

"What makes you think that any witch could be real based on what some kid said?"

She shook her head. "It's okay, Nora. I won't believe in witches."

"Good." I knew she was lying.

We were nearing home, and I was eager to get the girls inside and away from the eyes. Quickening my steps, I tried to think of something else. If I didn't acknowledge it, maybe it'd go away. It was like the doctor said: it's not really there. Everything was in my head. *You have to be stronger than your emotions, Nora*!

I looked up and down the street for something to divert my attention. The Dyne couple got a new car, a Porsche. Someone was going through a mid-life crisis.

As we passed the Mueller's, I noticed their newly painted fence, a powder pink.

Maybe the asylum *should* be called up, just not for me.

Mona took a deep breath, opening her mouth and closing it again. She did this two or three times before gathering enough courage to ask, "What about Aunt Nell? Wasn't she a witch?"

Screeching to a stop, I stared at her, aghast. "Who told you that?"

"*Pssssssssssssst.*" It was longer this time, and I let go of the stroller as if it were scalding. "Dammit!" I snapped, and Mona jumped away in fright.

"Nora," she scolded, her face ashen, "Mom told you not to swear—" Her foot knocked into an object just within the Belmonts' yard. The orange sky reflected off the glossy surface like a beacon.

It was a silver hand-held mirror, lying face down in the lawn.

"Oh, Nora," Mona gasped in awe. She let go of my wrist and bolted for it.

Mona lifted it in her delicate hands, her mouth

forming a perfect O of admiration.

It looked like a heavy antique, not something a Belmont child would use, considering they were closer to Caitlin's age.

Looking at the mirror, I followed the intricate swirls as they curled and swooped within the metal frame before twining around the thickened handle like metal vines. The mirror itself was dirty and smudged. It distorted our images, making us appear ghoulish and surreal. Mona entertained herself by making faces at her reflection.

Caitlin stirred but didn't wake when I asked, "Can I see it?"

Reaching out as if I expected Mona to bite me, I was quick to pluck it from her cupped fingers. I cradled it in both of my hands, afraid of its fragile appearance. Mona tipped herself up on her toes to watch.

My warped reflection showed a girl with dark blue eyes, her full lips pinched tightly together and light brown eyebrows arched in surprise. I reached up to touch my forehead; I didn't think I was raising my eyebrows.

"It's so pretty," Mona gushed.

"Yes, and it's not ours," I said gently. "We should give it back to the Belmonts…"

Mona gasped, sharp and shrill. "What?" I might as well have told her to cut off her hair.

I nodded towards the Belmont's door. "It's not ours." I tried to sound firm, though I heard the shudder.

My mirrored reflection shifted out of the corner of my eye, capturing my attention again.

The girl, who was supposed to be me, had changed. My hand reached up to touch my mouth to feel that my lips were still closed. She was still me, her distorted mouth opened in a silent scream. I licked my lips, but the girl in the reflection didn't move. "We should give it back," I told Mona.

"No!" Mona shrieked through clenched teeth. "I found it."

I looked back to my foreign reflection; the lips began moving around invisible words. A voice crackled in my ear as if someone had been speaking through a bad connection. The *pssssssssttt* overrode the words, making only a few syllables stand out.

With one hand, I slapped my palm over one ear to block out the sound. I didn't dare peek at my sister to see if she was doing the same thing. I couldn't tear my eyes away from the peculiar reflection as the words repeated themselves until the voice rose over the crackle. It wasn't my voice, I thought. It was hard to tell if it was female or male, but the words were taking shape.

"Offered death for once the brave."

Feeling my gut twist, I dropped the poisonous mirror.

Mona shouted, her hands swinging to catch it but missing. It fell to the pavement with a metallic clang. Facing the sky, the mirror went black as if it was turned off.

"What did you do that for?" Mona shouted.

I grabbed Mona's hand. "It's not worth it," I muttered and was forced to squeeze her little hand harder when she tried to wrench herself free. She squealed a protest and had to hop to keep up with me. I knew I should feel sick for hurting her, but I'd worry later and panic now.

We had to get away from that thing, away from the gnarled voice. The farther we got, the less it crackled and the safer I felt.

Mona had seen the mirror too, so it wasn't a delusion, right? But the *voice*. I swallowed hard, feeling the lump in my throat. Was she in danger just by being with me?

I'm not going to cry, I promised myself, feeling the pressure behind my eyes.

Mona cursed at me with words I didn't know she knew.

This episode or delusion, whatever it was, had happened right in front of my little sister.

This time, the message hadn't been in private. I watched her react to me. I saw the bewilderment play across her round face. It was painful to have it replay in my head, but it did, over and over.

Mona began to cry. Her frantic sobs haunted me all the way to the house. It wasn't very long before Caitlin was roused to join her.

Me barreling into the home with two screaming little girls was probably the last thing my mother wanted to hear.

I fumbled with shaking hands to unstrap Caitlin and passed her to our stunned mother, who had rushed to the door upon hearing the racket.

Mom blinked, her wild brown eyes flickering from face to face. "What happened?" she asked as calm as her alarm would allow.

Shaking my head, I threw up my arms in mute exasperation. I would leave Mona to do all the raving sobs. Mom would have to lecture Mona about possession.

I, personally, didn't want to be near the girls. What if I saw something that wasn't real and ended up hurting them? I didn't think I could live with myself.

I retreated to my room without an explanation. I couldn't deal with the questions right now. I felt like I'd done something awful, as if grease coated my skin, staining it for the weighty eyes to see—and they saw.

I locked my bedroom door, and the damnable gaze lightened just a little.

I saw the bear on the shelf beside me.

Mom hated that I still kept it. It was worn a little but not by use. I rarely played with it, but it made me feel safe sometimes. Plucking it off the shelf, I held it tight to my chest. "Okay, Damien," I cooed, my body shuddering, "let's try to be rational."

With my bear protector, I crawled onto my bed, and my foot hit the backpack, which was leaning against the side.

I turned on my bedside lamp and drew my knees and the stuffed animal to my chest. I was grateful that I couldn't see the eerie full moon, but the streetlights bled into the room. I thought about what Mona said about witches eating children. She had asked about our aunt. I hadn't seen that coming for miles—even my parents refused to talk about her—so where had Mona picked up the information?

What if something happened on the weekend? Maybe it wasn't just my sisters I should be worried about. I pulled and tugged at my shirt and realized what I was doing. I'd lost more clothes to the stupid nervous habit.

Slipping off the bed, I rummaged through my pile of dirty clothes until I found the jeans I had been wearing that day. I dug through the pockets until I found the wrinkled piece of paper.

All together, could they be some sort of poem? I stared at the words for what felt like forever, letting the words jumble together.

It didn't make any sense.

Dropping the note in my lap, I ran my fingers back into my French braid and pulled just enough to feel a bite of pain, something to reassure me that I was awake. I wanted to believe there was a connection with the messages, A vain hope that the words meant something.

Swallowing back my fears, I noticed my backpack's open maw. Within the gap, my notebook jutted out near the top. I could write them down for now, maybe find a connection between the three messages.

Reluctant but determined, I plucked the scribbler free and opened it to a blank page to purge the messages from my head.

The weighty eyes had disappeared entirely, leaving me to spend the next few hours staring at the words they'd left behind.

CHAPTER SIX

Friday arrived too soon. I'd spend several hours each day worrying and trying to figure out if I should go or not. It wouldn't hurt anyone if I didn't, and hell, I'd probably feel a little better about that, but I knew it would raise more questions, ones I didn't want to answer. If Phoebe wanted to, she'd hound me until I broke down.

I even called Aidan's cell at one point, but he didn't pick up, and I didn't know what to say for a message. He never called me back, either.

I adjusted my grip on the shopping bags and breathed in the fresh air. Maybe this weekend would be worth it. More than likely, I was overreacting. Wouldn't be the first time.

Phoebe nudged me as the city bus pulled around the corner. "Are you all right?"

Phoebe and I didn't live far from each other, and we'd agreed to bus it together to Aidan's.

"I'm fine," I replied automatically. I always hated that question.

Phoebe parted her lips, but she was interrupted by the shrieking brakes as the bus shouldered the curb and hissed to a stop.

To avoid Phoebe's curious gaze, I watched the bus doors folded open.

At first, Phoebe didn't budge. I knew she was watching me, and I motioned for her to lead. Phoebe was often rebellious with orders, but today she brushed past me to plod up the steps, the heavy pack bowing her spine for balance. We each paid and flopped onto empty seats, side by side, near the front.

The bus jerked to a start, and Phoebe spoke again. "So, seriously, are you trying to think up excuses not to go because of Aidan?" There was a twinge of disapproval in her low voice.

Squirming, I hugged the duffel bag on my lap. *Ah, hell, why not*? Before I could analyze what I was about to do, I asked, "Has anything weird happened to you lately?"

Phoebe shook her head. "Weird how?"

"Well," I struggled to collect my thoughts, "on Monday, you said you were having nightmares."

"Oh yeah." Phoebe looked startled, as if she'd forgotten. "I didn't tell you about those dreams, did I?"

"You started to."

"That's right. We saw Robin and blah, blah, blah." Phoebe sat at the edge of her seat, refusing to remove the hiker's pack. "It was kind of weird. Hadn't had that dream since I was a kid."

I thought of the spiders that had scampered through my last few nights. "What kind of dream?"

Phoebe started cracking her knuckles. "It was one where people were in my house and my family was being hurt and I couldn't do anything to help them and they kept trying to tell me things but none of it ever made sense."

"Do you remember what they were saying?"

She shook her head. "Sometimes when I wake up but that's about it."

"It's kind of a coincidence. I had an old dream about spiders." I played with the zipper on my bag.

Phoebe leaned back as far as her pack would allow. "I didn't know that. I remember that spider dream you used to have. With the scorpion, right?"

I hesitated, then nodded, feeling my heart skip a beat. I'd forgotten about the scorpion. "Has there been anything weird *other* than just nightmares?"

After a prolonged silence, I glanced at her, and she motioned frantically for me to continue.

"Messages." I paused, avoiding her stare. "I've been getting really messed-up messages."

"Like what?"

I told her about my notebook, the shower, and the mirror. I told her everything, keeping my voice down as I rambled for the rest of our ride. It felt good to tell someone. Inch by inch, I was pulling free from the anxiety.

Phoebe held her inquisitive expression even during the strangest portions of my story. I had hoped that she'd have an answer to solve my problem, but she wasn't offering any right away.

"I thought maybe it was a warning," I said.

"You didn't have any weird experiences yesterday, though?"

"No."

"Where's the note?" Phoebe asked.

I stared at her for several seconds, feeling the panic beginning to rise in the back of my head. She didn't believe me. Would she tell anyone else? The rest of the gang might laugh it off, but my mom wouldn't, and I had no idea how my dad would react. "Um…it's at home." I decided to omit the fact that I'd thrown it out.

Phoebe looked toward the back of the bus, not divulging a hint of what she might be thinking. "Have you told anyone else?"

"No," I said, too quickly. "Please though, Phoebe? Don't tell anyone."

She turned her head back to me, offering a slight nod, though she didn't make eye contact. "Maybe it was just stress, Fuller."

She *did* think I was nuts.

Only Phoebe and Cody knew why my family moved to Leland when I was younger. I kind of wanted to keep it that way.

"You're probably right." The lie strained my voice.

We fell quiet for several seconds, sitting side by side as the bus stopped to let on more people.

The snap of each one of Phoebe's knuckles was producing an internal flinch. I wanted her to stop acting nervous and support me, but she wasn't helping me like I'd hoped. Persistent, I tried to move the subject forward, hoping to jostle the protective Phoebe I had depended on all these years. "Thought about talking to him, but…"

She snorted, and the old Phoebe presented itself again. "You've always avoided him. He's not a bad guy, you know. He helped me when Re…" Her tongue seemed to tie itself.

So Aidan knew what was happening between Read and Phoebe. I felt the knife twist in my chest. Phoebe and I had been friends since we were kids; we told each other almost everything. When did this stop?

"At the Splitz party four months ago," Phoebe continued as if she hadn't stopped, "he paid for Robin and Cody's cab. Read seems to like him, and Read normally just likes things with tits. I mean, that in itself should say something. If you think about it, Aidan was always moved around because of his parents, so we're kind of his first friends."

"He told you that?" I asked.

"No, Read did once. Aidan's not out for pity." Phoebe snapped a disapproving glance in my direction.

Raising one hand defensively, I said, "Okay, okay, he's an awesome piece of work. I'm a bitch with low self-esteem or some lame psycho-analytical bull crap."

Phoebe burst out laughing, making me jump. She patted my arm as the bus pulled up to our stop. "Come on, you sarcastic psycho bitch. We have a party to start."

We stepped down the tall steps. We were on the four-lane avenue just a block from Aidan's—according to Phoebe. The houses were well kept and older with mowed lawns and rainbow-inspired flower gardens.

Phoebe waited for me to catch up and the bus's doors to close before she said, "I think you'll be just fine. Once the finals are over in a few weeks, we'll have all summer to avoid Aidan if you want."

I tried to smile and found it difficult. "I shouldn't be trying to avoid him," I admitted reluctantly. "I should be getting to know him. I just get a freaky vibe off of him."

Phoebe cocked her head to the side, her pale eyebrows raised in question.

I shook my head and waved it off. "Forget about it. It's not important."

Phoebe cleared her throat, and her playful tone darkened. "Well, don't go telling anyone else about the messages. At least not yet." Her dark green eyes met mine. "If you see or hear more, talk to me. Okay?"

I almost glared at her. This was the end of my argument. She wasn't willing to hear me out. Though if I were her, I wouldn't want to believe my friend was insane either.

After a hesitation, I nodded. "I'll talk to you."

The overcast of awkward silence hovered until we turned onto Shirley Street. Phoebe started to crack her knuckles again, and I tried to find something interesting in the older houses. One in particular had chalk writing on the individual bricks. A child's wobbly block writing proclaiming that it was the R-O-B-I-N-S-O-N-H-O-U-S-E. Then below it said: R-O-B-B-Y. Robby Robinson…poor kid.

"So," Phoebe whistled. "How did your essay go with Professor Chase?"

I could have hugged her. "I think I did okay, but then today she gave us another pop quiz."

"How exciting," Phoebe sneered. "I told you English majors were jerks."

I tried not to smile. "It would have been fine except for that random bonus question."

"Hey, at least you got a chance to up your mark. I don't think McCaully takes questions from our textbooks. What was the question anyway?" McCaully was a hated prof of Phoebe's. He taught a biology class while my Professor Chase taught my Classic Authors class.

"Kindness is the golden chain by which society is bound together. Who was that quote by?"

Phoebe snorted and popped a piece of gum in her mouth, offering me some.

"Yeah I got it wrong too." I politely declined the Juicy Fruit.

"Who quoted it? Shakespeare or something?" Phoebe stuck her tongue out, the gum wrapped around the tip. She crossed her eyes for added effect.

Rolling my eyes at her, I smiled. "Johann W. von Goethe."

"Bless you."

"Thanks."

"What did he do?"

"He wrote *Faust*."

Phoebe raised her eyebrows. "Forget I asked. I don't know how you can even study English as a major. You speak it, read it, what else is there to know? The way online trolls are now-a-days, no one in thirty years will know that the word 'you' contains more than one letter."

"Aren't you just glass-half-full today?" I said and was hip checked hard enough to stumble off the sidewalk.

Catching my balance, I giggled and realized I was feeling better. Phoebe and I talked about a few good memories from the past year, both of us careful to avoid both Read and Aidan's names. Phoebe was fond of the time the two of us and Cody sat around and mixed Pop Rocks with Pepsi. We were only eight at the time and were convinced we were badass until Cody freaked out and started to cry. He thought our stomachs were going to explode and wanted Phoebe to call an ambulance. Instead, we found Cody's dad, and all he could repeat was that Cody must have been constipated. That summer we learned that mixing Pop Rocks and Pepsi wasn't deadly but also the definition of constipation. We held that over Cody's head for an entire school year.

Shirley Street was a quiet little suburb with overgrown trees and lengthy front lawns. Unlike the newer areas, there was actual space between the houses.

Phoebe's cell phone went off, playing a Metallica song. "Cody?" she asked with a brilliant smile. "You better have gotten me my schnapps, or I'll be pissed."

We saw the house number, and Phoebe motioned for me to go ahead of her.

I stopped in my tracks. The Birket residence was a single-story brick home with brown shingles and overgrown shrubs. The windows were dark, leaving not hint of life beyond the glass. Twisting, I looked to Phoebe, pleading with my eyes.

She produced a very disappointed sigh and said into the phone, "Yeah, we're here already. Fuller was just about to let Aidan know we're here." Stepping into me, she shoved the flat of her hand into my back, pushing me up the walk. My sneakers clomped along the narrow sidewalk with the shove. I slowed afterward, hoping she'd be off the phone by the time I reached the door.

Unfortunately, I think she kept talking to Cody—who we all knew rarely spoke—on purpose.

Fine. I straightened my spine. *I'm not a little kid anymore. She was right to make me do this alone.* Though it didn't mean I'd have to like it. Maybe Read was here ahead of us. If Cody was on the phone with

Phoebe, that meant he and Robin were still behind.

A hair-raising prickle snaked under my skin. I smoothed out my camisole and jean shorts with one hand, trying to make my twitch look natural. Aidan was approaching the door, I knew.

Phoebe's voice droned on behind me between barking laughs and the occasional crude joke.

As I raised my free fist to knock, the door swung open.

Aidan popped into view, and I swallowed a shriek, jumping instead.

"Hi, Nora," he said, looking past me at Phoebe. Then that stare zapped me, and his lips formed a polite smile. "You're the first to arrive." He sounded pleased.

At least one of us was a good liar.

My attempt to match his enthusiasm was awkward, so I ditched the quivering smile. "Phoebe's just on the phone with Cody." I thrust a thumb over my shoulder. I felt like an idiot trying to make a conversation out of the obvious. I looked back and saw Phoebe wave at Aidan.

"Uh huh." Aidan stepped out of the way, inviting me in with a sweep of his arm.

Here goes nothin'.

I forced my legs to move until I heard the door latch behind me.

CHAPTER SEVEN

Though Aidan was behind me, the familiar vibration of his closeness made me shiver.

With a jerky hand, I brushed invisible hair behind my ears and looked around.

The house was small and convenient, retaining a lingering musky scent.

Heavy curtains were all drawn, the lamps attempting to brighten the dark space. I was pretty sure his parents had managed to collect every book with unrecognizable symbols and languages in existence, just to taunt a visitor's intelligence.

The walls were filled with graceful oil paintings beside masks from Africa and Asia. The house held a dim atmosphere, making it almost eerie. At my feet, there was a brown shag carpet, and at the far end of the living room, there was one wall that was entirely made of red bricks. Shelves were overflowing with foreign treasures. The furniture was (not surprisingly) dark as well. A sofa sat adjacent from a fifty-inch television screen, while a leather Lay-Z-Boy snuggled against the far wall beside a mahogany side table. I could almost hear my mother decorating their house.

Noticing my pause, he said, "My parents are archeologists. They're off in Mexico at the moment."

"Working?" I asked.

"No, vacation, but knowing them, they'll probably find another sponsor or project while they're there." Aidan motioned me to follow, leading me past the television and into the red and white kitchen filled with shiny appliances.

The kitchen almost looked like a show-home, especially compared to the living room. The contrast between the two rooms was almost like I stepped into an entirely new house.

I set my duffel bag of clothes on the floor and plopped my grocery bag full of chips, chocolate, and jujubes on the kitchen table.

Aidan tracked my movements, leaving ample room between us. He'd dressed in his usual t-shirt and jeans, but there was something different in his look. One thing I noticed right away was that he'd bothered to shave his stubble and his hair had been combed for once. I'd been so used to the disheveled, sleepy look that I realized I was staring and he was staring right back.

Rigid, I lowered myself into a white chair at the table. The looming silence rang more shrilly than the brakes on the bus. It made the creaking chair beneath me sound damn near explosive.

To alleviate the tension, I attempted a nervous smile. When he didn't smile back, I asked, trying to keep my voice soft so not to disturb the quiet, "We're not supposed to go, are we." It wasn't a question, and I'm not sure what made me blurt it out like that, except that the silence was making every second feel like minutes.

"What?" Aidan's straight eyebrows pinched before he pressed his fingers to his temples and looked away.

Sighing, I took a deep breath, preparing myself to say something that I wasn't entirely prepared to say. I had no intention of telling him about the messages, but maybe I could say what I was feeling? A smidgen of what I was thinking? Ooooh, that could be awkward afterward.

Luckily, Aidan raised his hand to hold me off and cleared his throat before he brought probing pale eyes back up to meet mine. "Nora," he said, as if saying my name might make his teeth stop gritting, "everyone is pumped to go. If you don't want to go, then don't. I'm not forcing anyone…"

He had a point. Though I wasn't sure I liked it.

"…Especially you."

Ouch.

"But I think they'd miss you." His shoulders wouldn't relax, and he stared blank-faced at the fridge instead.

"Why not have something at your apartment, or we could find a place near a lake?" I asked, wishing his fists would uncurl. I shifted in the creaky chair again and winced.

"For starters, this doesn't have noise constrictions, and it's free." Aidan opened the fridge. "Want anything to drink?"

The question was simple enough, though it somehow seemed inappropriate. My heart was beating a thousand times a second, my throat was closing up, and my hands were sweating. Of course I didn't want something to drink! "There've been nightmares…"

"You want me to tell everyone to go home because of nightmares." His eyes flickered over the refrigerator door and found me.

There it was.

"You too?" This time my throat did close, and the words came out a whisper.

Shutting the door with a jerk, Aidan leaned back against the cupboard and crossed his arms. "Everyone has nightmares, Nora."

Why was it each time he said my name it sounded condescending?

"Mine was about spiders," I said, trying to coax his out. "Phoebe's had some too."

Aidan's gaze turned icy, and he shook his head at me. "Listen, I know you don't like me."

I opened my mouth to politely protest, but nothing came out.

"And I don't know what reason I gave you," he continued, "but I would really like to go this year. I know it's selfish of me because they were your friends first, but I'm willing to keep out of your way, and I'm sure we can both have a good time."

I couldn't think of anything to say. To avoid his eyes, I focused on his boyish nose and clasped my clammy hands together on my lap. He'd caught on to my discomfort after all, and why wouldn't he? I didn't hide it as well as I should have. He'd probably be happier if I didn't go. It explained why he'd sometimes bail if I showed up unexpectedly to certain parties throughout the year. If I were him, I wouldn't want me there either.

What was I thinking, asking him to change the venue because of nightmares? Of course, he'd scoff at some silly girl with a head full of nonsense.

Not looking up, I croaked, "I'm sorry."

At the edge of my vision, I could see Aidan go rigid, as if he expected a trick.

I peeked at him, my chin tilted down to try and hide my scarlet face. "I didn't mean to make you feel that way."

Yes, I did and I knew that, but I wasn't about to tell him. I was already feeling rather disgusted with myself.

"No?" He didn't sound convinced. "I like you and your friends. You're some of the only people I don't feel like an outsider with. Have you ever been alone before, Nora? Like really alone?"

I didn't answer, couldn't. It would mean thinking about it.

Taking my muteness for a negative, he continued. "My family moved around so much I hardly had time to make a friend before we were moving again."

Not wanting to feel the weight of guilt any longer, I blurted, "I'll come. But only if you still want me to. If you don't, which I don't blame you, I'll tell everyone I'm sick."

Aidan hesitated before finally shaking his head. "I would really like it if you came."

"You're sure?"

He attempted a polite smile, which failed before he could look away.

The doorbell rang, and we both jumped at the same time.

"I'll be right back. Okay, Nora?"

He didn't look or wait for an answer before he headed through the archway.

Alone, I mulled over our conversation. *What a nice awkward beginning to a sleepover*, I thought, leaning my head back against the wall and rolling my eyes heavenward.

Phoebe's barking laughter from the entry made me feel instant relief. She and Aidan weren't alone when they walked into the kitchen.

Read was following close behind. "Hi, Nora," he greeted, sitting next to me. His dark hair was gelled to perfection. Why he wasn't a model or actor, I'd never know.

Phoebe plopped down opposite me and put her bare feet on my knees. Curling her toes, she stretched back like a cat, arms above her head. "Cody's picking Robin up. They won't be long."

Aidan offered them something to drink, but like me, they refused. I think we were all eager to begin. Phoebe and Aidan made polite conversation while Read wandered off to study some of the artifacts in the living room. Robin didn't bother knocking. She rushed inside, announcing their arrival with a booming, "Hello!"

She strode into the kitchen wearing a clinging green sundress and high-heeled boots that were laced to her knees to make her seem a little taller. I didn't know why she bothered. Next to Cody, she'd always be short— even in heels.

Cody stood in the living room, not bothering to join us in the kitchen. He looked tired even in the dim light. His baggy cargo pants made his butt look as droopy as the bags under his eyes. Even his t-shirt was rumpled, like he'd slept in it.

Aidan craned his neck to see Cody, and Cody nodded his greeting. Ever the tall mute.

Standing at six-foot-eleven, Cody could intimidate any tough guy. Though he was primarily skinny, he was all lean muscle.

I'd seen him play basketball—the sport that was paying his way through college—and the moment he hit the court, he was the badass his physique threatened he was. Once in Robin's presence, he was quiet and reserved. Phoebe once called him the modern day Jekyll and Hyde.

"Where's my schnapps?" Phoebe demanded with a grin.

"It's in Cody's car," Robin sang. "And we got beer and," she walked briskly across the kitchen floor, heels clicking loud and in charge, "vodka and whiskey." She opened the cupboard doors as if she owned the place, though she seemed to know what she was looking for. Despite the heels, she had to go on tippy-toes to pluck a glass from the cupboard.

"You been here before?" I asked Robin.

Robin filled her glass from the cooler, her chin-length chestnut hair swaying as she nodded. "Yeah, the party two months ago. Weren't you?"

Double ouch.

Phoebe changed the subject and jutted her chin toward Aidan. "So, where are we headed?"

"You'll see. Now that we're all here, I'm glad you could all make it." His eyes paused on me.

I realized I was blushing again and looked over to Cody. His light brown eyes were glazed behind golden, long lashes, and I was certain he had no idea someone was talking.

Phoebe pulled her feet off my legs, leaving pink impressions above my knees. "No problem," she said to Aidan. "Shall we head out then?"

"All right!" Robin finished her glass of water and put it in the dishwasher.

Phoebe was the first to head for the front door, while the rest of us gathered our things before following.

Aidan locked up the house while Robin talked of shopping adventures and bowling with a few of Cody's teammates and their girlfriends.

I helped Cody and Read with the large quantity of alcohol that was way more than we'd need for one night. Read's bottled beer, which he bragged to Cody about, looked expensive and possibly German. There wasn't a lick of English on the case.

Aidan opened his station wagon and helped pack it with duffel-bags and Robin's suitcase. I grabbed the last case of beer and shoved it beside Robin's suitcase on top of a blue plastic tarp. There was something underneath it, but I couldn't tell what. Shutting the back, I realized I got last pick for seats. The usual third seat in the back had been removed so we could stuff the car full of our junk, leaving the two bench seats.

Cody, Read, and Robin crammed into the back while Phoebe waited for me to hop into the front seat. "I called shotgun," she announced. I glowered at her, and she returned it with a playful tilt of her golden head.

With everyone waiting, I caved first. Starting an argument with Phoebe was often futile. Ducking into the car, I scooted next to Aidan, careful not to touch him.

We exchanged an uncomfortable glance before facing ahead.

Phoebe slammed her door shut, the hinges shrieking their protest.

Robin's high-pitched giggles bounced around the car as she initiated some type of poking contest that had Cody grumbling his irritation.

Aidan backed out of the driveway, somehow able to see around Robin's bobbing head. The girl might only be five-foot-one, but she was a bouncy one.

"So where are you taking us?" Phoebe pried, twisting in her seat to stare at Aidan's profile.

He didn't remove his eyes from the road. "Learn some patience." He chuckled when he popped the old car into *drive*. The whole vehicle *thunked* before lurching forward.

"Aw, come on Aidan, you can tell us now."

Aidan fell silent and serious, staring straight ahead.

"Give me a hint," Phoebe said, not phased. She jutted out her bottom lip in a pout.

Aidan took one look at her and laughed, actually laughed. I could hear something genuine behind it this time. It wasn't something to be polite or a social requirement. It surprised me what a nice sound it was.

"Okay," he said with a quirked smile that showed some teeth, "it's on my family's property, outside of town."

I had to look; he had very nice teeth. The real smile made him look kind of cute.

"Is it an old barn?" Phoebe asked casually, her attention partially focused on wrapping her fingers around the loose stitching along the back of her seat.

"Nuh uh!" Robin squealed in the back. "I'm not

sleeping in a barn!"

My head was turned enough to see Read's hand dart out and swatted Robin's knee, and she broke out into hysterical giggles that flashed smiles all through the car. Robin had a high-pitched, vibrating laugh. It reminded me a lot of Mona's, which had me a little homesick already.

Robin hit both boys' thighs before they could block her. Cody's lips stretched in what may have been a smile, but he didn't participate.

Twisting her body, Phoebe dropped her elbow on the other side of the seat. "So is it a barn?"

Aidan chuckled. "It's not a barn."

"Another hint," Phoebe urged. Her hand snaked out, slapping Robin's bare thigh; the sound cracked like a whip. Aidan and I winced just before Robin's shriek filled the car.

I twisted to see Robin flop forward gripping her legs, laughing. "No fair, I can't get you."

Cody, despite Robin being his girlfriend, looked relieved that the game was over. He leaned his spiky bleached hair on the window and closed his eyes.

Read reached behind him, opened his German beer, and cracked the top with a bottle opener.

"It was re-built in 1906," Aidan offered. His tone was low compared to Robin's boisterous voice, but it still snagged Phoebe's attention. "Hey, Read," he said, eyes on the rearview, "keep the beer below the window, will you?"

"A farmhouse?" Phoebe asked.

Aidan offered a noncommittal shrug.

"An Indian burial ground?" Robin offered, still babying her legs. The slapping game had ceased without retaliation, for now.

Phoebe snorted. "Are you kidding me?" she asked Robin.

We emerged from the small city onto the open highway. It wasn't long before we took an exit onto a narrow paved road. It had been repaired several times; each bump was evident under the car's poor shocks.

Sometimes, I wanted to be as carefree as Robin, not worrying about anything bad and just enjoying the moment. Robin was a pro when it came to keeping things entertaining, for herself and others. I could join the bustling conversation, but I didn't want to, not yet. There was a nagging at the back of my mind, an apprehension that kept me frozen in my seat.

Rolling my eyes up to the rearview mirror, I caught sight of Cody. He could have been sleeping the way his head jostled each time the car hit a bump. Robin sat up straight again, nudging his shoulder.

Brown eyes snapped wide, glassy and forlorn.

"Did you get any sleep?" I asked him.

His head didn't detach from the window as he muttered, his lips hardly moving, "No, I don't think I did."

Phoebe motioned to Robin but said to Cody, "What kept you up?"

I wanted to ask about nightmares but didn't want to ruin the mood either.

"How much longer? I'm getting hungry," Robin's loud voice demanded in the back seat before Cody could answer. She stuck her pierced tongue out at Phoebe, who returned the gesture.

"Not long," Aidan said.

"Get something from one of the bags if you can

reach it," I said. "There's lots of food."

"Ha!" Robin barked. "Phoebe will be tempted and look up my skirt."

Phoebe's lips curled. "No. Aidan will."

Cody's eyes narrowed, but he didn't say anything. Aidan's pale face flushed before sputtering, "I would not." He glared at Phoebe.

Phoebe couldn't resist her smug smile. "Watch the road, stud."

Read rummaged around in the back for a bag of chips for Robin, which kept her quiet for at least a few more minutes. Small talk was exchanged as Robin seemed to be flirting with Read while Cody slept, though I tuned most of it out.

The trees on either side of the vehicle were thickening. Fewer houses could be seen through them, and the shoulder of the road became nonexistent, replaced by a steep drop off.

Watching the forest zip past Phoebe's face, I didn't look forward until I felt the brakes. Aidan rolled the station wagon off onto an overgrown dirt road. Despite the slow speed, the car rocked hard, sloshing everyone inside from side to side.

"Hey, we must be close now," Robin said between jujube bites.

"What is it?" I asked.

Aidan took his eyes off the road, moving slower along the dirt path. The dust fluttered up behind us, blocking out the entire back window. "You'll see." Those blue eyes penetrated mine, making my insides squirm, and I looked away.

The vehicle fell quiet. Even Robin was hushed as we all watched the thick brush lining the road. If another vehicle happened along one of the sharp bends, there would be no room for both.

Outside the side window, I ducked my head to see the tops of the coniferous trees as they whizzed by. The orange sunlight made them appear to be glowing. The sun wouldn't be around much longer, which wouldn't give us a lot of time to set up.

The car slowed to a crawl, and it was Phoebe's sharp intake of breath that snapped my gaze forward.

We had finally arrived at our destination, and I could see *it*. I wasn't sure if I even liked *it*.

"Whoa," Read said from the back.

"I never expected this," Phoebe whispered to me.

Neither did I.

CHAPTER EIGHT

"Wooooow." Robin's breath warmed the back of my neck.

Slumping in my seat, I realized my mouth was hanging open and clamped my jaw shut with a snap. *We're spending the night here?*

It was a Victorian-style house. The sun-bleached brick siding was pitted with scars and scratches. A wooden front porch had faded to a sickly grey and tilted to the right. There were modern shingles on most of the roof, except for the rounded tower that was suctioned to the side. My eyes were drawn to the tower immediately. The roof bowed at a harsh angle and was littered with rotten shingles and last year's dead leaves. The tower hovered several feet over the new roof, looking like something out of a children's fairytale.

The windows on the first floor were mostly boarded up with plywood and two by fours, while the second floor's were new and crystal-smooth, reflecting the orange sun.

Rank, bare vines entwined the porch railing and clawed their way up the side of the chipped bricks, claiming the house as their own.

A draft chilled my right arm, and I realized Phoebe had stepped out of the car without me noticing.

Aidan and I were the only ones left in the vehicle. "I know it doesn't look like much," he said, "but we've been trying to make little improvements over the years."

I tried to smile at him, avoiding his haunting eyes, and crawled out the passenger's side.

I trailed behind the group as we stared up at the monstrous house, inching our way closer.

A cracked picket fence attempted to secure a front yard, yet it was overgrown with weeds and bushes.

"Have you been inside?" Phoebe asked Aidan. They were in the lead and the first to touch the splintering porch railing.

Aidan nodded and explained about the improvements he and his dad had done lately. "I used to live out here during the summers with my grandpa when I was a kid," he said.

"Aw," Phoebe grinned, "a Leland boy at heart."

Aidan didn't return the smile and wiggled the rickety railing instead. "You could say that. Always wanted to come back, maybe even live here one day."

Read sauntered up behind them. "That part looks the worst, though." He motioned with his beer bottle to the tower section of the house.

Tilting his chin up, Aidan squinted through the twilight. "Yeah, that part was off limits. Grandpa used to go up there sometimes, but I was never allowed."

Robin latched onto Cody's arm and asked, "Is it dangerous inside? Like, could we fall through the floor?"

As if it had been staged, a wooden shingle from the tower scraped off the roof and landed a few feet from Phoebe and Aidan. Dried dirt sprayed up on impact.

Dirt? With the overgrown grass, I didn't expect to hear it make a sound. Edging inside the gate, I hopped up on my tippy-toes to see dirt around the tower section. Not a single plant grew, no grass, shrubs, or weeds, just dirt spanning a foot from the brick.

Robin let out a breath, puffing her cheeks and looking at the rest of us wide-eyed as if to ask, *Really*?

Peering over her shoulder, Phoebe raised eyebrow. "Scared, Robin?"

Robin bit down on her glossy lip and straightened her posture. "No, of course not." I was close enough to see her fingernails dig into Cody's arm. His tired eyes winced but otherwise remained uninterested.

I couldn't blame Robin. My insides felt like mashed potatoes, but if I showed any anxiety, Phoebe would spend the rest of the night plotting to scare the crap out of me.

"Nah," Aidan said, "the inside has had a lot of work done. Hopefully, this summer the porch will be done." He wiggled the railing again, a disapproving line stretching between his brows.

"Hope someone brought candles and flashlights," Read said, flashing extraordinarily white teeth.

"I brought lots, and there should be a bunch in here still." Aidan stepped onto the creaking porch steps. He wobbled once he reached the slant, stretching his arms for balance. The grey boards creaked and groaned as he shuffled to the antique front door. Producing a key from his jeans, he unlocked it and pushed it open. The hinges shrieked their protest, imitating every clichéd haunted house.

Aidan hopped through the threshold and motioned for us to follow.

Read stepped up beside Phoebe. She glared at him, and without warning, he shoved her to the side and launched himself onto the porch. Spitting flames, Phoebe stumbled before darting after him. She came close to pulling his pants down as she fought to beat him into the house.

They slid on the slanted surface like Bambi on ice, entertaining the rest of us. The worthy struggle ended with Read winning the match. Phoebe was quick to complain about the false start as they clambered into the house, their voices carrying into a renewed argument.

Cody helped Robin along the porch. Her high heels weren't equipped for the dramatic arch. She cracked jokes about breaking a leg while swaying like a weeble-wobble doll. Reaching the front door, she caught Aidan's outstretched hand.

I could hear Robin's "ooos" and "awws" as I grabbed the shifting railing.

Aidan waited at the door as I climbed onto the slant. It seemed my sneakers would come in handy after all. Sliding a little, I made it to the doorframe. Aidan had offered his hand after a hesitation, but I didn't take it. "I'm fine," I told him as I landed on a solid wood floor, leaving the rickety porch behind.

Dusting off my hands, I could see that he was right about it looking better inside.

Unmarred drywall had been painted an off-white. The real hardwood floors held a thick film of dust, and now it had footprints. Read inspected the wood framing around every archway. It had been painted so many times there had to be half an inch of dark brown paint on them.

Robin was inspecting a claw-foot dining table in the room ahead of me while Cody stared at the wall.

It was like stepping back into history. The furniture was sparse, but little details like glass doorknobs and brass light-switch coverings were indicators of its time.

To my left, Read was talking to Aidan about firewood, and I followed them into what could have been a quaint living room. Devoid of furniture, it housed a brick fireplace and a window that wasn't covered with plywood. The window's glass was thick, almost making the world outside look a little off.

Behind me, Read blew at the mantel before coughing and sputtering. Looking over my shoulder, I saw the swirling dust fill the faded sunlit room like a fog. Read waved his hand from side to side in front of his face before plucking the dusty lantern from the mantel.

"We could totally have a fire," Aidan pointed out, serious. "Dad told me the chimney was cleaned last weekend and the flue still works, so…"

The dust was starting to tickle the back of my throat.

Read looked back at me. "Nora, you want to help me get wood?"

Robin started to laugh, and I almost choked. "Uuuhhh…"

"What's upstairs?" Phoebe's voice echoed.

Aidan brushed past me into the entrance. I turned to see Phoebe standing on the stairs, creaking them under her shifting weight for entertainment. The stairs turned behind her and disappeared from sight. The wood railing was cracked, and some of the spindles were missing.

"It's kind of messy. I don't know if you want to go up there," Aidan warned as she reached the first landing.

Phoebe flashed a defiant grin toward the second floor. "I can deal with a mess."

Before Aidan could protest, Phoebe disappeared up the stairs, her footsteps creaking the floorboards above our heads.

Aidan hesitated before grabbing the railing. "*Only* the second floor!"

Robin clicked her heels into the entry with us and looked to me, her green eyes wide and excited. "Are we going up?"

Before I could answer, Aidan was trudging up the stairs. "Might as well," he said, frowning. "Bring up some light, will you?"

The curiosity of this old house had hypnotized us all, it seemed. Perhaps Aidan's surprise weekend would be a hit after all. The seeds of guilt were laid as I thought of what a jerk I'd been. This was a great surprise, and it would make a great place for the weekend, maybe even more in the future.

Cody stuffed a handful of candles into his saggy back pocket while Read begrudgingly traded his empty beer bottle for a flashlight.

Read followed Aidan, then it was Cody, then Robin, who snatched my hand in her bony fingers to tug me along.

We traveled up the groaning steps in single file, not leaving anyone out of arm's reach. I was reminded of kindergarten recess.

Read hopped up on the top step, and a distinct crack snapped through the empty space. Robin glanced at me, her smile faltering and her bird-like fingers crushing my hand.

Breathing out slow so not to whimper, I said, "Robin, it's okay if you want to go back downstairs." I somehow hoped she'd say yes, but it only spurred her forward.

"It's okay," she whispered and took a few more steps behind Cody. "If something happens, Cody will save us."

Cody glanced back at the sound of his name, looking like an overgrown zombie.

Yeah, right. Even on a good day, I didn't think Cody could save us.

We reached the top of the stairs and were greeted by a hallway of doors, three doors on the left and two on the right.

Beside the landing was another set of stairs that curled against a circular brick wall.

It must be the tower, I thought and leaned closer.

It was shadowed and dark within, smelling like cold brick and something musty. That's what Aidan must have meant by 'only the second floor.' After seeing the roof, I doubted anyone would want to go up there anyway.

Robin gasped and didn't let go of my hand. Instead, she dragged me along with her. Jolted forward, I was yanked into a small room with her, our feet pounding on the wood floor.

Stumbling to a stop, I could see the source of her gasp.

An old crib was coated in spiderwebs and layers of dust. It appeared hand-carved, laced with intricate designs.

Above it was one of the new windows. I could see an overgrown pond behind the house. Cattails and long reeds encrusted the tree line before thinning into bush.

Robin pushed the crib with the toe of her boot, and it rocked for the first time in what could have been a decade.

The familiar hum bristled my hair, and I looked back to see Aidan walk into the room.

Seeing the crib rocking, he stepped inside. "Apparently, it was my grandpa's crib when he was a baby."

He was walking too close to me.

I felt my shoulders rise and refused to move. I wasn't going to show Robin that I was uncomfortable.

Aidan moved to stop the crib's rocking, and his hand brushed against mine.

That humming shock that I often felt around him became sharp. It electrocuted every hair on my arm and rocketed through my shoulder blades, giving me goosebumps.

It wasn't so much a physical shock as a vibration with a life of its own.

It wasn't my imagination. We both stiffened.

I met his shocking blue eyes to see them just as wide as my own and realized he felt it too.

CHAPTER NINE

Offering the little crib a sad smile, Robin shifted her eyes toward the only other piece of furniture in the room, a broken empty shelf. "Come on," she urged to me.

Staring at Aidan, I realized I should breathe.

He did at the same time, and neither of us moved.

When Robin reached the doorway, she looked back and paused.

Phoebe thundered into the moment. "Okay, you two! There's a third floor."

Aidan and I jerked apart as if stung.

Blushing, I spun around and almost bowled Robin over.

Luckily, Robin was spry enough to dodge, and we bolted past a bewildered Phoebe. The stinging thought followed Robin and me into the next room: *He felt that.*

I almost ran into the antique chest in the new room. A cracked mirror leaning against the wall gave Robin and me a distorted reflection.

Robin's green eyes were sparkling. "That was soooo cute, Nora."

"Ah, what?" I asked, hoping she'd keep her voice down.

"That was like a *moment*," she said, grinning so hard her face could split. "I mean, what if this turns out to be a romantic weekend? I would have been there when you guys first..."

"Stop," I hissed, and somehow, she listened.

She pinched her lips together with her teeth, but the excitement behind Robin's eyes didn't wane. She kept looking at me as I pretended to find interest in a chest full of mouse-chewed blankets. Robin had far too many romantic ideas. Sometimes I wondered how Cody could stand it. If he didn't bring flowers when he was supposed to, I bet she snapped.

"Phoebe..." Aidan sounded exasperated.

Stepping out into the hallway, I saw everyone was there, except Phoebe.

"It's starting to get dark." Read motioned to the window and flicked on his flashlight.

"Should we start a fire?" Robin asked.

Cody nodded.

"Nora and I were going to get firewood," Read said, pointing the flashlight at my feet.

Robin said, "Maybe Nora should help Aidan get it. He'll know where it is."

What a brat.

Aidan didn't seem to be listening to any of it. He was approaching the darkened doorway leading to the third floor.

"Where's Phoebe?" I asked.

Read thrust a thumb over his shoulder, not looking impressed. "Went exactly where Aidan said not to go." To Aidan, he said, bored, "I told you, man."

"Should we go up after her?" Robin asked, rocking from her toes to her heels impatiently.

Cody flinched and muttered in a slur, "Let's stay down here. Does anyone smell rain?"

Ignoring Cody's question, I asked, "Aren't you curious what's up there?"

Aidan turned his head like a whip and narrowed his eyes at me.

Shrugging my shoulders under the weight of the glare, I said, "I'm just saying," I held up my hands apologetically, "that if we're curious, she's ten times worse."

"True," Read grumbled, sounding bitter. "You can't keep that girl out of your business."

I waited, as it seemed he wanted to continue, but he swung his flashlight to the circular stairs instead.

"Phoebe," Aidan called and inched toward the open archway as if it would suck him in.

"What?" Phoebe's voice echoed against brick walls from above.

"Come back down," Aidan said, sounding worried.

"I'm almost at the top," she protested. "Don't you want to know what's up here, Aidan?"

Aidan rubbed his face with one hand, hard. "Well, yeah, but the floorboards are so brittle a pebble could fall through."

"Yeah, Phoebe," Read called, "we don't want to have to spend another weekend taking you to the hospital."

By another, he meant just one. Phoebe had broken

her foot falling out of a tree once, and her foot had decided to swell black and blue within the hour.

"I'm not scared," Phoebe said.

I could almost see the Cheshire Cat grin on her face. "Phoebe, we have to unload the car!" I shouted, growing impatient. I realized I wanted to go back downstairs. Cody was already starting down but stopped when Robin grabbed his arm.

I think Aidan mouthed, "Thank you," in my direction, but I couldn't be sure.

Phoebe said, "I'm going to look from the outside. Okay?"

"No! Stop fucking around and get back down," Aidan snapped.

I didn't think I'd ever heard him angry, like really angry before. He'd been annoyed with me, and sometimes Phoebe, though never angry. This time, I heard an edge to his voice, one that made him seem more like a twitchy finger on a loaded shotgun.

Read was grumbling, "Just let her go."

I could hear Phoebe's echo above. She was clucking like a chicken.

"What if she falls through?" Aidan demanded. "I don't even know where she'd fall. Cell phone reception isn't that great out here."

Cody pulled two of the candles from his baggy back pocket and held them out.

Aidan had the lighter.

Robin snickered as she carefully combed her hair with her fingers, smoothing it out to perfection. "We should go up there and scare the crap out of her."

Cody cracked a weary smile as Aidan lit two candles with a shaky hand and took one.

Everyone pretended not to notice, and no one moved to go first.

Concerned, my lips parted to ask, but Robin began to whine.

Whatever mechanism Cody had built into him instantly reacted. He grabbed Robin's petite hand and shouldered past Read, Aidan, and me. The two used the brick wall for support and started up the stairs. Robin frantically waved for us to follow.

Rolling his eyes, Read grumbled, "If it were one person to ruin a party, it'd be Phoebe." To Aidan, he said, "You want to start the car and I'll carry her out when she breaks her legs?"

"That's not funny," I said.

Aidan sighed, his eyes trained on the stairs, eyebrows pinching. "Looks like we're going up to the tower." He didn't sound the least bit amused.

I began to wonder how fast Aidan's clunker car could drive back to town if something did happen.

Read ducked his dark head and led the way up the steps, carrying the flashlight. I was next, then Aidan with his own candle. He cupped the flame in his palm to keep it from blowing out as he climbed the noisy stairs, leaving a few steps between us.

A cold draft from the circular tower sent a trail of goosebumps up my arms. *When we get back downstairs, I'm getting a sweater.* I should have thought of that earlier. There were gaps in the roof, after all.

I could see Robin and Cody just ahead of him. Robin was balancing on her toes so not to let her boots click, but I was pretty sure Phoebe knew we were coming. She was probably crouched up there waiting to scare the first person to walk through the door, which would be Robin and the worst candidate of our group. I hoped Cody had the reflexes to catch her, even tired.

With the faint light, I could see that the steps were thick four-by-eight planks that had been lodged into the circular brick wall. No railing graced the edge, and I was forced to use the wall as a guide. The gritty, cold brick sprinkled dirt past my palm.

If one of these planks was rotted enough, it could have a domino effect.

Phoebe was going to have to chill with the daredevil stuff or someone was going to get hurt.

As if in answer to my thought, the heart-piercing shout erupted from the third floor.

CHAPTER TEN

At the head of the group, Cody and Robin froze, stopping all motion on the spindly stairs.

It was Read who whispered an echo that was something like, "*Move*," and we lurched forward like soldiers. Robin's heels prevented a full-tilt run, which may have been helpful, considering the rickety stairs.

Cody and Aidan's candles went out, and I almost lost my balance in the dark.

I used the wall to steady myself, and the grit numbed my fingertips as I sailed up the steps as fast as Read would let me.

I used the glow of the swinging flashlight overhead as a guide.

I bumped into Read's back in my concentration. The smell of the burnt wick crowded my nose.

Swaying to catch my balance, I gasped, "Phoebe? Are you okay?" Cody's lanky, tall body was blocking most of my view.

No one answered. No one even moved.

Read, Cody, and Robin peered into a room through an arched brick doorway, never stepping inside, stranding Aidan and me in the creeping dark. The itching, spying dark.

Trying to peer over Read's shoulder, I could just make out the open trusses of the ceiling and slivers of moonlight filtering through the holes.

"What is it?" Aidan whispered close to my ear. His warm breath had me gulping back a squeal. He was careful not to touch my skin when he tapped me in the middle of the back and asked again. "Nora? What's going on?"

"I don't know," I confessed.

He sounded worried, and I couldn't blame him. There were people he just met a year ago looking into his family's business, and they weren't reacting—at all.

I thought about what it would be like if everyone gutted my own family's affairs? If everything I'd held secret was laid out on the table, I'd be expecting some type of judgment, scorn, or pity. I didn't want any of that, and I was certain Aidan didn't either.

Taking in a deep breath, I shouted, "*What the hell is going on?*" Cody cringed at the blistering echo that shot back at us.

"I'm okay," Phoebe called, her voice echoing past us along the stairwell.

Well, that was a relief, but it didn't change the fact that Aidan was still behind me. Standing on my tippy-toes, I was still unable to see Phoebe. I was about to ask Cody, Read, and Robin to move when Robin interrupted me.

Twisting her petite figure in the tight space between

the two tallest, skinniest guys, Read and Cody, she faced us in the dark. "You're sure you've never been up here, Aidan?"

Read swung the flashlight back, blinding me. Raising my free arm to block it, I squinted over my shoulder to see Aidan's confusion. "Yes, I'm very sure," he said slowly, testing the words one by one.

His handsome face screwed tight, Read moved forward at last, leading the pack into the room. Aidan practically mowed me over when we reached the last step and entered the circular tower room.

Inching along the wall, allowing space for the others, I swallowed my alarm.

The brick wall across from me looked like it had been chipped away, like some sort of graffiti. It wasn't a natural pattern.

Read's flashlight swept over the far wall.

Feeling light headed, I snapped my hands out to steady myself against the gritty wall and keep the room from tilting. *I don't want to be in here*, I realized in a sharp panic.

The weighty eyes were hiding in the dark. I could feel the dirty gaze and took a deep breath.

Phoebe was across the circular room, inspecting the walls. A pattern wasn't gouged into the brick. It was *the* words.

Dismal is the Demon's Grave was the one nearest to the ceiling, followed closely by *Offered death for once the brave. One soul of blackened sin.*

Then there was another sentence, one I hadn't seen before.

Railing torment lies within.

In the center of the room, two oversized wooden

chairs sat back to back. They reminded me of the electric chairs featured on TV, minus the wires and headsets. There wasn't anything fancy in their construction. They were blocked pieces of wood that were old but held a finish to prevent rot. One faced a tiny window that was no bigger than my hands.

The second large wooden chair was tilted toward me, and I could see the leather straps on the arms and legs. Were they used to hold people down? Was there something about this room that Aidan wasn't *supposed* to know?

I pressed back into the cool, gritty wall; it gave me a sense of stability, a sense of this all being real.

My muscles tensed as a foreign heat swelled near the surface of my skin. The grainy wall chilled the unexpected wave, and I wondered if I was going to throw up.

Cody stumbled a little and flopped onto the chair facing me. At first he held his arms up, inspecting the shiny surface on the chair. The wood, especially where the hands would rest, was lubricious. *Was it age or repetitive use*?

My legs began to vibrate from the inside out, and my knees threatened to buckle, but I didn't fall.

"Nora," Aidan whispered beside me, "are you okay?"

Just moving my head flashed little black spots before my eyes. I hadn't been feeling this dizzy down below, but then, I hadn't felt the weighty eyes either. I wondered if the run had affected me in some way, or maybe the room.

Aidan was watching me. I hadn't really seen him worried before, but his face was pinched, body rigid, as if he expected to run.

Read asked, "Do you need help?"

I could only imagine what I must look like to them. My arms nearly spread eagle, hands clawed against the brick, and legs tight together. I confessed hoarsely, "I don't know if I can stand." I was certain I didn't want to sit in the other chair.

Barely touching my arm, Aidan's fingertips were icicles against my hot skin, and I shivered, unsure if it was the initial sensation I had felt when our hands touched or if it was just a feverish reaction. Aidan's pale eyes shifted from my arm to my face, and he paused before motioning for me to lean on him.

"It's okay, buddy," Read said. "I got her."

One of his hands caught around my waist; it was easy for him to pull me away, and I pushed more of my weight into Read than I normally would have.

Leaning my shoulder to Read's t-shirt, I felt his warmth, and I almost preferred Aidan's cool hands.

Gripping my waist as if I might pitch forward, Read drew me closer to the chair behind Cody's. I couldn't help but watch my feet to make sure they didn't cross over each other and I'd land on my face.

With Read's flashlight pointing down, I noticed the floor was spotless, dust-free. Not a single footprint. The floorboards weren't straight; they formed a pattern. A series of triangles that all pointed to the middle, to the chairs.

I hadn't realized I had Read's shirt knotted in my first until he helped me sit down. I collapsed, and my legs and arms sighed in relief though the room still tilted.

"Thanks," I muttered and noticed Phoebe watching

us, her mouth pinched.

"What do you think these chairs are for?" I asked.

Aidan gave a careful shrug. "My grandpa collected antiques. He…" His eyes widened, and he looked from them to me. "You don't think that he used these, do you?"

Not feeling well enough for an argument and slightly embarrassed that it had been my first conclusion, I scoffed. "No, of course not."

"They were probably just too heavy to put in the auction," Aidan said.

If no one had been up here, why was the window shiny and floors swept? Only the bricks and chairs seemed affected by age and the weather.

Phoebe asked, "You've never been here before?"

Aidan looked to Phoebe, affronted. "No, I told you. Grandpa said it was too dangerous."

"Not you," Phoebe said, "*her*."

I realized she was talking to me and froze. "You're joking, right?" My eyes betrayed me as I glanced at the writing on the wall.

I had asked her not to tell, begged her! What was she doing?

Saving the day, Read almost ran into Phoebe. He was touching the red walls with his palm, as if he could absorb what he saw. "Have you guys noticed this?"

Robin sat down on the floor and crossed her ankles. She seemed to have noticed the lack of dust as well; otherwise, she'd never have risked it. She was facing Cody and me in the chairs when she snapped at Read, "Kind of hard not to."

"No, not the writing. The wall!" When no one reacted, he continued, "It's warm in some spots, ice cold in others, and even hot sometimes. It almost hurts to touch it."

Phoebe touched the wall, patting her way around the room to confirm. "He's right."

Bewildered, Aidan joined them, and the three slapped at the bricks, discussing the unusual temperature changes.

Robin tapped my arm with a manicured nail. Careful not to turn my head too fast, I squinted over at her. "Nora, your initials are carved into the back of this chair."

"What?"

"That could be anyone's initials," Cody slurred. I wasn't sure if it was because he was dizzy like me or if he'd drank while downstairs and I hadn't noticed.

"N.E.F. is written here." Robin pointed at the chair.

"My middle name is Jean."

"Your name is Nora Jean?" Robin imitated a southern accent with a half-smirk.

I would have swatted at her if I thought I could aim, but the wavering room wouldn't allow it. "I don't think I want to be up here anymore," I said. "I don't feel well."

"Me neither," Cody echoed.

Ignored, Phoebe spoke up, the urgency in her voice demanding attention. "What's this? This wasn't here before, I swear. I walked around the whole room, like, twice."

I turned the other way in my seat to look. Instant dizzying waves slapped me in the face, and I touched my cheek, feeling that my skin wasn't just warm; it was hot. Dropping my face in both hands, I wondered if I needed to vomit. Peeking up at my friends through splayed fingers, I said, "Guys, we want to get out of here."

"Wait a second," Read said.

Aidan took three strides toward Phoebe and Read to study the new find. "It's a door," he announced.

That's it, I've finally lost it. I'm wandering around in my head right now, and I bet Phoebe is back downstairs explaining to the rest of my friends that I had a family history of hallucinations and it was bound to happen one day.

This strange door was small, maybe four feet tall, if that. I was reminded of the one from *Alice in Wonderland.*

Off the deep end, here I go. I giggled behind my hands at the thought.

Our new door had a brass knob that was as big as an eight ball. It wasn't wooden like the door downstairs. It was a pale-blue marble, the color of…the color of Aidan's eyes. It was as smooth and shiny as glass, reflecting the candles and single flashlight. I could see Phoebe and Aidan's reflections in the gleaming surface.

"Open it," Phoebe whispered loud enough for us all to hear, though she was talking to Aidan.

Aidan looked back at me. "Should I?" he asked.

I wasn't sure why he was asking me. Maybe because he knew I wasn't feeling well and wanted out too.

My eyes trailed to the messages. I shook my head but at the same time said, "Sure, why not?" The minute they escaped, I knew those words weren't mine.

I touched my mouth with my shaking hands. My lips felt numb. I wanted to yell, "No!" Instead, I wheezed.

Down, down, down the rabbit hole.

Aidan had turned back to the marble door and

reached for the knob.

He turned it as if it might crumble beneath his palm. It sounded like two smooth stones grinding together. I jumped out of the chair, spooking Robin. She toppled back as I tried to scream.

Not even a whimper escaped my throat.

"Guys," Robin called, her eyes on me while everyone else seemed focused on the new find. Everyone except for Cody. He was trying to get out of his chair behind me but seemed to have lost control of his legs. He couldn't run, and I couldn't scream to warn them.

The swelling panic brought on a strange warmth inside my stomach. At first, it was ignorable, until I felt a pinch of pain, as if the warmth were growing too hot. Maybe I really did have to vomit.

Grabbing the armrest with my fingernails, I prepared myself to retch over the side when something happened. I could only describe it as a burst of energy escaping.

One second I thought I was going to vomit and the next, the hot acid rippled up my throat and was gone, as if it were never there, but I was weakened somehow. The dizziness that almost had me to my knees evaporated along with it.

Choking, I half expected pain when I swallowed but instead found my voice. "Stop!" The hoarse scream was worthless.

Aidan swung open the door, and a shrieking wind exploded into the room.

CHAPTER ELEVEN

Aidan's sneakers grazed my knees as the wind lifted him off his feet and threw him against the opposite wall.

The candles were snuffed, leaving a swinging flashlight and faint moonlight.

Gripping the armrest, I twisted to try and see Aidan. My ponytail whipped past my temple like a spear.

It took a moment for my eyes to adjust before I could see that Aidan wasn't falling. The wind wasn't strong enough to lift me out of my chair, but it had pinned Aidan to the wall. He was red-faced, and his arms were above his head, one leg poker straight and the other bent at the knee. Neither foot touched the floor.

The flashlight rolled in front of me.

Moving to catch it with my foot, I heard Robin scream, "Get away from..." Her voice melted into the howling.

I missed the flashlight as it swung past my foot, and I scrambled out of the chair to catch it. All the energy I had before climbing those stairs had returned. The wind didn't lift me up but shoved at me as I chased the flashlight toward the stairs. My fingertips grazed the round handle before I was snagged. The wind twisted around me like a funnel.

Jerked upright with the force, I was spun around before I had enough time to comprehend what was going on. Flung like a rag doll, I twisted to face the room again, my mouth opening, but I couldn't scream through the oxygen-stealing wind.

I squinted to find Phoebe not far from me, standing stiff as a board. Her face too was red, and her hands were balled into white-knuckled fists. Read was beside her at the wall, his hands up to his ears. The hollow whistle tore through my eardrums, and I tried to wiggle my arms.

I couldn't.

Moving my head wasn't a problem, but every other part was impossible. My fingers would barely twitch on command. I stood as frozen as a statue, deaf and sucking in small breaths where I could. Something had just taken my voice and balance seconds before, which left me to wonder: what else was it capable of?

I felt a quiver begin at the base of my spine and rattle through my body, working its way through the back of my head and echoing like a gong.

I wanted to ask Aidan if he was all right. Tilting my chin up, I saw he was still pinned to the wall, immobile and struggling. What would stop it from doing that to me? To anyone in this room?

Swallowing hard, I tried to ignore the panicky

sensation to run. Trying to twitch my legs, I knew I couldn't but kept trying. *You're trapped*, an evil voice in my head hissed.

Stay calm, I rationalized in response. The spidery feeling of dread was edging my mind. Was this it? Was I dead? Insane? Could this even be real? All I knew was I wanted to leave.

Robin had already let the hysteria take over. I could see her screaming but couldn't hear her over the roar.

Cody's long arm was frozen as he reached out for his petite girlfriend, his bleached spikes blown tight against his scalp.

As abruptly as the wind had begun, it vanished.

Stunned, I took a deep breath, hearing frantic gasps and Robin's shaky sobs fill the tower.

Testing my limbs, I found I still couldn't move. Every inch of me was a statue.

"Run for the exit!" Phoebe commanded. She was in the same position she had been when the wind had hit her. "Read!" Phoebe screamed.

Read was *moving*.

"Read, run!" I joined in. Just finding my own voice was glorious. He was the farthest from the marble door other than myself.

His eyes were locked on Phoebe's before he bolted. Racing toward me, he brushed past and on to the archway. As he reached it, I heard a sharp slap.

I jumped and lost my balance. The shock of being able to move again threw me off.

Stumbling, I saw the stairway was replaced by the same smooth brick as the rest of the circular room.

Standing straight, I tested my limbs, curling my fingers, moving my legs, stretching my arms. Such simple actions sparked incredible relief in me.

Aidan had fallen from the wall, landing awkwardly on his feet.

Read slapped the bricks, testing their integrity. "What is this?" he demanded. "We have to get out of here." A wild fear had sparked in his grey eyes, and he slammed his shoulders into the bricks.

"Read, stop, you'll just hurt yourself." Aidan's voice was strained.

"What was that, Aidan?" Cody asked, his voice shaky and soft.

Robin looked up, tears streaking her thick foundation make-up. "Cody?" She sobbed, shaking so hard I was surprised the floorboards didn't shudder beneath her.

Cody twisted, stood, and reached for Robin in one motion. Though he was still pale, he didn't seem as sick as before. He pulled Robin up in his arms, protecting her, and I felt a pang of longing.

Fearful, my eyes flickered back to the wall where the door had been. The window was too small for me to crawl through. Even then, it was a three-story drop.

I looked to the opened marble door.

I didn't move closer to see where the mystery wind had come from. I wanted to sink into the floor and disappear. This type of craziness didn't happen to real people—to sane people.

I pinched myself hard and winced as the pain throbbed in my forearm. It didn't feel like a dream. *Or was it all a hallucination? Maybe this was all in my head right now.*

In a feeble attempt to calm myself, I took a deep breath through my nose, releasing it through parted lips, and stared at the only escape, now filled with an inky darkness.

The marble door hadn't disappeared, but beyond it was a black pit, giving no hint to what it hid.

Phoebe spoke first, anger and fear searing her voice. "What the fuck."

"What is this?" I croaked.

We all waited for an answer, tensing with each delayed second.

Phoebe took a cautious step forward. "Where's the flashlight?"

"It must have fallen through the doorway before the…" I motioned to the bricks Read was leaning against.

Phoebe sighed through her nose.

I heard a lighter spark to life, and a blaze of color erupted beside me.

Aidan was at my side. I hadn't even known he was there, and it took all I had not to jump. I'd always known when he was close; what had changed?

Aidan's pale eyes narrowed on the darkened rabbit hole as he lit one of the discarded candles.

The mysterious opening was still dark. The door should have led outside. The main house was only two stories high while the connecting tower was three. At least that's how it appeared from the outside.

He raised his candle higher, but no shadows cast within the marble doorway. He didn't move any closer, and I didn't blame him.

My imagination presented me with a variety of gruesome ideas.

"Maybe we can get to the roof through the window," Cody said.

Read was shaking his head. "Who'd fit through there?"

Robin started to raise a shaky hand. "Maybe?"

Aidan stepped forward, closer to the hole.

I gasped, and my hands clawed out to catch him. "*Don't.*"

Aidan paused, stretching the candle toward the doorway as far as he could without stepping closer. Not even a shadow revealed itself. There wasn't a floor or walls, just blackness.

Phoebe grabbed my arm and whispered, "Come on, the window."

I reached for Aidan, snagging the back of his shirt. He didn't resist as I pulled him back.

It was as if a gunshot went off when we all bolted for the window at the same time.

Read had reached the window first, but his hand never touched the glass. Instead, he hit brick.

I ran into Phoebe, and Aidan ran into me. Cody and Robin skidded just behind Aidan, almost colliding with the group. It could have been comical any other day.

All around us, there was a solid wall. The single candle provided the only light. I looked up to see the patchy room was sealed above.

It was plain luck that the flame hadn't been snuffed in our race.

Robin's breaths came loud and raspy from behind, each one a struggle.

No one dared to speak, but what would anyone say?

I touched my forehead. If I'd finally cracked, I should be the one panicking, not Robin.

I turned slowly, my eyes falling on the little doorway again.

If it were possible, a darker shadow stood in front of it. "Guys," I hissed.

Everyone turned and froze.

Aidan raised the flame and revealed a human-shaped shadow without a source. Defying all physics, the shadow didn't disappear when struck with our candlelight. It remained perfectly still. There were no features other than the human shape. It seemed two-dimensional, and it was definitely male. Broad shoulders and narrower hips, short hair (I think), even the stance seemed masculine rather than feminine.

"What the hell is that?" Phoebe's eyes were wide and feral.

Robin was sobbing so hard that Cody shushed her.

Read inched forward. "This is a nightmare," he whispered. "Just like early this week. It's all just a dream."

"Then it's my dream." My lips felt numb.

The perfect shadow had remained still against the bricks until I spoke.

It lifted off the wall and began to shift. The darkness within the shadow swirled like a living mist, reflecting Aidan's light.

Read looked to us. "What do we do?"

That was a good question, but no one answered.

As he turned back to the spectacle, it began to gain color, texture, morphing from a shadow into the shape that held it dormant.

It was faded at first, and I strained to see more, wanting to see every piercing feature before it manifested itself fully. My fingers had dug deep enough to peel skin near my elbows.

Then the shadow was gone, replaced by a man.

Chapter Twelve

There were few explanations for what I was seeing.

I was either crazy or bat-shit-crazy. I'd have to decide later.

Instead, I peeked at my friends to see the same shock.

It was a minor relief, but it proved that I wasn't completely mad. Right?

Blinking rapidly as if it could clear the illusion, I realized I'd just watched a shadow morph into a solid man who didn't appear much older than us, though I doubted that was the case. Nothing that rolls out of shadows could be like us.

He was breathtaking, and as hard as I tried, I couldn't look away.

I've never seen a day-old corpse before but I wouldn't be surprised if it had skin like his, deathly pale and flawless. It made a shocking contrast to his midnight hair, like he was digitally remastered instead of real.

Without thinking, I stepped forward and spoke past the awkward lump in my throat. "Who are you?"

Even his voice sounded dark, low, and resonating. "The question is who are *you*?" His obsidian eyes sought me out, and I unexpectedly felt violated.

Read was the first to recover and knocked on the bricked-up window. "*We* are just about to leave."

I glanced at the strange man dressed all in black. The t-shirt beneath the vest subtly revealed broad shoulders, chest, and arms. One had to look to notice, and I was quite sure every female in the room noticed.

The man could have been dreamy if he hadn't just popped out of shadows. Nothing that beautiful should exist, except maybe in a fairy tale, to tempt stupid, young girls into some perverse, sexual game.

"You can't leave," the shadowed man rumbled, "yet."

Before any of us could stop him, Read stepped in front and shouted, "Hey, man, what's your problem? We don't belong here! Let us out."

The man in black smiled without showing teeth. "Well, *man*, as an illegal transgressor, you became my problem." He managed to mimic Read so well, I had to replay the scene in my head several times to register what shadow-man said.

Gritting his teeth, Read lurched forward, fists white and tight. If it hadn't been for Phoebe's firm hand, he might have made a move he'd regret. "There's six of us and one of him," Read hissed at Phoebe.

"Yeah, one of him," Phoebe echoed, "but I don't suppose you noticed that he used to be a friggin' shadow that came out of a four-foot door?"

With a violent jerk, Read pulled free. Phoebe looked ready to grab him again but bit her bottom lip and stopped.

Vibrating, Aidan sounded indignant. "Trespassed? This is Birket property."

The shiny black hair that fell over the man's forehead shook, and he motioned to the marble door. "This is my place. The doorway to my world."

He was darkness. I could *feel* it. I was certain he was responsible for the wind. What else was he capable of? He'd paralyzed my body, forced words out of my mouth, and basically scared the crap out of me. What could we possibly do about him?

"You opened a forbidden gateway," he said in a low rumble, practically a seductive purr.

"We didn't know." Robin's usually loud voice was numbed.

"Yes, I see that. Now you will have to come with me."

I shook my head and noticed everyone else was too. "You can't make us," I said. It sounded feeble, even to me. Of course he could make us. We were helpless flies in honey.

The man in black laughed, actually threw his head back and laughed for several heartbeats. "If you stay, you'll starve." He swiped his hand as if he were decapitating all of us with his fingers. "I've given ample warning."

Blinking away the numerous questions, I focused on one. "What warnings?"

Phoebe's arms slapped to her sides. "Oh God."

I thought she was going to mention the messages I had received, but instead she said, "I'm so sorry. I thought I was just imagining things…"

Read grabbed her shoulders, facing her before demanding, "Imagined what?"

"I thought…" Phoebe swallowed so hard I could hear it.

"When I got up here and shouted for you guys, I thought I saw myself, sitting in that chair." She pointed to the one Cody had fallen in when we'd first arrived. "I was strapped in, and there was blood." She rubbed her forearms and hands. "And the writing on the wall…" Her eyes shifted to me.

Read glanced at me before saying, "It's okay, Phoebe, you didn't know." Turning his attention to the man in black, he tried to take charge. "We didn't know, all right? Just let us go. We'll never come back, I promise. We'll board up the room and never come back."

Nodding in unison, our little group tightened together.

The hungry smirk on the beautiful man's face gnawed at my insides.

"It's too late for that," he said. "Not only did I give a standard warning…"

"A standard warning?" Phoebe's hands dropped from her mouth, her eyes filling with anger. "That was terrifying!"

Calmly, as if he hadn't been interrupted, he continued. "A standard warning in accordance to the rules. Also, some of you sensed the doorway the minute you stepped into this room, *my* room."

The dizziness and nausea…

I glanced at Cody, who returned my pointed stare, affirming my suspicions.

"Then my grandpa didn't write those words on the walls?" Aidan asked under his breath.

"Let me get this straight!" Phoebe demanded. "We opened a doorway to your world, and now we have to go with you because of some rules we don't know or even care about?" She paced the room but kept a safe distance from the shadow-man.

His eyes stalked Phoebe's every step. "Because you opened the door, you must face the Challenge."

"A challenge?" Aidan repeated, strained.

The man in black nodded, his hair sweeping across his low brow as he did. "If you win, you can return home safe and sound. If you fail, you belong to me."

"To you?" Aidan asked.

I twisted to see if Aidan was trying to piss him off. Instead, I found myself staring at someone entirely different.

Aidan's eyes were glassy. His mouth hung open, and his already pallid skin had been drained of all conceivable color, including his lips.

"Yes, mine for eternity."

"Yours?" Aidan echoed so softly that I barely heard him.

"Aidan?" My hand touched the top of his fingers, and I prepared myself for the tingling sensation. When it didn't happen, I curled my fingers around his hand, waiting for the sensation to shoot up my arm like before. I didn't realize I was squeezing until he flinched and looked to me. Those vacant, pale blue eyes didn't seem to be seeing me, though.

My heart plummeted. Pulling my hand away, I forced myself to look at the man in black. "You didn't answer my question about who you are."

To my sickened horror, I realized he had been watching me before I'd turned. "I am the darkness between worlds."

Something about those words rang a warning in my head. My eyes flickered to the words, *Dismal is the Demon's Grave* behind him. *Dismal and dark...*

I had heard this before. But where? It was like the day I found the note. There'd been a cold chill of recognition, but in my mind, the memories remained misty.

"You're from the Demon's Grave then." I pointed to the messages. "We're the braves?" I hoped not. *Offered death for once the brave.*

Phoebe snapped, "But that still doesn't tell us what you are."

That cold stare left me, finally. "What could possibly live in a Demon's Grave?" He mimicked her tone.

It was shocking to hear something so perfect say something so condescending and so...human.

"A demon," I blurted.

Phoebe whirled to face me.

The demon clapped his hands two or three times, beaming at me as if he were a proud teacher and I his pupil.

The demon gestured to the marble door at his back, seemingly bored. "In each world, there is a doorway, but not everyone can enter. You cannot."

"This is bullshit. We weren't going to anyway," Phoebe hissed, glancing at the rest of us.

Somehow, the demon had heard. "I am also someone you don't want to upset." Despite the calm politeness, there was a black inferno in those eyes.

Phoebe snapped her fist up with a single distinctive finger ready.

"Phoebe, don't." Read jumped forward and clasped her wrist, swinging her around to face him.

She stopped on command, and her gaze fell on Read, eyebrows furrowing. "We can't just go," she whispered. I could see the worry sinking into her, inch by inch.

My hands balled into fists. *If this were all in my head, then I should have some control, shouldn't I?*

Before I could think through a plan of action, his voice interrupted my thoughts. "If you don't go and take your chance, you forfeit and lose."

A chance to promote my delusion. I hid the smirk behind my hand. Feeling a little giddy, I held back the laugh. I really, *really* just wanted a hysterical release.

I bit down on my lips harder, praying the pain would take the hysterics away.

I glanced at Robin. Her face was buried in the crook of Cody's arm, and she was holding very still while I was vibrating on the inside.

"What do we call you?" Cody spoke for the first time.

Sighing through his nose, shadow-man finally said, "Call me Damien, for now."

Like the little demonic kid in The Omen? *Of course I'd pick that name for a demon.* That movie scared the crap out of my sister and me as kids. And against my protests, she named her stuffed bear after him so it wouldn't scare her anymore.

Read's grey eyes narrowed. "Why should we be ready? No one else got these warnings."

Damien gestured to the wall. "I sent these, to be

specific."

Phoebe glanced at me again. "What if only one of us got them?"

Sucking my cheeks in, I tried to will her eyes away from me.

Damien raised his straight eyebrows. "You all received the messages. The subconscious is a path of communication."

I wondered which was more impressive, the part about everyone having nightmares or the part about different worlds.

Phoebe's eyes were trained on me. "And what about people who saw them without dreams?"

Damien's eyes followed Phoebe's to me.

The hysterics were shattered by the wrecking ball that was his stare. I coughed to try and hide my unease.

"What exactly is the Challenge?" Phoebe continued.

Read was still holding onto her arm, but neither seemed to notice. They were a pretty couple, I decided. The exact height and nearly the same build. Phoebe with her full lips and flawless olive complexion and Read with chiseled cheekbones and thick, dark hair. An hour ago, they would have barked at each other rather than be that close.

Just another pair who had someone to lean on, I thought and glanced at Aidan, who was still looking stunned. *Nuh uh.*

"It is simple," Damien said, gaze sweeping. "You survive six Challenges and you're set free. If you fail, you're trapped."

"What kind of challenges?" Read and Phoebe asked together before glaring at each other.

"Once you pass through this door, your thoughts

will be open enough for me to know certain," he paused, taking a moment to gauge us, "nightmares and longings."

Snorting, Phoebe was already shaking her head. "This is disgusting."

I tried to give all the information ample time to sink in, but it wasn't absorbing well. It had hit us so fast. We were having a good time just a half an hour ago and now…now, I'd gone off the deep end. *This couldn't be real. A demon, a Challenge, and a secret doorway in an attic. Yeah, right.*

I wonder where it started. Was I hurting people outside of my mind right now? My stomach clenched at the idea. I tried to plead with Phoebe with my eyes. *Please, knock me out, throw me out of the house, tie me down, take me into the hospital—anything to make this stop.*

"Join the Challenge or die here." Those were his last words. As swift and smooth as his former shapeless shadow, he faded out of sight.

I gazed into the darkness of the small doorway. Sometimes lightning would flash through in purple, blue, and yellow colors. Soundless bolts without a pattern, without thunder.

"What do we do?" Aidan croaked.

When no one answered, I replied, "I don't think we have a choice."

Phoebe started cracking her knuckles and was the first to move. Shuffling closer to the door, she stopped cracking long enough to extend one hand, palm open to the darkness beyond. Legs bent, she positioned herself into a fighting crouch.

"What are you doing?" Read hissed, embarrassed.

He always hated it when she showed off her fighting poses.

She turned back to us and attempted a confident smile. "The Challenge." Before anyone could protest, she bent at the waist and launched herself into that darkness. It swallowed her whole, leaving no trace. I couldn't even hear the sound of her footsteps.

Robin gasped so sharp and hard it could have been mistaken for a shriek.

"Where'd she go?" I demanded. "Why'd she do that?"

Read took two rigid steps forward. "We can't just let her go in there alone."

"Yes, we can," Robin squeaked.

"The demon said we'd starve waiting here." Read flung his arms up. "If these Challenges are based on our nightmares, do you really want to go in there weak and starving?"

Flinching, Robin pressed herself harder into Cody. If she wasn't already crying, she would have started.

"Ease off her." Cody's low voice held no room for an argument.

Looking up at Cody, Read shrugged. "What do you want me to say? You want to leave Phoebe out there?"

"What if we get separated?" I asked.

"We already are," Aidan said.

No one could argue with that.

Read started toward the doorway again and glanced over his shoulder at us, fear glistening in his eyes. "For the record, I think we should have stayed here."

"I can't believe that we're doing this," Aidan mumbled to me.

Shivering against the warm breath at my neck, I

held out my hand to him. "Come on, Aidan. It'll be over soon when they give me drugs."

He stared as if I'd offered a hand grenade. After a hesitant pause, he took the two steps toward me and took it. Again, no charge coursed through us. In fact, the hum that I often felt whenever he approached wasn't there, either.

"What do you mean, 'give you drugs'?" Aidan asked in a low voice.

Poor Aidan, he was hoping for a great weekend party, one that we would all enjoy, but it turned around and blew up in his face. Well, rather, *I* blew up the party. That's me: tick, tick, tick…

Robin was peering up at Cody. Her fingers had knotted themselves in his shirt. "Go?"

Lost for words, Cody returned her gaze, helpless to answer.

Read came around us and took my other hand, giving it a reassuring squeeze.

I squeezed back, feeling how sweaty both of our palms were, while Aidan's fingers were ice on my other hand.

"You guys coming?" I asked Cody.

Cody jumped when he realized I was staring at him. Beads of sweat frosted his forehead. "If I stay here, do you think something will happen?"

"Yes," I answered as honestly as I could. "And I don't think it would be good. The Challenge might be my only way out of this mess."

"*Our* only way out of this mess," Aidan corrected, eyeing me incredulously.

"And Phoebe's in there," I added.

"We can't just leave her there," Read said.

Robin whimpered and peeked at the door through splayed fingers. "Let's just stay. Maybe he can't force us in. He could have been lying. Anyone consider that?"

Cody patted the bricks where the door leading downstairs used to be. "They're right, we have to go. We'll just be trapped here instead."

Courage, remember these people need a leader, I thought, though it felt foreign. Phoebe shouldn't have gone so quickly; she was the brave one.

I nodded to Read. "Robin, take Cody's hand and Read's. We'll all go together." At least I wasn't doing this alone.

Robin reluctantly peeled off Cody's chest, gripping his hand already. Taking small, uncertain steps, she drew closer, assessing the dark doorway.

With a deep breath, she looked to the three of us and slapped her free hand into Read's as if it was a last-minute decision.

"He said *if* we could beat him," she said, her voice cracking in experimental optimism.

Smiling as best as I could, I felt Aidan tug to lead the way. I realized how grateful I was that I didn't have to head into the dark first.

Aidan glanced back as he reached the door. "Duck."

I gripped Read's hand tighter as Aidan slowly melted into the darkness. The colors in his face half mingled with the inky black before fading into it, almost looking as if he were being pulled apart, like the shadow-man had done.

Hunching over to fit through the door, I hesitated, my face inches from the black pool.

Aidan's hand pulled on mine, and I let it inch into the dark.

It was chilled but not cold. The air felt thick, like walking into a mist, except it wasn't damp. Taking a deep breath, I inched forward and felt Read squeeze my hand again.

"You're doing great," he said, pressing close from behind. He was warm against my hip and shoulder but so close I didn't dare look back.

Be brave, I thought, *like Phoebe.*

One cautious step was all it'd take, and I closed my eyes to do it.

Chapter Thirteen

Pins and needles prickled every pore.

Overwhelmed, I opened my eyes and found myself staring into darkness.

Wiggling my fingers to adjust my grip on the hands, I realized I couldn't feel them. I tried to turn my head when the sensation of weightlessness hit me like a baseball bat. I couldn't feel the floor beneath my feet. It was like I was floating.

Parting my lips, I realized they felt fat and fragile, as if too much movement may cause them to explode. No sound escaped as I tried to form Read's name. Something had stolen my voice again.

I had been so relieved before we stepped through that doorway that I wouldn't be alone, and here I was, alone.

The panic didn't have enough time to take root when a pale light flashed in the distance. *Am I dead?* I wondered. Wasn't this what people saw before they died? The white light at the end of the tunnel? This wasn't much of a tunnel, just an endless stretch of darkness, but the light was at least a destination.

Somehow, I was gravitating to the glimmer.

As I drew closer, I could make out a room within the light. Grey walls, green floors, and people were beginning to form through the warbled film-coated entrance.

I recognized two people. Phoebe was awkwardly holding Robin, who was crying. How had she gotten there before me? I wondered. I couldn't see Aidan, Cody, or Read in the room yet.

I drifted into the light. My limbs were still numb when I reached it.

Pitching forward onto a green carpet, I felt myself jolted into reality. My cheek pressed to the carpet, and I took several panicked breaths before I could compose myself.

I shifted my arms, feeling the warmth of my skin. The prickling sensation subsided, allowing me to sit up without grimacing. Read and Aidan had been behind me. I wasn't sure if they followed me through or had been there the whole time.

Read stood up in alarm, wiping sweaty palms on his jeans.

Aidan sat closest to me. "Is everyone okay?" he asked, his voice gruff as if he were fighting a cold.

There was a muttered reply amongst us few, each struggling to clear the cobwebs.

I stood up and Aidan followed, standing very close to me as we both inspected the cramped little room. There was a horrible, dirty, thin, green carpet at our feet. I wiped my face as I could still feel it there. The four walls held no entrance or exit, trapping us within. I turned to see if the portal to the room was still there, but it was nowhere to be seen.

Aidan leaned closer to me and whispered, "Where's Cody?"

I hadn't realized he wasn't in the room with us.

"What happened?" Read asked.

Robin tilted her head up. Her face had lined itself with blackened tears from her mascara. "Cody never came through. It's all my fault!" Sobbing between each word, she managed, "I didn't believe him when he said he got that message."

"Robin?" Read took a cautious step forward.

Phoebe's arms dropped, her compassionate expression hardening. "What message?" Her eyes rolled up to find me.

Shrugging, I held up my hands as if to say, "*How should I know*?"

Wiping her nose with the back of her hand, Robin edged away from the cold voice. "Cody told me about a message that he got last night," she said stiffly. "It was the same one that was on the wall. I thought it was a prank."

"Which one?" Phoebe growled. There were two black stains on her sweater where Robin had leaned.

Still refusing to look over at her, Robin replied, "The torture one."

Railing torment lies within.

Aidan cursed under his breath.

Robin seemed to remember her makeup and wiped at her face.

"Who else got a message?" Aidan demanded.

I crossed my arms over my chest and stepped away

from him. Phoebe's pointed stare targeted me, and everyone's attention shifted.

"Why didn't you say anything?" Robin's voice hit a shriek that made me wince.

"Why didn't you?" I shot back. "Or Cody for that matter?" The moment I snapped, I realized I shouldn't have. Robin's wounded expression had me refocusing my attack. Taking a deep breath through my nose, I tried to catch the reins of my emotions. I felt a weight in the pit of my stomach. It twisted like a boulder suspended by a string, ready to drop.

"I had my reasons," I said at last. "It's not like this is real anyway. Right, Phoebe? Remember when I told you?"

"You both knew?" Robin squealed.

Phoebe's eyebrows pinched. "*You* knew about Cody's message," she accused.

Read was shaking his head, ignoring the girls' back and forth. To me, he said firmly, "This is all real, Nora."

His grey eyes were the most intense I'd ever seen them. He was staring at me as if I might shatter, and he could keep that from happening. No wonder the girls crawled over each other to get him.

"This isn't happening," I said to him. "Right now, in the real world, I'm having a nervous breakdown and you are all probably worried half to death."

Phoebe and Robin were still toe to toe, screaming at each other. "It's your fault!" Phoebe jabbed a finger at Robin. "If you didn't tell him what to do all the time, he might have said something to one of us."

Robin recoiled. "I don't tell him what to do all the time, and you didn't say anything either." Then she struck like a snake and shoved at Phoebe to push her back. Taken off guard, Phoebe stumbled.

Read grabbed my shoulders, snapping my attention back to him. Frustration lined his handsome face. "Nora, this *is* happening."

I jolted and saw Aidan jump past us and between Phoebe and Robin. "Don't do this now. She didn't know."

Read shook my shoulders for my attention. "We're stuck in some grave thing with a fucking demon."

I tried to wriggle free as his fingers dug into my shoulder. "Read, stop it." I spoke but couldn't hear myself over the fight. Read's fingertips pressed against bone, and I bit back the panic. Do I yell at him? I had never seen him like this before.

Read's wild eyes focused when Aidan grabbed his wrist.

"She didn't know either." Aidan jerked on the arm holding me.

At first I didn't think Read would let go, until something in his hardened expression cracked. He flung his arms away, the finger impressions leaving a bruise-like throbbing. Backing away from me, he shouted, "If you're going crazy, maybe I am too." Snapping his head toward Phoebe and Robin he shouted, "*Will you two shut the fuck up?*"

The jarring sound silenced everyone. Read often spoke in smooth, even tones, never this.

Phoebe stalked away from Robin in the bitter silence, arms crossed and back rigid. Robin's fists were white knuckled, and she looked ready to sputter an insult but trembled instead. The room thrummed with emotions and was too small to get away from them.

"The messages." Aidan held up his hands in a truce for everyone to see. "They must be connected somehow."

"You're right." The foreign voice penetrated the room.

We all twisted in the same instant. He was standing in the middle of the room, amid us all.

"The messages are connected." Damien's smirk was both seductive and sardonic.

Robin voice cracked in its shrillness, interrupting my confusion.

"*Where is he*? Where is he you, bastard?"

The sudden outburst startled us all.

I jumped, bumping into Aidan just as Phoebe caught Robin from behind.

Wrapping an arm around Robin's narrow waist, Phoebe pulled back before she could barrel into the demon at our center.

Robin was normally a pretty and primped girl, but with streaking make-up and the hostile twist of her full mouth, she was a frightening sight. Baring her teeth at Damien, she began to wiggle and twist, her sundress riding up to dangerous heights.

Phoebe tried to hold her tighter, and Robin fought harder. I knew I should help her, but I couldn't move. Not because I couldn't, but because I was scared.

Damien stared at Robin, stone-faced.

She didn't crumble under the gaze as I would have. "Cody! I'm talking about *Cody*, you idiot," she screamed, mistaking his blank stare for ignorance. She burst free of Phoebe's weakened grip and raced at him. Petite, frail Robin was diving at someone twice her size with a blind determination. Phoebe stumbled, swinging her arms only once. She didn't follow too closely before slinking back to her corner.

Damien deftly caught both of Robin's wrists in one hand.

Crying out, Robin twisted like a wild animal, kicking and shrieking.

It was Aidan who stepped forward first, grabbing Robin around the waist to pull her away.

Damien tilted his head to the side, studying the tiny girl for a moment. He spoke calmly, though somehow his voice echoed inside my skull over Robin's booming words. "Don't attack me again." I wasn't sure what he did to make her drop to her knees, but Robin's bare, shaking legs buckled, almost dragging Aidan down with her.

Releasing her, he took a step back as Phoebe helped Robin to her feet and back against the wall, the farthest they could get away from the demon.

Chewing on my lower lip, I felt helplessness threatening to creep in. How the hell were we supposed to win a game against a demon? The messages. It all had to do with the messages, like Aidan had said. They held a key to our escape; they had to. "I want a piece of paper and a pen."

I looked up at Damien. His hands were curling up into fists, on the brink of losing his temper. He reluctantly tore his attention away from Robin, who was creating quite the show now that she started clawing at Aidan, begging for him to get her out. Surprise flickered across Damien's surreal features when I repeated my request.

"Well, can I?" I shouted. Under his stare, I managed to keep my feet firm beneath me and tried not to show

how scared I felt.

He nodded, his original stoicism replacing the surprise in an instant as dark eyes drifted to the floor.

I looked down at my feet to see the white pad of paper the size of my palm. Laid neatly across it was a black ballpoint pen. I recognized them both from my dad's study at home. Mona had recently taken up doodling, leaving little notes to our father until he told her to stop and locked the pad and pens away in the top drawer.

I picked up both items, feeling their weight in my hands. Maybe Damien did see into my mind after all. This minor detail from my dad's study at home made me wonder what big details he might have gleaned.

Aidan moved closer, passing Robin to Read, who didn't appear very pleased. "Do you remember them?" Aidan asked me.

Phoebe sidled along the wall to join us.

I nodded to them both and began scribbling them down.

Dismal is the Demon's Grave. The first message on the wall. *Dismal and dark*, the words drifted back into my mind before I could stop them.

One soul of blackened sin. Offered death for once the brave. I grimaced at the familiar words.

Railing torment lies within. Cody's little contribution. I wished he had spoken up sooner, but that wouldn't have been like Cody at all.

Robin's voice was like nails down a chalkboard, and I caught Phoebe's eye. Somehow she got the message and snapped, "Shut up, Robin. We have to think, and you're not helping."

Reducing the squeals to breathy sobs, Robin held

back the curses for a moment. Lips quivering, she collapsed into Read and covered her face with her hands.

"Did anyone else get any messages that weren't on the wall?" I asked.

Everyone shook their heads, including Robin.

I stared down at the pad of paper in my hand, turning it around for some clue. A message within the message, and yet I couldn't see it. I tried squinting, counting the letters, using every other letter to form words.

"Anything?" Phoebe asked, casting an impatient glance over her shoulder at the demon.

Damien's eyes met hers, and she quickly looked back to us.

Aidan looked over my shoulder at the words I had written down. "Hey," he said softly and reached for the pen.

I didn't stop him as he crossed out what I had written and began anew.

Dismal is the Demon's grave,
One soul of blackened sin,
Offered death for once the brave,
Railing torment lies within.

Shaking my head, I glanced up at Aidan. Instead of writing them across the page, he had written it like a poem. Which made sense, it all rhymed but…

I gaped at the discovery the moment I saw it.

Aidan was already beaming. "This is it. The messages are a message."

CHAPTER FOURTEEN

Phoebe crowded close. "What message?"

"Door," I said.

Phoebe's barking laugh held a maddening edge. "And that tells us what?"

"What are you guys talking about?" Read asked, softer now that Robin was in his arms.

"It's like an acrostic poem," I explained. "The first letter when positioned vertically spells: Door." I didn't take English Literature for nothin'. I smirked.

Aidan held up the piece of paper, eyes bright and hopeful. "Does it really matter? I figured out the message in the messages."

You? I thought. *You mean we*?

Aidan turned to Damien. "Was that one of the Challenges? One of the six?"

Even I knew that it couldn't possibly be the Challenge. It was too easy. There was something about a demon in a magical realm that didn't ooze freebies.

Damien's lips curled unpleasantly. "That was not even the beginning of the Challenge. Now you've figured out what you must go through."

Aidan deflated. "Doors? This has to be a joke."

Damien pointed toward the wall behind Robin and Read.

Without warning, it caved in.

All five of us scattered to escape the dusty debris. Plaster, drywall, and splintered wood crumbled in a U-pattern, revealing the same heart-shriveling darkness that had been beyond the marble door. I wasn't sure I wanted to walk through it again. Who else would we lose if we did?

In his low baritone, Damien explained, "Within each door is a Challenge. Face it until you find the black door, which will lead to the next Challenge. If you survive them all, you're free. But, if you fail or die, you're trapped."

Or die…we could die. I didn't exactly enjoy the idea of being in this part of my brain, but to die? What if, for a moment, I could believe that this was all real? What were my last words to my mother? My sisters? Mona was still mad at me about the mirror when I left.

Would they think I was kidnapped, or would Damien throw my body back out into my own world?

"What's in the last door?" Read asked, eyes snapping to Aidan and me, then the demon, as if one of us would reveal something.

"Your world. You'll be free," Damien said.

I asked, "And where is Cody? You took him somewhere."

"I never touched your Cody. He wandered off into the darkness."

Robin wiped at the running mascara, her voice cracking and meek. "Will I ever see him again?"

"If he makes it. It's really up to him." Damien waved a dismissive hand. He might as well have said, "*I wouldn't hold your breath.*"

Sneering, Phoebe said quietly, "Let's get this over with." As we turned toward the opening, the darkness within the vacant hole began to evaporate into smoke, the black tendrils fading and twisting upward in a mass, clouding the ceiling from view. The walls beyond the hole began to take shape.

Damien ducked inside a long hallway, and Phoebe followed, though she kept a watchful distance, hands up and legs bent as if she expected him to turn around and grab her. The hazy walls around her vibrated as if they weren't quite solid or real, but she stepped within the hallway and didn't fall through the floor.

Phoebe was the only one to follow Damien. The thin layer of snaking mist was disturbed by her steps.

I held my breath as Phoebe slipped closer to one of the walls to touch it. The fuzzy surface reacted as if she had poked her finger into stagnant water. Thickened ripples expanded outward, getting bigger until they hit a corner and stopped short, smoothing out the wall's surface once more.

"Whoa," I heard Aidan breathe.

It was like nothing that I had ever seen before.

Read joined Phoebe through the doorway, signaling for the rest of us to follow.

Without arguing, we stepped through the gap. Robin was the only one who didn't have to duck through. Our feet kicked up the rest of the mist on the floor.

The same grey walls and green carpet stretched down the narrow corridor. Phoebe's finger poked a solid wall this time. She patted it as if to reassure herself that it was real. Mimicking her, I patted it as well. It was cool to the touch, not heated like those in the tower.

One side of the hallway was bare with cracks and dents in the dry wall. The other side, however, held dozens of doors. Each was painted black with strange markings. Some of the carved symbols took up the entire door; however, most were smaller patterns that I'd have to get closer to see.

I moved to the other side of the hallway, pressed my shoulders to the wall, and reached out. The door in front of me was so close my fingertips could almost touch it.

The feeling of being watched had me looking to Aidan, but he was pressing his face close to one of the numerous symbols. His distinct jawline was sharper as he jutted his chin forward in concentration.

There had to be forty or more doors staggered down the long hallway. Were we supposed to choose?

No one made an attempt to open one. Most of us were trying to set each symbol to memory.

Past Aidan, I caught the unblinking obsidian eyes narrowed in on me. My stomach dropped, and I crossed my arms tight to suppress a shiver.

His square jaw set into a thrilling smile, and despite my better judgment, I broke eye contact first. It was either that or run, and there was nowhere to run. "Which door do we pick?" I asked, happy that my voice didn't crack.

Damien said, "One of you has the key."

"The key?" Aidan demanded. "What kind of cryptic bullshit is this?"

"Are all the doors locked?" Phoebe asked.

"Don't open them," I hissed when she reached for one. Her hand snapped back like she'd been stung before she glared at me.

"How else are we going to find out who's got the key?" she demanded.

Read pulled the weight of those eyes away. "Well, I guess we're going to have to split up. Six Challenges and five people, right?"

"Split up?" Robin gasped. "We can't split up. What if one of us disappears just the way Cody did?"

I wanted to say to her, "*Cody is all right*," but I didn't know for sure. Instead, I held out a hand to calm her, but she took it as an invitation. I almost lost my balance when she wrapped her narrow arms around me and began to shudder like a leaf. Eyes round, I glanced up to see Phoebe shaking her head in distaste. "It'll be okay, Robin," I said, licking my lips. "It's just a suggestion."

Damien shook a finger at us as if we were troubled young children. "No tricks. You try to betray this Challenge, you will betray one of your friends. Perhaps you should split up, find your way faster," he said, his body statue still. I couldn't tell if he was joking or not.

How the hell could we betray the Challenge? If this were in my head, had I created a loophole in my fantasy? And if it were real… "You mean there's a way to escape?"

Aidan's eyes widened. "Whoa, whoa, what? How will we even know if we're cheating?"

We all glanced at each other, fear and apprehension dancing between gazes. There was a way to get out early? It seemed impossible at this point, and even if I figured it out, I'd be putting someone in jeopardy. I didn't think I could live with myself if I did that. Fantasy or not.

I shook my head. "If we split up, how would we find each other?" If there was a way to escape, we needed to do it together.

Phoebe sighed through her nose. "We stay in groups, of course. It makes sense that we'd meet back here to pick another door. Read can come with me. Aidan, you and Fuller are together. Maybe we'll have a better chance of finding something. And Robin." Phoebe looked at the little weeping girl.

It hurt to look at Robin when she untangled herself from the hug. Her face was swollen from tears, her head lowered. A thought struck me like a sledgehammer. *She has let the fear in. It's in her eyes.*

What if this was real, just like Read said? Would I imagine Robin like this? Seeing her panicked expression reminded me of being a scared kid. I hadn't let my own fears in yet. One look at Robin told me that I shouldn't, I *couldn't*.

Robin's tears soaked through the shoulder strap of my camisole, wetting my shoulder. I inconspicuously wiped it away. I didn't need a reminder of fear other than Robin, not now.

Raising his hand for attention, Aidan said, "We shouldn't split up. Who knows where we'll end up?"

Phoebe started cracking her knuckles.

Read frowned. "We're wasting time arguing about this."

Aidan lifted his arm and showed his wristwatch to me. The first and second hands were twisting from left to right, left to right, left, right.

"I don't think that time is our problem," he mumbled. "I agree with Robin. I think if we split up, we're screwing ourselves."

I jerked my head to ask Damien, but he wasn't there.

Following my gaze, Robin asked, "Where'd he go?" Her voice shook with her body.

"I think that she's in shock," Phoebe said and wriggled out of her sweater. Her lean body looked as if it belonged in a fitness magazine with just the tube top and shorts.

Read gave her a quick up and down before frowning and looking back at Aidan. He was still staring at the doors, making his way down the hallway.

Appreciative, Robin popped inside Phoebe's oversized sweater, still shuddering and wringing her hands. She immediately started to snuggle closer to Read.

Phoebe turned and grabbed a silver doorknob.

"Phoebe!" I shouted.

She twisted it, but the knob wouldn't move. "It's locked." She huffed and glared. "We aren't getting anywhere by just standing here, you know."

"She's right." Read stepped forward, away from Robin, and tried another door. It too was locked. Shuffling down the hallway, he twisted the knob of the fourth door, and it swung inward by a hair.

Phoebe rolled her eyes. "Great. The locked ones are probably our way home," she grumbled and gave the closest locked door one last kick.

I hated to admit it, but she could be right.

Noticing that they had an open door, Aidan stalked toward us. "One of us has the key. What about..." He noticed Phoebe's lack of clothes and stammered to a stop.

Oblivious, Phoebe pushed Read out of the way. To my surprise, he moved without complaint, and we watched as she kicked the open door inward with all of her strength.

It flung open, hitting something on the other side with a *bang*. It was so loud that I could have easily mistaken it for gunfire.

Phoebe flew back in surprise, her spine hitting the opposite wall. Aidan was so close to me I could feel him jump at the same time that I did. Robin squeaked and shuffled behind Aidan.

Attempting to slow my heart after the violent jump-start, I shuffled closer to see the same darkness beyond the threshold. "What about the key?"

Aidan started counting the doors. "There's maybe three dozen doors in here."

Phoebe edged closer to the opening.

I shook my head. "I think we should figure out the clue first." I grabbed Phoebe to turn her around to face me, the dead dark just over her shoulder.

Phoebe crossed her arms over her chest, her skin brushing against me. "We're wasting time. We can figure it out as we go."

"We got the clue now," I protested.

Aidan was nodding along with Robin.

Read said, "Well the last four doors were locked. What if we each try them? Maybe only one of us can open certain doors or something."

"That would suggest that this is Phoebe's door," Aidan pointed out, "but how can we be sure?"

Rolling her eyes, Phoebe flung open her arms. "We're wasting…" Her voice cut off the second she saw me slam back against the wall.

The long squid-like tentacle whipped into view behind her, disturbing the misty dark so that it spilled into the hallway at our ankles.

Robin screamed shrilly, falling to the ground. She crab-walked backwards, and I heard Aidan shout, "Phoebe move!"

She barely had enough time to turn around.

The rubbery flesh smacked against my stomach before constricting around Phoebe's slender waist.

Her forest green eyes grew wide, and she opened her mouth.

I heard the sharp intake of breath before the scream that never came.

In a flash, Phoebe was ripped back into the dark.

Chapter Fifteen

Everything came unglued.

Without thinking, I stepped toward the darkness when the door slammed shut. The rushed breeze hit my face, smelling rancid and sickly sweet, like rotting food.

At the same time, Read grabbed my arm and pulled me back hard. Losing my balance, I hit my head on the drywall, and I clutched the back of my skull, hissing.

"Shit," he said. "Are you okay?" Read's fingers probed over mine, which hid the throbbing shriek at the back of my head.

"Oh God, oh God, oh God." Robin quivered on the floor, her legs curled up to her chest. "It just *took* her!"

Aidan twisted the doorknob to find it locked.

Read asked, sounding both angry and concerned at the same time, "Why didn't you grab for her, Nora?"

Why didn't I? It seemed so unreal! Reasons fumbled through my mind, knocking into each other. *I couldn't believe what was happening. I didn't think, I couldn't move, I didn't save her*! "I don't know," I said in a whisper. *Had there been enough time to grab her?*

Robin began to cry again. "First Cody, now Phoebe. We have to get them back!"

Please let this all be in my head. Let it be a dream.

"Nora," Read said low, his eyes level with mine. He wouldn't continue until I looked at him. "You realize this isn't a dream, right? Phoebe is really gone. Something just took her. Cody is really lost. Our friends are gone."

Had I spoken my thought out loud? I opened my mouth to reply, but the uncertainty on his face seemed impossible to assuage. "I'm sorry," I said. "It happened so fast."

Read turned, letting me go. "Someone help me break this door down."

I started to shake my head, but my brain felt like it sloshed around, and I stopped.

Aidan said, "I don't think that's a good idea."

Read glared at us over his shoulder. "Our *friend* is in there."

"She thinks this is a dream?" Robin choked. "Like the ones we all had earlier this week?" Her eyes began to widen at the possibility. "They did seem real. This could be a dream."

"Oh yeah?" Read barked. "How is it we're all dreaming at the same time?"

Robin just stared at me, eyes glistening, until I was forced to look away. *How could this possibly be real?* I glanced at my friends, feeling the shame swell in my chest. *Phoebe is really gone.* It circulated like a warbled record.

"How did you wake up from a bad dream before?"

Robin asked, getting to her feet with the help of the wall. Phoebe's sweater was a sack on her petite frame.

I shook my head, trying to think. "I, uh, pinch myself, I guess. But the messages weren't dreams…"

Before I could back away, she stomped up to me, her previous sadness fluttering behind her like a memory. Robin pinched my arm, then twisted so hard I shrieked.

Jerking away, I held my flaming forearm in my palm. It throbbed as if Robin had put a cigarette to me instead. Eyes narrowing, Robin motioned to me. "Did you wake up?"

"I get it," I shouted to keep her away.

Read slammed his shoulder into the locked door. The wall shuddered, but otherwise, it didn't budge.

Slipping past Robin, I put my shoulder against the door with Read. "On the count of three," I instructed. My insides felt like someone had punched me, but at least my head didn't throb as much. Besides, if I didn't do something, I'd go insane. I understood at last why they were so angry with me. Phoebe and Cody were gone. Not my imaginary friends, my *friends*.

"One…two…*three*."

Together we rammed our bodies into the door. A shooting pain zipped through my shoulder blade and down my spine and shook the teeth in my gums all at the same time.

The door, however, didn't budge.

Aidan's voice rose before we could do another count down. "If we're going to get her back, we can't just go barreling into the dark like Han Solo on the Death Star. You heard Damien, if we fail or die, we're stuck here."

Robin looked to me, eyebrows raised as she

mouthed, "Death Star?"

I shrugged.

Read stalked past us and studied the doors. "How can one of us have the key?" he demanded, not looking up.

Robin hurried after Read. She spoke softly as they marched down the hallway together. I think enough of her nerves returned for her to try and comfort someone instead of everyone trying to comfort her.

Rubbing the place where she pinched me, I pushed off the door.

I wished I could be of more help and stared at the watery symbol on Phoebe's door. If only there was something in those carvings that would lead us to our friends.

If it weren't for me, maybe Phoebe wouldn't be lost. If I had just talked to Cody a little longer, maybe, just maybe…

Aidan was studying the doors beside me when he whispered, "I'm sorry." His pale eyes flickered toward Read and Robin; they were too far away to hear.

"You didn't do anything to be sorry for. I'm the jerk here."

"I got you guys into this," he said piteously.

Here, I was blaming myself, and I felt the weight of it, heavy, brooding and chock full of self-pity. I hadn't thought about what Aidan must be going through. It was his house. He'd opened the door, and here we were. It wasn't that I blamed him; I knew there was a part of me that could, but I didn't. If I started pointing fingers, where would it end? Where would it get us?

Tightening my lips, I realized we weren't going to win this way. Turning, I caught Aidan's shoulders, determined to face him squarely and honestly. "Listen, there is nothing to be sorry about. You didn't know. We all didn't know. I agreed to open that marble door. We're in this together."

It wasn't completely true. I said *yes* when I didn't want to. Could it be Damien had forced me to say those words to get us here? Those weighty eyes that I felt in this hallway weren't any different than the ones I had felt in my own house. Remembering the shower, I shuddered and let Aidan go.

Aidan hung his head, his thick reddish-brown hair bobbing. "I could have stopped Phoebe from going upstairs."

"I doubt it," I said and licked my lips before asking, "Do you think your grandfather knew about the Demon's Grave?"

Sighing, he looked up. "It's been bugging me, but I don't know."

"Are you going to give up on me, Aidan?" I demanded in a hushed whisper.

He shook his head, clarity gradually sweeping the shadows from his expression. "Course not. Are you?"

I let his shoulders go. I could feel the muscles in them tense just before I released him. "No," I answered. "Listen, first we have to figure out that clue. It means something."

Aidan leaned against the wall opposite the doors and slid down until he sat on the floor. He couldn't stretch out his legs in the narrow hallway. "Maybe it's a clue for later, like in one of the Challenges."

I nodded, watching him. "But then, which door do we pick? There's too many."

"I still think that the door we should go through is a

locked one." Aidan gestured toward the door that had a little dent from Phoebe's kick. The symbol that was carved deep into the wood looked like four smooth waves that were blocked off by a vertical, almost like a dam.

"What could these symbols mean?" I asked, though I knew that Aidan wouldn't have the answer.

"Maybe some dialect," Aidan said. "Who knows if it's even decipherable?"

"Wish we had your parents' living room. Bet there's a book in there that could tell us."

The corner of his mouth tugged at an attempted smirk.

Any other day, this might not have warranted humor, but I think both of us were eager to break the tension, and I was grateful for the small smile. I started rummaging through the pockets of my blue jean shorts.

"What are you doing?" Aidan asked.

"Looking for a key."

Aidan shook his head. "Would be a bit absurd."

"Look where we are," I countered.

His smile vanished, and he shoved his hands in his pants pockets. Neither of us found anything.

"Okay," I said, hearing Read trying doorknobs down the hallway. He didn't open any that weren't locked. Read had pulled his car keys from his pocket and marked the doors that were locked. Aidan and I didn't move from the floor. Their distraction helped numb the erratic voices in my head. *Phoebe and Cody were in trouble*. This all felt so wasteful, but if we rushed and got the wrong answer, where would our friends be then?

Robin and Read came back toward us. "Only five of

them are locked," Read confirmed.

Aidan was counting on his fingers, unresponsive.

"What do we do now?" Robin asked, hands shoved in Phoebe's kangaroo pouch.

Sighing, Aidan dropped his hands. "There has to be a connection somewhere. What if we walk through the wrong door…Robin, what's wrong?"

Robin's eyes bulged as she eased her hands from the sweater's pocket and showed us a glass key that fit in the palm of her hand.

Leaning forward to inspect it, no one moved to touch it.

Finally, Robin squeaked, "Oh my God! Phoebe had it this whole time?"

It was a key but made from what looked like glass. It had a slender, circular neck with a square tip, much like old-fashioned skeleton keys.

Robin was dancing from foot to foot, heels clomping. "Well?"

"This is great, as long as it doesn't break in a keyhole," I said.

Aidan's frown deepened at my words, and he took it from Robin's palm. She didn't move to stop him, only whispered a warning. "*Don't* drop it."

Aidan's eyes rounded as if it hadn't occurred to him, and he froze.

"Which door?" Read asked.

I plucked the key from Aidan's fingers before he could react.

Jolting, he didn't move to snatch it away, just watched me.

I gestured toward the doors. "Let's see which one this thing opens."

Aidan nodded silently and stood at my side. Working down the hallway, I tried each door that Read had already marked as locked. Carefully placing the glass key in each, I wiggled the lock. Each of the five doors denied the key.

"Uh oh," Robin whispered. "Maybe you're not doing it right?"

I glanced at the door Phoebe had disappeared behind. It wasn't marked by Read, but it'd been locked before.

"Crap," Read muttered as we shuffled closer to the door.

Turning the key in the keyhole, I heard the distinct *click.*

Robin shuffled closer to me while Read stepped back.

Feeling the tension from my friends behind me, I pulled the key out, hearing the clinking while the glass shuddered in the keyhole in my nervousness.

The symbol on the door was three water-like symbols that rode through a triangle.

I pocketed the key in my shorts. I didn't want to leave it behind just in case we'd need it for any other locked doors. I'd just have to pray it wouldn't break in the meantime.

Aidan reached in front of me and grabbed the doorknob. I felt his chest at my shoulder and forced myself to look at him. He raised his eyebrows as if to ask, *Ready?* We each took a deep breath in preparation. *What were we about to walk into?* The question was heavy, almost too heavy to dwell on.

Nodding at Read and Robin behind us, Aidan twisted the knob, and pushed it inward.

Chapter Sixteen

Aidan and I exhaled at the same time.

There was a room in front of us, a familiar one instead of the inky dark.

Robin spoke to Aidan softly. "This isn't so bad. It's your folks' house."

It was indeed the Birket living room, the same one we'd left behind before piling into the station wagon.

Every detail was immaculate. There was the brick wall, dark furniture, masks, and overflowing bookshelves. For a moment, it felt like we were back in our world—and safe. It was the green carpeted hallway we crowded within which reminded me otherwise.

Aidan stepped through the doorway first, and I followed with Robin. Read was close behind me, breathing down my neck, his hands hovering over my hips.

Stopping just within the threshold, we listened to the sounds of a seemingly empty house.

When the door didn't slam behind us the way it had Phoebe, I looked over my shoulder. Where the front door should have been, there was a sneering wooden mask. It was three feet tall, not exactly intended for a human face.

"This is uncanny," Aidan whispered, eyes wide.

"It's like we're actually at your house again," Robin confirmed, still keeping her voice low.

Neither had seen the mask for a door behind us, though Read had and gave me a pointed stare before walking up beside me and keeping one hand at my hip.

Mildly uncomfortable with the move, I stepped away. I followed as he tip-toed to one of the bookshelves.

No one spoke as Aidan carefully pulled a faded green book from the closest shelf. The spine was nearly broken, but the title on the side was legible: *Talking With Spirits*.

"This isn't ours," Aidan whispered, then snatched another book like a praying mantis. This one was newer, the paper jacket still smooth. The cover read: *Bending Time & Space*.

"Another clue?" I asked. My eyes darted from the books to the room, searching for anything out of place. Having only been to his house once, I knew I was at a disadvantage.

Having flipped open *Bending Time & Space*, Aiden muttered into the pages. "I don't know. Neither book has an author or publisher, so I'm assuming so."

Robin took the *Talking with Spirits* book from Aidan and opened it. "Half of the pages are blank," she told us.

Read walked around us before collapsing in the

brown recliner. His thick, dark eyebrows pinched together. "There's no kitchen either," he said.

Looking up, I saw there was a wall where the doorway used to be. "What else looks out of place?" I asked. "Other than blocking off our only two exits."

The heavy curtains were closed, allowing no light through. Our only illumination came from one of the intricately designed, tall lamps. It had an imitation wood neck leading to the light-brown cloth shade. It was something that I'd seen in the ol' country stores my mother frequented during a decorating phase.

Robin began to grumble and slapped the book closed. "It just keeps talking about a Ouija board."

"What about the window?" I asked.

Aidan stopped me by grabbing my wrist in his chilled hand and pulling me back. "Wait a minute, Nora."

I began to protest when his grip tightened.

We stepped back together, shuffling around the coffee table.

Alerted to a disturbance, I held still, searching the shadows, the walls, and the scary masks for any signs that we weren't alone.

Robin, who was close to me, gasped.

A jerking step back had me hitting the couch behind my knees. Taking Aidan with me, I plopped unceremoniously back onto it.

"That wasn't here a second ago," Robin said, easing in beside me on the couch.

Laid out on the seventies-style coffee table near my knees was a Ouija board.

The letters and numbers were the usual, along with the giant YES and NO. In the center of the board was the planchette—the teardrop-shaped wooden piece—that acted as the indicator. I remembered a Halloween party as a teenager where they had one out. I refused to play along but watched from behind the couch as my friends squealed and gushed whenever it happened to spell a nonsensical short sentence.

"What is that doing here?" I picked up the planchette and turned it around in my fingers. It seemed like an ordinary game piece, no scary symbols or anything.

Read was leaning forward in the chair, hands clasped in front of him. "So we get to talk to dead people," he said dryly.

Robin closed the *Talking with Spirits* book she'd been holding. Setting it beside the game on the coffee table, she whispered, "Like…*real* dead people? Ghosts?" She looked to Read.

"I think that this is our first Challenge," Aidan said. "My parents had this very same game. They used to hold séances for the neighbors when I was a kid."

I reeled back for a second. To expose your own child to something as morbid as calling the dead seemed wrong to me.

Robin's eyes were round. "That's dangerous, isn't it? I mean, they didn't believe in what they were doing, right?"

Aidan shrugged, not looking up. "My parents are…different." He swallowed and kept his face turned away.

I immediately felt ashamed. He was probably embarrassed, and we weren't helping. "Sorry," I whispered.

"Me too," Robin said. She added, after a moment's

pause, "Actually, it's kind of neat. Maybe people really did get to talk to ghosts in your house. Plus you'll know how to play this."

Aidan took the teardrop-shaped planchette from my hand and put it back down on the board. "This doesn't seem right. According to my parents," he said the last sentence slowly, "you have to be careful that you don't call up something dark."

"Like what?" Read asked guardedly.

Aidan almost smiled. "Like demons."

Read barked a laugh, probably the loudest sound to have pierced the little room since our arrival. I'd be lying if I said I didn't flinch.

Aidan continued, "Poltergeists, dark spirits, you know, the seedy underworld sort. Our neighbors at the time were convinced their apartment was haunted. Turned out it was bats in the walls."

I frowned and decided to veer the conversation back. "We can be specific on what we call up, right?"

Aidan jerked his head up. "I don't know." He offered a helpless shrug. "Like I said, my parents dabbled in this when I was young, not me."

"Well, I watched one once." I glanced at Read, knowing he had been at that party. When he gave me a blank stare, I continued. "Uh, so I remember a little ceremony they read off the pamphlet, and then people would ask to contact a spirit. They have to touch this, though." I put both my fingers gently on top of the planchette. "I remember Phoebe yelling at Read to keep his touch light."

Mentioning her name swept a moment of stillness through our group.

Robin's eyes were wide when she whispered, "You

did? When was this?" Instead of asking me, she asked Read.

Read nodded. "Yeah, I remember now. It was high school, before we met you."

"What kind of ceremony?" Aidan asked.

I let go of the planchette and ducked my head to peek under the four-legged coffee table for a box or instructions but couldn't see either. "Um," Feeling silly, I glanced at Read for help.

Read shrugged. "I barely remember the party, let alone the ceremony." This was plausible. Read was drunk most of that night. "I think we had to ask for something that wouldn't wish us harm or something like that. Then that weird goth-chick—remember her?—she did that thing with the candles."

I remembered her running her hand over them and dripping wax on the planchette, but that part wasn't in the pamphlet, according to Phoebe.

Swallowing, I realized no one was saying anything, and it would be up to me. Tilting my chin up so I wouldn't have to look at anyone, I said to the room, my voice cracking, "We need to use this board, but we only want to talk to something that doesn't wish us harm." Hell, I felt like a moron. I knew Aidan was watching me and didn't look at anyone.

Aidan cleared his throat. "What she said," he joined, in followed by Robin's meek, "Ditto," and a grunt from Read.

I smirked, feeling a rush of giddiness. "I think we have to touch it. That's all I can think of for a ceremony, considering we're all out of candles."

"And I thought I was so prepared for this weekend," Aidan muttered wryly.

Robin giggled, and Read and I cracked smiles. It felt good for a little humor to interrupt the seriousness. I think we would have laughed at the smallest joke at this point. Anything to break the tension.

"Okay," I said. "On the count of three, we all touch the planchette."

"Okay," Robin whispered, her hands hovering. We all leaned forward, crowding shoulder to shoulder as I started the countdown.

"One, two…three."

We all reached out to touch the game piece at the same time when it darted out of our reach and to the opposite end of the board.

Robin scrambled off the couch in a blur and peeked above Read's chair. "What the hell!"

Read and I fell back into our seats. My back pressed against the couch, getting as far away from the board as I could.

"Whoa," Read breathed, eyes wide.

Aidan had frozen. He was the only one who hadn't moved, and he stared at the game piece, puzzled. He reached out slowly, but the piece didn't move again. He brought it back toward us, and I hesitated before scooting forward in my seat. "Try again?" he said.

In a hoarse whisper, I warned, "But it moved!"

Robin nodded vigorously, unable to speak.

Read was already leaning forward, hands out to touch the planchette. "Come on, Robin."

At his request, Robin inched her way around the chair and smiled at Read weakly. "If you say so," she said to him softly.

Aidan's eyes met mine, encouraging me to reach out.

Robin eased back onto the couch beside me and sat close enough that I could smell her shampoo.

Together, we floated reluctant fingers over the teardrop shape, glancing at one another, waiting for someone to chicken out.

Robin took a deep shaky breath and nodded to me without looking.

"One," I said slowly, eyes darting to each of my friends. "Two…three."

The minute our fingers brushed the top of the game piece, it darted away.

Though I had an inkling that it might happen again, I still screamed and jumped on top of the couch cushions. "This is stupid!" I barked, my hand over my chest to slow my heart.

Robin had darted off the couch again and was halfway across the room when she finally realized there was nowhere to run. Read was standing now, hovering over the Ouija board, looking startled.

Aidan had jumped this time but otherwise didn't move. "I guess we can't all touch it at the same time?"

Balancing on the dark cushions, I waited for Aidan to grab the planchette and put it at the base of the board, away from all the letters.

The shape didn't move, and we just stared at it trying to decide what to do.

"Ask it a question," I whispered from my high vantage point.

Aidan frowned and asked the most obvious question on all of our minds. "Will Damien give our friends back?"

The plastic teardrop twitched before taking off across the board. Each pause was swift, and at first I didn't realize it was spelling something out until halfway through.

Robin's hand rose to her lips, staring at the magical game piece. Easing back to us, she didn't sit on the couch, rather knelt on the other side of the coffee table to watch.

The clear, plastic window stopped over a 'V', then it went to an 'E', then to an 'R'. I watched in petrified fascination as the planchette stopped cold.

"Never," Read growled. "It said, *never*."

Feeling my shoulders sag, I crawled down to sit next to Aidan again. Damien will *never* give our friends back? "Can we win them back?" I asked.

YES.

Before anyone could ask another question, the device began to spell out something else.

W-E-A-K.

Robin inched forward on her knees. "Weak? We won't get them back because we're weak or they're weak?"

"No, we're not weak," I reassured. Glancing toward the coffee table pointedly, I argued, "And we'll be getting through this. We'll get our friends back, with or without Damien's help." I stopped myself. "I can't believe that I'm fighting with a game."

Aidan tilted his chin up, piercing eyes alight. "Or with the entity controlling the game."

That was eerie.

Y-O-U-W-I-L-L-D-I-E, it said.

"Die!" Robin hissed. "Of what? How?"

When the planchette didn't twitch, Aidan repeated her question.

Y-O-U-R-W-E-A-K-N-E-S-S.

"No." I shook my head at Robin. "It's lying, Robin. Don't pay attention."

"Let me take it." She didn't look at Aidan as she spoke. As she reached to take the planchette from him, her eyes were bright with unshed tears. When Aidan didn't move, she looked up at him. "Please."

Aidan looked at me, then her, before easing his hand away. He didn't seem warmed with the idea.

Taking it, she asked in a shaky voice, "How will I die? What is my weakness?"

"Robin," I protested through gritted teeth.

C-H-E-A-T, it spelled.

I grabbed the planchette away from her before she could ask another question. "You won't cheat, Robin. We don't even know how to cheat here."

I placed the piece back on the board, and my fingertips were on it when it began spell.

"How do we beat this?" I demanded. I had to force myself from moving it to where I wanted it to go. It was strange to feel it shift beneath my fingers, slashing toward each letter and pausing before flinging across the board.

S-A-C-R-I-F-I-C-E, it said.

Beneath my fingertips the planchette went dead, leaving me with that ugly word. I hated that word.

"What does that mean?" Aidan asked. "Does it mean just for you or all of us?"

I shook my head, staring at the game piece. "I don't know—" Before I could finish, the game piece began to move again.

O-R-T-H-E-Y-D-I-E

Maybe we should have listened to Damian and split up. Would Phoebe still be gone if we had? Even so, she wanted to go without figuring out the clue. At the same time, it had been the right door all along, but how were we to know then?

The teardrop beneath my hand began to move again. I jerked my head down as it started to spell: **B-L-O-O-D-S-A-C—**

I heard footsteps beyond the walled-up kitchen and jerked my hands free of the planchette.

Stiffening on the couch, Aidan laced his fingers in mine and squeezed, trying to keep me calm—probably trying to keep us *both* calm. Robin darted around the coffee table and latched onto Read's arm. "What is that?" she whispered.

Unable to answer, I stared at the bare wall as it began to waver and wobble like it was made of Jell-O.

First an arm broke through the warped wall, then a foot, a shoulder.

I braced myself, gripping Aidan's hand hard as two people entered the room, stepping through the wall where the kitchen doorway used to be. Behind them, the wall gained density, appearing just as solid as it should be.

The faces were very familiar, and I had to choke back my gasp.

There was a blonde girl with a round face and blue eyes the color of dark jewels. The boy had wild reddish-brown hair with a light scruff on his face and electric blue eyes.

CHAPTER SEVENTEEN

It was us.

A translucent Nora and Aidan stood against the wall, facing our group. It was surreal staring at my face. She made the familiar expressions I'd seen in photographs.

The Smokey Nora and Aidan wore our clothes, but they were rumpled, dirty, and wet. The other me was soaked, her dyed blonde hair matted to her skull and water dripping from her fingertips to the rug. The other Aidan was similar, pale and wet, though his roan hair was sticking in all directions. Together they were chilled, hazy, unhappy, and dirt-stained.

Uncertain, the real Aidan and I glanced at each other. At the same time, our clones turned to glare at each other.

Robin breathed, "Whooooaaaa."

Aidan detached himself from my hand and touched the planchette. "Who are they?" he demanded of the

Ouija board, agitation stiffening his shoulders.

Y-O-U, the Ouija board answered. **A-T-T-H-E-E-N-D**.

"At the end?" Read asked slowly. "Why is it just you two?"

I had no way of answering and bit my lips together.

At the same time, Aidan and I stood up. I just knew that if he was moving, I was too. It would be better to be closer to my friends than the doppelgängers.

Taking in a deep breath, I saw Robin grab Aidan's other hand and squeeze until her knuckles were white. Her other hand was still latched onto Read's arm.

"How should we get rid of them?" I asked Aidan in a hushed tone.

Before he could speak, Other Nora answered. "If Aidan did his duty, we wouldn't have failed." Her voice was mine, though like a recording, it sounded minimally different coming from someone else.

Other Aidan's eyes swept the room, despondent and grim. "I will never see this room again because of her," he grumbled, gesturing to the Other Nora in disgust.

"Shut up," she snapped. It was eerie hearing my own voice so full of revulsion. "It's because of *you* that they died. You were supposed to guard the tower."

Aidan—our Aidan—held up a hand to silence their bickering. "They? They died?"

The Other Nora sneered at him. "Yes, Phoebe drowned, Robin was eaten by spiders, Read…"

"Make them shut up," Robin squeaked. She was looking to Read.

The Other Nora continued as if Robin hadn't spoken. "…Read burned, and Cody well, we never found him."

Other Nora tilted her head to the side and spoke in a low voice. "And it is all because of you, Aidan. You killed us all by bringing us here," she hissed, raising the hairs on the back of my neck. "It was your job to keep everyone away from this place."

Aidan took a step around the coffee table toward the fake us. I didn't like the separation and whispered frantically, "What are you doing?"

Cody had wandered off in the dark; Phoebe had separated from us by opening doors. I didn't want to lose someone else because we couldn't stick together.

Ignoring me, Aidan edged closer until he stood beside the boy who looked like him. Every feature was in place. The color of his eyes, the serious straight-thin lips, dark, straight eyebrows, and the thick roan-colored hair, it was all the same. To the two of them, he asked, "Are you the future us? That's why the *Bending Time* book appeared in the bookshelf?"

"We are," Other Aidan replied, his eyes narrowing as he looked at me. "We made it but couldn't get through the swamp. If it wasn't for her crazy family—"

Other Nora moved to slap him. Teeth bared, she shrieked through them, as if it could contain the rage that flushed her cheeks. At the same time, their bodies appeared to solidify, their translucent quality fading little by little. I hadn't noticed until I couldn't see light through Other Nora's flailing arm.

The slap was sharp and echoed through the living room. Other Aidan's head turned with the hit, and he kept his face turned away, the bitter smirk betraying his amusement.

The swamp? I swallowed hard. Was that why they were so wet? Did they—I mean *we*—die in a swamp? It also meant that Aidan knew about my family. Out of all of the outcomes, that one bristled my hairs the most. Irrational, I know. I assure you, I'm completely aware that I am.

"How do we stop it?" Read asked the peculiar doppelgänger, his voice steady.

Other Nora's eyes shifted to the real Aidan, though she made the small gesture seem difficult.

"We need a sacrifice," she said. "They can all go home if someone takes their place. Someone worthy of the sacrifice."

My muscles grew tense and still. A *sacrifice*, the very word was a jagged cut down my spine. I didn't think there's a dirtier word out there. To the Other Nora, I argued, "That would be cheating. Damien said we couldn't win this way. We had to beat the Challenge." I remembered how Robin had been called a cheat. Could she try to sacrifice herself? Or worse, someone else?

Other Aidan was trying to protest, grabbing his throat trying to speak, but no sound escaped. The Other Nora seemed pleased, though I wasn't sure what was going on between them.

"I'm sorry, Nora," Real Aidan spoke up, sounding as if he meant every word. "Maybe this is my Challenge. Maybe we have to separate after all."

Aidan waited for me to catch his pointed gaze before asking, "What if we kill each other? This is my fault for running us in here. I should have looked upstairs before—"

I shook my head, stopping him with a frantic flutter of my hand to keep him quiet. "You won't kill me, Aidan." Fear was evident in my voice, and I wished I could sound confident, like Phoebe.

"You can't," Read announced to Aidan, his tone smothering the whispers. "Nora's right."

Read's back up gave me some relief. He'd listen to Read before he would me.

I started to nod when a book flew off the one of the shelves. The hardcover volume sailed at Robin's head. Gasping, I slapped a hand on her back as a warning and ducked with her.

I felt the pages ruffle my ponytail before the book slammed into the bookshelf behind us.

Robin screamed so loud that my ears rang. I shouted to the Others. "I know Aidan won't kill me because he didn't mean for any of this to happen. How many parties do you think were invaded by a demon? How would he know?" I looked to the bookshelf for any sign of a disgruntled book before looking to Aidan.

Aidan, the real one, was staring at me aghast, while the Other Nora grumbled something about being an idiot.

The second her eyes met mine, another book launched itself from the same shelf, spinning like a top.

I tried to duck again, but the corner caught my bare shoulder. It bounced off of me, hitting the Ouija Board with a *thud*, sending the planchette sailing.

Out of the corner of my eye, I saw Aidan jerk to rush toward me, but something stopped him.

The impact wasn't hard enough to break bones, but it stung. Cupping my throbbing shoulder, I picked up the book and flung it away as fast as I could. It made my nerves shake with its closeness. Glaring over my shoulder at the others, I realized they were dry, no longer drenched from the swamp. Their clothes weren't as rumpled either. "If we die, I won't blame you,

Aidan," I said out of the side of my mouth.

He attempted a crooked smile, though it was strained.

Pointing to his legs, I asked, "Can't you come near us?"

Aidan's fingers twitched, and he stuttered through his teeth, making futile grunts in response.

"Oh God," Robin whispered.

Read started forward, pausing when he heard me hiss a warning.

Aidan face reddened, but he managed a single step. It looked labored and stiff, as if his legs were filled with hardening cement.

Three books launched a concurrent attack. Shrieking, I dropped onto the floor in a ball, hugging my knees tight enough to make my fingers cramp. I heard Aidan shout my name as one book out of three hit me in the middle of my back.

Yelping, I straightened, grabbing my throbbing spine, only to be pelted again in the arm and the hand. Curling back into a ball, I felt Robin's fingers snake around my ankle. She clung to me, and I at least knew she was all right. It was a small comfort when a book grazed my ribs, scraping as it went by.

I wished that Read and Aidan could somehow let me know they were okay. I waited for something to hit my temple and knock me unconscious. I waited, with dread, for Robin's fingers to go slack.

The dissonance of pages, books, and crashing items filled the room, making hearing a shout impossible. Peeking above my knees, I watched the country-fried lamp tip over the couch, crushing itself into the cushions.

Another book cracked into the middle of my back. It took all my will to remain still and not straighten to make myself a bigger target.

That's when Robin's fingers let go, nails scraping my ankle. I thought I heard her scream but couldn't be sure.

I swatted out an arm to grab her when a book hit the back of my arm hard enough to sweep my hand back around my knees. "Robin?" I called, my voice useless.

Something glass shattered. I heard the sound of a crash, maybe a bookshelf, and then all went silent.

Waiting for a noise, I hesitated. Was it really over? Or was this the calm before the storm?

I peeked past my knees and saw scattered books coating the floor like a second skin. Lifting my head, I looked around to see that only a few hard-covered books resided on the bookshelves. They seemed stationary, for now. One of the bookshelves had toppled over the Lay-Z-Boy. The mountainous pile of books at the base of the chair made me think of Read. Was he trapped beneath?

Daring to stand, I groaned and staggered, feeling the impending bruises.

Wobbling to the books, I heard myself shout, but I wasn't the one speaking.

"Read, help him!"

Twisting, I saw Robin edging toward Other Nora on the floor. Other Nora had been transformed in an instant. The dirt had vanished, leaving a smooth ponytail and dry, ironed clothes. Robin looked to Other Nora for reassurance, and that's when I realized what was happening. My friends thought she was me.

The shudder of the wall, as if someone slammed

into it, turned my attention to the Aidans. They were grappling with each other and dodging another flying book from the last shelf as it sucker punched them.

Read darted forward again. He grabbed Aidan's arms, struggling to pin them behind his back. I wasn't sure if he had the real Aidan or the Other. Like Other Nora, this doppelgänger appeared just as Aidan had when he'd stepped into the room.

Jumping over the coffee table, I clumsily knocked over the game board. I couldn't let the Aidan nearest me swing at Read's apprehended Aidan if...Bloody hell, this was confusing.

Scrambling over the mess, I swung my arms around the Aidan that Read didn't have and hugged him from behind. Clamping my hands together, I leaned back and ducked my head to avoid being smacked in the nose with the back of his head. I pulled him away using every bit of strength my body would allow. I believe he managed to hit every forming bruise except the ones on my back. Read and I pulled them apart. I hadn't realized that my Aidan couldn't breathe until the sharp intake of air.

Somehow we were successful, until the five books propelled toward us.

Robin scrambled to her feet and ran behind Other Nora for protection. I wanted to warn her, but Aidan lifted me off my feet, breaking my hold on him. Stumbling, I nearly fell, but he grabbed me around the waist. I thought I should scream until I realized he was protecting me from the books.

I heard three of them hit Aidan's back, dropping to the floor with heavy *thunks*. He grunted in pain, but he didn't whine as much as I had. Read took one in the shoulder, staggering back a few steps. He rubbed it with a grimace, losing the grip he had on his Aidan.

"The board lied to us," I whispered, realizing he wasn't letting me go. Could this be my Aidan or the Other Aidan? "I wouldn't try to hurt you, and I don't blame you for anything that happens." I could eat these words later, but they seemed important for him to hear, whether this was Other Aidan or the real one.

"No!" my doppelgänger spat. "That's a lie. You always felt strange around him, and you know it. You have good reason not to trust him. Ask him how he felt about you when you first met him. Nauseous? Sick? Go ahead, ask!"

I pointed at her. "If the Aidan there killed you, then I'm sorry. But we're not going to end up like you." At least I hoped not.

Aidan unwrapped his arms from around me and coughed.

I pivoted just in time to see the Aidan near Read cough as well.

Read and I exchanged a curious glance as the two of them reached for their chests simultaneously.

"What's happening?" I asked Other Nora, but she was gone, leaving Robin stunned and alone. She backed away from all of us, nearly tripping over a book at her heels.

I wanted to go to her, but both Aidans fell to their knees between Read and me. They were gasping in loud, ragged breaths.

Read scrambled for the Ouija board on the floor.

I caught the planchette on the floor and tossed it to Read.

Fumbling a little, he caught it and slapped it on the

board. Placing his hands hastily over the piece, he asked loud enough for me to hear, "What's happening?"

W-H-I-C-H-O-N-E, it replied, taking a painful amount of time to spell it out.

Glancing up, I saw the skin on the Aidans' faces begin to writhe. It was as if fat finger-width worms were wriggling just beneath their flesh. I tried not to stare but couldn't seem to look away, either. Their faces contorted and rippled, the cheekbones stretching so far that identical splits in the skin was visible on their left cheeks before the skin stretched again in another direction.

At the wall where the front door should be, Robin was screaming.

Read pointed at both of them, his eyes on me. "Which one is the real Aidan?" He had to shout over Robin to be heard.

I hadn't considered that the Ouija board was making us pick. I glanced between them just as the Aidan closest to me tried to shout, producing an inhuman, wet gurgle.

"He's dying, Nora," Read warned, glancing between them frantically.

Why did I have to choose? I suppose it would be easier than having the death of a friend on his own head. I ground my teeth together. The one closest had blocked me from the books. Would the Other Aidan have done that to trick us?

I opened my mouth to answer, but instead I yelped. Alongside Aidan's temple, a spine-like bone rippled up into his hairline, stretching skin until it was white. Within the confines of his arms, I could see movement as if something were laced with his muscles, changing shape. His chest even arched up as if his heart were pulsating on the outside of his chest. *Thump, thump, thump.*

"That one!" Read pointed to the Aidan furthest from me.

"No!" I shrieked, holding out my hands as the Aidan nearest me collapsed. Well, they both collapsed, but I caught mine.

He was heavier than I thought, and I fell, cradling his head as best as I could so it wouldn't hit the floor. I landed on my tailbone and stiffened. The paralyzing pain tore through my back, but I didn't drop his head. My fingers dug into his scalp, real bone instead of something shifting. Looking down on him, I realized nothing could have prepared me for what I saw.

His mouth was hanging open, as if the jaw had been broken. It was unhinged and slightly lopsided. His open mouth and eye sockets were empty. There was no eyes, teeth, or tongue to be seen. There was nothing, just darkness.

Read hovered over the two bodies, inspecting both, while Robin inched toward the Aidan nearest Read, balancing on the discarded books.

I wanted to be angry with Read, but I couldn't. He asked me to choose, and I waited too long. Aidan was suffering, and I hesitated. This wasn't like losing Phoebe or Cody. They just disappeared; I didn't have to see them…like this. The Aidan closest to Read moaned, his feet twitching.

Feeling tears stinging the corner of my eyes, I looked back down at my Aidan and screamed.

I dropped his head and scrambled away, wriggling out of reach. The body didn't move to grab me, but the head lolled to the side to face me again.

An oversized eyeball had been peering at me through the opened mouth. It filled the entire gaping jaw. The large eye was white except for the pupil, which had dilated upon focusing on me. It rolled around as I scurried away, peering around the room before arching up to focus on me again.

A stabbing terror streaked up my body when the eye suddenly disappeared into the hollowed darkness of Aidan's skull. His chest pumped, and the writhing skin slowed before the body stopped altogether, lying perfectly still.

The dreaded silence didn't remain long before I heard Aidan curse.

He was sitting up with Robin's aid. Clutching his chest with one hand, he stared at the monstrosity in his…suit. "Just like that fucking dream I had," he choked.

I remembered he hadn't indulged the details of his dream before our trip. I suppose I wouldn't want to talk about it, either.

Read chose right, I suppose. *If this was the real Aidan.* Read helped him to his feet, and I felt relieved that I hadn't had to choose.

I crawled to my feet; my legs felt like I'd spent the last half hour doing jumping jacks. Aidan was helped to his and nodded to me. I tried to smile when I saw everyone was looking at me…no, past me.

Twisting, I saw the black door again. It hadn't been there before.

Our way out!

As I took that first step toward it, a rumbling alerted us to the bookshelves all around the living room.

"Get down!" Aidan shouted.

No one hesitated this time. I landed hard on the floor between the coffee table and the couch. I wheezed for a breath, staring at the floor as the entire room erupted with the sound of flapping paper and raucous crashes.

The heavy hardcover books slammed against the opposite walls. One hit the back of my thigh, stabbing a Charlie-horse sensation through my muscles. One skidded over my head, slapping up against the couch. I was lucky to be relatively sheltered between the table and couch this time. I tried to lift my head to see where the others were but couldn't make them out. I could just hear Robin's shrieks over the explosion. A book knocked me in the back of the head, shooting blackened stars through my vision and forcing me to duck again.

It seemed to last a lifetime, longer than the last assault, before the explosion faded.

Lifting my head guardedly, I croaked, "Is everyone all right?"

Aidan's eyes were open, and he was breathing, but he was grimacing.

"Yeah, I'm fine," Read said sarcastically, having been hit by a few himself. As he sat up, several books toppled off of him.

"Robin?" I asked, standing again. The Charlie-horse had turned into a cramp, and I tried to rub it out.

She murmured something noncommittal but lifted her head with a groan. She was fine. I reached out to help her to her feet.

She staggered upright and helped Read. I reached down for Aidan.

He accepted my hand, staring at the black door at

the other end of the room. Unbalanced, he wobbled away from me and toward Robin and Read.

The body of the Other Aidan was completely obscured by layers of books, or he had disappeared, just like the Other Nora. The old shag carpet wasn't even visible anymore.

"Skinwalkers," Aidan whispered, eyes wide and searching.

I blinked at him. "Sorry?"

"Nothing," he murmured, avoiding my stare. He had barely made eye contact since coming to. Was it really our Aidan?

"The door." Robin sniffled, smiling a little. She pointed toward the black door that had appeared on the opposite wall from where we'd come in.

Aidan produced that irritating polite smile. "I'm telling my parents to buy paperbacks from now on."

Read chuckled. "Screw paperbacks. E-books, man. Then the next Challenge might not be so painful." He reached for his back, the humor slipping as he winced.

The four of us stumbled and wobbled over the debris of scattered books without a backward glance.

Aidan reached the door first. "This is the same symbol, but look," he mused, reaching out his hand to trace the waves and triangle. There had been three watery lines, and now there were two.

"A countdown?" I asked, reaching forward to grab the doorknob. The motion cracked a stinging pain through my shoulder. *This will bruise*, I thought.

Twisting the knob, I pushed the door inward. I didn't want to stay any more than Read. The idea of seeing my angry doppelgänger again made me squirm. The image of that eye staring at me from Aidan's opened mouth was bad enough. *No, the Other Aidan's mouth*, I corrected myself. At least I hoped it was. Aidan said a skinwalker was a monster that could reside within your skin? Someone that looks like you, talks like you—that sort of thing? The idea made me feel a lingering betrayal. What if the skinwalker was still here? And he looked just like Aidan?

The Other Nora said that Aidan felt as uncomfortable around me as I did him, but he had felt nauseous? Sick?

Shuddering, I stepped back, hugging myself.

I didn't have to look up to know Aidan was staring at me. I could feel it.

CHAPTER EIGHTEEN

When we left Aidan's deranged living room behind, I couldn't see anything at first, only vague outlines in the dark.

Dread itched in the back of my mind as I wondered what might be watching us, waiting for someone to notice it crouched in a corner.

Shoving the unpleasant thought to the side, I fidgeted in place and waited for my eyes to adjust.

Read squeezed my hand, and I pressed mine against Robin's, knowing she was looking up at me. I was grateful that it was dark; she wouldn't be able to see my smile waver.

The small window to our right allowed a little moonlight.

Blinking away my surprise, I saw the squared, heavy-set chairs sitting back to back in the middle of the circular room. Dark brick walls curved around us, but the little marble door wasn't in the room anymore.

Robin tugged at my hand to catch my attention.

With my vision filtering the dark, I could just make out her wide eyes. "Have we won?" she asked, her voice rising with a false hope.

I had to be strong for Robin. Maybe she was the only reason I hadn't run screaming. It reminded me of when Mona would get scared. I had to be the adult, the one in charge, the one with all the answers. Sighing patiently, I said, "I don't think that guy would give up so easily."

"Five Challenges left," Read told her, and I felt her shoulders sag beside me.

Detaching himself from the group, Aidan jogged to the arched doorway and leaned in as far as he could without tumbling down the steps. "It's really dark, but if we keep to the wall, we should be able to get to the second floor."

"Maybe we should see what's outside first," Read whispered.

Still attached to one another, Read, Robin, and I shuffled to the window. The moon, half hidden behind a cloud, slowly emerged from the gloom. I waited to see the pond that had been behind the house but could only see the outline.

As the full force of the moonlight shone into the circular room, I heard a distant scraping. Startled, I instinctively pulled Robin closer.

Her head jerked from side to side, and she hissed, "What was that?"

Holding up my fingers for her to see, I whispered, "It'll be—"

Aidan grabbed Robin by the arm and yanked. Still attached to me, Robin jerked me back to the wall fast and hard, and I choked back the rest of the words. Hell, I'd forgotten what I was about to say.

Aidan spun us around. His pale eyes were wide, but his voice whispered, instilling a fear all the way down to my knees. "Something's coming."

Read stood near the chairs and craned his neck to look through the darkened archway. "What could it be?"

No one answered, leaving only Robin's whimpering to fill the void. Robin and I found the wall and stood with our backs to it. Aidan stood in front of us, and I had to duck my head to look past his shoulder.

Robin's body hunched as she pulled her hand out of mine to put them to her face. "I can't take anymore of this."

Aidan warned Robin to keep quiet, and she clamped her hands over her mouth hard enough to leave dents in her cheeks.

In the stillness, I listened.

At first, it was just a shuffling or swishing sound. Gradually, it grew louder, closer.

It reminded me of a straw-bristled broom against concrete, except it was coming up the stairs.

I almost didn't hear Robin. "...to get out of here. Someone think of something."

Her panic was infectious, the opposite of what I needed.

Aidan hissed at her to be quiet again, and Robin began to whimper behind her hands.

Unable to take it anymore, I moved to hug her when they burst in like oily floodwaters.

Dozen of the arachnids, no hundreds, maybe more, rushed into the room. There were large hairy tarantulas and smaller spiders of all shapes and colors and sizes. I recognized a few daddy-long-legs but they weren't small. This particular variety was as big as the tarantulas.

Aidan must have seen that peculiar spider at the same time.

"You know what I heard?" His voice shook as we backed to the wall beside me. "The daddy-longlegs spider is the most poisonous spider in the world, but their mouths are too small to infect people."

"Very reassuring, Aidan, but that's a myth." I almost sounded calm and received a side-ways glance. I wasn't calm. though; I felt panic shaking in my guts. My dream, the nightmare that haunted my youth, had showed itself into reality; there was no waking up from this. I needed something to do or some avenue of escape to turn to.

I scraped at every available corner of my mind hoping for a hero moment but found only fear caving in whatever logic and common sense I had left.

Robin, who I thought would be screaming by now, had frozen stiff, staring at the eight-legged mob without uttering a sound.

Read batted at his pant legs as he danced his way toward us, dark little spiders clinging to his jeans.

The hero moment was passing, fast.

Aidan and I pressed our backs against the chilled bricks. *We could run past them, squish a few; they won't all attack at once, right?* In the childhood dream, however, they all attacked when I ran.

A black, hand-sized scorpion propelled its way over the sea, moving with it and even squishing some of the smaller spiders under foot.

I heard a whimper and looked to Robin. She was still frozen against the wall, and it took me several seconds to realize it was me who'd made a noise.

The spiders crawled all over each other to reach us. I felt the little tickles near my ankles, then my arms and shoulders by those that had taken to the walls.

My skin crawled without their assistance, and I tried to focus on the facts. When I was suffering from the spider nightmare as a child, my mother thought it would be a good idea to learn about them. *You can't fear what you know*, she said.

Though right now, I could argue that point.

Some spiders could produce milk. Okay, that was distracting enough for a weird fact. What about that spider in the South Pole that could withstand a lot of heat?

There was a tickle in my ear. Every thread of willpower prevented me from moving. I took a deep breath through my lips before closing them and thought, *They have disjointed limbs to move fast and no spinal cord.*

The venomous scorpion skittered past Read and over Robin's boots, then over my sneakers before stopping. *Scorpions are considered arachnids too*, I thought.

Arching its intricate, segmented body, it almost appeared to be looking up. The tail wobbled with the oversized stinger.

One pointed foot drew itself down my shin, the tiny hairs on its legs tickling mine and almost making me flinch.

Go away, I pleaded in my head while at the same time trying to stay a statue.

I couldn't take my eyes off the curled stinger, sharpened and ready to strike. I realized it would be comparable to a pocket knife.

"Guys." I struggled to keep every limb from shaking. I didn't want to startle my new friend. My hands, legs, and body were beginning to constrict to the point where I had to struggle to stay upright. *Please don't fall*, I begged my legs. *Please don't fall.*

The idea of falling headfirst into a sea of spiders made me dizzy, but the idea of falling into the scorpion was enough to remind me that I could die here.

My eyes flickered to the writhing mass that was the spiders, trying to distract myself as three of the scorpions sharp feet pressed hard into my upper thigh, trying to gain purchase on my flesh.

"Hold still, Robin," Read muttered a few feet away, though I couldn't see him out of my peripheral vision. But I could see Robin. The only movement on her was the shifting of the spiders as they messed up her hair and crowded Phoebe's sweater. If she could do it, so could I.

"Keep your back at the wall and keep yourself very…still." Aidan swallowed in between his last two words. A tarantula stopped its trek up the front of his shirt to watch his mouth move with several glassy eyes.

As I pressed my back against the wall, my knee almost slipped. The abrupt jerk stilled the scorpion. I needed both of my hands against the bricks to keep steady and tried to move very, very slowly.

Robin's silence was making me nervous.

Hairy spider legs brushed over my bare calves and thighs, joining the scorpion that was testing its grip on my jean shorts. They tickled my arms and fingers and tugged into my hair. I squeezed my eyes shut, waiting for the nightmare to be over.

* * *

There was a calm.

The shrill silence forced me to let go of my held breath, and I listened for any movement, any voices, any sign of life.

It was then that I realized I was lying on my side, my head propped up but leaning on something hard. My hand tingled with pins and needles beneath my body, like I'd been there a while.

My eyes snapped open, and I found myself staring at the legs of the wooden chair on the third floor. I was still in the Birket house. But I didn't feel the spiders, the crawling, the blanketed terror…

Back to back, the two heavy chairs were illuminated by the moonlight from the window behind me. The carved letters were only a few inches from my face. Robin had mentioned them earlier, I remembered.

NEF.

Licking my dry lips, I whispered croakily, "My middle name starts with a J."

The presence was heavy, weighing around me like a blanket.

I rolled my eyes up the wood and saw a large hand gripping the armrest.

Another hand slapped down behind my head, making me jump.

I could feel his body hovering, but it wasn't warm; it was just there, an instinct that prickled like knowing someone was watching you. He was almost touching along my hip and shoulders—almost. Despite the lack of touch, he was trapping me to the floor, lording over me that I couldn't move; he must have known, must have felt, my helplessness.

I dared to turn my head. I found myself staring into two bottomless eyes that were so close I was surprised I couldn't feel Damien's face. Our noses should have been bumping together.

It took a second to realize I was staring into the demon's eyes, and something finally snapped.

As I drew in a breath to scream, the small window of stillness vibrated a tension through the silence.

"You shouldn't be here, Nora."

* * *

Something skittered across my face.

The rustling erupted in a wave, and I let out a wheezy scream.

Eyes squeezed tight again, I listened to my blood pumping in my ears. The calm had vanished, a distant dream. Had I passed out for a second? I felt the cold wall at my back instead of the wood floor or the pins and needles. I was back in the nightmare instead of the silence of the third floor.

Four spiders took to racing across my face.

Fear coiled down my spine until my knees buckled.

One stopped on my eyelid, and another wriggled up my nose.

I couldn't fight it any longer.

Screaming, I kicked my legs and slapped something wet off my cheek in my frantic flailing.

Swinging my head back and forth, I almost lost my

balance and was forced to open my eyes.

I dug my hands into my hair to shake the spiders loose.

The scorpion flew off my legs and landed on its back near the heavy chairs.

In my frenzied attempt, I tried to stop screaming, but my voice wouldn't cease.

Tears stung the corners of my eyes as the spiders came back for me, faster than before.

I shoved my back against the wall and felt something wet against my right shoulder blade. Nausea shuddered through me.

"Hold still!" Aidan's cry was muffled but alert. "They'll kill you if you don't! Just hold still!"

I turned my bleary vision to him, attempting to resist the urge to twitch.

Aidan was pressed tight against the wall, spiders all over him. They were in his hair and on his face, arms, and legs. They crawled all over each other, and one big brown one dropped from the ceiling and landed on his shoulder.

I winced, but Aidan stood still, his face half turned toward me.

"Hold still 'til they're less aggressive," he said. A smaller spider crawled into his ear.

Out of the corner of my eye, I saw Read had imitated Aidan, his back pressed to the wall, eyes closed, nostrils flaring.

It took me a second to realize that Robin was curled up on the floor with her hands on her head, still silent and stronger than me.

Moaning, I tried to do as Aidan suggested. I held my arms and legs together to avoid anything crawling up where I probably wouldn't be able to keep my cool.

My palms pressed to the brick so hard my shoulders threatened to shake. Even as I moved, I could feel the spiders already regaining their claim on me.

Hairy feet crawled up my legs and arms, but luckily, I didn't feel any stings.

A tarantula on my shoulder touched my chin with one slow limb. I felt two spiders land in my hair with fat *plops*. My legs felt weak. They wobbled, and I didn't have time to catch myself before I twitched hard enough to cause a ruckus. I felt the first sting in my kneecap. It burned sharp and hot, bringing tears to my eyes.

The tears ran down my face, unaware of the eight-legged dangers, and dripped off my jawline.

Holding my body rigid, I calculated each breath through my nose. *Iiiiinnn, ooouuuut. Iiiiiinnnnn…*

Focus! a frantic voice in my head demanded. *Think about how to get out of here, not about the spiders.*

I took a deep breath and obeyed; I had no other choice. In the dream, they'd rip at me if I ever moved, and there was never a place to run. Even if we broke for the archway, we'd be filled with venom by the time we got to the stairs. In my nightmare, they were poisonous, all of them. How would I wake myself up? There had been a way. There was one way out of the silly nightmare.

But this was *not* a silly nightmare. This was *real*. And I could die in it if I didn't act smoothly. I could kill Aidan, Read, and Robin with me.

I thought of the doppelgängers. They said that we would kill each other, and there wasn't any trust. Other Nora had said, *Robin would be consumed by spiders.*

The sting on my knee was getting hotter, almost unbearable.

Spiders were crawling under my shirt and up my shorts; thank goodness I'd worn underwear.

In the dream, it was a phrase I'd say to myself to wake up. *It's only a dream?* That didn't seem quite right, but it was close.

"Robin!" I shouted through clamped lips, making it sound more like, "*Ruuhhin.*"

No one answered. No one dared.

This isn't really real. Damien just made it all up so that he could scare you and stop you from winning the Challenge, the helpful voice in my head reasoned. Unfortunately, when the voice of reason showed up, so did its insidious counterpart. *You can barely stand; there's poison in you. You can't do this, Nora. What about Robin? She's covered and isn't moving. What if she's dying? Maybe she's already dead.*

With my eyes closed, the room felt like it was tilting, and a strange heat swelled within my stomach. I thought for a moment it was from the lack of food.

Skin on my forearm snagged on a clawed foot. The twitching pain offered wood, in the form of panic, to the fire in my stomach.

Without warning, the memory switched on. The fire in my belly writhed and burst with enough energy for me to open my mouth and say, "This is only a nightmare." And for a single moment, I believed it wasn't real.

Despite the belief and the words, the throng of arachnids thickened. I stifled the panic as my face began to crawl and itch. *Just take that step, Nora, and let them kill you,* I thought. The tears welled up in my eyes again, threatening chaos if they were to fall.

"Say again!" Aidan's voice shouted through his closed lips.

At first I was confused, trying to weed through the terror to remember what I had said. Straining through the panic, I shrieked through the edge of my lips, not wanting to open my mouth again. "Only a nightmare!" My stomach didn't empty its contents, and the heat from within dissipated with the words, a release.

My voice fueled the feverish agitation. I was certain I was covered from head to toe. My body itched, and my fingers twitched involuntarily.

I heard Read shout, "Ei ju' a nighmer." The conviction in those words made me relax just a little. I felt a warmth inside my stomach return with the spark of hope when I heard Aidan say the same words.

The warmth spread, like a bad case of heartburn up my chest, but there was nothing there, and it felt as if it weren't restricted to only my organs. Even my skin felt hot with it.

The tickling of a spider in my ear was almost too much. I screamed this time and moved away from the wall. Despite the danger and the hissing warning, I shouted, no longer afraid of what might crawl into my mouth—well, for just a second, I wasn't. "This is just a stupid nightmare!" The warmth in my body oiled out of my skin as I threw all of my energy, my hope, and my fear into those words.

Suddenly, there was nothing.

The shuffling noise evaporated, leaving the air noticeably lighter.

Little hairy bodies, scraping feet, and the insistent tugging all stopped. My hair stopped moving with bodies, and my face didn't itch against tiny feet.

I opened one eye and peeked through lashes.

The floorboards were bare, devoid of arachnids, dust, and everything else.

Opening my eyes wider, I took a chance and looked down at myself. With my vision clear and the dizziness subsiding, I straightened my posture with slow, meticulous motions just to test it out. My knee was swelling and showing off a combination of dramatic reds and whites. There was a cut, but it wasn't as deep as I thought it would be. It didn't hurt much either. My skin felt stretched and a little sensitive to touch, but otherwise, I could move it without any trouble. There were a few bites, though none compared to the colors on my knee.

My arm had a scratch, but it was minor and about as deep as a cat scratch. I glanced over to see Aidan brushing his pant legs, making sure that the spiders were gone.

Read stepped away from the wall, eyes wide. "Robin?"

The hardwood where Robin had crouched was stained black.

CHAPTER NINETEEN

Aidan inched forward and tested the burnt spot with his foot. "Where'd she go?"

"She didn't say anything," Read said as if his tongue were too thick to form the words. "Half way through, I thought she might have passed out."

Robin would be consumed by spiders.

"Robin?" I called uneasily. "Robin, where are you?"

There weren't many places to look, and we ended up staring at the floor before I asked, "You don't think she's dead. Do you?" *Consumed, maybe?*

"You'd think there'd be a body," Read answered, his eyes never tearing away from the spot. "It's like the weird Nora said."

I looked up at Read, uneasiness clawing inside my head. Other Nora said Read would burn, and I knew Read was thinking it too as he stared at the empty spot on the floor.

Aidan asked, "That was your nightmare?"

It took me a second to realize he was talking to me. "An unpleasant one from when I was little."

Aidan grimaced. "Can't say that was pleasant for me, either."

I tried to smile and failed miserably.

Our eyes rose to the arched brick doorway. It appeared to be the only way out.

"Should we go?" Aidan asked.

Casting one last glance at the burnt spot in the floor, I immediately regretted it as a new wave of guilt crashed headfirst onto me.

"I guess," I said, knowing I didn't sound helpful. "There's no black door anyway to tell us to go somewhere else." My gaze settled on the two chairs. The initials carved into the wood weren't there, I realized. Remembering Damien hovering over me, I wondered how long I'd passed out. Was that what happened to Robin? Did she pass out and they…

They didn't consume her, the reassuring voice in my head sang loud.

Aidan and Read were talking, and I realized I wasn't paying attention.

"…our only choice, Read."

Read ran his hands over his dark hair, flattening it to his skull. "This isn't fucking right, man."

Aidan started toward the stairs. "Maybe if we make it to the end, we can get our friends back."

"Or find them along the way," I added, hope straining for traction.

Read didn't appear convinced. He muttered something under his breath before following.

No one spoke as we felt our way down the spiral stairs. Each step echoed off the walls, a grim reminder of our vulnerability. Even with Aidan in front of me to test each step, I was cautious. All I could imagine was Damien creating a hole where there wasn't one before and us plummeting into that floating dark. I didn't want to lose anyone else. I wanted to know that they were okay.

In the pitch black, I kept my hands on the wall, listening for Aidan's steps ahead of me and feeling Read's breath tickle the hairs on top of my head from behind.

The gritty brick crumbled under my fingertips, numbing them the further we descended.

When light began to seep into the stairwell, I was relieved, and our steps quickened. We reached the second floor of the old Victorian house, unscathed.

It was still dark, but at least lights were coming through the windows.

Lights?

"Are those streetlights outside?" I asked, squinting as if that would help. It really didn't. There should have been a dark little pond amongst hanging trees, not multiple city lights.

Aidan stepped up to the only window that wasn't in a bedroom and cleared his throat. "It's city lights," he confirmed.

It would appear we weren't done with this particular Challenge.

I straightened my shoulders, and Read cursed under his breath and glanced at me. Catching my eye, he offered a small smile, though it betrayed him and he looked away.

"Any more nightmares you want to brief me on?" Aidan asked as he stepped away from the window.

Did living nightmares count?

"Nothing that sticks out."

Read shook his head. "I don't dream," he said before his eyes bulged. "Except that one before we came here. Think that might…?" He didn't dare finish.

I shook my head, hoping that would be enough to console him—it wasn't.

Aidan said, "No use just hanging out up here. I don't want to be covered in any more spiders. No separating." The last two words hung in the air as he turned his icy-blue eyes to Read and me.

We nodded together, and I twisted my camisole in my fists, knowing I'd probably stretched another shirt already.

Aidan led the way down to the main floor. My swollen knee stretched each time it bent, feeling fat and stiff. I tried to camouflage my hobble. No use worrying about something I couldn't fix right now. In my research, I'd learned that scorpion stings were recoverable without a hospital. Unless I went blind or lost all feeling, I could survive.

On the main floor, I could make out the fireplace in the next room, the scattered bottles, cans, and sleeping bags all laid out the way we had left them.

"He's pretty big on details," I said, unsure if I was impressed or not.

Read rushed on tip-toes to the living-room. "Yeah, but our bags are gone."

I guessed the sweater I'd wanted earlier was no longer an option.

Aidan made his way to the tall window closest to the front door and inspected the outside lights.

After several drawn out seconds, I asked, "What's

next?" Inching closer to the tall, narrow window Aidan was peering out of, I tried to weave my head to see around him, but it was a futile effort.

Aidan glanced over his shoulder as Read joined us in the entry. "I think the black door's somewhere out there." He motioned to the window.

He didn't bother addressing me, just Read. Frowning, I ducked and shouldered Aidan out of the way to see the city street. I could feel Aidan's breath on my shoulder as he asked, "What do you think it is? Any ideas what nightmare this could be?"

Numb, I shook my head, then realized he wasn't asking me.

"I told you, I don't dream. Any you might have had, Aidan?" Read asked.

The station wagon wasn't there. The trees had been replaced by concrete, dilapidated apartments, pawn shops, litter, and potholes. In the distance, I swore I heard a siren.

Collectively, we pressed our faces against the narrow rectangular glass alongside the door. Read's chin brushed the top of my head, and Aidan wove behind us to get a better look.

"Awesome," Read muttered unimpressed. "We're downtown."

There weren't many people, but there *were* people. They didn't linger in one place for long. One man was jogging into an alley while another stumbled out of it in a drunken stupor, hitting every car and wall until he disappeared around a corner. I wondered if they were part of Damien's little world or if they were trapped like us. Could they be doing a Challenge, or had they failed and had to make sure we failed? I shuddered at the idea.

The streets were lined with bulky old cars that I'd seen in movies set in the 1950s. Most were rusted with flat tires and were multi-colored—different hoods and mismatched doors. It matched the rest of the street that seemed to be fighting between a glossy new shop and crumbling apartment. It was typical downtown, minus the 1950s decor.

Read touched my shoulder. "Is that…"

Without warning, a grisly face slapped against the opposite side of the glass.

We all shouted with a start.

My head hit Read's jaw, his teeth snapping shut and sending a pressurized throb through my skull. But it didn't stop us from running away from the window.

Aidan hissed for Read and me to stop.

I was halfway to the stairs and Read was ready to run through the dining room to the back of the house. "He's saying something," Aidan whispered.

Freezing by the stairs, I held my breath to listen over my heartbeat.

The haggard thing was barely loud enough to hear through the window. "Very bright out here. Very bright indeed. Very bright out here. Very bright indeed." He wore rags that draped over his bony frame and were useless against the cold. He hadn't shaved in weeks, and what few elongated teeth he had were stained yellow.

What scared me wasn't his clothes or peculiar speech; it was his eyes.

He had none.

There weren't eye sockets or eyebrows bristled above, just a wrinkled layer of flesh where eyes should have been.

The deformed old man seemed to be looking at us

while repeating, "Very bright out here. Very bright indeed."

The chill ran from the base of my spine and up through my shoulders, and I remembered to take in air again.

Aidan waved his hand to get our attention before whispering, "We need to get out of here before Damien finds a way to force us out."

I knew he was right, but at the same time, I felt a brittle safety in here. Out there, we were walking targets. There were too many eyes—or lack of eyes— and they were all watching us step into their minefield.

Shuffling toward the front door, Read whispered, "What about him?"

The old man kept his face close to the glass, croaking his phrase.

"We run across the street if he comes after us," Aidan said.

"To the alley?" Read asked.

Aidan nodded after a pause.

"You mean where the drunk guy stumbled out of?" Read asked.

Aidan's icy stare didn't go unnoticed.

"Wherever we can then," Aidan said with tight lips, "but we stick together."

"Can you run?" Read asked.

It took me a moment to realize he was talking to me. I reached back and bent my knee, stretching my thigh. The skin felt tight but again, no pain. "It feels fine. Just looks ugly."

Read eased closer to the door. "We need a better plan."

Aidan frowned. "Like what? Wait for this place to

catch on fire?"

I flinched at the harsh words, but he was right. We had to move, but I didn't have to like it. Read caught my hand and muttered, "Here goes nothing." He swung the door inward, exposing us to the run-down street.

Read stepped outside, then stopped short.

Ready to run, I collided with Read's back. The eyeless stranger didn't acknowledge our presence, still pressing his face to the window of the Victorian house. Determining that the old man wasn't a threat, Read started to walk between the cars and toward the road.

Sneakers scraping on the sidewalk, Aidan and I watched the old man while Read kept his face turned to the opposite side of the street, pulling me along. Somehow my sweaty palm didn't slip from his.

The only sound behind us was, "Very bright out here. Very bright indeed."

The roadway was cracked and pitted. Traffic lights changed, but no vehicles were running.

I didn't recall having any nightmares in the city, but anything was possible.

We reached the other sidewalk unnoticed. Read asked, "Any ideas?" He squeezed our slick hands together.

I glanced at Aidan; his face had gone ashen. "What is it?" I asked.

Shaking his head, Aidan darted his gaze up and down the empty road. "I just realized that this is my nightmare."

CHAPTER TWENTY

Read turned with an impatient shrug. "So what are we looking for? Should we be hiding somewhere?"

"Maybe from them?" I asked and pointed to the street corner opposite the Victorian house.

A group crowded around polished motorcycles. Unlike the cars on the street, these bikes looked as if they'd just rolled off the assembly line, though they still held the antique flare of the rest of the vehicles. The oversized headlight, thin handle bars, large tanks, and skinny wheels were nothing like the modern variety I'd seen zipping around Leland.

Read and Aidan looked up the street in surprise and ducked at the same time.

Following their lead, I scurried behind a Chevy with a purple bumper. Clustered together between two vehicles, we could hear the raucous laughter fill the street ahead.

"Aidan," I whispered, "what happened in your

dream?"

Aidan motioned for me to be quiet.

I followed his gaze toward the Victorian house—which was crammed between two gloomy apartment buildings. The haggard old man shuffled inside, his verbiage trailing behind. "Very bright out here. Very bright indeed." He didn't seem to have any interest in us whatsoever.

"Aidan," I insisted in a whisper.

A few car lengths north of the Chevy, a stereo crackled to life, filling the air. An echoing voice sang, followed by a choir of voices *doo de doo'ing* in the background. The slow song sounded like something from the 1950's.

Read and I exchanged a curious glance as the echoing main voice mentioned a game. Read pulled his hand from mine, and we both wiped our slick palms on our jeans.

"What is it?" I asked Aidan. "What should we be looking for?"

He didn't answer. His eyes kept wandering to the cars then down the street and to the motorbikes; apprehension creased his youthful features.

Read's shoulders sagged, exasperated. He looked ready to say something when the roar of an engine smothered the music as well as my yelp of surprise. It stopped Read cold.

Aidan jumped and grabbed my arm as if *I* were the one to save him.

Craning my neck to see if there was a single vehicle taking up the roadway, I saw none. It had been so loud I couldn't pinpoint the direction it had come from.

The music began to take over the street once more,

a new song erupting from the crackling speakers.

Between shallow breaths, Aidan said, "Come on."

Before Read or I could question him, Aidan stood up and started in long, purposeful strides, the kind that was harder to stop.

Read shoved me to move. Panicked, we hurried to catch up to Aidan. Looking to him, our pace quickened to keep up. Aidan stared straight ahead. His lean figure was rigid, but he hadn't slowed.

Keeping close to the buildings, we passed the occupied car playing music. I could see three teenage boys inside. The muffled vintage music carried through the window.

I felt a scream choke in my throat as we passed. The passengers didn't have eyes.

Their shapeless pale faces lacked not only the eyes but also mouths. The skin where lips should have been had stretched horizontally, sealing any opening. The only portion of their faces that was noticeable was the lump of their nose—without nostrils. Even their hair was all the same color, styled the same, with a part in the middle, and they wore the same collared shirt and slacks.

I thought to myself, *It's just a few of the faceless, nameless people of this city, like any other...right? Maybe the demon had a sense of sick, very sick, humor.*

I could hear the eerie chorus of voices within the car, making it all the more surreal.

The three boys in the car watched us pass, as is if they could see. They turned their heads as we hurried along, and I found myself staring back for as long as I could.

Nearly tripping over my own feet was the signal to

stop.

I realized that Aidan was aiming for the biker types at the same time as Read, who growled under his breath, "I don't think we should be going this way."

"What are you doing?" I asked in a hoarse whisper. Was he insane?

Aidan didn't answer.

I tugged on him as hard as I could and dug my heels into the concrete, getting Aidan to halt. He jerked back and stared at me like I'd fouled some important scheme.

"What is it?" I asked. "You're freaking us out."

Read nodded. "Dude, you have to tell us what's going on."

Aidan looked past us and then up the street before licking his lips and shuffling from foot to foot, nervousness drawing his pale skin taut. "If…if this is going the way…" He held up a hand and started again, still not looking at us. "If this is my nightmare, then I don't want it to end the same."

"What happened?" Read asked.

Aidan sighed, his pale gaze continuing to shift. "There was a car…" He began to wring his hands together. "In real life, it belonged to my cousin, Adam. When I was a kid, he was driving me home from a baseball game when a drunk driver T-boned us.

"Afterward, I started having nightmares that Adam's car was trying to run me down. Like it was getting back at me for taking too long. He had to pick me up from practice… well, you know, it was guilt stuff." Aidan avoided my sympathetic stare and turned to the bikers, who were beginning to take notice of us.

"What happened to your cousin?" I asked.

Aidan kept his face turned away. "Died in the

hospital."

I felt an empathetic twitch in my chest. "How old were you?"

"Nine."

By the way, he shoved his palms into his jeans pockets and deflected my gaze. I wasn't sure if I should tell him I was sorry or avoid it altogether.

"What did you do? In the dream, I mean."

The question got me a glare that could have melted ice. "I ran," he said as if I was slow.

All right, it was a bit of a dumb question, but I had a point. "Do you ever get away?"

"I usually woke up." He watched the bikers, and they watched us.

"Aidan, we have to get out of this alive. And if you didn't get away by running, then we need an alternative."

Then without thinking it through, I blurted, "I'm sorry about what happened."

Aidan winced, and Read frowned as if I had broken some man-rule.

"It wasn't your fault."

"Never thought it was," Aidan growled, shutting me down. "But this nightmare still exists. I just didn't think that I'd be repeating it for real. To top it off, I'm dragging friends with me."

"You're not dragging us anywhere," Read said with certainty. "We said in that first Challenge that we'd do this together."

I glanced at Read, hoping to catch his eye.

Aidan looked away, scowling. For an instant, I saw the anger that emitted from the doppelgänger in the previous Challenge. The creeping suspicion returned. If this was the real Aidan, which I believed it was, he could still turn into that bitter guy soaked through and blaming me for everything. The Others had been right about Robin. Before I could indulge the idea further, my thoughts were snapped out of their focus.

"Listen," Read said firmly, "I'm just as freaked out as you two, but we need to keep our heads."

"Aidan…"

Aidan held up his hands to silence me before crossing them over his chest. "I'm thinking."

Read gave me a *"We have to think up something fast"* raise of his thin eyebrows.

Twisting back around, I reached up and touched Aidan's cheek with my fingertips to get him to look at me. The moment his piercing eyes swept to meet mine, it all felt far more intimate than I intended.

Drawing back my hands as if I'd been slapped, I stuttered, "Auh-Auh-all we had to do in mine was admit it was a nightmare. Maybe it'll work this time?"

Aidan's eyes shimmered with doubt. "If something happens to anyone…" He frowned, refusing to finish his sentence, but he didn't have to.

The pressing silence turned our attention to the group of bikers on the corner of the street.

These people were no different than the other occupants of this world. Two of the five had eyes this time—well, at least three eyes all together—but still harbored other deformities.

Aidan nodded to them. "I was on foot in my nightmare. I don't want to try and outrun a restored Maserati A6G, especially if this is going to be real."

Read whistled, impressed, though I had no idea what a restored Maserati looked like. I could only conclude it was fast and expensive.

I inspected the heavy-looking bikes and frowned. "You're going to steal those bikes? Do you even know how to ride one?"

"I do," Read volunteered.

"All three of us can't fit on one bike," I pointed out. "And there's five of them against three of us."

Read grimaced. "Then let's hope one of you is a fast learner. At least one of the bikes should fit two."

Seeing me gape, Aidan held up his hands for me to see, attempting to keep me calm. "I didn't say we'd be stealing them. These people weren't in my dream. Maybe it's how we can find the black door."

Before I could utter a word, Aidan started for the bikers again. I realized he hadn't answered my question of whether he could actually handle a motorbike. I knew I couldn't. The craziest thing I'd ever driven was my mom's sedan. Rebellious, right?

Shuffling behind Aidan, I looked up to see the only woman—who could be in her mid-twenties—peel back her lips in a toothy, sardonic smile. "Well, well, if it isn't Hansel and Gretel."

I had to bite my lip from blurting, "*Are you the wicked witch*?" For all I knew, she could be.

She wasn't deformed like the rest of her posse. Her face could have been pretty if she pulled it out of the permanent lip-sneer. Her dark brown hair was pulled back in a tight ponytail, and she wore actual black leather chaps and a jacket. She paid particular attention to Read—most girls do.

I half hid between Aidan and Read as the five began to circle us.

Aidan offered his friendly smile to the witch-woman. "Actually, we need a ride," he said in a casual off-hand tone.

The woman glanced at the three of us and rasped a laugh. "You serious, kid?"

Kid? We couldn't have been more than a few years younger than her, maybe even the same age. The five had completely surrounded us at this point. One of them was standing disturbingly close to my left. I could feel his body heat against my bare shoulder.

My chin had to tilt up to see his face; he was much taller than me—than any of us. Aidan was our tallest, and he was almost a head shorter. The tall man sported a shaved head riddled with an oversized black tattoo of what could have been a skull, but I couldn't make it out from my angle.

He had at least one eye, which blinked long lashes at me.

I grimaced before attempting to control my expression. His left eye had been smoothed over, like it had never existed. He didn't have eyebrows either.

He licked his lips at me slowly.

I jerked my head away before my face could betray the disgust roiling in my stomach. Taking a new grip on Aidan's arm, I stood oppressively close. Any closer and I'd be shoving him.

Read gestured to their parked bikes. "Where are you off to?"

A teenager, maybe fifteen, replied. He stood on the other side of Read. "We're going to the next city." He flicked a cigarette butt onto the sidewalk then blew smoke through the triangular hole where his nose should have been.

I had to give Read credit for not coughing when he

spoke. "We're looking for a ride."

"It'll cost yah." The girl looked him up and down, arching dramatic, pencil-thin eyebrows.

I had to hide my face in Aidan's shoulder to stop the persistent tickle from the lingering cigarette smoke.

"How much?" I heard Read ask.

Peeking, I saw the teenager smile wide, showing all five pristine teeth. "A hundred bucks." He tilted his head and looked at Aidan and me. "Each."

I believe Baldy behind me chuckled, or maybe it was indigestion; I couldn't tell.

We didn't have that kind of money. I had ten dollars and a glass key in my pocket. I wasn't sure what Read and Aidan were carting around with them, but it certainly wasn't three hundred dollars.

"No, problem," Aidan replied, not missing a beat, even sounding confident.

The two silent bikers on either side of the woman were quiet for a reason. Both of them resembled the boys in the AM radio car, no mouth or eyes, but they nodded when she glanced at them.

We're so dead.

CHAPTER TWENTY-ONE

"Where is it?" the woman asked, scratching her shoulder, and I could see her deformity at last. Her hand was fat, warped with scars, and her fingers were stubs, no longer than my toes but much thicker and without nails.

I caught a name on the sleeve of her leather jacket: *Viper*.

"It's in the next city down the line. I have some dealings there. If you take us directly to the…soap warehouse on Ninety-seventh Avenue, you can get your three hundred bucks and a bonus," Aidan answered, aloofly.

I struggled not to act surprised when her scrutinizing gaze landed on me, then Read.

Aidan pointed down the street behind us. "You see, our car broke down, and I can't be late. These are important people."

How did he learn to lie like that? I wondered. The

soap warehouse was a little fake, but it seemed to work on Viper. If I got out of here, maybe I should invest in watching gangster movies. My heart thumped as she mulled it over. After a pause, she nodded to Baldy behind me.

"I think that we should do it, Frankie," she said. "Not like we're doing anything else tonight."

"And what if there's no money?" one-eyed Frankie asked.

One of the mouthless men leaned close to her ear. There was no way he could have spoken, but Viper tilted her head as if to listen anyway.

Afterward, I understood why her nickname was Viper. The smile that curled her lips reminded me of a serpent.

"Then we can kill 'em," she told Frankie.

Perhaps Viper wasn't the ringleader after all.

I wanted to lean up to Aidan and say that we still had a chance to back off but lost my nerve. This was his nightmare, after all. He would know what to do better than me.

Aidan nodded to Viper and her faceless associates. "We have a deal then?"

Viper pulled a jagged hunting-knife from her belt and twirled it in her fingers expertly, watching Aidan before tossing it in the air and catching the blade with her good hand. "Deal." She threw a wink in Read's direction. "You know the price."

Aidan didn't remove his friendly, shielded smile. "Shall we?"

Head high, she tossed her ponytail and motioned to their bikes. "Time to ride, boys." She looked Read up and down before purring, "You can ride with me."

Read's steely eyes shifted to the bike, and he stepped toward her. The group around us began to separate, and I felt a draft where Baldy—or rather, Frankie—had been standing.

When neither Aidan nor I moved, Viper jutted her chin at Aidan. "You go with Paul." Her narrow eyes scanned me with a scowl before she said louder, "Where should Miss Muffet go?"

Frankie leered from his bike. "Muffet will come with me."

"No detours this time, Frankie." Viper was smiling all too pleasantly.

This time?

They straddled their bikes, and motors rumbled to life. Kickstands were kicked and bikes righted as the riders waited for the three of us to join them. I forced each finger to detach from Aidan's arm and hoped this was a good idea.

I was close enough to hear Aidan tell Viper over the engines, "I don't want to be far from them. We can't separate."

Something shadowed over Viper's eyes, but as soon as it appeared, it was gone. She turned her sharp chin toward the eyeless man and nodded as if hearing him. "You won't be," she answered, sounding disappointed.

Aidan started for the young punk's bike, and I took the few shaky steps to Frankie's. He'd better be a damn good driver, without detours.

Frankie scooted back in his seat, like he wanted me to sit in front of him. The letters AJS were scrawled across the oversized gas tank.

Oh that wasn't going to happen.

Viper must have noticed Frankie pat the narrow

section of seat between his crotch and the gas tank. "Play time later, Frankie."

How about never, Frankie?

The oversized cyclops was frowning, but he scooted up.

In the distance, the ear-splintering, engine-roaring barrage erupted.

Read shouted something from the back of Viper's bike. She was already backing out of her space. Her motor was low compared to the intensity of the nightmare-car.

I bolted for Frankie's bike just as a red classic sports car raced around the corner beyond the Victorian house. Straddling Frankie, I held tight. "Go, go, go!" I shrieked, pressing my cheek to his shoulder.

The bike skidded to a start, and I wasn't entirely prepared.

The violent jerk almost snapped my grip like a twig. As we picked up speed, the engine was hot against my bare legs, feeling more intense near my swollen knee.

The other bikes raced alongside us, roaring their engines in unison, but even they couldn't drown the bellow of the Maserati sports car.

Read and Viper were just ahead of us. Both of them lay low on her bike as the wind blinded Read with her ponytail.

Aidan was beside us. Hunched, his face was turned toward Frankie and me.

The cherry red sports car was easily gaining on the group. A white stripe arched up the hood, but it was splattered with a dark crimson that didn't match the color of the car.

The Maserati inched closer to the fifth biker, one of

the eyeless/mouthless ones. I looked back and saw the headlights of the car nearing the back tire of his bike.

The sports car looked as though it was getting ready to pass when it swerved.

With a shriek of tires and smoke, the fender knocked into the motorbike—hard.

The rider soared while the bike fell to its side, spinning out of control and skidding between two parked cars.

The airborne rider landed on his head, crunching down like an accordion against the pavement. His arms attempted to cushion the fall, but from the violent twist of his body, I was sure he didn't make it. Biting down on my lip, I tried not to scream. The fall looped in my memory even as I looked away.

Frankie and I passed Viper's bike. Aidan and the teenager were inching ahead of them as well.

The heat of the engine wasn't warm anymore; it was burning. Wincing, I tried to hold my bare legs out to avoid scorching them, which felt like they were cooking from the inside out. It reminded me of standing next to an oven or fire pit with a nasty sunburn.

"Faster!" I urged Frankie. I wasn't sure if he could hear me, but I was certain he got the idea.

The bike's engine revved as I heard a crash barely muffled by the machinery.

Looking back, I saw the red car had eliminated yet another member of their gang and was gaining on Viper and Read.

Viper glanced back just in time to see the Maserati's bumper collide with the back of her bike. Read's mouth opened in a scream, but I heard nothing over the bike.

Viper struggled to gain control of her vehicle. She

and Read wobbled violently before veering to the side. The speeding car could have hit them but, before I could see, Frankie took a sharp turn down an avenue, leaving Read and Viper out of our sights.

Aidan and Paul were inches ahead of us as my driver struggled to pull up beside them. *Say the words, Aidan,* I pleaded in my mind.

The shrieking tires had me looking back, hoping to see Read and Viper. Instead, it was the Maserati skidding on the wide turn and emerging from the billowing tire-smoke.

At first I was certain that we could get away. A few more turns and we could probably put enough distance between the car and us. But I was wrong.

The Maserati launched forward the minute it had a straight road again.

The car neared the bikes at an alarming speed. I could hear myself screaming long before I knew it was me.

Squirming to inch closer to Frankie, I saw there was nowhere to run or take cover.

The bumper crept closer, only a foot from touching the motorbike. We had to make a turn, *something*.

I searched the Maserati for a driver, but I couldn't see anyone beyond the clear shimmering glass. The only movement was the streetlights playing off the darkened windows.

All I could imagine was my face slamming into that shimmering windshield.

Squealing, I braced myself for the impact, wondering which way I'd fly.

Behind the car, a movement caught my eye.

Viper and Read rounded the corner, their legs

almost scraping concrete on the turn. *That was too close*, I thought in relief. Then Frankie's entire bike jerked.

It wobbled dangerously beneath us, and for the second time, I almost lost my grip.

A sickening warmth churned in my chest and stomach, and I heard the distinct sound of metal scraping metal.

I was going to die in a Demon's Grave away from everything I knew, everything familiar, and everyone I knew.

I'd become another headstone for my parents to purchase.

Part of me wanted to bury my face in Frankie's back and wait for the jarring smash. The other part had to watch.

Twisting my neck, I watched as the Maserati sped up for another go at the bike.

Stiffening, I prepared myself when I realized we were pulling farther away.

I craned my neck to look over Frankie's shoulder; I could see him catching up to Aidan and Paul. Or were they slowing down?

I tried to shout at Aidan to hold on as we came level with them, but it was too late.

He knew it was coming. I could see it in his face.

The Maserati hit Paul's bike with more force than it had hit us.

I watched the collision in helpless horror as Paul lost control.

The motorbike began to twist. The tires smoked and skidded, the distinct smell of burning rubber hot in the air.

Paul lost his balance, and they tipped onto their side.

Aidan's leg must have bent before it could be trapped. He detached himself from the nose-less teenager and rolled.

Paul wasn't so lucky. His leg stuck between bike and pavement, he spun into a parked car. Paul and his bike hit hard enough to lift the rusted car and wedge part-way underneath.

On the opposite side of the street, Aidan had rolled under a parked pickup truck.

The minute Aidan disappeared, the Maserati slammed into the side of the truck. It missed him by a millisecond, spewing sparks into the air.

The back wheel of Frankie's bike slid out to the side, twirling until we faced the scene we'd left behind. We skidded to a stop, and it jostled my insides.

The Maserati shot past us in a blur, and I turned my head to see it screech around the corner and out of sight. Smoke had filled the air, and I breathed through my mouth to combat the overwhelming stench of burning rubber and exhaust.

It took a second or two for me to realize I could get off the bike.

Using Frankie for leverage, I swung my legs. In my urgency to get to Aidan, I nearly tangled them on the seat. My legs wobbled as if molded from gelatin, and I struggled to jog towards the pick-up truck without eating pavement.

The dented, scratched metal glared in the streetlight. The driver's side door would be impossible to open. The center was caved in, and shattered glass had fallen onto the pavement.

Aidan hadn't come out yet, and I felt a chill at that fact.

Dropping to my haunches to avoid the glass, I anticipated the worst.

It was dark under the truck, and I could make out the outline of Aidan's body near the sidewalk.

In the shadow, I saw eyes blinking at me.

Touching my chest with my hand, I wheezed, "Aidan, can you move?"

After a pause and several rapid blinks of those eyes, he shifted his arms and legs slowly, testing each digit in his hand.

"Nothing's broken," he said, his voice soft and far away.

Pounding footsteps behind me straightened my spine.

Turning, I saw Read as he skidded to a stop and dropped to the pavement beside me. Seeing Aidan, he breathed out a half-laugh, half-sigh of relief. "Shit, dude, I thought it hit you."

Rolling, Aidan drew himself closer to us. Read and I shuffled back, pushing glass out of the way with our feet.

Aiden stopped in mid-roll. His eyes glazed, and I could see the damage for the first time. A nasty gash on one leg had torn a hole in his jeans, exposing the bloodied combination of skin and gravel. I couldn't tell how deep it might be. I only saw the blood soak in his jeans in a deep, unhealthy crimson.

A cut within his hairline had left matted blood on the left side of his head, trickling a few droplets across his temple. The one day he decided to make his hair look presentable and it was twisted and spiked all over again.

"Crap," Read muttered. "Dude, is there anything broken?"

I shook my head at Read but said to Aidan, "Stay awake, all right? Don't fall asleep."

Aidan muttered something before looking down at his bloodied leg. His languid eyes almost shut, and I patted his arm. His t-shirt was ripped as well. Along the shoulder were minor scrapes from the pavement, nothing any of us hadn't endured as children.

"We have to find something to clean his leg," I said to Read. Then I asked Aidan, "Can you stand?"

Aidan flexed his wounded leg and nodded. "It's not broken." As if remembering what had just happened, he jerked his head up and asked, suddenly alert, "Is it gone?"

"Yeah, it's gone." Read bent over and put Aidan's arm around his neck, helping him to his feet. The little bits of glass tinkled from his clothes, and Aidan staggered before leaning against the pickup.

Breathing in deeply, Aidan pinched the bridge of his nose, squeezing his eyes shut. "That sucked."

I couldn't help but glance in Paul's direction.

Bloodied streaks led to his motionless body, still trapped beneath the bike and half under one of the parked cars.

Behind us, Frankie remained seated on his bike. He was staring at Viper, who was dismounting hers like a sleepwalker. She didn't seem interested in anything other than the damage on her motorbike.

Aidan winced as Read helped him hobble onto the sidewalk.

No one spoke as we edged farther up the street and

watched the bikers talk. They no longer seemed interested in us. If we were lucky, they'd forget long enough for us to get away.

Shuffling along the sidewalk, I listened for the motorbikes to roar to life, for them to give chase. There was no sign, even as we rounded the corner and ducked out of sight. I peeked one last time to see them distracted in conversation.

"What happened?" I whispered once we were halfway down the second block.

"I just said that this was a nightmare." Aidan cringed. "Then the bike slowed down and the car hit us."

"But you're okay?"

Aidan bared teeth as he grumbled, "It's just a scrape."

"No need to get all macho on us, Aidan," I whispered.

He narrowed a pointed stare at me before testing his leg. He could walk on it easier if he used Read for support; otherwise, it was a slow and visible limp. "Nora," he said, looking down, "this isn't some fancy, happy story where if we work together, everything will work out. We'd be naive to think that. Instead, let's focus on getting out alive, huh?"

I blinked in surprise. *I was being naive?*

I wasn't sure how to respond when the glacial eyes met mine.

Uncertain, I offered to walk on Aidan's other side so he could brace himself between Read and me, but Aidan refused.

Hurt, I backed away.

It made me feel awkward and estranged from the

two of them, as if I were the outsider.

Falling back a few steps, I let them move ahead and kept a watch behind us. I didn't need his judgment right now. I looked to Read but found no support.

"It's about time," Read said.

To our left was a darkened alley littered with garbage, but beyond all the discarded rubble and shadows was our salvation.

In the center of the alley was a wooden fence that had to be eight feet tall between the two stone apartment buildings. Within the fence was a black door, illuminated from the light of a first floor apartment.

"Guess it's a good thing you don't dream, Read," Aidan said as we wove our way around the dumpsters and strewn cardboard boxes.

Read smirked, flashing his ridiculously white teeth. "Yeah, you two are messed up."

Story of my life.

CHAPTER TWENTY-TWO

The door slammed shut behind us.

The bang rang in my ears long after the door disappeared and left purple and black striped wallpaper behind it.

Read muttered, "Is this where Goths come to die?" He nudged me.

We stood at the edge of an oak table that was almost too big for the dark dining room.

Illuminating the space was a black candelabra situated on a white doily that took up most of the table. A matching oak cabinet was stuffed in the corner, encasing dark-colored dishes, vases, and goblets. There was barely enough room to sidle around the table and chairs.

The only escape was an archway leading to a dark, could-be kitchen.

I was distracted from the décor when Read help Aidan into the high-backed chair at the end of the table.

Aidan eased into a sitting position and gripped the armrests hard, stretching out his injured leg gradually with a sigh of relief.

Read stepped back, and I rounded the chair. My hip brushed the wall before I crouched to inspect Aidan's leg. I had to squint to make out the gravel-infested divots.

Aidan's lips creased in what could have been a smile...or maybe a grimace. "God forbid there be anything bright and peppy around here."

Read grinned. "It's Mary Poppins's house on depressants."

I hummed "A Spoonful of Sugar" before rolling a rock free from Aidan's punctured skin.

The boys snickered until Aidan jolted in his chair in pain.

"Alcohol abuse jokes aside," I plucked larger chunks of rock and pavement from the wound, hearing them sprinkle on the carpet, "I need to wash this out."

Aidan hissed through his teeth, "Do you know what you're doing?"

I shook my head. "No," I answered truthfully, "but at least I'm trying." Resentment gurgled just below the surface. What if he couldn't run without one of us carrying him? This could kill us all, and he had the nerve to ask if my help was worth it?

Standing, I avoided his eyes so he wouldn't see my anger and turned to the only doorway in the room.

From where I stood, it appeared to be a kitchen, though there were no lights other the candelabra to prove otherwise. "Be right back," I grumbled. Then I added, "Don't wander off."

Aidan snorted, though it didn't sound sarcastic, just

amused.

Read followed me to the doorway and leaned against it so he could watch us both.

The room wasn't very big, and to my relief, there was a lantern on the nearest counter. The flame had been drawn down low, making it difficult to see the rest of the room.

Ducking so my face was inches from the tin base, I adjusted the gas lever the way we'd done back at the Victorian house, and the flame rose to life. Blinking back the dancing dots in my eyes, I snagged the metal handle and lifted it above my head.

It was a kitchen all right, with raspberry countertops, black cupboards, and an island where the lantern had been sitting.

Rounding the cupboard, I opened a stiff drawer in search of a rag, dishtowel, paper towel, anything to help remove the gravel. The first drawer held thick butcher knives. One was splattered with a dark crust.

I shoved the drawer closed, listening to the utensils clattering together inside. *What the hell had been chopped up in this kitchen*? Paranoid, I turned around in a full circle. No other door was visible in the room. There was a window over the sink behind thinning curtains. The only other doorway was where Read watched me. "What is it?" he asked, jutting his chin in a nod.

"Nothing," I lied.

The kitchen was a mess. Pots lined the cupboards near the window. Dried herbs hung from the ceiling, and some of the leaves had sprinkled the raspberry counter.

"Is Aidan still in there?" I asked past the lump in my

throat.

Read nodded, crossing his arms over his thin chest.

"What?" Aidan's voice came from the dining room. He was just out of my line of sight, which made me nervous.

"Just making sure you haven't run away," I said and went to the next drawer, revealing broken bottles and a moldy pancake.

"Oh har-har, funny," Aidan said. "What's taking so long?"

Read pushed away from the doorway. "I'll help."

I sighed, not wanting Read to lose sight of Aidan, and opened the next drawer. It had dish towels decorated with red flowers. "I got it." I drew the towel out, waving it like a flag, keeping Read in place. I pivoted on my heels to face the sink. The motion made me well aware of the tightness in my swollen knee.

With the help of the lantern, I inspected the swelling. It didn't seem to be getting any worse, but it wasn't any better either. The continuous throb I felt from the heat of the bike was gone again, leaving a faint stiffness in my skin. Maybe that meant the poison was going away. Not all scorpions' stings were fatal to humans, after all. I should count my lucky stars, if I had any left.

Lifting the lantern back over my head, I saw the sink was brimming with dirty pots and pans. As I turned to say something to Read, my foot slid on something slick. Yelping, I swung both arms out and caught the island with my free hand. The lantern emerged unscathed.

As I righted my balance, my somewhat steadier foot supported all my weight.

Following my elephantine display of stealth, Aidan called uncertainly, "Is everyone okay?"

Read was around the counter in seconds, and he grabbed my elbow to help me stand straight again. I lifted the flickering lantern to see the floor near the sink. There was a strange lime-colored liquid all over it. It reminded me of dish soap.

"I'm okay," I called back to reassure Aidan. "I just slipped in…goo." I wiped my defiled sneaker on the cupboard.

"What the hell is that?" Read leaned over and stared, palms propped on his thighs.

Tip-toeing past it, I muttered, "I'm pretty sure I don't want to know."

Jerkily, I twisted the tap, and green water burst from the spout. I reeled back a few steps in disgust, managing to avoid the goo but dropping the towel on the floor. The backs of my knees banged into something solid, making a gong-like sound. Already moving too fast, I had little time to react.

The lantern was flung over my head as I toppled backwards.

My butt hit part of the mysterious bubble behind me, and I shrieked and slid down the slope onto my back. The lantern's glass shattered a few feet above my head, and darkness shrouded the kitchen. My feet were propped up on the rounded object, my shoulders on the floor.

As the initial shock subsided, I groaned. The developing bruises from the books reminded me of their presence.

"Jesus, Nora," Read chuckled.

"What happened? Are you guys okay?" Aidan

called from the dining room.

"Yeah, just a sec, dude," Read shouted back. "Just have to pick up our resident klutz." After a heartbeat, he added, "Again."

"Shut up, Read." I wriggled until my butt hit the linoleum floor.

What else could go wrong? I felt awkward and embarrassed. I had my clumsy moments, but this was becoming ridiculous.

Read grabbed my arm to help me up.

"But a cute klutz, right?" I tried to tease.

"Always," Read said and started to pull me up when he paused. "Nora, stand up."

Through the window's curtains, a dim light began to wax, like the moon was emerging from the clouds. I could see enough to make out the overturned cauldron.

"Holy shit!" I spat, grabbing wildly for the counter. If it wasn't for Read's grip on my arm, I might have fallen again. There wasn't much hope that Read would be able to lift me. He wasn't the strong type; he was— as he often boasted to anger Phoebe—an endurance-type. I'd be lying if I said I didn't wonder if this were true or not.

"Guys?" Aidan called.

Read eased his grip on my arm before letting me go. "Yeah, so, let's get another rag and—"

Water spilling over the counter and onto the floor stopped him cold. I hadn't turned off the faucet.

I hopped over the large pot with the help of the island, avoiding the goo, and fumbled for another towel. The water from the tap wasn't green—according to the moonlight—and I soaked the towel through.

"Guys?" Aidan repeated, his voice strained.

I turned off the tap, but the water kept spewing. Twisting it in the opposite direction didn't seem to help either. The water flowed unhindered; it neither increased nor decreased in pressure.

"Just leave it," Read whispered.

"Guys!" Aidan called more sharply.

Dancing back to avoid the water that snaked along the linoleum, I made it around the island with Read following closely.

"Guys, there's something you should see," Aidan insisted.

Read darted into the dining room in three steps.

I wrung out the towel as best as I could and hurried behind Read.

There was nothing out of the usual at first glance. Aidan was twisted in his chair to look behind him with his leg still extended toward us. "This probably isn't a good thing," Aidan said, not looking back.

I slapped the wet dish towel onto the table and slowed my step. *Did I really want to see this?*

I gripped the back of Aidan's chair and stretched to see past him.

It took a moment for my eyes to adjust to the extra light from the candles. I froze as I made out the outline of a plump body on the floor.

It was an old woman, from what I could tell. Lying face down, she was dressed in a dark cloak, her long, greasy white hair splayed around her matted skull like a batch of snakes. When Read had pushed me back to help Aidan into the chair, she would have been a mere foot away from my sneakers.

Aidan stood up on his own, using the table for support. "Do you recognize that person?"

"No. You?" I lowered my voice along with his. "Read?"

Read shook his head. "Why is she here?"

I motioned to the kitchen where we had left the cauldron. "She's a witch," I said.

"A *witch*?" Aidan cried, not whispering anymore. "Considering she's dead, she can't be a bad one."

To the corpse, Read asked, "Are you a good witch or a bad witch?"

"Read." I rolled my eyes.

Aidan opened his mouth to say something, then seemed to change his mind.

Read gestured to Aidan and me. "We have to clean out your leg before anything spontaneous happens."

I took one step and felt the carpet squish under my sneaker, sounding soggy and wet. We all looked down to see the carpet was soaked. The water had already seeped into the dining room.

"That's impossible," Read cried. "It would take a couple of hours for that little sink to flood the dining room."

Aidan hobbled in a half turn. "If time doesn't exist here, why should physics?"

I took the towel from the table and ordered Aidan to sit back down. "Bring your leg up so I can see. We have to be fast."

He dropped into the high-backed chair and propped his foot up on the table. "Shouldn't we be getting out of here?"

"We might not get a second chance to clean this," I replied and dabbed at the scrape with the towel, not concerned with hurting him anymore. The important thing was to get him able to run and at least prolong infection from setting in.

"Read?" I asked, not looking up, "is there a way out other than that stupid window?"

Aidan leaned forward carefully and ripped the exposed threads near the hole, making it bigger for me to see. His thigh had taken the brunt of the fall. I was no doctor, but it almost seemed deep enough to need stitches.

With shaky hands, I picked out glistening chunks of glass, rock, and clumps of dirt while Read paced the two rooms, kicking up the water as it rose high enough to squish water between my toes.

When I was finished, I turned the dish towel around and put the clean side to his skin.

The water was warm around my ankles.

I fumbled in tying the towel around Aidan's leg. During my third failed attempt, Aidan stole the cloth and tied it expertly into a knot. "Spent a year on a yacht," he explained.

Rolling my eyes, I snapped, "Could have told me instead of watching me." I wasn't really angry at him, but the demand to get out was weighing heavier.

I snatched Aidan's wrist, jerking him hard to his feet. The water had almost reached my knees, churning and swirling faster around my legs.

We trudged through the water, encumbered by the new current. Long, slow strides led us to the doorway and into the kitchen. Read grabbed my wrist, leading the way. I reached back and took Aidan's cool hand. By the time we reached the doorway, the water had risen halfway up my thighs.

Read gestured to the window just above the sink. "That's the only possible exit."

The curtains were opened wide enough to reveal jagged glass, like someone had thrown a rock through it.

"There wasn't any glass on the floor when we had been in here before," Read said, gritting his teeth as he fought for another step. "I think it was broken from the inside."

A chill ran down my back. "We'd have heard it break," I protested.

Read tugged on my wrist. "It's the only way we can go."

He was right; we'd have to risk it. I gave him an apologetic wince, and we battled the flood.

Making our way around the island, I pushed Aidan toward the window. Terrifying images of someone grabbing my ankles in the deepening water plagued my imagination, but I didn't want him lagging behind.

Aidan looked back at me, eyebrows pinched. "You should go first."

"Go," I insisted with enough authority to make him step closer to the sink. Despite my previous animosity, I'd feel pretty damn bad if he were swept away in the water.

"Yeah, you two argue," Read said then climbed onto the cupboard as if to finish his sentence with, *While I do something smart and get out of here.* He knocked out the last loose bits of glass with a cast-iron pan. Upon closer inspection, I could see blood on one of the jagged little pieces, reflecting in the moonlight.

Read eased through the window, careful not to cut himself. His shirt rode up to his armpits while he escaped feet first. If the water around my hips wasn't so distracting, I might have paid attention to that.

I struggled to stay upright as an undercurrent picked at my ankles, pulling my feet up whenever I wasn't focused.

Read turned back around to help Aidan through.

"Just go!" I shouted at his second glance back.

With the water around my waist, we didn't have time to play the polite game. Standing was becoming a pain. I stumbled, gripping the cupboard to keep from drifting. Part of me wanted to let go and float—see where the strange river would take me—though I knew it would separate us and I'd be in the same predicament as Phoebe, Robin, and Cody.

Aidan pushed himself up onto the cupboard, wobbling before sitting at the edge of the counter. His legs kicked at the clutter of dishes and pans in the kitchen sink.

Read beckoned Aidan forward. "Put your feet through," he instructed. It felt like forever, though it probably took less than a minute for Read to help Aidan slide out without any injures. They tried to avoid dragging him against the edge, which still sheltered a few rogue shards.

The water slapped against my stomach.

I was beginning to lose my footing. The current was able to lift my left foot completely off the floor, and it took all my balance and stubbornness to get it back down. As I gripped the flat kitchen counter, my fingers cramped, desperate for something with more purchase.

"All right, quick, Nora!" Aidan reached his arms through the window for me.

Eager, I let go of the counter, aiming to snatch his hands.

Our fingers brushed when the current yanked my

feet behind me.

Pitching forward, I screamed, but it was cut short when I gargled water instead.

CHAPTER TWENTY-THREE

I felt a hard floor at my back. I wheezed a harsh breath and opened my eyes.

The ceiling above my head had vaulted upward with cracks allowing in fresh air.

No water, no kitchen, no fear.

Glancing to the window, I saw the moonlight had faded. I wanted to sit up but couldn't bring myself to move. The beauty of being safe was something to savor.

I took a deep breath. The air moved my chest up and down. What a relief. I took another and another until my hand touched one of the chairs sitting back to back in the circular room.

I had thought it was a dream. How could I have forgotten when the spiders were attacking? I was here before. Was this all a dream? A hallucination? Where was everyone?

"Phoebe?" I whispered. "Read?"

Dead air shattered under my voice, and when my ears stopped ringing, no one had answered. "Cody? Robin?" I turned my head into the chair, my forehead bouncing off the wood, and I winced.

"You ask for everyone but one." The mellifluous voice echoed in my ears, but my eyes wouldn't adjust to see him.

Blinking several times, I realized he was a shadow pacing the wall near my feet. His broad shoulders were hunched, and his hands were clasped behind his back with his head tilted down. From that angle, he could have been watching me.

"Where am I?" I asked.

The pacing stopped, and he straightened slowly. "You don't know?"

If I didn't know better, it sounded as though Damien were smiling.

* * *

Warm water assaulted my mouth and nose, striking through my sinuses like twin daggers.

I clawed at the water to reach the surface. One of the currents shoved me against the island, shooting pain through my bruised back.

Instinct took over, and I shouted in bubbles. I clawed at water as if it were a mountainside or a tree.

It wasn't until after my gurgled scream that I realized all my air was gone. With a jolt of panic, I planted my shoes against the island.

Pushing off with all my strength, I aimed for the window, praying to break the surface.

Stretching my fingers, I strained to feel Aidan's

hands. I could see his watery, warped face above, could see him reaching for me.

As my feet found the island to push off, a second current shoved me back. I skidded over the island as the water's flow flushed me away from the kitchen.

Kicking and swinging my arms, I tried to find the surface.

Panic heated within my chest, my lungs started to ache, and my throat convulsed for something, *anything*. It took all my concentration to not take a breath.

One frantic kick landed against something solid beneath my foot. Pushing off, I rose. My muscles leaked of energy with each labored stroke.

My fingers broke the surface first. I didn't think I could rise fast enough before my head broke free. I took a shrieking breath. My lungs felt as if they'd been caved in. My arms wind-milled for something to grip.

I didn't want to go under again, but I had to get to the window.

Taking another greedy breath, which still didn't feel like enough, I twisted until I realized I wasn't in the kitchen anymore. The undercurrent had swept me into the dining room. The water was over my head. The archway to the kitchen was almost submerged.

My flailing arms eventually caught the top of the china cabinet. My fingers cramped to hold on. My sneakers flattened against the wall, preparing myself for another swim. Several breaths and heartbeats passed before I found a smidgen of courage to try again.

Aim for the archway, I thought. *One thing at a time.*

With that, I bent my knees for a leap off the wall.

It was now or never.

Jumping to bypass some of the water, I landed a

foot away from the archway. Pushing hard, I used my burning muscles until my hands grabbed the doorway. Another rush of water attempted to knock me back.

As I gripped the wall, my arms and legs strained and ached.

All I wanted to do was stop, but I didn't want to deal with the consequences. The window was my only way out.

Somewhere far away, I heard what could have been my name, but it was muffled.

I immediately thought of Damien. *You shouldn't be here, Nora.*

The water should have been flowing out of the window by now, but it kept rising to crush me against the ceiling.

Dragging myself through the doorway, I crawled until I was rolling against the kitchen wall. I tried to find the next place to jump before the current snagged me again.

I couldn't see the island in the kitchen anymore. If I could launch myself off the wall, I might be able to grab it and pull myself closer to the window, but if I missed, I'd be back in the dining room.

All I could hear was a roaring, splashing river. Gathering up bits of my nerves, I took a deep breath, which still wasn't enough, and plunged under.

I counted the long, fighting strokes and hoped I'd find the counter sooner rather than later. *One, two, three...*I started to feel the familiar strain. The arch in my right foot began to cramp, and I tried to roll my toes back in my sneaker to prevent it.

The fourth stroke was a struggle. A current pushed me sideways, and I had to flail to right myself.

Five...six. I had to release some of my held air in my efforts.

The window was barely visible. As I drew closer, I could see nothing was pouring out of the cracked glass, as if an invisible barrier was there. I had to hope it wouldn't hold me in, too.

The cramp in my foot began to spasm pain up my leg, making my swim awkward and slowed. My lungs burned and convulsed for air, making me feel heady and my limbs weak.

My hand smacked onto the top of the counter. I could still see the moonlight streaming through the window, making it an easier target. Beyond the window, I could make out two watery silhouettes.

One of them thrust hands through the window and its invisible barrier.

Pushing off of the island, I used the last of my reserves. If I missed him again, I wasn't sure I could make it back to the opening.

I stretched out my hands, wishing my arms would grow longer. I strained in agony.

One of Aidan's hands grabbed my right wrist. He was half submerged in the water. He'd plunged his shoulders and face through the window's opening. His hair floated around his head in the current.

I could have shrieked in joy, and I gripped his wrist in return. His other hand managed to snatch my waving free hand before he dragged me from the current that tangled in my feet.

I wanted to help by kicking, but the cramp seized everything in my foot, seeming to cripple my leg in the process.

Air.

The coolness struck my hand first, and Read grabbed my right forearm to help Aidan pull.

My head was freed, and I inflated my crippled lungs, but it still wasn't enough. I gasped again, my cramped foot useless, and I could only kick with one leg to help the guys pull me free.

I tumbled into Aidan; he cushioned most of my fall in the violent crash.

With a wheeze, I slowly rolled off of him and landed with a wet *plop* in the clipped green grass. Exhausted, we all heaved and watched the stars.

Read sat up first, having fallen to the side. "You okay?" he whispered.

Why hadn't he been the one plunging through the invisible barrier for me?

I nodded, unable to speak. My foot contorted and twisted in its cramp, and I let the pain stab at me only because it meant I was alive. Also, I was too exhausted to care.

I let the air touch my wet skin, chilling me until I started to shiver. Again, I didn't care.

Catching his breath, Aidan said, "That's the last time I listen to you. Next time, you go first."

I choked on a laugh that sounded more like a gargle.

Sitting up was a chore, but once I had, I tore off my shoe and grabbed for my toes. Stretching the cramp alleviated most of the pain. The balancing effort on my hips had me rolling onto my side, but I didn't dare let go of my foot until the pain was all gone. My forehead bumped into Aidan's damp chest, and I tried to joke, "You wouldn't have been able to swim with that leg."

Aidan touched the top of my head. I looked up at him, and our eyes met, holding for a second or two longer than it should have in our proximity. I saw pain in his pale blue eyes that shut me up.

Read cleared his throat loud enough to make me jump. "Can you stand?"

I wasn't sure who he was asking but nodded anyway.

Rolling away from him, I sat up with a few grunts and groans, putting my wet shoe back on. I would have much rather stayed on the soft ground. The exhaustion tempted sleep, but if I stopped now, I doubted I'd get up at all.

My muscles wavered as I crawled to my hands and knees. Grass and dirt clung to my arms and back and tangled in my ponytail.

Aidan hobbled to his feet and reached down to give me a hand. He staggered a little when I put too much of weight on him. We must have looked like quite the awkward pair.

Balancing on my own two shaky legs, I wrung out my hair as best as I could. My jean shorts dripped no matter how much I squeezed out the edges.

I realized Aidan was staring at me. When I met his gaze, his cheeks flared red, and he turned away as if he'd been slapped.

Looking down, I realized my camisole was clinging to my stomach and bra in crinkles. I tried to pinch the shirt away, but it suctioned back to my skin. I was slim but by no means like Robin or lean like Phoebe. Thinking of Phoebe, I was grateful that I wore a bra today; her tube top probably wouldn't have made it through that. Ironically, I remembered the Others saying that Phoebe would drown. The reminder sucked the humor right out of the idea.

Glancing back at the window, I saw that it remained broken and the water still didn't escape.

The outside of the house revealed just how tiny it truly was. It appeared large enough to contain the kitchen and dining room only. It was slapped in a clearing, surrounded by twisted trees. It had a shabby roof with missing or loose wooden shingles and chipped, abscessed, dark purple siding.

The full moon brightened the clearing enough to reveal no door to get in, at least not on our side.

Coughing, I felt the water from the house burn my throat. Disgusted, I didn't want to swallow it again and, without an ounce of grace, I spat. People made spitting look easy, but apparently it took some practice. I wiped the spit-strings from my lips with the back of my hand.

"Mona teach you that technique?" Read was smirking.

Instead of something intelligent, I issued the routine come-back. "Shut up."

Aidan detached himself from us, wandering toward the trees in a zig-zag pattern. One might have thought he was looking for the perfect entry or drunk, though I think his limp was throwing him off balance.

"At least he can walk okay," I whispered to Read.

"That's a plus," he said, grey eyes flickering to me so many times that I finally looked at him. "Are you okay?" he asked, serious.

"Yeah, I'll be fine."

Read looked me over before nodding. "When this is all over, you and I should hang out more. What you did in there was really brave."

I tried to smile. Did he mean hang out, or did he mean date? Or was I over thinking it? I realized I was blushing.

"What are you doing?" Read called to the trees.

Looking over his shoulder, Aidan said, "Going into the forest."

"I see that, but why?"

"Maybe the door's in there." Aidan pointed into the shadows. "It's not out here, and I don't think I like being out in the open when I can't run." He tested weight on his injured leg.

Despite the bright moon, I still had the sickening feeling that something could come flying out of the sky and scoop us up. "Aidan's right," I said. "We can't stay out where we can be seen."

Read shook his head, peeking at my shirt. "Guess not."

I pulled it from my skin again.

Aidan hesitated along the tree line. He didn't look back when he asked, "Why?"

"There is something in there." Read's grey eyes narrowed, his handsome features going rigid and still as he concentrated straight ahead.

I strained to see through the shadows. "How do you know?"

Aidan answered instead, limping back toward Read and me. "We kept hearing things move when you were in the house."

"Then I bet the door is in there," I answered. "Wherever there's danger, that's where our escape will probably be."

"Escape?" Read raised his eyebrows indignantly. "You mean new Challenge where we can almost die again." He thrust a thumb over his shoulder at the house.

"Do you want to get through this Challenge or not?" I snapped.

Read nodded at me like I was stupid. "Yeeeeaaaah, but I want to make it alive."

Sighing, I dropped my arms. They were too heavy to hold up anyway. "What do you suggest then?"

Aidan watched the two of us, pausing in his step. "Why don't we wander around the perimeter?" Aidan made a circular motion with his hands. "Then we can—" He stopped so suddenly I realized he wasn't looking at me anymore but past me.

I didn't want to—I *really* didn't—but I turned my head to look over my shoulder.

Only a few feet away, within the shadows of the tree line, was a tall silhouette.

It appeared to be human, standing with its head high and arms akimbo. We stared at each other for the longest time before it lurched forward.

"Run!" Aidan initiated the alarm.

Together, Read and I spun on our heels and bolted.

I heard the shuffling leaves and snapping twigs as the figure leapt out of the shadows and raced toward us.

He was shouting something that I couldn't hear over my own panic.

The maniac was gaining fast, and I knew I wasn't going to outrun him.

CHAPTER TWENTY-FOUR

I wasn't sure what thought process ran through my head when I realized I wasn't going to make it. I'd read about flight or fight and had always wondered which one I was. I wanted to be a fighter, like Phoebe, but was certain I'd just run. Life was disappointing that way.

Hearing his breath close behind, I could practically feel the heat of his body.

One warm hand grabbed my bicep, and my fear turned to liquid, taking my limbs with it.

Skidding to my knees, I curled up in a ball on reflex.

The pursuer staggered, letting me go, but didn't have time to stop.

Dirt sprayed just as a foot hit my leg and his shin collided with my side. Luckily, it didn't hurt as much as I expected.

Calling out, he toppled over me and crashed onto the ground.

Like a drunk, I attempted to wiggle out from under his shins and to my feet. I had to start running, but my attacker was quick to recover.

The assailant wrapped his arms around me from behind, already on his feet. I lifted my legs, hoping I'd drop and he'd lose his grip.

The bear-hug gripped me so tight that I found myself gasping, my ravaged lungs whistling.

A familiar voice cried, "I can't believe it!" He let me go.

Spinning around, I gasped while still trying to catch my breath. "Cody!"

Slapping my hands around his neck, which almost required tippy-toes, I hugged him to make sure he was real. There had always been an adamant whisper in the back of my mind saying that we'd never see him again. Pressing my cheek against his chest, it was almost surreal. He smelled like dirt and honey, though I wasn't sure why they'd be together.

Aidan limped closer, his suspicious gaze appraising Cody. I couldn't blame him. I should have considered that Cody might not be the *real* Cody before flinging myself into a hug. But I was far too relieved to think differently.

Read slapped Cody on the back, smiling widely. "Took you long enough."

Cody didn't back away from my arms the way the old Cody would have, and he ignored the fact that I was probably soaking his clothes.

Cody provided me that ounce of hope I needed, hope that Phoebe and Robin could be found.

I was the one who pushed away, craning my neck to look up at him. "*Where* have you been?"

Cody looked back at the woods after fist bumping Read. "Here. I can't believe that you guys came back for me. Where's Robin? Probably waiting on the other side, right? How did you get so wet?" He tried brushing off his shirt, but it was already damp and dirty.

Aidan spoke first. "What do you mean by, *came back*?"

"Well, when you completed the Challenge of course. And you did!" He threw his arms up as if he just scored a touchdown, at least until he saw Read's pointed frown. "What?"

"We're still playing, dude," Read said.

Cody's smile faltered. "You mean you guys haven't left?"

I shook my head and winced as Cody's expression plummeted.

"So," he rubbed his face between his palms, "did…did you lose the Challenge?"

Aidan's eyebrows furrowed. "What are you talking about? We only made it through two so far."

Cody looked from Aidan, to me, and to Aidan again, astounded. "I've been here for over three weeks and you've gone through *two*?!"

"Three weeks?" I cried.

Cody's fists rose to his temples, pressing hard.

I noticed for the first time that his shirt was torn and tattered. Fresh blood blemished the left arm of his shirtsleeve, and old bloodstains splattered his shirt and down the left side of his jeans.

His once bleached, spiked hair was matted with mud and dirt. It was almost like he was telling the truth.

"We've only been in the Challenge for maybe four hours or more," I guessed, seeing Aidan nod his agreement out of the corner of my eye.

Cody pressed his fists harder on either side of his head.

"How do you know that you've been here for three weeks?" Read asked guardedly.

The question snapped Cody from his trance. "Damien told me one night." Then he barked a strangled laugh that covered a surge of emotions.

"Damien visited you?" Aidan and I said together and peeked at each other.

Cody's eyes were suddenly wet, and he looked away.

Read patted Cody's back, looking uncomfortable. "Well, you're with us now. You can help us beat this Challenge."

Cody snapped straight. "Shit! *Robin*. Where's Robin?"

Aidan took an automatic step back. Read looked scared, as if Cody was about to burst into tears.

Clearing my throat, I said softly, trying to sound calm, "She, uh, disappeared in the last Challenge."

Cody stared at me, unblinking for several seconds.

I squirmed, wanting to move away from the mute accusations.

"This isn't supposed to happen!" he shouted, startling all of us. Hell, to put it in perspective: Cody rarely spoke. He spoke even less since dating Robin, who never stopped talking.

I wasn't sure what to say to him; '*I'm sorry*' didn't seem to cut it. I glanced at Read and Aidan for support, but they'd seemed to have found something interesting on the ground.

Cody took a deep breath, before saying, "Damien

said that if there was a split in the group, we wouldn't all make it home."

The omen blanketed a bitter silence.

Cody whispered, "I hope it's Robin that makes it."

Though the words damned the rest of us, I still wanted to hug Cody, reassure him that what Damien had said was likely a lie. But why would Damien lie? To confuse us?

Aidan was the one who changed the subject. "What happened in the house?" He gestured to the water-logged building behind us.

Looking away from the midnight sky, Cody glanced at the house and chewed his lips together before beginning. "I found this place and the witch. She seemed okay for the last...I guess, two weeks, 'til I realized she had been putting these spells on me when I slept. She wanted to sacrifice me or something."

I winced as there it was again. *Sacrifice.*

Cody swallowed loud enough for me to hear. "Yesterday, Poline came at me with a knife." Pausing, he squinted at the house. "I, uh, knocked her out with a chair."

Our eyes lingered on the swaying flood within the broken window, and Aidan said, "Actually, I think she's dead."

Cody paled and opened his mouth to speak, but no words came out.

Aidan and Read found the ground interesting again.

I put a damp arm around Cody's shoulder. "Listen, it was an accident, and it was in self defense, plus she wasn't..."

"I didn't mean to." Cody's freckled face reddened.

I shook Cody's arm imploringly. "*Listen.* At least

we found you and you're safe. She wasn't a real person, Cody, just part of the Challenge. Now we need to find a way out of here."

I hoped my words were true.

Cody shook his head. "You might as well not bother. Poline let me wander. We're trapped in a crevice, I think. There's this dirty wall that goes all around this area."

Read looked around them. "Can we climb out?"

Cody shook his head again.

Read stepped back, frustration grinding his teeth.

"You think we're stuck here?" I asked, feeling a lump in my throat.

Cody shrugged, looking away.

"So what do we do now?" I crossed my arms over my chest, trying to warm myself. I felt the nightly chill without the adrenaline to keep me warm.

Read and Aidan began to talk about options all at once, waiting to see Cody dismiss or approve each idea with a shake of his head.

It was hard to focus on just one without being pulled into another.

The low growl to our left deadened the chatter. Our eyes caught each other's in apprehension. Had we all heard it? The time to think up a plan was demolished, our temporary safety gone with a single sound.

Reluctantly, I turned my eyes before my head, scared to move too fast. A white wolf was hunched outside the tree line. Its head was lowered, its shoulders bunched.

The wolf growled, which bared pointed teeth and spiked the white hair around its collar.

I backed up and bumped into Aidan.

The large wolf's ears pinned back, and its eyes glowed as it padded forward.

"I found one in the woods once." Cody touched his shirt where the dried blood had been splattered.

As if our minds were linked, we all stepped back at the same time. The wolf slunk forward, snarling and snorting.

"What does it want?" I asked in a whisper.

"Meat," Cody replied, then before I could react, he broke off in a run.

Aidan, Read, and I didn't hesitate.

I think we were all prepared for it on some instinctual level. We twisted to speed after Cody; he already had a good head start. He aimed for the opposite tree line behind the witch's house. It was the closest escape that wasn't water filled.

The wolf howled long and loud before loping after us.

As we zipped past the house, I saw a lattice we could have climbed to the roof, but it was too late. Before I could shout, the house was passed and the wolf too close for us to turn back.

Aidan was already falling behind, and I screamed at him to keep up. I didn't want to lose him and knew I wouldn't go back for him. The coward in me would win that argument.

I glanced back and realized the wolf wasn't wasting any time shortening the space between us. It moved at the same intense speed as the Maserati.

In the distance, a chorus of howls filled the night.

Any second, my heart would surely smash its way through my rib cage. I felt my knees getting weak.

The white beast slowed to howl a rough response to

those in the distance. *He's calling them*, I thought.

It was a minor lead but enough to allow hope to spring. I was never a great runner. Cody was the runner and athlete, not us.

Read wheezed to my right, beginning to fall back with Aidan.

I supposed his claims of endurance had been slightly exaggerated.

The resonance of hungry ululations pierced the night in unison. It could have been my imagination, but they sounded closer.

Cody was speeding ahead. Would he come back if we fell? I somewhat doubted it. He knew these wolves. He knew what they were capable of, and if we were caught, would he even know?

The twisted trees ahead extended branches low enough for us to climb. Wolves couldn't climb trees. At least, I was pretty sure they couldn't…in our world.

Pointing to the greying giants, I shouted above the haunting clamor, "Climb!"

I just hoped everyone could hear me as we drew closer. I got ready to jump. I couldn't miss, I couldn't fall, and I couldn't stumble, unless I wanted to be eaten alive.

At the idea, I stumbled, almost losing my footing. My ankle rolled painfully, though not enough to send me sprawling. Even Aidan managed to pass me, hopping as if he were in a three-legged race.

Cody vaulted into a tree on my right, his height proving useful as he hardly had to jump. He pulled himself up onto the first branch, making it look easy.

Aidan reached the tree I was aiming for before I did. He jumped and cracked his injured knee into a branch. Bellowing, he didn't slow and scrambled for precarious safety.

I was running so fast that, if I didn't time this right, I'd end up slamming into a tree trunk.

Taking a giant step with my momentum, I pushed with my leg as hard as I could, my fingers straining for the first thick branch.

My sneaker found purchase on the scratched trunk, propelling me upward.

It was enough to snag a low branch.

I dug my fingers into the grey wood and let the adrenaline pull my body the rest of the way up. I could feel the strain burning in my muscles—every muscle. Though I didn't stop until I was straddling the lower branch and looking down.

The wolf's yellow eyes were narrowed on my dangling shoes. I wasn't sure how high he could jump but didn't want to risk it.

Out of the corner of my eye, I saw Read climbing higher. At least he'd made it.

I lifted my legs out of harm's way. I heard the snapping jaws below, then Aidan and Cody's shouts from above.

The wolf just below me was scratching at the dry wood, scarring the dying tree as if it could dig its way to me.

CHAPTER TWENTY-FIVE

Curling my legs up to my chest, I hugged them, breathing in relief and staring straight ahead. No way was I looking down again. My ankle throbbed but wasn't badly hurt from the roll. The bruises on my back hurt worse, so I figured this was a plus.

"Jesus, Nora, you *enjoy* these close calls?" Aidan's voice floated down, and I pretended not to hear the sarcasm in it.

I pressed my spine against the trunk and listened to the multiple growls from below. I squirmed, feeling far too close to them, even at my height.

Glancing up, I saw a thicker branch next to Aidan's perch. "Are there a lot down there?" I asked, standing on shaky legs, keeping close to the tree.

Aidan nodded, his reddish brown hair matted to his head with sweat. "Maybe four…no, five now."

I wiggled my way up next to him without much trouble, grateful for the extra distance.

My throat was dry. "Thirsty," I admitted.

"Should have drunk some of that water you almost drowned in," Aidan replied, his eyebrows raised.

"You're a riot." I wiped the sweat from my forehead and saw Aidan smile out of the corner of my eye.

Cody waved from his tree, whose branches intertwined with ours. Read sat just below him, clutching his chest and swallowing every second. He had paled dramatically. He looked ready to ralph.

"Now what?" Cody asked, distracting me from Read.

One wolf snapped its jaws below, and another bellowed, raising every hair on my arms.

Taking a deep breath, I gripped the branch between my legs and dared to look down.

Three had their front paws against the tree trunk and locked eyes with me, their hunger gleaming. They stretched as if it could get them closer while sniffing the air furiously.

I noticed for the first time how gaunt these ones seemed. They had ribs like washboards and pointed hip bones beneath fur that was falling out, leaving patches of pink flesh exposed. Only the first one, the one that had run us down, appeared healthy. It paced between the two trees, watching and calculating. For a second, I believed it was working out the details on how to knock us down.

In the distance, beautiful singsong ululations split the night, drawing dangerously close.

Squinting in the dark, I could make out moving shadows through the trees. As they neared, I counted six. They were black and dark brown mostly and each as thin as the next.

"What now?" Cody repeated edgily.

"Well," Aidan licked his lips, "we can wait up here until we starve or fall out of the tree."

"There has to be a door somewhere," I said, picking at threads of hope.

Read finally lost it and hurled vomit over the side. Gripping the branch, he lay on it on for dear life, shuddering.

As the splattering chunks hit the ground, my throat closed enough to tickle my gag reflex. I had to look away and touch a finger to my lips to warn myself not to vomit. I needed to reserve all my energy, not lose it. Especially when the wolves crowded around it and started lapping.

"You okay?" Cody asked, sounding a little green himself.

Coughing and spitting, Read grumbled, "Yeah, sure. Fucking awesome."

"There has to be a way out of here," I insisted, wanting to get away from the smell of stomach bile. Craning my neck, I peered into the trees, trying to catch a hint of a door.

"We need some ideas," Aidan concluded. "You've been here for a while, Cody. Can you think of anything?"

Cody looked around, the veins in his neck throbbing. He finally shook his head, not looking at any of us.

I tried not to glare at him. He had to know something. He'd been here for three freaking weeks! Instead, I gripped the branch with my knees and watched the monsters below with the others.

The wolves started to lie down, watching us from

their sides.

Minutes began to stretch by, and I leaned back against the trunk of the tree, waiting for an epiphany.

"I got away from one once." Cody almost sounded as though he were thinking out loud and stopped.

We all stared at him, waiting.

When he didn't continue, I cleared my throat. "What happened, Cody?"

He scratched his arm, straining his eyes to see into the distance. "There's a small lake just north of here. I just ran into water after it ambushed me."

Read asked, "You think they're afraid of the water?"

"I don't know, but I ducked under and held my breath. When I came back up, it was gone. Thought maybe it was because it couldn't see or smell me."

Aidan frowned. "Or it was afraid of whatever lived in the water."

Interrupting the debate, I asked, "You mean that if they can't see us, they might go away?" It didn't make a lot of sense to me for hungry wolves to give up so easily, except this wasn't a common sense type of world.

Cody shrugged with a pained expression that seemed to say, *It's all I got*.

"What about up there?" Aidan asked.

Tilting my head back, I followed Aidan's gaze. Higher up, the branches weren't as sturdy as the ones we were on. I doubted we could hide on bare branches.

"There aren't enough trees for cover," I said.

Falling silent again, we watched the trees above and then the wolves below until Cody swung a long arm out to point.

I followed his finger past the wolves. It took me

several seconds to see the moonlight gleam off a glossy dark surface. Along the edge of the tree line where we had burst through and a few oaks to our right was a black door. But it wasn't upright. It was lying flat on the ground with leaves scattered on top, almost obscuring it from view. No wonder we didn't see it earlier.

"How do we get over there?" Aidan asked, glancing down at his tender leg.

Cody swung his head left and right so hard I thought he might lose his balance. "The trees are close enough. Maybe we can climb through."

Read swayed, looking exhausted. "We could do that, but those things will probably follow us."

"What about a distraction?" I asked.

We looked at each other for ideas. It wasn't until Aidan broke off a smaller twig from his branch that the idea took form.

His legs gripped the tree as he twisted for a good throw.

The twig sailed past the door, and three of the darker wolves bolted for it. They fought each other, their nails scrambling over the slick door. Only one caught the twig in its jaws and snapped it in half. Their disappointment was taken out on each other, snarling, biting, and wrestling.

I began to smile and repeated, "*Sooooo*, we need a distraction."

"Sticks?" Read was staring down at the milling bodies, unconvinced. "They're wolves, not house dogs."

Aidan grabbed for another branch. "Then maybe they'll go for these and we can have a chance to get out."

I could only foresee one problem. "You think they'll

all fall for that?"

Aidan frowned, turning to Cody. "Cody, do you think we could climb through these branches to the big tree and get to the black door that way? If we're close enough to jump down, then we won't need to distract them for long."

Cody obliged Aidan's curiosity with a demonstration. He lifted himself from his branch to one of our higher ones as if they were monkey bars and dropped onto a branch above our heads. "Follow me," he instructed.

Read sluggishly went first, his grip almost faltering as he made his way across the branch, legs dangling.

Holding my breath, I didn't relax until I saw Read land on the branch above. If he could do it, so could I.

Aidan followed Read. His eyes kept turning back to me, making sure I was there.

As Cody was on his way to the second tree, we all watched his every move and did our best to mimic him.

Climbing through the trees was almost like being a kid again, though back then, wolves weren't below waiting to rip us apart. I tried not to think about falling and focused on my steps instead. When I felt shaky or unsure, Aidan was the one who turned back around to encourage me. I found it somewhat surprising that he took so much effort into securing my safety. I supposed the scare with the witch's house had gotten to him. I wanted to let him know that it was all right and tried a reassuring smile whenever our eyes met.

Before I knew it, we were standing over the black door in the earth with the wolves trailing below. They were entertained by the movement above and crowded beneath us.

My hands felt raw with promised calluses by the time I reached the final tree limb. The guys had spread out to other branches, allowing me room on the nearest one.

Cody was smiling by the time we were all overlooking the door. He snapped off a larger branch. "Ready?" he asked.

Aidan, Read, and I all grabbed branches that might fly a little farther than the thinner sticks.

"On three?" Read suggested, sounding unsure.

Aidan nodded. "Yeah, but should we all throw in the same direction?"

"Shouldn't matter." Cody shrugged, shifting on his feet. He gripped a branch above his head for balance and started the countdown.

The height was making me shake the longer I stared at the ground. *I hope I can throw far enough.* Recalling the calamities that were my baseball practices as a kid, I almost missed my cue.

"Three!" Cody threw his branch as hard as he could into the clearing.

One dozen heads turned, but they didn't move.

Aidan, Read, and I threw ours.

Mine and Aidan's made it to the clearing while Read's tangled in another tree.

The largest, a white wolf, yipped and bolted forward. Whatever that one wolf initiated, the rest followed. Tongues lolling, they bounded away.

"Now!" Aidan whispered harshly so not to distract the predators.

We all jumped from the trees. I jumped from a little too high. The impact quivered like a metal rod against my joints. Ignoring the shock as best as I could, I scrambled for the door.

Cody wrenched it open, and it hit the ground loud enough to draw the wolves away from their pursuit and back to us, bounding at full speed.

Cody jumped first. I was going to wait for Aidan when I felt a hand shove me from behind. Unprepared, I was airborne, falling through the doorway, arms flailing.

Tumbling inside, I didn't have time to scream, and I landed awkwardly. I think I managed to elbow Cody in the stomach as I fell on what felt like carpet.

As I rolled onto my back, one wolf snapped its jaws, almost catching Aidan's foot as he fell through. Before he hit the ground, Read moved to jump.

I saw Read's body fling back so violently that I screamed.

The door above our heads slammed shut, sealing out the wolves and Read Wallace.

CHAPTER TWENTY-SIX

Aidan landed between Cody and me.

One flailing arm almost caught the side of my face when the door above slammed shut.

Stunned and panting, we sprawled on the floor, staring at the ceiling.

Did we just lose Read? I knew what I'd seen, but it haunted me, replaying in my mind in a loop until I could convince myself of what had just happened.

Slowly, I pressed my palms into the carpet behind my shoulders and eased into a sitting position. My gaze never shifted from the door embedded in the ceiling. It had a tribal wolf carved into the wood.

I wiggled my limbs. I didn't seem to be hurt beyond scratches and bruises. I glanced at my companions, who seemed no worse for wear. "Think we can get back up there?"

"Where's Read?" Cody looked around the room.

Aidan pointed to the door above while staggering to

his feet. Baring gritted teeth, he limped a few steps, catching his balance against a grey wall.

Cody stood up too fast and wobbled back a few steps. His focus was above our heads, and he reached for the doorknob—being the only one tall enough to do so—just as it evaporated inches from his fingertips.

Rolling, I started to stand but found my legs too weak to attempt such a feat. "Maybe the wolves didn't get him. I just saw him pulled back," I said.

I looked around the small square room with grey walls and green carpet, which was very similar to the one we first fell into here.

"She's right." Aidan's glassy gaze shattered. "I didn't see a wolf behind him."

Cody stared at the empty ceiling where the door had once been. "What if it did?" His eyes rolled to Aidan and me, hardening. "I heard those teeth before the door shut."

Then he's dead. The harsh words itched in the back of my mind until I pushed them away.

"Nora."

The haunting voice didn't belong to either of the guys with me.

Jumping with a start, I twisted my head back hard enough to crack my neck.

Standing behind us was our elusive Master of Nightmares. The shock of seeing something so perfect froze me in place.

I wasn't in the tower room this time and wasn't alone, either.

Damien gazed down at me, his obsidian hair framing his shocking pallor. Hands clasped behind his back and shoulders squared, he could have passed for a gentleman, though that didn't suit what he *was*. He wasn't smiling, but his eyes were bright, making my stomach flip.

It was easier to try and stand the second time.

I rubbed the crick in my neck and heard Aidan limping up behind me while Cody edged closer to my side.

"How did you like the wolves?" Damien's intense gaze never left me. His voice didn't echo inside my head like before.

I waited for a clever quip from Aidan, but when he didn't say anything, I looked down, trying to sound nonchalant when I muttered, "Challenging, I suppose."

Straightening my damp camisole and shorts, I made sure Aidan and Cody's feet were in my peripheral vision.

The silence stretched, forcing me to look back up to see the demon still watching me, unblinking.

He must have liked the answer. Damien flashed a charming smile that was almost as jarring as it was foreign on him.

Aidan brushed up against my shoulder, and gooseflesh prickled my arm.

"I began simply, didn't I?" the demon asked, serious all over again. Without waiting for an answer, he continued, his eyes not straying far from me. "And now we're working our way up to difficult. Kind of like those…er," he twirled his fingers searching for the word, "console games I saw in that one's head." He motioned to Cody.

Cody's voice barely squeaked above a whisper. "Where's Robin?"

"And Phoebe?" I added.

"And Read?" Aidan finished.

Damien blinked as if the questions were shockingly idiotic. "They lost," he said, finally sweeping his glossy black eyes to the others. "They're *trapped*. I explained all of this." Then seemingly to himself he muttered, "Perhaps I didn't start out simple enough."

The swell of frustration closed my hands into fists. "What do you mean, they lost? They were taken."

At the same time, Aidan's voice melted with mine. "They weren't even given a chance! Are they dead?"

A shadow stretched across Damien's sculptured features before he growled as if speaking to an antagonizing child. "I said *trapped*."

I felt my shoulders start to sink, feeling the strain in my muscles relax just a little. *He didn't say dead. This meant we could save them, right*? I thought about the sacrifice the Others referred to.

To Cody, I tried to sound positive. "See? They're okay."

Cody didn't look at me. "Then where are they?"

Damien obliged. "They submitted to Challenges, the same as you."

Eyes wide, I looked to the demon. "Meaning they could still die? They're not safe?" Frustration was beginning to boil upward, a warmth in my stomach expanding like a balloon.

Damien's mouth twitched as if to hide a smirk. "I explained the rules clearly. If you cannot win against the Challenge, you end up dead or *trapped* here."

The smug tone must have triggered something. The next thing I knew, I was shouting. Heat radiated off my skin where it had once been covered in goosebumps. "There wasn't a fighting chance. You just *took* them!

Now they're stuck in Challenges? That's basically a death sentence."

"It is the Challenge." Damien didn't waver at my aggression. "Cody wandered off and ended up in a Challenge not directed for him. He skipped ahead and had to face the consequences. I'm following protocol."

Protocol? This was the word he used to sum up the terror, the fear, and the pain. It was so cold in comparison that I knew this demon had no idea what we were going through.

"He could have died in a Challenge not meant for him." It took all I had not to launch myself at him. My hatred for him went beyond glaring; I wanted to hurt him. I knew I couldn't, but the idea was deliciously inviting. *If I can find a way, I will.* I let the anger carry me just a few feet from the demon, just out of reach.

"Nothing is fair, Nora. I thought that you of all people should know that." Damien lowered his voice, letting his raven-jeweled eyes bore into me as if we shared a secret.

Our eyes locked for longer than a few seconds, and I realized my mistake. I was trying to piss off a demon. What the hell was I thinking?

"What does that mean?" I forced myself to simmer the heated emotions. It was harder than I thought.

"What is your age on your world?" Damien asked.

At first I didn't know how to respond. The simple question was about as effective as a slap. Straightening my spine, I plucked at my shirt, tugging it down. "What does that have to do with anything?" Neither Cody nor Aidan spoke.

"I was curious how long it's been for you," he said and released one arm from behind his back.

Feeling the warmth rise in my cheeks, I didn't answer, too afraid of his goal.

Aidan betrayed me by saying, "Just answer the question."

I glanced at Aidan, annoyed. He wavered under the snap of my gaze, electric eyes flickering away before he whispered, "What if it's a clue?"

Turning back to Damien, I answered honestly. I could have lied but didn't, at least not yet. "I'm twenty-one."

"Sixteen of your years then? Is that correct in how you gauge time?" The way he said it meant he already knew the answer.

The hairs on the back of my neck bristled. The pent-up anger began to evaporate, replaced with dread.

"Sixteen years?" Aidan asked doubtfully. "What does that mean?"

I wasn't sure who he was asking but lied to drown the silence. "I'm not sure."

Perhaps Aidan sensed the trembling in my voice, but I could see it in his face that the wheels upstairs were turning in a new direction.

My hands wrenched on my shirt, straightening and twisting to keep them moving.

"Is there something wrong?" Damien asked, feigning innocence.

I didn't answer the question. Instead, I caved to Damien's first assessment in a grumble. "You're right, nothing's fair."

"Nora?" Aidan whispered. Out of the corner of my eye, I saw Cody nudge Aidan to keep quiet.

I wanted to spin around and tell Aidan it wasn't his business.

In my family, we hid most of the family pictures from when I was young, locked away the past, the questions, and the pain. It wasn't until five years ago that Mom put up one picture in the back hallway where no guest would see.

Aidan ignored Cody's nudge and said to Damien, "What do you mean, 'It's been sixteen years'?"

"Since we've met," Damien answered coolly. "I admit, I didn't recognize her at first. It's peculiar how the exposed always come back."

"What are you…" It wasn't until the words started leaving my lips that I absorbed what he had said and staggered back, knocking into Aidan first. "Met? We've…what?" *Oh crap, his angle*. He was going to turn them against me. I felt the panic seize in my chest the moment Aidan backed away from my touch, hands up. Cody wouldn't look at me.

Damien's eyes sparked at my reaction. I was giving him exactly what he wanted.

Taking a deep breath, I tried to control the mixed emotions that sang through my blood. He had no right to butcher me through my past. "You're lying," I accused.

Cody stepped in front of me, almost blocking my view of Damien. "Look, if this isn't a clue, then it's not important."

I tried to give Cody a grateful smile but couldn't muster the strength. All my energy poured into controlling myself before I could do something stupid.

"But *I* know," Damien spoke up. His voice quiet but carried throughout the whole room, ringing in my head as if it were its own megaphone. "I know everything."

If he could see into our minds, then he knew about

me. He knew about my twin sister's death sixteen years ago. I had to wonder how he'd twist a lie into that story. Not everyone was privy to my family's loss. We were careful to avoid questions, always. It wasn't that we couldn't talk about Neive. It was that we couldn't talk about her death.

I wanted to ask Damien what he knew but not with Aidan and Cody around. He was talking about the night of the murder, but I would have remembered a demon. I remembered scattered images from a five year old's perspective but there'd just been the five of us that night.

The silence stretched during my contemplation, and I realized everyone was staring at me.

Cody had moved to my side to touch my shoulder, and I flinched. If Damien wanted to tell my family secret, what would stop him? And what would it matter at this point? I'd seen Aidan's worst nightmare, after all. Secrets were falling fast.

Shifting from foot to foot beside me, Aidan asked, "You remember him?"

"No." I crossed my arms over my chest.

Damien's eyes reflected a devilish shine. "If you truly believe that, then there could be problems ahead."

"What sort of problems?" Aidan asked, leaning away from me. It was an unconscious gesture, but it revealed what he was thinking all too clearly.

I felt sick to my stomach.

I hadn't met Damien before; of this, I was certain. "He's lying." I held my chin high. "What are you up to, Damien? Do you need to embarrass me? Maybe loosen their trust so we'll separate again? What the hell does this have to do with getting our friends back?" I managed to keep my tone low and thought I sounded damn smooth.

The rage was starting to twitch again, building and twisting with the warmth. I had to clench my fists, fingernails biting into my palm to hold it from overtaking me.

Damien stepped forward, making the hairs on my arms stand on end and sending a shudder through the air that buzzed in my head. As he closed the gap between us, I saw Aidan limp back, his eyes wide.

I wasn't sure what held me in place. Perhaps it was fear. I'd like to think it was a shot of bravery, though I'd be lying to myself. My insides were vibrating into liquid, and my skin crawled.

Aidan grabbed my shoulder to pull me back.

"Birket." Cody hissed a warning, sounding surprisingly like Phoebe.

The demon's cold, inimical gaze shifted to Aidan. I tried to step back and realized I couldn't. Damien leaned in so close I thought for an instant he was going to kiss me.

Flinching, Damien stopped inches from my face, eyes alight.

Lips lingering just over the bridge of my nose, he whispered, still not looking at me, "Don't move." With a flick of his hand, Damien sent a sudden force through the room that spread outward in a gust of wind.

Aidan's hand jerked from my shoulder, and I heard two thuds followed by muffled shouts.

My body teetered at the impact, but I didn't step back, determined to stay still as I strangely felt more relaxed. The buzzing irritation I felt earlier was receding.

Turning my head, I saw Aidan and Cody suctioned to the wall, like they had been in the tower, and jerked my eyes back to Damien. I took a ragged breath to focus.

The warmth in my chest and stomach had vanished. I didn't want to let him know he was making me nervous, though it proved impossible.

In a voice too low for the others to hear, he hissed, "Your past has everything to do with why you're still alive."

Swallowing hard, I shook my head and moved my numbing lips. "I don't know what you're talking about."

"Don't you?" He raised his eyebrows at me, unbelieving. "Don't you wish for justice for your sister?"

I snapped, "You only know about her from rooting through my head."

"I did," he said, "but it was buried deep. I didn't see it until you showed me when you were covered in spiders. Still hopping back and forth between worlds?"

In the house and when I was with the spiders. I remembered the wooden chairs back to back. How could I have forgotten? Breathing through my nose, I tried to wrap my mind around what he said—about what it *meant*.

"Am I going crazy?" I asked. "Is this all made up?"

Damien's stony expression revealed nothing.

"You—you saw what happened. You don't know me," I said to fill the quiet. "What do you want?"

"To see what you can do," he answered. "To see what Nell promised."

Of course he'd remember her name. "And what can I do?"

"If I knew, I wouldn't have to test you."

"Test me for what exactly?"

An apprehending smirk twitched at the corner of his mouth. "You called Nell insane."

"She is."

"What about you? You believe you suffer from the same delusions?"

My heart twisted. "That's not funny."

"It wasn't meant to be." The smirk fell, and he reached up one hand, palm cupped as if to touch my cheek, but he didn't touch me. His hand hovered close enough that it shadowed my peripheral vision but didn't give off a heat. "Perhaps what you perceive as crazy isn't necessarily the truth."

"What is it called, then?"

Damien canted his head. "To some it is a gift, to others, a curse."

"And you call it?"

"A threat."

The words made my blood run cold, and I took a step back.

So many questions—insane questions—raced through my head that I wasn't sure what to ask or where to start. I tried to push aside the cloudy images that clogged my memory. I recalled the two men Nell had with her, one a bulky blonde and the other a thin redhead with the initials JWD on his jacket. Both were sadists. but they were human, and despite their hazy faces in my memory, I was positive neither could have been Damien. "Which one were you?"

"Which?"

"Of the men who helped Nell abduct us? Neither of them was found." Only Nell had been locked up, found naked on the side of the road two days after I had been recovered.

Damien shook his head at me. "I wasn't one of the men."

"Nora," Aidan's voice wheezed behind me.

His voice sent a jolt through me.

I had forgotten about them!

I started to turn to my companions when Damien's cupped hand forced me to look at him. His hand was cold, smooth, and distressingly strong. He had my attention.

"We're not through." He said it as if it were a threat. "I know of your past, but he doesn't." Damien's eyes flickered over my shoulder, and I knew he was looking at Aidan.

"He doesn't know," I confirmed.

"Keep it that way for now."

"What? You already told them you met me."

His fingertips buried in my hair above my temple, and I bit my lips together.

"Don't tell the Birket about Nell," he said. "Haven't you ever wondered if he felt strange around you too?"

Bullseye.

"Start to." He slipped his hand away, tracing fingers that buzzed with electricity down my cheek.

I stepped away, leaving a fair gap between us.

Ignoring me, Damien said louder for everyone to hear, "Time's wasting."

A black door materialized behind the demon. His supernatural gaze fixed on me as I backed away. I had wanted to ask him about Aidan, about Nell. Questions whistled past, but instead I pivoted toward my friends, toward safety.

I had to remember who was more important here. My friends were alive, unlike my past, which was long dead.

CHAPTER TWENTY-SEVEN

Cody and Aidan stepped away from the wall, brushing themselves as if they'd been coated with spiderwebs.

Aidan's electric eyes were seething. "What did he say?"

I didn't have to look over my shoulder to know that Damien was gone. "He was trying to intimidate me," I answered. It was mostly the truth.

Cody eyebrows pinched. "What did he mean by infraction? I thought the three weeks was the punishment."

"I'm sorry, Cody," I said. "I shouldn't have freaked out."

"Why did you?" Aidan asked, his voice low.

Taken off guard, I answered him with a strained stretch of my lips. I could only hope it looked like a smile. "He makes me nervous. Let's get this over with. I don't want our friends to be trapped any longer than they have to be."

Aidan didn't press his issue any further and shouldered me aside without seeing my glare. He twisted the handle and pushed the door in. The door scratched along the floor, stopping short. It didn't reveal much through the two-inch crack.

We paused, using every sense to locate signs of immediate danger on the other side. The seconds ticked by. I started to move when Aidan blocked my way. He leaned his shoulder into the door, forcing it to scrape the already scuffed floor.

Cody stayed behind Aidan and me. He'd be able to see over both of our heads anyway.

Inside there was darkness, though that didn't surprise me.

Dismal and dark... Just the way Damien liked it.

I was reminded of the tentacles that shot from the darkness for Phoebe and took a deep breath. Ducking, I pushed past Aidan to get inside first. If someone were to go missing, it would be me. I was being tested after all, wasn't I?

"Wait!" Aidan hissed before snatching my wrist hard enough to make me flinch. He followed close, his eyes darting left and right, his cool hands moistening.

The light from the room behind us revealed the narrow walls on either side and a dark wood floor.

Muttering, Cody stepped in behind Aidan. The door slammed shut, making me jump. I kept my free hand close to my body, tugging at my damp camisole, as if it could keep me safe.

We froze at first, not daring to move, and listened to our collective breaths.

I inched forward, one foot testing the ground before the other. There was nothing but darkness above, below, and ahead. I started swinging my arm from side to side when Aidan let go.

Gasping, I opened my mouth to say his name. A fluorescent light began to flicker overhead. Wheezing out the fading word, I looked back to see Aidan standing next to a standard, everyday light switch. His eyes were looking up at the ceiling in relief.

We stood in a hallway. It had warm-brown walls with a mural of cherry blossoms gracing every inch of free space. The hallway felt welcoming.

Perched on white pedestals on either side of the door were two white, Chinese-style vases.

"The door hasn't disappeared," I whispered.

Cody twisted to inspect it before shaking his head and saying, "Doorknob."

I had to do a double take, but he was right. The doorknob was missing.

That meant we could only go one way.

Turning, I noticed the sign above the archway ahead. It would be the only thing to mar the warm atmosphere. In large, uneven letters, dripping crimson, it read: *Museum*.

Aidan asked Cody, "Any nightmares about museums we should know about?"

Cody gaped in confusion. "Should I have?"

My insides were still reeling from my encounter with Damien, and I wanted to get this over with quickly. Without waiting for them, I started forward, my sneakers squeaking on the polished floor.

As I approached the gruesome museum letters, I could hear the boys trailing after me. I tried to prepare myself for anything. This could be a museum of horrors. Maybe there were monsters that would spring to life or stuffed animals that would be waiting to devour and skewer us on horns and teeth.

All right, first look for exits and try to herd everyone toward them, I thought.

I stopped just before the archway and peered inside, straining to see as far as I could. Dim overhead lights illuminating the gigantic room.

There weren't any windows or doorways that I could see, but they could still exist amongst the obstacles.

The displays were like any others in a museum: warm colors, pleasant, with titles, captions, tags and all closed off by red rope or glass. I was surprised at how normal it was.

Cody peeked over my shoulder and breathed out slowly. His breath was atrocious, and I leaned away from him. He didn't move past me but was close enough I could feel his body heat at my shoulder. He swallowed and whispered, "At least it isn't a museum on wolves or the history of witchcraft."

I smiled wide. "Or Ouija boards."

"Or spiders," Aidan contributed dryly.

I couldn't help myself. "Or a killer Maserati."

Aidan looked away, eyes narrowed in thought.

Bewildered, Cody glanced between us.

Feeling the tension coming off of Aidan, I patted Cody's shoulder reassuringly. "It's nothing," I said more softly and stepped through the threshold.

Veering to the left, I found myself amongst busts of ancient goddesses and gods as white as bleached bone. Tables with pale cloth showed off spotless golden discs, intricate jewelry, and pottery reciting ancient stories from Greece or Rome.

I ran a finger along the edge of a glass, which held golden jewelry, bracelets, necklaces, and rings, each carved with a meticulous hand.

Aidan stopped at one of the busts. It was of a warrior-like woman. She wore a helmet with a Mohawk top. On her right shoulder, holding up her garments was a decorative disc. He read the tiny golden plate at the base of the glass casing. "Pallas Athena, Patron of Athens."

This was only the first section, and as interesting as it was, it didn't reveal anything of our Challenge. Each area was separated by thin, temporary walls taller than Cody.

"Come on," I whispered to them. "We need to find a way out."

Agreeing mutely, Aidan was closest to the next opening and stepped through.

Following close behind, we ended up in an Egyptian-themed area. The centerpiece of the room, which caught everyone's attention, was the open sarcophagus. The golden lid depicting a pharaoh's noble figure leaned against the casket. Stone-faced and holding a scepter close to its body, it was vibrant with colors even in the dim light.

Aidan hobbled around the glass casing without us.

I wanted to stop him but knew I'd be too late if something were to leap out and nab him.

Shuffling to a stop on the other side of the sarcophagus, he breathed, "Woooooowww."

Cody and I scrambled to catch up.

I'd never seen a half-covered mummy that wasn't on TV before.

The face was partially revealed, showing the dark,

paper-like skin stretched over the cheekbones and forehead. The eye sockets were empty but weren't gaping holes; instead, they were two slits that were too dark to see inside. The lips had decomposed and peeled back to reveal a row of crooked, yellow teeth. One hand was wrapped tightly to the chest while the other was free, revealing not just the browned, dead flesh but brittle bone as well.

Cody recovered first, reading the gold plate on the glass casing out loud. "Ramses II, third king of the Nineteenth Dynasty."

"Come on," Aidan said as if he wished he didn't have to. We backed away into the next room, unwilling to tear our gazes from the mummy until it was out of sight.

Cody backed into something metal.

Slapping a hand over my mouth to stop a scream, I jumped and turned to see shiny medieval armor on a mannequin, a lance held firmly in one metal hand.

Aidan and Cody studied a display of long broadswords while I peeked at all the heavy crusader stones with crosses carved out of them. Still, there didn't seem to be a clue about our Challenge.

We had separated in the small flimsy room, drawn to all four corners, and I started to think about Damien's visit. He'd mentioned he'd be testing me, and there'd been something about me and Aidan…

I pinched my lips together and watched Aidan press his face to a glass case filled with deformed and twisted stones that didn't look like anything I'd seen in our world.

He wasn't supposed to know about my past, but I remembered the spark in Damien's eyes when Cody called him *Birket*. The house we'd been in had belonged to the Birkets.

"Aidan?" I whispered, glancing over my shoulder to make sure Cody was still distracted.

"Hm?"

I took a deep breath, remembering how we'd felt that strange shock when our hands touched outside the Victorian house. "Have you ever felt strange around me?"

"Hm?" He scratched his head until his hair spiked in its usual, wild fashion.

I nudged him and hissed, "Like when our hands touched at your house. You don't remember that? I know you felt that. I mean like before that. Have you ever felt like…like maybe you knew I was coming, or close, or just weird?"

Tearing away from the glass case looked difficult, but he managed, pausing before asking, "What are you talking about?"

This was useless. Maybe Damien had told me that to throw me off. Perhaps this was the test. "Nothing," I muttered.

"Is that what you guys were talking about? You and Damien?" Aidan straightened, keeping his pale eyes level with mine.

Kind of. I shrugged.

Aidan's shoulders sagged as if I'd insulted him. He looked away, peering over his shoulder to see where Cody was before taking a deep breath. "I don't know."

Before I could ask further, he turned his back to me and walked away, head down.

He's shutting me out, I realized.

Shaking my head to clear my thoughts, I tilted my

chin up to see the back wall of the large room. The display areas, which were the size of two of my living rooms, had taken us farther away from the black door than I'd expected.

Inching into the next display room, I saw it was mainly Celtic. There were pictures of Stonehenge tacked to the walls, while displays of tools, stone, and an assembled hut took up most of the space. There were displays of the Green Man and items featured in druidism.

Despite all the fascinating items, my attention was drawn to a door just beyond the exhibit. I was about to shout back to the boys when something stopped me.

The door was cracked open. It wasn't the traditional Damien-black-door, and no symbols decorated the front.

As I slipped closer to investigate, I could hear the boys approaching the Celtic room behind me. They whispered back and forth, though I couldn't hear what they were saying.

Unwavering, I clasped the doorknob and pulled it toward me. This was wrong too. Damien's door always swung in.

Blinking, I tried to make out the details of the new room, but it was too dark, like staring down a well. I'd have to call the guys to help me investigate. It would be stupid to go in alone.

Before I could turn to call, a faint lime-colored glow flickered to life.

Like a switch, it revealed a little of the new room. It wasn't much but enough for me to make out a metal examiner's table, like something I'd seen in vet clinics before. The glow blinked but didn't go out before resuming a steady rhythm: *on*, off, *on*, off.

After only a second, a large light over the metal table flashed on. It was bright, probably the brightest I'd seen in the Challenge yet. I squinted back the pain and lifted an arm as a shield.

To my relief, nothing happened. Nothing jumped out of the shadows or roared to life. Everything was still, except the hum of the powerful lamp reflecting off the metal table.

A thin, beige curtain surrounded the tiny room like a mask.

The glowing light was on a smaller surgical table. It was the size of a D-battery and shaped in a cube. As it flashed the green light steadily, I realized it was calling me. I felt a tug in the center of my stomach that was like pulling.

I began to feel light-headed, but my eyes didn't leave the enticing little light. It wanted me to go and pick it up. *Something that small couldn't be dangerous*, I thought dreamily. It was rather pretty, and wouldn't it be nice to have something like that with me? We could have something to show us through the dark. Maybe then Aidan would stop doubting me, stop pushing me away and trust me a little.

I heard Aidan and Cody's voices getting closer, but neither seemed to notice the door. If I didn't hurry, they'd get the crystal before me. The idea sent a pang of jealousy through me so sharp and fierce that I bolted into the room without a second thought.

My head was a haze, like walking into a dream with only one focus: *I had to have that little light.*

I took three leaping steps around the empty examiner's table and scooped it up.

It was cool in my warm palm, calming, perfect in every way.

Elated, I could barely take my eyes from it as I hurried back to the doorway. I knew I should have waited for my partners, but I couldn't help it. Clutching the cube in my hand, I dared to inspect my new prize.

Uncurling my fingers one at a time, I savored the little light as it flickered *on*, off, *on*, off.

My heart ached at the idea of losing it, leaving it behind, letting anyone else see it. I would have to hide it from Aidan and Cody. *Especially Aidan. He's had it in for me from the beginning*, I thought, panicked. If he saw this, he would try to take it away. I knew it. We weren't meant to be friends; we both knew that from the very beginning. I glanced up, hearing the two of them whispering just out of sight, in the Celtic area.

I should hide it, but I wanted to look at it one last time.

The color had changed from the brilliant lime to a pink, which darkened to a blood red. Blinking, I transferred it to my fingertips, holding it up to the light. Each flash darkened the color. It began to fall into a deeper and deeper red until it was almost black.

I half expected it to gradually heat up in my palm, but it remained cool.

This didn't seem right. I wouldn't have to *give* it to Aidan and Cody, just have them take a look at it, right?

Maybe they'd know what it was doing, but I'd make them promise not to touch it. Sighing in defeat, I took a deep breath. "Ai..."

A cold, steely hand clamped over my mouth from behind.

CHAPTER TWENTY-EIGHT

My cry was muffled when a second arm wrapped around my stomach, trapping my arms to my sides.

As they dragged me back into the room, my spine crashed into something hard that creaked and clattered like…metal?

I twisted and struggled, but it felt as if the arm were squeezing me tighter until it was too painful to twitch.

My chest heaved against the constriction, and my head swam. I felt hysteria settling in for a visit. If I hyperventilated, I'd pass out, and that would mean losing the cube.

Concentrating on my increasing heartbeat, I closed my eyes, daring it to slow. Each deep breath against the metal hand made the fingers against my cheeks slick with condensation.

The bright light over the examiner's table snapped off, and my eyes opened. The light shone from the museum outside, shadowing Tin Man and me.

Inhaling deeply, I knew I had to warn them. I screamed against the hand, twisting my head at the same time. The fingers almost slipped away before digging painfully into my jaw.

It whipped me around. My feet left the floor, and my head couldn't keep up. Darkness twirled, and heated nausea struck the back of my throat, stiffening my jaw and strangling the scream. Tears sprang to my eyes, and I tried to blink them away.

Out of the corner of my eye, I saw the door to the museum close on its own. It locked out the light so only a sliver crept in beneath. I tried to focus on the little light; otherwise I wouldn't know if I were upside down or right-side up in the dark. If Tin Man wasn't holding me, I would have fallen.

The cube warmed my sweaty palm, a small comfort that showed I was still alive. It marked divots into my palm, but I was determined to conceal it. Holding it to my thigh, I hoped the light didn't peek through my fingers.

This must be why Tin Man came after me. It wants the cube back. I could hand it back and take my chances, but I didn't think I'd be released so easily. Besides, the cube was mine now.

Screaming against the steely hand, I breathed through flaring nostrils to stop the room from spinning. I needed more oxygen.

I'm going to die, I thought. *Right here with Tin Man, he's going to wait for Aidan and Cody to leave and then take the cube.* I somehow hoped Damien would steal me and let me join Phoebe, Read, and Robin, but that didn't seem to be happening.

At the same time, the thought made me angry. I had

to wait for a demon to save me? What was wrong with me? I had a chance to help save them, and I was giving it up so easily. There were Challenges harder than this.

Lifting my right foot, I kicked back for a leg. *Won't take me down so easily*, I thought.

The clang echoed against my soggy sneaker, but my attacker didn't react. There wasn't a grunt of pain, a flinch, or a step back. Only the metallic ring still hung in the air.

Somewhere to my left, I heard metallic footsteps approaching.

There were two?!

Breathing deeply and frantically through my nose, I sensed the air grow sharp as something touched the fabric of my shirt. Something sharp.

As I twisted in the anaconda grip, the point rose up and caressed the edge of my collarbone. It was a pointed, wooden tip from something held by Tin Man Number Two, though he stood several feet back. In an instant, I remembered the knights from the medieval display. One of them had held a lance.

My captor leaned me into the tip of the lance. It was surprisingly dull but pressed to my skin, scratching the splinters beneath my collarbone.

I raised my foot and struck at the loud shin behind me, frantic for noise—a lot of noise. As I pounded at it, the room vibrated with the echo until the door flew open.

"Nora?" Aidan's voice shouted through the blinding light.

Hope split into fireworks inside my head, and I screamed to warn him.

I was such an idiot! I wanted to drop the little cube

of light, but I couldn't. I wished I could say that I wouldn't, but my fingers couldn't uncurl around the object no matter how hard I tried. The corners dug so deep in my palm I wondered if they were breaking skin.

As I blinked away the harsh light, I saw Aidan's wild hair silhouetted in the doorframe. He froze before shouting, the urgency snagging every syllable, "Cody!"

The lance stopped pressing to my collarbone, and the shiny knight, who I could finally see, turned to the intruder.

Cody skidded in beside Aidan, his smile barely visible until he looked into the room. He opened his mouth as if to say something, but nothing escaped.

Aidan and Cody stared at the two knights, and the knights stared back at the two strange boys as if deciding what to do.

Unable to twist in the steely grip for fear the pressure would break bones, I watched helplessly, hating the sensation, and scrambled for an idea.

The lance-wielding knight turned his head back to me, armor squeaking. Shoulders rising, he lifted the lance, aiming for my chest.

My heart beat so fast it made my chest feel too small to cage it.

The knight dove with the lance poised, and I heard Cody and Aidan shouting within my spinning world.

I waited for the pain to spike my chest. It just felt like I was falling. The room tilted, and I was floating. In my confusion, I didn't think of screaming, I just stiffened, waiting for the worst.

I landed hard on the metal shell. The armor *crunched* and *clanged* against the polished floor.

The arms released me.

Surprised, I almost forgot to move. The split second of hesitation resulted in a clumsy scramble. Rolling off the mound of metal was the easy part. I landed on my stomach with a *splat*. My body felt inflated once released from the weighty arm.

There wasn't enough time to stand. Twisting onto my back, I saw the lance-wielder had fallen too but was getting up much more quickly.

My sneakers dug into the floor in a clumsy crab walk. I still clutched the cube. "Help!" I called.

It was Aidan who grabbed my arms from behind and swung me from the floor. We staggered into each other until we regained our equilibrium.

"Out!" I heard Cody squawk.

My free hand gripped Aidan's shirt sleeve to keep the room from spinning. Glancing over my shoulder, I realized what pulled the knight to the floor—inadvertently saving me.

Ramses II swayed on his feet over the metal-clad knights.

Aidan seemed to see him at the same time, and we paused in the doorway to see the mummy grab the surgical table.

It tore off one of the metal legs as if it were made of twigs. It tossed the rest of the metal aside, hitting the beige, medical curtain. The table didn't hit a wall behind the curtain; it flew straight back into darkness and was swallowed whole.

The mummy gasped strangled, unrecognizable words: "*Nii heeeel.*" It could have also been a language I wasn't meant to understand. The lack of lips made speech slightly more challenging for this one.

I was still attached to Aidan's torn sleeve when he

decided to run. I was yanked from the doorway and tried to not let go.

The last thing I saw was the mummy swinging a metallic table leg.

It could have been comical, this frail mummy beating the crap out of a metal suit, but each stroke hit so hard the armor dented. The lance-wielder swung an arm back, which the mummy barely avoided.

Snapping back to reality, we ran.

Cody was ahead, using all of his athletic ability to stretch the distance between us and him.

We tried to keep up. Aidan's limp had lessened enough that the shrill, clanging metal was receding. Racing through the still-life displays, we pivoted just in time to avoid smashing any of them.

A strong wind whizzed between our heads, and a thrown lance plunged into the hardwood floor ahead of us.

Splinters sprayed at our ankles, and together we screamed.

I careened around the corner, and Aidan narrowly dodged a Roman pottery case.

I peeked over my shoulder. The knight wasn't there. Instead, it was the mummy, just a few displays back.

The rail-thin creature moved slowly and calculated each step. Its head tilted back as if it were blind, arms extended with stretched fingers. Strips of loose gauze floated off its body in a hypnotic dance.

Cody was in the hallway, heading for the door that we had come through originally.

"We'll be trapped," I panted to Aidan. We launched ourselves after Cody, seeing no other alternative.

Cody struggled with the new rattling doorknob that

hadn't been there before. It was locked.

Glancing over my shoulder, I expected to see the mummy. Instead, it was one of the knights, struggling for traction around the corner. The metal suit clanged noisily, the lance poised to strike.

Aidan grabbed my arm and pulled me out of the way of the lance just in time. We both hit the wall with a *thud*, jarring the wind from my lungs.

Cody jumped out of the way and hit the opposite wall, facing us. His gangly arms held themselves high as if to avoid a second impact.

At full momentum, the knight slammed into the black door. The lance tore through as if it was cardboard, and splinters exploded.

Aidan grabbed one of the Chinese vases by the doorway. With all of his strength, he heaved it into the knight's head. It shattered into fragile pieces and left a small dent in the helmet, but otherwise it was a useless effort.

The knight spun around, unharmed, and balled up metal fists. He swung an arm at Aidan. The movement was slower. The weight of the heavy metal probably saved Aidan's life.

Aidan ducked and pushed me forward. I stumbled and fell to the ground, my knees skidding along the hardwood and vase fragments with painful squeaks.

I wobbled to my feet. My knees burned, but that wasn't my biggest threat.

Twisting, I saw the mummy creeping around the corner. Red, beady eyes narrowed on us through gauzed slits. Its jaw barely moved as it slurred, "*Aw keeell.*"

I grabbed the second vase that sat in the doorway as Aidan and Cody struggled with the knight behind me.

As I threw the vase, I realized it was a bit heavier than it looked. I had to use the knuckles of my cube-hand for added momentum.

The tall, elegant artifact collided with the mummy's neck and shoulders instead of its head and shattered into a thousand pieces. The sound almost drowned out the screeching metal behind me.

Shards of the white vase cut through the brittle fabric and flesh. The mummy hesitated as if expecting pain, then began its advance again, staggering from side to side with one very clear focus. It banshee-shrieked, "*AwwwkeEELL!*"

The warmth touched my stomach, and I felt the cube warming as well.

No, it was growing hot!

The mummy was only a few feet away. The smell of dust and mold tickled my nose.

The cube was a throbbing black. I shook it close to my ear, and I swear I heard liquid sloshing about.

The mummy took another step forward, and I felt like a trapped animal standing between the clattering knight and this mummy.

Aim for its head, I thought desperately.

Bellowing a battle cry, I charged, hunching my body as I rammed into the flimsily wrapped bones.

It was easier than I thought. The mummy either hadn't expected it or was too slow to react. It flew back, skeletal fingers clawing at the air.

Gritting my teeth, I threw the cube, surprised that it left my fingers so willingly. I had expected stabbing jealousy, but it hadn't been mine to begin with; it had been Damien's.

The glowing crystal bounced off the mummy's chest

and clattered to the floor.

In the heat of the build up, I hadn't quite considered that it might not work. Shit.

The mummy roared a throaty cackle that echoed in the thin hallway.

Just above the cackle, the little cube emitted a buzz, like an electric charge.

The mummy and I froze, staring at it, dumbfounded.

It didn't seem so little and harmless anymore. Especially when it puffed up like a square balloon.

The cube inflated to over twice its size, and its electrical charge was growing louder. I shouted, "Run!"

Hunching my body, I bowled the mummy over again and leapt out of range of his claws. Darting through the Museum archway, I was sorry that I didn't look back. I just kept running as the cube hit a curiously high-pitched note, growing louder and louder. I felt my hands reaching up for my ears unconsciously.

Frightened, I dove behind the thick pedestal that held the bust of Athena. Huddled up, I clutched my knees just as Aidan skidded in beside me. He curled up against me, holding me against his rather comforting sweaty, coppery smell.

The harsh noise of the cube began to screech at deafening levels.

"Cody?" I shouted, peeking around Aidan.

He wasn't near us when the explosion hit.

CHAPTER TWENTY-NINE

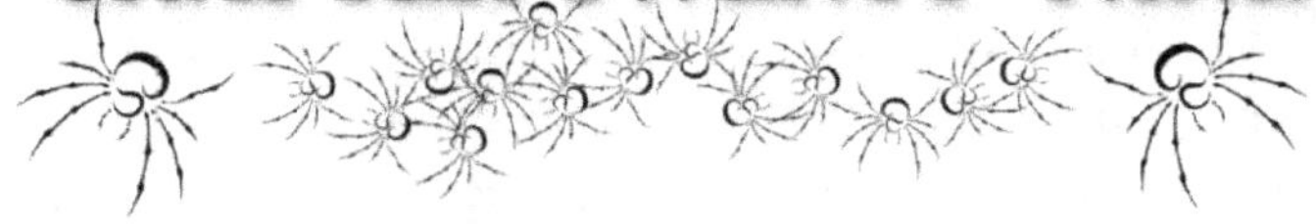

I've never heard an explosion before, at least not in real life.

It rocked every nerve, shook my teeth, vibrating my gums, and made me very aware of what little control I had. The sheer panic wouldn't allow me to move, even if I tried.

Despite my palms suctioned to either side of my head, my ears felt as if they were being stabbed with hot pokers.

Ducking our heads together, Aidan and I pressed into one another hard. Neither of us looked up as the ground lost all sense of stability. The walls and ceiling rained plaster on our heads and shoulders, and I waited for that final blow of something heavier.

Aidan grabbed my arm, and I realized the shaking wasn't as violent.

I slapped a hand on top of his and squeezed to let him know I felt it too. We waited as the world began to right itself again.

The ground was still, but my body jittered with phantom vibrations. My eardrums replaced the sound of the explosion to a droning hum.

I didn't know how the brunt of the blast missed us. As I wiggled my body, plaster fell off my head, coating my legs. I waited for any new pains but felt none.

I peeled open my eyes, one at a time. My limbs were visually still attached, and Aidan was sitting up. Catching my stare, he mouthed, "You okay?"

Nodding, I asked him the same thing, and he nodded.

I shifted to my knees, hearing bits of the ceiling fall off my lap. I squinted over the sturdy pedestal we'd ducked behind; the room was foggy with plaster. I swallowed the tickle in the back of my throat. The bust just over my head had taken a bit of a hit. Pallas Athena's helmet wasn't as pristine. A chunk out of the face and helmet head marred its beauty.

Aidan pointed to the hallway where dark dust mingled with rags. That must have been all that was left of the mummy.

The wall was charred black and had expanded three times its original construction.

The cube caught my eye. It was still in the hallway, but instead of just a little red light, it was calling out metallic beeps, like a timer. *But didn't it already explode*? It had depressed back to its original size, but the sound was unnerving.

"Cody?" I called over the ringing in my ears.

Searching the debris of scrap metal, busts, broken pottery, and rags, I didn't see any real body parts, which was a relief. I didn't think I'd be able to take seeing

Cody like that.

Aidan helped me to my feet with a jerk and immediately let go.

The rhythm of the metallic beeping was quickening, and I felt my heart picking up with the beat.

"Cody!" I kicked at the debris, hoping to spot him through the plaster. "There's a bomb!" *Please don't be dead*, I whispered in the back of my mind, feeling the ache of tears coming close. *Did Damien take Cody instead of me?*

Cody's voice alerted both of us to the displays. He said something unintelligible, but it was *his voice*.

Without thinking, Aidan and I ran through the displays. Aidan shouted Cody's name just as Cody stumbled through the fog, coughing and sputtering.

Seeing him alive and ghostly in the plaster's dust, I ushered him to follow us. "We have to get out of here. That little bomb could go off again."

"The hallway." Cody pointed over my shoulder. "The doorknob was on the door."

"It was locked!" Aidan protested. "There must be another way."

I glanced over my shoulder and shook my head. There was no time to search up and down the museum for a black door when there had been one just beyond the bomb. It would just mean running past it.

The beeps had drawn closer together. There was only a half a second between each metallic alert. "Let's go," I said, and without their consent, I ran.

I knew Cody was close behind me. I could feel his coughs hitting my back.

The red cube illuminated the entrance to the hallway, and Cody pointed over my shoulder. "There!"

Nestled and untouched against the new ash-and-sunder decor was the shiny black door. Exactly where we'd left it.

The intensity of the beeping rose to an almost unbearable volume. My ears throbbed as we shouldered our way into the hallway. As I slowed, Aidan shouldered past both Cody and me and snagged the door. The carved symbol was the same watery dam symbol on the door that had taken Phoebe.

"Wait!" Though I knew he wouldn't.

Aidan tore open the door, and I thought someone was shouting, "*Go, go, go!*" But I couldn't be sure.

Aidan, Cody, and I tumbled through the doorway without the preliminary safety checks. If something had been waiting for us, we'd have been meat.

The door swung behind us as if a gust of wind had caught hold of it, slamming it shut.

Behind the door, there was a very faint boom, like a large explosion that was very, very far away. It shook the carpet at our feet and shuddered through the surrounding walls but didn't rock them enough to throw us off balance—not like the first.

Crowding close together for protection, we ducked our heads until the room went still. Tilting my chin up slowly, it seemed like minutes had passed before anyone ventured to speak.

"Uh, guys?" Aidan broke from the circle first.

Cody and I looked up to see a polished staircase. With the black door at our backs, we stood on an oversized welcome mat that read: *Home Sweet Home.*

I snorted at the little mat and saw Cody and Aidan's feet step away from me.

Looking up to the wide staircase, I could see it was

grand in design. A dark varnish and dainty, thin steps led to a second floor. No photos or paintings adorned the lifeless grey walls, though an extravagant chandelier glowed with candles and crystals overhead.

I reached out and touched the nearest wall with a tentative twitch, fearful that it would wobble like the very first one. It was solid. I pressed my palm to the cool surface.

Aidan asked, "Guess we go up?"

Cody and I grunted our replies. The second balcony was shadowed by the chandelier. Anything could be up there waiting for us.

Aidan reached down and touched the rag around his leg. I had almost forgotten about his injury.

"How is it?" I asked, glancing down at my own poisoned knee. The swelling had decreased and the redness dulled to a pale pink.

Aidan made a point of not looking at me. "Hurts," he replied with a weak, closed-lipped smile.

Cody used his chin to point at the bloodstain on the rag. "What happened?"

"Long story. I'll tell you later," Aidan said. He turned his electric eyes to me. "Come on and no wandering off this time."

I glared at him, though it didn't matter. He turned away before seeing it.

Aidan led the way up the stairs with Cody close behind.

Seeing me hesitate, Cody glanced back and ushered me closer with a snap of his wrist. He wouldn't move until I followed after them. Each stair was only wide enough to fit the balls of our feet. One wrong move and we'd all be sent tumbling down.

Using the railing like the two ahead, I made it to the last step. The balcony overlooked the entrance and was encased in the same regal wood railing.

The hallway spanned in two directions. We could go left or right. It was strange considering all our other Challenges kept us on one path. I realized we'd never been given a choice before, and we all paused, looking left and right.

Aidan sighed after several seconds. "Which way should we go?"

At both ends of the hallway, there were shadows clouding the possible horrors. Whatever surprises waited, we weren't supposed to see them.

Nobody moved. If something terrible happened, whoever made the choice could be held responsible. If I chose, I'd be risking my friends' lives. But that was what this Challenge was, wasn't it? One big gamble that would drain our resources until we finally succumbed. I thought about Damien's test—the cube. It almost cost us all our lives. I didn't trust myself with any further decisions and looked down the first hallway as far as I could. There was nothing but shadow.

I turned to peer down the other side and saw only shadow. No movement, no twitch, no blinking lights—only shadows.

Aidan stood fidgeting beside Cody. He took a deep breath and pointed right. "Let's try that way."

Neither Cody nor I could argue and followed him to our right.

The hallway wasn't affected by the light of the chandelier. Wisps of inky fog spilled prematurely at our feet, eagerly coating the floor in its haze before we reached the obsidian archway.

Cody hooked his finger into the belt loop of my shorts while I reached out and grabbed Aidan's arm. Just before he stepped into the darkness, Aidan glanced back at me. Worry wrinkled his poker-straight eyebrows together.

I linked my fingers with his. It was strange, in a way; just a few hours ago, I'd have cringed at this.

I squeezed his hand and tried to smile at his frown. He'd made the decision I couldn't, and I felt the guilt that accompanied that. If something were to happen, Aidan shouldn't shoulder it, though I didn't want to either.

I glanced behind me as Aidan started forward and saw the perspiration coating Cody's forehead, clumping the excess plaster from the museum's ceiling. He didn't look down at me, only forward, and I finally did the same to realize that Aidan had disappeared behind the wall of darkness. If he wasn't holding my hand, I might have thought we'd lost him.

I held tight to his fingers, feeling his hand twitch, reassuring me of his presence.

Behind me, Cody drew closer, and with just a few steps, we were drowning in the dark.

Our breaths echoed back at us. I kept my free hand out, swaying it from side to side to try and find something solid, something to follow. I could hear Aidan's hand scraping against the wall ahead of us. At least I hoped that was him.

Cody hissed, "Does anyone have matches still?"

"No," I whispered back. *Read had the lighter*, I thought. The thought of him made my heart ache. I hoped he was okay with the others.

Cody leaned closer and said in a hushed tone,

"Maybe we should turn back."

"Keep going," Aidan mumbled. "Keep quiet."

He was right: we were making enough noise just breathing.

As we kept shuffling along, Cody kept stepping on my heels. He grunted an apology.

I ignored him. After a while, my heel had gone numb anyway.

I wondered if we were going to find anything at all. Maybe we'd just walked into our own doom and we were all lost in the Demon's Grave. I took a deep breath as my pendulum search pattern bumped into something.

Startled, I faltered in my step, and Cody stepped on my heel again.

Swinging my arm back, I found the same soft object. It wasn't hard, like a wall. It felt almost squishy and warm.

Tugging back on Aidan's hand, I whispered so softly I barely moved my lips. "Wait…"

I pushed my fingers forward and felt it move, like…skin.

My hand jerked back, but it wasn't fast enough. A beefy, damp hand caught my wrist with cat-like reflexes.

I cried out, and my voice was a bombshell, echoing crisp and shrill in the hallway.

"What is it?" Aidan demanded over my yelp.

"Something has me," I wheezed through my teeth, twisting my wrist to free myself.

Cody released my belt loop and wrapped his arms around my waist, pulling me back, but I wouldn't budge. My arm felt as if it was being pulled out of its socket, and I pleaded for Cody to stop until he released me.

I jerked free of Aidan and heard him gasp a protest.

Balling up my first, I decided to try out something that Phoebe taught me back in junior high.

The knuckle of my middle finger stuck out a little farther from my fist, and I twisted my body in preparation and hoped for good aim in the blindness before punching.

To my surprise, my protruding knuckle hit flesh. The impact shuddered all the way up my arm, and if it weren't for Cody's arms, I'd have fallen off balance.

Phoebe's specialization in "dead arms" must have worked, because the grip on my wrist released, and there was a growling complaint in the dark, the kind that made me think of a feral dog.

Aidan caught my arm and demanded if it was me as Cody grabbed my other arm and yanked. I made a noise similar to a whimper, and together we staggered back the way we'd come.

I scrambled into a jog, keeping my shoulder at the wall. We pitched out into the dim light that was nearly blinding to us.

The chandelier near the stairs was hard to look at, but at least we were in the light again.

Stopping in the lit sanctuary, we turned to the darkness, expecting something to come lumbering out after us. Only our footsteps and movements disturbed the mist.

Several seconds ticked by before we caught our breath and began to relax.

"What happened?" Aidan asked me.

I pointed with a shaky hand toward the darkness. "There's something in there. It grabbed me and wouldn't let go until I gave it one of Phoebe's *dead arms*."

"Those *hurt*," Cody attempted to joke.

I didn't have the strength to laugh, and Aidan just looked confused. "Dead arms?"

"Yeah," I said when Cody didn't offer an explanation. "She'd hit a pressure point with her knuckle, and it would go all numb and tingly."

Aidan's sour expression stopped me. He gestured to the darkness. "Nothing is happening. You don't think that's weird?"

My eyes wandered back to the ebony abyss, waiting for a sign—for something to burst free and find us sitting in the hallway ripe for the picking.

After a few seconds of silence, Cody motioned to our left, growing somber. "Maybe we should check out the other way."

My eyes grew wide. "No." I grabbed Cody by the shoulder, fingers digging. "We should find light first, something to guide us through."

Cody smiled as reassuringly as he could muster. "It's okay, Nora. Aidan and I will check it out."

And just like that, Cody gently shrugged my clawed fingers away. I was ousted.

"We can't separate," I insisted, letting my hand fall. My arms were feeling oddly languid and tired. Crossing them over my chest, I glanced between the guys, chewing on my bottom lip.

Cody shrugged and said to Aidan, "We won't wander far."

Aidan was staring down the unknown hallway. "It's not like we got far the other way."

I didn't want them to go and leave me alone, but I also didn't want to wander into the dark again. The memory of the fleshy cushion beneath my fingertips was still vibrant.

"Can we wait here?" I asked hopefully. "Maybe it'll come to us in the light."

"We can't do that," Aidan said. "We have to keep moving."

I wiped the sweat from my brow, coming away with bits of white plaster. "I can't go," I admitted, avoiding their eyes. "I need to rest for a bit." I could feel them both staring at me and hunched my shoulders with my hands tucked under my armpits.

In the silence, I babbled, "That thing is waiting for us. We have to go right, and you know it. There is no easier route here."

I balled my hands into fists and took a deep breath. This wasn't fair. We needed a rest. *I* needed a rest from all this.

"Here," Cody said.

He held out a white string. I followed it with my eyes and saw it was attached to his t-shirt. I frowned. "What is this for?"

Aidan was already close to the darkened hallway to our left. "Cody and I will go a few feet in and see what's up," he said.

Did they discuss this while I had my head down? I glared at them. "You want to leave me behind?"

"No," Cody flashed his best brown puppy eyes, "it's not that. We just want you to feel safe. Listen, this stupid string has been trying to unravel for days. I'll tug at it every ten seconds so you know we're there."

"Not even," Aidan said, holding his hand out to the hallway as if testing if the darkness were real.

"What if something happens to you?" I asked.

Aidan glanced over his shoulder. "Then we shout and run back."

And run off without me!

Uncurling my fist, I pinched the white string in my fingertips. My stomach did a flip. "Why not just sit for a second?" I protested. Neither of the guys seemed to share my views and stared at me as if I was just a silly girl.

I felt them about to cave to my weakness, and to avoid the look they were sure to give me, I snapped, "Every ten seconds, got it? If I don't feel one, I'm coming after you both, and if something happens to me, it's on your heads for not wanting to rest for fifteen minutes."

I'm such a wuss. I wanted to tell them to whistle or sing something to ensure they were all right, but whatever was in there would be listening to them too.

Cody nodded to me and patted my shoulder before snagging the back of Aidan's shirt as a signal for him to lead.

Hobbling, Aidan didn't look back at me. Maybe he was hoping I'd be swallowed up, disappear, or just leave them to their Challenge. Despite his leg, he probably thought he and Cody had a better chance.

Watching Cody disappear into the looming darkness, I hoped I was wrong and everything would be all right. They'd come back for me and we'd continue. Maybe we could outwit whatever was waiting and just skip ahead. No harm or foul, just a lucky break.

The string in my fingers tugged, and I leaned against the wall, the small reassurance only lasting a second. The moment they were gone, I couldn't hear their footsteps or breaths. I felt the strain of being alone.

Since we had stepped into this Challenge, I'd always had someone with me, someone I could count on to have my back and I theirs. Safety in numbers and all that. But this felt wrong.

If something came racing towards me while they were gone, what would I do? I glanced to the stairs, then to the hallways. None were ideal escape plans.

The second tug of the string lessened the worry a pinch, and I leaned against the wall opposite the staircase. Regulating my breathing, I kept glancing at the shadowed hallway to my left. I could hear them talking in whispers. Then I realized the whispers had changed direction.

Freezing, I listened as I turned my head slowly, trying to pick up where they were coming from. They weren't coming from the hallway to my left; they were coming from downstairs.

As I strained to hear the words, I could tell that several voices had joined in. They melded together in soft tones, then a buzzing took over. Every once in a while, I would catch a word. I scarcely allowed myself to breathe in case I might miss a string of something recognizable, a sentence, a clue, *anything*.

Amongst the rumblings, I heard what almost sounded like Robin's voice. Taking a sharp breath, I heard, "...we never...again?" It sounded exactly like Robin Thurston.

Pushing away from the wall, I caught the banister overlooking the entrance with my free hand. Were they here? Had we met up after all?

The little string in my fingers tugged again.

"Robin?" I called, my voice cracking. But no one was at the base of the stairs.

The whispers continued to bounce off the walls, swirling dizzily.

An unrecognizable hiss voice echoed louder. *"Dismal and dark is the Demon's Grave."* The rest was muddled and camouflaged with the other voices.

"Dismal and dark..." I clapped a hand over my mouth to stifle the words.

The whispers drew closer, or maybe they were louder. It was as if the murmured drone had been given volume-control, and instantly they were blasting through the space at decibels that hurt my head.

I tugged at the string hard, hoping to get Cody's attention, then covered my ears.

I shouted through the amplified cacophony, "Stop. Stop! Aidan? Cody? Come *back*."

The room began to spin as if the voices were stripping me of my balance. I wobbled, trying to keep my hands up against my ears, then realized that I wasn't standing anymore. My body was pitching forward, toward the stairs. I screamed in surprise, releasing the string.

Arms flailing away from my head, I closed my eyes and prepared myself for pain.

Someone caught my hips from behind, digging fingers in. My fall was halted as abruptly as the voices.

My torso jolted forward, but I was able to grab a railing and pull myself upright. *They came back for me*!

The silence was almost as shrill as the voices, and I struggled to focus on the banister to regain my balance. It wasn't coming very easily this time, and I twisted in the grip. My shoulder bumped into Damien.

CHAPTER THIRTY

Damien released me before I could slap him away.

I stumbled, and my back hit the wall, knocking my knees together. Every muscle quivered, begging for relief. Unable to hold myself up, I slid until I was sitting on the floor.

I raised my hands, discovering they moved slower than I commanded. Flexing my fingers in slow motion, I stretched out one leg, but it wouldn't straighten the way I wanted. I touched my temples with both hands. The vertigo hadn't lost its edge, and it felt like marbles were racing each other against the inside of my skull. "What's going on?"

Damian stood just a few feet away. I rolled my eyes up to see him staring down at me, the chandelier at his back. "You're being punished for someone else's mistake." He almost sounded apologetic, which made me giggle.

Like a sneeze, it escaped, and I quickly squashed it

297

as black dots danced between us.

My hands touched the floor on either side of me, and I realized I was tilting to the right.

Trying to concentrate past the bumping marbles, I remembered Robin's voice and asked, "What mistake?" *Robin had been called a cheat by the doppelgängers.* "Whose mistake?"

"That doesn't matter right now," Damien answered softly.

Nausea heated my face and clamped down on my jaw. Closing my eyes only made the spinning worse. I realized I'd dropped the string. Warning Cody and Aidan wouldn't work. I couldn't hear them in the darkness. No whispers, talking, shuffling of feet. *Where are you guys*? I opened my eyes.

"What are you doing here?"

Damien was inspecting my outstretched leg. The red swelling on my knee had faded to a heated pink just seen under the mud that crusted my sneakers and calves. "You're very lucky to have survived this long."

"This long?" I hissed his last words, my voice dripping with venom. "This is bullsh…" I choked as hot saliva moistened my gums, forcing me to swallow. *I'm going to ralph right in front of Damien…son of a bitch.*

"Your nightmare," Damien mused. "Did the spiders and scorpions turn out well? I see that you've been stung without much consequence."

I didn't bother following his gaze and glared at him through the tangle of loose hair. The warmth in my stomach fought alongside the nausea. I remembered it from our last encounter, but it wasn't making things easier.

"Control your emotions," he advised coldly.

"Humans are so weak with their feelings. It's an enigma how your race made it in your realm."

Gritting my teeth, I choked down the anger, taking his advice even if I stubbornly didn't want to. As I took a deep breath, I felt my heartbeat begin to slow, just a little, the heat in my belly quaking but not squeezing.

Uncomfortable, I shifted against the wall. "We didn't trespass, did we? You made us come in because you were, what? Lonely? Psychotic? I didn't tell Aidan to open that door. Someone else did."

Damien's smile disappeared. Something tenebrous flashed across his face, and I realized I might have hit something. He recovered quickly, the pretentious expression dancing back in place. "I didn't make Aidan open the door. You spoke those words not of your own free will?"

At first, I thought he must have been pulling my leg. Blinking back the surprise, I shook my head. "It was like someone else was controlling me."

"I'm insulted you'd think I'd stoop so low."

My eyes narrowed. "You shouldn't be. All of that crap that you just threw us into…" My stomach clenched with the return of the heat against my insides, and I swallowed the building saliva, desperate not to vomit.

"That *crap* was what the Challenge offered. May I remind you that you received the messages and you still opened the door despite the Keeper's warnings plain on the wall," Damien said and stepped closer.

The instant he did, the meager control I held over my stomach loosened.

I twisted in time for my stomach to convulse, and the first wave of vomit slapped the floor. My eyes teared, and I gagged when I saw the long, dark hair amongst stomach bile.

Before I could blubber my horror, another throe struck, and I was subjected again. Wave after wave hammered into my stomach until I was left with a sore throat and a mixture of tears and snot dripping off the end of my nose.

Spitting, I rocked back, kicking myself away along the wall. The smell was overwhelming, and I held my hand to my face to try and protect myself from another attack.

My entire body was shaking, and my skin prickled with a chill.

My head felt inflated, and I asked through my hand, my voice high pitched and shaking, "Whose mistake was that? Shit, Damien, shit!" I choked on the bitterness; I'd rather lick the floor than taste what was left in my mouth, but I thankfully restrained myself.

Damien didn't answer. Bridging the gap between us, he knelt.

The back of my head smacked against the wall when he reached up but didn't stop him from placing a hand on my forehead. It was cool and inviting compared to the throbbing heat. I could almost imagine steam twisting off my skin when his chilled fingers cupped over my forehead. Part of me was scared, letting the demon touch me, while the other was relieved that the torture was ebbing.

How bad was the mistake to lose their hair? It had been long and dark, which could have meant Robin's, but her hair wasn't that long. The worst part was that it had been in my stomach. My hand still up to my mouth, I tried to disguise a popping gag reflex with a cough.

Damien's touch soothed the heat in my skin, and I met his eyes.

Shaking, I felt the tears welling, this time not from the strain of vomiting but from the fear bubbling to the surface. I didn't want him to see me like this. It was like giving him some inappropriate compliment for getting to me. But that's what he did. He got to me.

When we spoke last, he said I was a threat and he wasn't sure about me, and here he was. He was comforting in a twisted way, but it didn't make sense. He gave me this punishment; he shouldn't have been trying to make me feel better. But he was.

I tried to read what he might be thinking, but his eyes were just black and watching mine, as if trying to read me at the same time.

Sniffling, I looked away, to the messy floor. "Was it Robin? Was that her hair?" I licked my lips behind my hand and tried to hold back the wave of emotions. I struggled to keep them deadened, like him. "Is Robin dead?"

Placing three fingers on my wrist, he lowered my hand from my mouth, making me look at him. He said soberly, "Robin is not dead."

My eyes narrowed, searching for a sign of a lie. His lips didn't twitch; his eyes didn't brighten in amusement or look away.

He got to you again, Nora, a voice whispered in the back of my mind.

Pulling my arm from his touch, I latched it around my stomach. "Why are you here?" I demanded, blinking back the watery vision. "Was it just to watch me play out the punishment?"

Damien removed his hand and stood up fast enough

I'd have gotten dizzy. Turning away, he said in a calm, even tone, "There is a game you mortals call 'hide and seek.' It is very simple, and I know that you all know how to play. I think that will be your next Challenge."

I shook my head, confused. "Why are you telling me this?" I asked, happy to feel the swelling in my head evaporating along with the dizziness. My stomach still felt as if it had taken a beating, but it could have been worse. It could still be in the beating.

Damien spoke with his back to me, facing the banister overlooking the entrance below. "Don't let him catch you in this one."

"Concerned?" I mocked, though the smug smile wouldn't surface. It could have been such a good hero moment, but let's face it, I was no hero.

He didn't answer, didn't move, just stared at what lay below.

"Great. Thanks," I mumbled, then added quickly, "Damien?"

He looked over his shoulder at me as I sat up slowly, testing out my shaky limbs. The chills were leaving me, but I was still feeling weak.

"When we were in the last Challenge, what was that little cube?"

"The crystal that disintegrated the mummy?"

I nodded once, afraid I might set off my stomach again.

He seemed pleased at the question, though he didn't smile. "That was a technological device formed in the Brenhenos province. It will first destroy all life visible, then it will count down for an explosion to destroy the area of the kill, to leave no evidence. Activated by a..." he paused, "...a certain touch, it has been responsible for the deaths of thousands of Brenn tribes. Nearly knocked them into extinction."

I frowned. "So I activated it."

He didn't respond.

"Did…" I rolled onto my hands and knees, easing back onto my haunches. "Did you come here to help me?" It didn't make any sense, unless he felt guilty. Did demons feel guilt? Or maybe he wanted me to trust him.

The broad shoulders rose as he looked me over, distaste crinkling his nose and lips up. "I don't…know why I came," he said, sounding earnest.

"To watch a punishment?" I offered.

His eyes flickered away from mine, and he started to speak, eyebrows pinching together. "There's something about you."

"That's rich. First, you insult my family and tell me I'm a threat." I tapped my head against the wall to shake the marbles loose. "Then tell me that I can't say anything about Nell."

"You won't."

"I won't?" I felt the smile before I could stop it and snickered, hearing the edge of hysteria until I coughed.

"No, you won't." Damien's jaw twitched, and he crossed his arms over his chest. "If you truly feel the need, know that there's a blonde I'm particularly fond of. Her death would more than suffice for your lapse in judgment."

Stiffening, I stared at him, afraid to move.

Damien nodded as if we'd come to an understanding, but I didn't think it was the same one. "What about Aidan?" I asked. "You didn't seem to like his last name much."

"That is between him and me," Damien said in a way that ended the conversation.

I pushed off the wall and tried to get up, but my rubber legs kept me from getting past my hands and knees. "Just a second. What does Nell have to do with anything? Does she have something to do with Aidan?" *Something important to this Challenge*, I thought.

Damien's dark eyes narrowed, and I realized my mistake.

I shook my head. "How?" I swallowed, trying to find the words I didn't want the answer to. "How is this supposed to end?"

At this, he raised his eyebrows. "Don't you know? You'll end up staying." The obsidian eyes flickered over my shoulder. "I think it's time your friends returned."

The gruff scream from the hallway was my first hint of a presence. I struggled to my feet but needed the wall for support.

Aidan limped from the shadows, eyes wide and frightened. He grabbed my camisole and dragged me down the stairs without waiting. I stumbled, my balance still off.

Damien was nowhere in sight.

"Where's Cody?" I cried, looking over my shoulder, waiting for our friend to emerge from the shadows.

Aidan didn't reply, breathing heavy enough to wheeze. He yanked me around the staircase where a new door stood beside the old one. I didn't get a chance to see the carving on the front before we were stumbling through in a blur.

Aidan let me go and slammed the door shut. He locked it using the large deadbolt above the doorknob. Twisting around to face me, he leaned against the door, gasping for air.

"Aidan!" I cried, feeling the weakness in my arms as I grabbed his shoulders.

He flinched at first, raising his hands to fend me off.

"What happened to Cody?" I burst, panic rising. "We just locked Cody in that Challenge, Aidan!"

Hitting the back of his head against the door behind him, he gritted his teeth and wouldn't look at me. "*Railing torment lies within.*"

The words from the wall, the only message I didn't get before entering the Demon's Grave. They sent a chill down my spine, and I wasn't sure why.

Stepping away from Aidan as if stung, I noticed the new room for the first time. It was like stepping back in time.

A brown, stained-glass lamp shone light into the room, revealing an old seventies-style couch and matching chair decorated in orange and brown flowers against the wood-paneled walls. A flattened brown shag carpet cushioned my feet, but there was a foot traffic trail from the couch to a small room across from a set of stairs.

It appeared we were safe for now. Turning back to Aidan, I asked again, trying to make my voice sound rational. "What happened to Cody?" Maybe there was something we could still do to save him. The door hadn't faded out of view yet; there was still time.

Aidan took a deep breath, wiping away the sweat on his brow. "Cody and I found ourselves outside. We looked all around and finally found the door that we apparently came through. We were about to open it when it began to rain and snow at the same time and hard. Cody began to get panicky and told me not to open the door. So I didn't."

I realized my legs were shaking and led Aidan away from the door. Circling a brittle-looking coffee table with a single lit candle in the middle, we sat down on the couch.

The ease of sitting made my muscles sigh. "Then what happened?" I urged, cupping Aidan's arm hoping it was comforting, but I could have strangled him for stalling.

"Then we just stood there, and suddenly we heard these whispers. They just came out of nowhere. They began to get louder and louder. They told us all of the messages that spelled DOOR and said that we were going to die. Suddenly, Cody began to scream and shouted that they would not get him just like in his dream. Then this shadow," Aidan made a wavy motion with his hands imitating claws, "it came from nowhere and stopped right in front of Cody. I didn't know what to do, so I opened the door and grabbed Cody to pull him in. But he was gone. He was just sucked into the shadow." Aidan rubbed the front of his face with his hands as if to rid himself of the image. "Like it ate him."

His last words struck me odd. The shadow man had swallowed Cody up without a fighting chance, just like the others. Damien was picking them off one by one but not killing them. Why?

Aidan moaned, "I couldn't save him. I ran."

"It's okay, Aidan. It wasn't your…"

"It's not okay," he hissed through gritted teeth. "I got scared and ran before it could get me. If only I didn't listen to Cody. Maybe he'd be here with us instead of in that…that…" Aidan shook his head, unable to continue. Instead, he turned to me, face red. "Where are we?"

I stiffened and glanced left and right, pondering our escape routes. *Hide and seek. Don't get caught*, I thought.

Aidan asked, "What?"

Oh crap, did I speak out loud?

"I, uh…Damien told me about the next Challenge," I said, eyes darting from the stairs to the little room that looked like a bedroom from my angle.

Aidan's spine straightened so quickly his arm jerked from under my hands.

I wanted to change the betrayal I saw on his face and spoke quickly. "He told me that we were playing a game of hide and seek."

Aidan's pinched mouth opened just enough to say, "Now the demon is giving you personal attention. We were out running into shadows, and he was talking to you?"

I hesitated; it wasn't like that.

"He…" I suddenly decided not to tell Aidan about the punishment. He was worried about Cody. He didn't need to be thinking about who else could be hurt. "He just told me about the next Challenge."

Aidan stared at me, his gaze swimming with suspicion. "What is going on, Nora? What is it he knows about you? And don't say 'nothing,' because I know you're lying."

"Aidan," I pleaded, feeling the urgency of our situation.

"*Don't*," he snapped, glaring at me. "You're going to tell me how you know Damien."

My lips formed a thin, tight line of disapproval.

Breathing through my nose, I tried to calm my initial reaction, which was to start yelling. Damien brought it all up and left me to deal with this. "I barely remember what happened. He's tricking you by saying my past is somehow involved and that I had met him before. I would have remembered."

"Nora," he warned.

I took a deep breath. "We don't have a lot of time."

"I'm not moving until you tell me what's going on." He crossed his arms.

If his pale eyes could hold sparks, they did today, and I realized that if I didn't tell him, the small bits of trust we had collected over the last few Challenges could be shattered. We'd end up like the Other Nora and Aidan.

Don't tell the Birket about Nell, he'd said and then did this to me. He was making the rift between us widen.

Clearing my throat, it took more effort than it should have to speak, but I pronounced each word carefully, having not said them for over a decade. "They murdered my twin sister in front of me when I was five."

CHAPTER THIRTY-ONE

The silence stretched, and though Aidan finally decided to look at me, I didn't want to look at him. The last thing I wanted was sympathy or worse, the accusations in his eyes.

"Aidan?"

He grunted.

Twisting my camisole in my hands, I asked, "Remember when you said you sometimes felt strange around me?"

"You've asked this already," he said.

"Was it like you knew I was coming before I got there?"

"No." He sounded serious and cleared his throat. "It was more like there was something wrong with you."

Surprised, my eyes snapped back to him to see if he was serious.

His chin lowered as he glowered at me. "Like you didn't belong here, like you were never meant to be in the same room as everyone else, but you were." He took a deep breath through his nose. "I guess I don't have to ask you about your experience."

Like I didn't belong? I gaped at him, unsure how to proceed. *Don't tell the Birket*, Damien had said.

At my silence, Aidan stood up and began pacing the small room. Behind him, the black door was replaced by a white one. "You said *they*…"

"What?" I stood up with him, clenching my fists around the bottom of my shirt, desperate for something to do.

"You said *they* killed your twin sister."

His back was to me, and I felt the chill from where I stood. Licking my lips, I nodded, knowing he couldn't see me. "There were three of them. A woman and two guys, and no, neither of the men was Damien." I stalked toward the white door and tried the handle. It was locked.

He still wouldn't look at me as he paced the rectangular room, his shadow following along the wall so I could track him without looking.

"What if one *was* Damien? You were young and…"

Tugging at my shirt, I sighed. "One was a fat, blonde guy and the other was a skinny guy with a stupid jacket that had JWD on the sleeve. Besides, I already asked Damien."

"You asked Damien?" Aidan paused in his pacing. I could see his shadow face me before he snorted, "Because a demon wouldn't lie."

I held up my hand and counted on my fingers, still facing the white door. "Neither talked like Damien. They didn't look like him, and we weren't even close to your grandpa's place. It was a different city entirely." I grit my teeth and snapped, "Remember, Aidan? The place where *all* this started. How come you're not on trial?"

Aidan stopped pacing. I had hit the nerve. I seem to be getting good at that.

With enough courage to turn around, I let my emotions guide my attack. "Cody, Phoebe, and Read are trapped off in some shadow. Robin could be seriously hurt or worse."

"Why would Robin be seriously hurt? You don't think she's dead?"

I had slipped up, but I wasn't about to stop. "And I can't tell you about my family tragedy because he'll kill Phoebe. Do you know how many shrinks my parents threw me at? I don't think there'd be enough in the world after this!"

"Nora, stop, please," Aidan began.

"Stop? You wanted me to start!" I shouted so loud the back of my throat ached and my already weak legs wobbled. Slapping a hand to the wall, I waited for the scathing retort. I couldn't even look at him as I'd already said too much and my head was pounding with adrenaline that should have been put to better use.

If I wasn't too tired, I might have just decided to cry. Not to get him to shut up, but because I needed a release. All this pressure had been building with no escape valve.

Aidan's soft voice said, not far away, "I shouldn't have accused you."

Frustration launched me away from him. *He doesn't mean it,* I thought.

To get away, I stepped into the only other room, a bedroom.

I took a deep breath through my mouth, letting it out slowly. I heard the shudder in my chest. *This was stupid.* I couldn't let my emotions get the better of me, just like Damien said. I touched my stomach, feeling it twist and warm, though I wasn't sure if it was out of hunger or anger.

This could be what caused the rift for the doppelgängers, not the story of my sister or Damien's lies. Crossing my arms, I surveyed the little bedroom, trying to form a logical solution. Weapons, I needed weapons and a hiding place. *Couldn't get caught, couldn't be controlled by emotions.*

My bottom lip quivered, and I tried to make notes of the room to distract myself. Black candles crowded the bedside tables, the shelves, and the dresser, snaking tendrils of wax over edges and to the floor.

In the center of the room was a black four-poster bed with a sheer, lacy canopy. Just seeing the fluffy, dark comforter seduced my every muscle to lie down. After my massive puke-fest, my body felt as if it were filled with sand.

Sitting on the edge of the bed, I rested but wouldn't allow myself to lie back. My nerves were shot, my emotions running so deep and hard I was exhausted. I was puttering on low fuel and knew I should be focused on hiding. Ahead of me, the stairs beckoned me to keep moving. Turning my head, I noticed a stone crucifix on the wall above the headboard. To my right was a window, though outside it was a blurry grey as wet snow splattered the glass.

Aidan mentioned that, before Cody disappeared, it had started to rain and snow at the same time. Could Cody be outside right now? Or in here with us?

"Aidan?" I asked, watching the window. In my fascination, it took me a moment to realize he hadn't answered.

Standing slowly, with the help of one of the bed posts, I poked my head out into the living room to see Aidan sitting on the couch. His body was hunched with his elbows on his knees, careful to avoid the bloodstained towel tied to his leg. Peering over his fingertips at the white door, he was ashen.

Glancing at me, his eyes widened before he motioned me to stay quiet.

Leaning against the doorway, I listened.

Footsteps squeaked against what sounded like packed snow. They were pacing in front of the door, back and forth.

Stiffening for several seconds, we waited for the next move. The footsteps kept pacing, and I thought of our warning. We had to hide. I motioned to Aidan to come to me.

He stood up, eyes darting to the door. He ventured a single step, but a new noise froze him before he took a second. Mumbled words could be heard through the door.

Don't get caught.

Flailing at Aidan to hurry, the doorknob twisted, and my heart stopped. I think I stopped breathing until I heard the lock rattling, but the door remained closed.

Aidan jerked off the couch and limped on tippy-toes across the living room.

The instant he was in arms' reach, I grabbed his shirt and pulled him close to whisper in his ear. "We have to hide."

Aidan nodded and peered inside the bedroom. "Let's

go outside before it can come in," he breathed and limped to the window.

Flipping the lock at the top, Aidan gripped the small handle at the base and tugged, gently at first. The window shook but otherwise didn't budge. Taking a deep breath, he strained, his face reddening with the added force, and this time the window slid as if layered in grease and slammed into the frame above. He might as well have just held up a sign that said: "*Victims Seeking Abuse: Sign Up Sheet Here.*"

A single, icy strike snuffed most of the candles. Bullet-sized rain and snow pelted my face, numbing skin.

Jumping back, I held up my hands to protect myself and staggered into the archway. Stealing a glance at the main white door, I saw splinters beside the doorknob as if the Hulk were on the other side.

"Aidan, we have to go upstairs," I said, though my voice disappeared in the wind. The steps behind me reached a landing before curling up along the wall. The second floor was probably where we should hide.

Struggling to close the window, Aidan jerked hard on the handle, and it slammed shut, the sound echoing in my head.

Before I could tell Aidan about the door, there was a sharp *snap* from the living room, and I noticed the doorknob was gone, leaving splinters on the floor. The door slammed inward followed by a rough, male's triumphant cry.

Racing into the bedroom before I could be spotted, I pointed to the bed and dropped to my belly.

The shrieking wind ceased as the front door shut, and I could hear boots clomping in the next room.

"You can run, but you can't hide," came the husky voice from the living room.

Together, we slid under the box spring, shuffling to the middle before turning our faces to the archway. I half expected Aidan to grab my hand, but this time he didn't. His hands clutched the carpet, his focus on the doorway.

The leathery creak of wet shoes and deep rasps in the living room was all we could hear. We should have run for the stairs while we had the chance, I thought.

I stopped fidgeting when two black combat boots stomped into view.

They paused in the threshold as I heard the man say between heavy breaths, "Come out, come out, wherever you are." He sounded like a long-time smoker.

The boots plodded toward the window, and I heard the latch *click* back into place. He paused there, facing away from us. "You're not out there," he concluded, self-assured.

Rigid, I clasped my fingers together, digging nails into the back of my hands. Any second he'd poke his head under the bed and see us lying here like sitting ducks. Was he going to be deformed like the people from Aidan's nightmare? Was he a cannibal? A ghoulish monster? My imagination was abruptly interrupted by his voice.

"Are you here?" the voice asked, but it was far away. Blinking, I peered around the bedroom to see he wasn't with us anymore and breathed out.

Aidan and I were locked in place.

Until Boots went upstairs, I didn't think either of us would budge. Even then, where would we go? For all I knew, Boots could have freakish hearing and find us the moment we shuffled.

"All right, don't worry. I'll find you." There was a crude snicker in the next room. "Actually, maybe you should worry, because I *will* find you."

Chapter Thirty-Two

"Hey, Aidan," said the man in a sing-song voice. "Yeah, it's me, Aidan. You've gotta remember me. I was that kid you gave that little video camera to. We were pals, right? Gee, that camera sure did come in handy." There was the raspy snicker again. "So did that money I found in your backpack."

Aidan tucked his arms closer to his body and didn't respond to my glances.

Casually, the man kept talking as if Aidan and I were standing right in front of him. "Yeah, you know, it's me, Jordan Peterson. Remember when you kissed the bathroom floor by the urinals on Valentine's Day? Just so you know, that was totally piss. I know that weasel Jake tried to say otherwise. The whole thing was Mick's idea, funny as Hell. You remember Mick, right?"

I prayed that he'd walk up the stairs, but he didn't. He kept talking and pacing just outside of the room, taunting my patience. "Or the time we stuffed you in your gym locker? I heard the janitor found you hours after the school was closed." He rumbled a gravelly chuckle before stepping back into view.

"Hey." Jordan sounded like he was smiling. "From what I hear, you have a sweet little thing with you. I'm sure that she doesn't want to be there with you. Just like Tracy Domo in the eighth grade. Though you could have kept that one."

Aidan winced as Jordan stepped farther into the bedroom again, and I could smell the sharp sweetness of a cigar.

"Fuck, she was a terrible lay." Jordan chortled.

In grade *eight*? I looked at Aidan, but he hadn't flinched.

Jordan wandered to the side of the bed where Aidan lay. He dropped to one knee, and I realized we were done.

I scooted over and nudged Aidan to follow. We could get to the other side of the bed and maybe make a run for it. It was doubtful we'd make it, but it was better than just sitting here.

A hand shot under the bed. It latched onto Aidan's calf and yanked.

Aidan cried out as he was dragged away so fast that I barely had time to react. Clawing my hand out, I barely touched Aidan's arm before it was ripped away. His piercing, wide-eyed gaze caught mine just before he disappeared, and Jordan was back to his feet.

My breath was quick and panicked as I shuffled closer to the other side of the bed before a hand could snake around my ankle too.

I heard slaps and Aidan's cries, then a massive *thunk*

that shook the bed and Aidan groaned.

Slapping a hand on the bed, I used it to help me stand. Moving too fast made my head spin, but I had a barrier between the two guys and me.

Jordan was tall with an ample amount of muscle in his arms, despite the beer gut. He had a dark buzz cut to go with the combat boots, camouflage pants, and green wife-beater. I bet he had a collection of knives in his parents' basement, too.

Jordan was holding Aidan upside down by his ankles.

"Hey!" I cried, catching Jordan's attention. I couldn't see Aidan's face; it was blocked by the bed.

Jordan looked up, revealing numerous pale scars against his dark tan. Maybe he played with the knife collection, I concluded. It was either that or enough knife fights to intimidate the crap out of me, and *that* was working.

"Hey, this must be your girlfriend." Jordan shook Aidan's ankle for attention.

"Let him go!" I shouted, more out of reflex than common sense.

Unconcerned, Jordan shook Aidan hard enough to make him gurgle and blow spit bubbles. It didn't sound good, and Aidan wasn't struggling the way he should. Remembering the sound I'd heard, I hoped he wasn't too out of it.

"Hey, darling, how about you come with me?" Jordan's brown eyes met mine, and he started to leer but stopped. "Are you as dirty as you look, girl?" He even laughed at his own joke.

Awful.

My eyes flickered around the room for a weapon.

The wax on the candles might be hot enough for a distraction, the holders looked flimsy and plastic, but the stone cross on the wall above the bed…

"I said, let him go," I repeated, clutching the bottom of my camisole with one hand.

"Me? Let geek boy go? But we have so much catching up to do. Look at who you're hanging out with, sweetie." He swung Aidan a little again. "He can't defend himself, let alone a girl."

He said *girl* as if I were a lower class. I wasn't easily offended, but that last part stung. If I were to face off against Jordan, I'd probably lose, but I didn't plan on being unarmed—not if I could help it.

With slow, careful movements, I stepped up onto the bed. The bad side was I was within arm's reach of Jordan. The good side was I was closer to the stone crucifix. One good swing with that against Jordan's face might give us a head start, if Aidan were faking it. *Please be faking it.*

"Jordan, let him go." I gritted my teeth, balancing so that my move would come as a surprise. I hoped. If he saw it coming, he'd have us both. In that moment, I realized I really didn't know what I was doing. Everything could go wrong.

Jordan raised his eyebrows. "A little hostile, aren't we, sweetie?"

Repressing a sneer, I asked, "Why won't you let him go?"

"Because," he said simply.

"Why not let him go?" I repeated as patiently as I could. I reminded myself that it would have been the same response my seven-year-old sister would give if she wanted to stalemate me and save her hide.

Jordan looked at me and smiled. "You're a curious one." He looked back down at Aidan. "Isn't she, Aidan?"

Aidan moaned; the blood must have been rushing to his head. From my new angle, I could see his face was scarlet.

"Can I have her?" Jordan chuckled, looking down at his victim.

My hand shot out, grabbing the stone cross. It was heavy, and I dropped it behind my back as Jordan swung Aidan one more time. I wasn't close enough to attack, plus being higher meant he'd see it coming.

I needed a surprise—I needed to hide.

Jumping back off the bed, leaving the obstacle between us, I said, "Sure, you can have me. But you have to let Aidan go first." I forced a smile. He was stronger than me, faster, and probably had plenty of nasty ideas in that thick head of his, but if the focus of the game was hide and seek, I'd find my opportunity. At least I hoped so. I sprang for the doorway, careful to keep the crucifix out of sight.

"You can't carry him and catch me at the same time!" I shouted and raced from the other room.

Taking two steps at a time, I scrambled up the staircase. I wasn't as fast as I knew I could be. My body wasn't allowing any more strain, and by the time I reached the top, I wanted to collapse.

Luckily, this new hallway wasn't entirely shrouded in shadows, but the one on the left still was. It was similar to the previous Challenge.

My choices were simple: lose Jordan in the shadows or take my chances with the light and find a place to lock him in or hit him with something better than the stone.

Peering down the stairs, I saw Jordan skidding to a stop at the base. Aidan wasn't with him, which worried me.

The second our eyes met, Jordan bolted after me.

Veering right, I saw three closed doors to choose from. I opened the second one and closed it behind me with a jerk just as I heard the heavy combat boots reach the top of the stairs. Or maybe that thudding was my heart.

Spinning around, I faced a sitting room, much like the one downstairs, except it was classier. There were dark chairs and a velvety sofa surrounding a heavy black coffee table. Thick, dark curtains that touched the floor and were wide enough to hide a person framed a bay window.

Scurrying to the maroon drapes, I swept them away from the wall before slipping behind. They fluttered back in place, settling around my body as I pressed my back against the wall. I prayed I didn't make them look misshapen.

My knees buckled, and I squeezed my eyes shut, begging my body to hold me up for just a little while longer. I strained to listen over the rain.

With brute force, Jordan burst through the door, making me jump.

My cheeks puffed as my swear stopped cold.

"Hey, baby, I'm here," he gloated.

Holding my breath, I squeezed every muscle to be still. His combat boots squished with water against the carpet, drawing closer.

I barely heard him sigh over the thunder in my head.

I waited for the curtains to move violently to the side. If he found me, I'd be trapped. My hand readjusted on the crucifix at my side, slowly, carefully.

Outside the curtains, Jordan swore under his breath, and I heard a jolting thump as a piece of furniture slammed against a wall. His heavy footsteps began to fade, but he didn't close the door behind him. I wondered if I was going to get off that easily.

I waited, my fingers restless and wiggling, until I heard another door open with a bang. "Where are you, sweetie?" he roared in filthy delight.

I peeked out from my hiding spot. Jordan was nowhere to be seen.

Creeping from the drapes, I tip-toed to the open door. Was he out there waiting to pounce like a wildcat? The idea would have been comical if it were anyone but Scar-Face.

Silence haunted the hallway, and I poked my head out. I could hear those boots squeaking in the first room I had passed.

"Come on, little girl," Jordan snapped from Room One, his patience wavering.

Unexpectedly, I saw his boot thump out of Room One.

Flinging myself back into Room Two before I could be seen, I pushed my back up against the wall, trying to sink into it. I tried my best not to fidget as the heavy footsteps came closer, echoing in the hall. My heart outpaced his steps five to one, and I shied away from the threshold. Watching the door, I wished it had a lock on it.

I saw one of the chairs shoved to the wall. It must have been what he had pushed on his way out. I could hide behind that for a while, but if he came within a few feet, he'd see me.

As I decided what to do, Jordan passed my room.

I peeked along the wall, watching as he stalked in the direction of Room Three. The door flung open, and he laughed. "Don't be afraid, girl. I won't hurt you, much. You might even like it." With that, he erupted in loutish hee-hawing that propelled me into the hallway.

I glanced at Room Three and noticed the edge of the black door. It was wide open, and I knew Jordan was inside by the sound of his voice. He was uttering chiding nonsense. All the other doors were white, except for door three. Creeping forward to get a better look, I tried to hasten my steps. As I drew closer, I could make out a carving of what looked like a plume of smoke or a cloud.

It was our door, all right.

I could just run through it alone, but the idea of going through a Challenge without Aidan made my stomach turn. As much as I wanted to save myself, I couldn't leave him behind on purpose. He could be hurt downstairs.

Dancing on tip toes, I made my decision and darted away from the black door. Keeping my footsteps light and noiseless in my sneakers, I shuffled down the stairs, hoping that a step wouldn't creak under my weight.

Above, I could hear Jordan's distant shouts as I rushed into the bedroom where Aidan was floundering to climb to his feet.

Blood trailed down his face from a gash in his forehead, staining the bedspread. Wiping at his face, he smeared the crimson across his temple and cheek and sniffled. Looking to his hand, he stared at the bright red as if it were bright green instead.

Hurrying to his side, I put his arm around my neck and helped him to his feet, leading him to the doorway. My legs screamed a protest, and each step was agony with his weight leaning against me. I wrapped an arm around Aidan's waist, pressing the crucifix to his side.

Aidan attempted to lift his own weight, fresh blood accompanying the streaks down his face.

"Come on, Aidan," I whispered. "We have to get out of here."

Aidan made a feeble noise; he was trying to move his legs faster, but it didn't help much, and I couldn't just carry him out of the bedroom.

We fumbled to reach the stairs when Aidan breathed in sharp.

My head snapped up to see Jordan at the top of the steps, brown eyes blazing. His bulk filled the entire passageway.

A shot of fear punched my guts, and I almost dropped Aidan.

Jordan reached into his back pocket and produced, with the snap of his wrist, a hefty switchblade.

Gesturing at me with the knife, he started to plod down the stairs. "Found you. The game's over, sweetie," he said. "You're mine now."

Chapter Thirty-Three

I glanced at Aidan. We could try and run to the front door and into the storm, but I didn't think we'd make it. Our black door was up those steps past the bully, and I was certain he was going to make it difficult.

Aidan squinted at me before closing his eyes.

"Stay awake," I said.

His head bobbed in what could have been a nod before he whispered, his voice barely audible, "You can't carry me."

At first I thought against it, but the way my thighs trembled, I knew it would be easier to save my strength for the fight. What little strength I had anyway.

In the process of setting Aidan on the floor, I collapsed with him. I wanted to give up, I realized. I wanted the weakness and hounding consternation to end and never be felt again. I wanted to be warm and safe in my bed and know that my family and friends were safe. How could I have taken those things for granted? I sat on the floor, feeling the shag carpet against my legs. *What could I do?* I thought despairingly.

Jordan's clunky boots descending the stairs pinched me from my daze. I looked up, and my stomach dropped upon seeing the triumphant smile on his scarred face. He stopped at the landing, looking down at us like he'd won, the handle of his hunting knife turning in his anxious hand.

No, a voice urged in my head. *You can't give up to his guy. What about Robin, Phoebe, Read, and Cody? What about Aidan?*

Aidan's was drawn tight and pale. I couldn't just give up. There had to be some escape. Renewed with a sense of defiance, I asked, "Why are you doing this?" I gripped the stone in my hand tighter, though I wasn't sure how effective I'd be at wielding it. Jordan had a knife, and I had a bloodied college guy.

Jordan smiled. "The little dork didn't tell you?" he asked.

It felt like my brain sloshed when I shook my head, and I winced.

"Well, I guess that that would be understandable." Jordan glanced between us. "I wouldn't admit I was a loser like him, either."

"Oh?" I asked, feigning interest. I inched back on my knees, gauging a proper swing.

"Have you ever wondered why Aidan came to Leland? Of all the places he'd been before, he chose some small city to go to college? That doesn't seem a little fucked up?" Jordan cocked his head to the side.

I swallowed hard. "His family moved around a lot. It's also none of my business." I scooted back until my ankles were level with Aidan's hip.

"Yeah," Jordan snorted. "I forgot you two aren't supposed to like each other. Sometimes, an inheritance can call to a person."

I shook my head. "You're talking gibberish," I said and glanced at Aidan. He wasn't moving, which sent alarm coursing through me.

Leaning forward to take Aidan's hand, I squeezed, waiting for him to oblige me with a response. He didn't.

Jordan's gravelly voice cut through what self-control I had left. "I met Aidan when we were in junior high. He made the mistake of insulting me in front of Mariah Fields, of all people."

Keep stalling, a voice inside my head urged, though the other part wanted to panic. Every instinct said to run and hide, tugging at me with ghostly finger. Instead, I stalled. "Who's Mariah Fields?"

Jordan snapped a harsh laugh and paused in his descent. "She was this girl I tried asking out, but Aidan got in the way."

I frowned. I couldn't imagine Jordan's borderline hostility impressing a girl. Aidan was always helping people, it seemed. It would be only natural for him to save a girl from being bullied into a date. I felt a little swelling of pride for my new friend. He had always tried to protect me even when he made it clear he was suspicious.

Jordan swaggered down the last few steps, leering unpleasantly. "So I paid Aidan here a little visit." He kicked Aidan's foot, which flopped, making my stomach crawl. "After that, I got quite fond of the kid. He always had money and some cool merchandise that went like crazy on my own little market."

"Like the camera," I said flatly, glaring.

Jordan shrugged. "He fought back when most of the others would stop after a while, if they tried at all."

The aspiration of revenge writhed in the back of my mind. I hated that I'd been was so distant before. Even if he did feel like I didn't belong, he hadn't acted on it, and I had. I tried to exclude him whenever I could. I'd cast him out the way Jordan had. What kid would play with the one who wore a bull's-eye?

I gnashed my teeth. I knew I'd have to move fast for a good swing. I'd have to aim for his head, eventually.

My gaze landed on Jordan's knees instead. I'd have to get him to fall first. The living room was devoid of any weapon other than the lamp, and I didn't want to jeopardize a source of light. The pale candle atop the thin candleholder might be a weapon, if it was heavy enough. If the holder was as cheap as the furniture, it could be useless.

Taking a deep breath, I shook my head. "Why aren't we supposed to like each other?"

Jordan paused on the last step. "Opposites don't always attract in the animal kingdom."

"Awesome. You're a real wealth of information," I snapped. "Just another one of Damien's make-believe bad guys, eh?"

The muscles in Jordan's shoulders bunched. "Make believe? This is too rich to be a dream." Jordan leapt at me.

My muscles were prepared, even if they were a little weak. Rolling to the side, I made a clumsy swing that missed by a foot and bounced off the wall next to the bedroom.

My head spun, and I realized that Jordan wasn't

going for me.

Instead, he grabbed Aidan's hair, lifting his head off the ground. He smiled at me like a hyena.

"What do you want with Aidan?" I asked, my voice shaking as I crawled to my hands and knees, hoping that the spinning would stop.

Jordan paused, thick fingers positioned on the handle of his knife. "I think I should make him as pretty as me," he growled softly.

If he'd shouted it, I'd have considered it an idle threat, but the low rumble and glint in his eye sent chills down my spine.

Jordan's eyes trailed from the handle to the deadly tip, entranced.

The room was charged with electricity, and I could scarcely breathe as the knife hovered over my friend's face. "*Don't*," I hissed, struggling to my feet.

In my rush, my head spun out of control. I'd stood too fast. Gasping, I hit the wall, my voice jostling.

I didn't think after that, just moved.

Stepping forward, I lifted the crucifix over my head and forced it down, using my weight and gravity to form the arc. I knew the knife was tipped to Aidan's hairline but couldn't risk watching the bloodletting even if it meant I might make things worse.

The corner of the stone collided between Jordan's shoulder and neck.

Crying out, he swung the beefy arm holding the knife at me. I swung the cross like a baseball bat and miraculously caught his forearm before being gutted.

Howling, Jordan ducked to avoid another blow and swatted at my wrist with his free arm. My grip on the crucifix wasn't as firm as I'd hoped.

It flew from my grip and landed near the couch; the collision with his arm threw me back at the wall on shaky legs.

As I fell back, the blade glimmered past my stomach, almost snagging my shirt.

That was close.

I didn't check for damage. I was too busy flailing for balance and to retrieve my weapon again. As I staggered past Jordan and Aidan, I saw the knife again as Jordan rolled to his feet. I also saw the glassy, hot hatred. It was like Jordan wasn't seeing a person but a cold-blooded enemy.

Ducking, I scooped up the crucifix and twisted in time to see Jordan swing at me. I was forced to back away, keeping my arms up to avoid a slash.

The couch caught the back of my knees, and I tumbled into the cushions, narrowly avoiding another volatile swing of the blade. From the lack of pain, I could only assume that I wasn't cut.

Moving fast, I grabbed the candlestick on the coffee table and stabbed blindly at the looming figure. It was a surprise the candle remained lit in the swing.

Pressing my back to the cushions, I held the flame before Jordan's face, gritting my teeth and awaiting the pain. His arms were longer, and I couldn't back away any further.

To my surprise, he stepped back, looking angrier. My insides shook, but I kept a firm grip on both of my weapons as I scooted to the edge of the cushions. I glanced at the knife. If I could knock it out of his hands, I would have it.

Seeing my gaze, Jordan flashed teeth in a ferocious grin. "Not going to happen, sweetie. If you're done playing girlfriend, I have a carving to finish."

Turning to the side to keep me in sight, he edged toward the limp, pale form on the floor.

"Aidan!" I shouted. *Please let him wake up.* "Don't sleep, Aidan. The door is at the top of the stairs!"

On the floor, behind Jordan, Aidan's wild hair stirred. Maybe he was coming to.

Seeing my distraction, Jordan dove at me.

I wasn't ready this time and ducked.

Rolling off the couch, I dropped to my hands and knees and heard Jordan crash on the couch.

I was careful not to move the still-lit candlestick, but the pause proved to be a mistake. A flying boot from the couch knocked into my hip.

The hard shove sent me sprawling. The candlestick skidded out of my hands as I landed on my stomach. I still gripped the crucifix and could feel it grinding between my lower ribcage and the floor.

As I tugged to pull it free, I felt the oppressive weight cover my entire back. Gasping in a breath, I realized it was Jordan. The muscular forearm pressing down on the side of my face, attempting to crush it into the carpet. The glass skeleton key reminded me of its presence in my pocket when it ground into my hipbone.

Don't get caught, Damien's warning echoed, instilling fear.

I wheezed for a breath. It was almost impossible with my chest being ground into the shag carpet. As I wriggled, I wondered when I'd feel the knife. How bad would it hurt? I'd never been stabbed before. I tried to pull out the stone, which was jammed between my ribs and the floor. I needed to have something to swing back if Jordan's head came into my peripheral vision.

I had to think of a better plan, I realized. In pain and trying to reserve energy, I stopped struggling. I needed to analyze a move that would get me somewhere instead of just tiring myself out. One thing was clear: I wasn't going to be able to haul Aidan up those stairs with Jordan chasing me. I had to knock him out somehow.

One hand fumbled at the back of my shorts. He gripped them so his grimy fingers were inside the waistline at my side, and he tugged, hard.

The waist of my jean shorts dug into the opposite hip, and I felt the branding fear.

"Aidan!" I shouted, hoping he'd wake up, but he remained motionless by the stairs, face turned away from me.

Pulling harder at the cross where it had wedged between my belly and the carpet, my wrist twisted until it hurt too much to continue. I didn't dare let it go, despite the pain. Overwhelmed, I could hear myself trying to scream, could smell smoke, but everything was starting to blur.

Jordan jerked down on my shorts again. I felt something give in the front, and they were pulled halfway down my hips on one side.

I kicked with renewed energy; the heel of my sneaker stabbed the back of his thigh. I couldn't let this happen. Part of me wanted to scream for Damien. He'd told me to hide, but I couldn't anymore.

The warmth in my stomach burned, and I wondered if I'd vomit again.

Jordan grunted at my sudden kick, his ankles snaking around mine from above, his knees on the outside of my legs. His arm pressing to my ear, the hand letting go of my shorts and messing around between his crotch and the bare skin of my lower back. He hadn't even raped me yet, and I felt the slimy sickness of being tainted—used.

I had contemplated dying in the Challenge; I'd considered being maimed or injured or seeing friends die, but raped?

Don't let him catch you.

Twisting my head under the arm's pressure, I looked for the knife and spotted it by his knee. He'd let it go, freed it for me to take.

Grinding my teeth together, I shouted and tried to slide beneath him, my free hand reaching. I felt the carpet burning the side of my face as I dragged it under the weight of his arm.

Stretching my fingers as long as they'd extend, I urged the knife closer, pleaded with it. I didn't want to be helpless again, not like when I was younger.

Jordan grabbed my shorts and tugged again with a growl.

I squealed a protest and stretched my fingertips, feeling the familiar warmth in my gut swirling, charging, and igniting within. *I needed that knife.* My wrist, trapped beneath me, felt as if it were about to break in two, but I refused to let go of the cross, my only weapon. Ironic. I'd never been very religious in the outside world.

He tugged my shorts half way down my butt. I felt the sharp open zipper of his pants against bare flesh. His hard-on was pressed there, still covered in a fabric. That would give me a few fleeting seconds of hope.

"Does this seem make believe to you?" Foul, hot breath heaved into my ear.

I screamed, the tangled fear escaping with the building warmth within. As it raced down my arm, it was like hot ants under my skin. The pain was easily ignored as I called for the knife to extinguish the helplessness.

Nothing was touching the hunting knife when it shuddered on the floor, nudging toward my fingers.

The charge that had started in my stomach danced its way through to my fingertips. It felt as if someone had cracked elastic bands against the tips of each finger. My fingernails ached as if crushed, but the knife was only an inch away from my hand.

"What?" Jordan asked. "*That*?"

I held back frustrated tears, sniffling back the snot that came with them.

Jordan's big combat boot lifted from my ankle. He kicked the knife away, sending it clattering into the wall.

While he lifted his foot to kick the knife, it gave me enough time to arch my back and free the stone crucifix.

Twisting like a corkscrew, I swung in a wild arc.

I missed with the stone, but I connected with my elbow. Every ounce of shame and fury at his attempt exploded with the peculiar warmth within. The pressure on the side of my face released the moment my elbow made contact with his temple.

I watched his brown eyes shake inside his mangled head. For a moment, his eyes glazed, distancing him.

I was able to roll onto my hip, and his body flopped off mine with a groan.

Sitting up, I used the momentum and swung the stone, missing him by almost a foot. My aim was completely disoriented, but the damage I'd done had almost ended it all.

Jordan coiled away from me, going for his knife.

On my knees, I grabbed for my shorts, self-consciously jerking them and my underwear back where they belonged.

The adrenaline coursed and seethed. I didn't recognize anything I did. I just moved.

Following him, I batted the stone across the back of his head. I heard the cracking impact as he fell into the couch. Knife in hand, he stabbed a hole into the cushions, the tearing sound reminding me that that could have been my flesh instead.

The sound fueled enough rage to keep me upright and wouldn't allow my shaky legs to buckle. While his back was still to me, I swung the stone again, catching him mid-spine. He shouted and stood to make a grab for me.

I was too close, and his arm snagged me in the jaw.

I had little sense of where I was falling. Dots trailed through my vision before I realized I was on the floor and the warmth in my belly had evaporated. The strength I had left faded.

This was it. I had lost.

The smell of smoke had grown stronger, and I glanced up to see the metal neck of the candlestick. Dots played games in front of my eyes, and I lifted the holder slower than I wished. The candle hadn't broken, and its flame still flickered. I considered that it could have been protected by an invisible shield, like the one in the witch's window.

Jordan turned to stab at me without looking, his expression livid until the flame of the candle caught on his camo-pants. Licking the material, it curled up his knee. I realized it had done the same to the edge of the carpet on the far side of the living room, near the wall, though those flames weren't nearly as greedy as the ones that had Jordan's leg.

Dropping the knife, he swatted at the hungry flames with both of his hands.

I rolled onto my hands and knees, feeling the heat above my head.

Curling my fingers around the heavy handle of the discarded knife, I got onto my knees. Gripping the handle with both hands, I lunged at the closest thing to me, Jordan's thigh. The blade entered almost to the hilt, and the handle jabbed my ribcage.

He screamed in gruff surprise, the sound quickly morphing into pain.

Jordan swung a beefy hand at me, knocking my knife grip loose, and I fell into the side of the couch.

Blinking, I felt heat at my feet and tried to clear the haze in my head. Wrenching away from me, Jordan flailed to remove the knife, stepping directly into the spreading flames. Greedily, they rose in a feeding frenzy.

The opposite side of the old couch began to crackle as the fire caught the corner. Groaning, I tried to get up, every muscle protesting, and I collapsed back onto the carpet.

The heat against my calves alerted me that it was either succumb to exhaustion or get Aidan up the stairs before the fire spread. Jordan was distracted, at least.

As I crawled on my stomach, my arms and legs were laced with lead and the healing bite on my knee ached, along with my jaw, where Jordan hit me.

A lifetime passed before I reached Aidan, it seemed.

He was still conscious but barely. He blinked at me, attempting to clear the blood from his eyes. "What…?"

"Get up. I can't help you," I demanded. It was true. I wouldn't be able to half carry him again. We were on our own this time.

I tried to stand, falling on my first attempt. My jaw throbbed, it hurt to speak, but I screamed at Aidan anyway, hoping he could hear me over Jordan's horrific screams. "Get up or…" I decided to poke at the hero in him. "Or I'll be alone in this Challenge because you left me!"

Shame, shame, double shame.

The fire was spreading behind me, and Jordan was spinning on the carpet in a fiery ball, spreading the flames. It was only a matter of time before he spotted us near the stairs. The distinct smell of burning hair and skin prodded my gag reflex.

I had never smelled burning flesh before. It was similar to cooking meat and, mixed with burning hair, made it hard to take a breath with gagging or choking.

I wobbled to my feet; Aidan crawled to his and wavered in a Frankenstein-fashion as he took each step.

We fought to keep our balance as the smoke swirled around our heads, choking us. We made it to the first landing as the fire tasted the walls, reaching higher and higher.

Jordan hit the railing of the staircase.

I coughed hard enough to make my chest hurt, and Jordan's shouts were reduced to an almost feminine shriek. Agony tore through his throat in a way I'd never heard before.

Looking back, Aidan's eyes widened. "Down, onto

your stomach," he coughed.

I barely heard him but agreed. We crawled up the stairs to hide from the smoky fumes. Jordan had gone suspiciously quiet when we finally reached the top.

The smoke on the second floor was even thicker. I hacked and wheezed, but no amount of coughing could rid the rattle from my chest. I reached back for Aidan, realizing I couldn't see him anymore.

It wasn't until his hand slapped on top of mine that we followed each other's lead.

We were forced to lower our bodies to the floor, writhing like worms on our stomachs.

I caught his hand, and he wriggled up beside me. "Last door in the hallway," I said, my mouth feeling like it'd been cleaned out with cotton.

Moving together, we made sure we'd reach out for one another with each struggling shuffle. I felt the first door, then the second. My hopes rose as high as my doubt as we inched toward our suffocation.

My already weakened muscles screamed, and my body begged to collapse. A few times, it almost got its way. I kept thinking of Jordan's screams; it was the only thing that kept me from stopping.

Finally, my hand touched a closed door. I could only assume it was black and hoped that it hadn't changed since my adventure downstairs.

"Here!" I choked to Aidan, who bumped into me.

Clawing upward, I lifted myself into the haze, feeling the round smooth doorknob. As I twisted, it swung inward, and I fell with it. Landing hard onto a carpet, I paused before crawling inside on my hands and knees.

Aidan was close behind, wheezing, pale and still

bleeding from his forehead.

The smoke billowed inside with us until our feet were out of range of the swinging door, and it slammed shut.

Collapsing simultaneously, we sputtered and gulped clean air only to choke on it.

I coiled onto a ball on my side. My trembling body grew still, and my eyelids drooped. They felt far heavier than I remembered. The grey walls of a small room surrounded us. There wasn't anyone else; we were safe.

I glanced at Aidan; his eyes were already closed. I caught sight of the gash on his forehead again. The one I helped Jordan make with the knife.

"Aidan," I croaked, "don't go to sleep."

"Sleep," Aidan murmured and caught my hand in his.

"You can't," I protested. "I know 'cause I want to sleep too, but we just can't." I pushed at him with my free hand. My arm muscles protested before flopping to the floor and so did my head. I lay there, breathing, then coughing.

The smoke here was gone but still haunted my lungs. Heavy layers of exhaustion clung like a parasite, and I realized Aidan was sleeping.

My eyes closed, for only a moment.

CHAPTER THIRTY-FOUR

Dreams buzzed like insects in the sweltering summer.

First, I dreamt of Phoebe and Read. They were huddled together in a corner. Both were scared and clinging to each other. Phoebe had her long legs cramped up against her chest, careful not to extend them toward the mist that was closing in.

Read clutched Phoebe so tight that she cringed but didn't tell him that he was hurting her. I heard him whisper that he was sorry, but Phoebe wasn't listening.

Across the room, Robin was screaming in fits of hysteria, screams eerily similar to Jordan's just before he fell silent.

Robin stood on a single child's bed with crumpled, rose-printed sheets. Mascara tears stained her cheeks, and she wiped her nose with the back of her hand before picking up a pillow. Using both hands, she swung it, wafting the mist away.

"Fight it!" I shouted just as the picture died away

and was replaced with a new one.

* * *

The sandbox was warm, and I looked down to see the start of a sand castle.

"What do you think we'll get for our birthday?" a child's voice asked.

Jerking my head up, I saw a little girl I recognized from the one photograph in our hallway.

Startled, I opened my mouth to say something to the familiar dark-haired little girl when the backyard gate swung open.

Neive and I froze as a burly man with a blonde ponytail and unruly beard stepped into our backyard. His girth mushroomed over his jeans, and he filled the whole opening. Beetle eyes focused on us immediately.

I recognized him, and every muscle in my body locked in place. I hadn't seen him for sixteen years, and yet every detail was sharp as if I were seeing him for the first time. I craned my neck to peer past him for his brother, but if memory served, he'd be waiting in the yellow car.

The patio door closed behind us with a snap, and I jumped.

Looking back, the petite, pretty brunette with a round face and full lips flashed a charming smile. A small part of me thought I should be relieved to see our aunt, but I consciously knew it was a memory.

Neive pointed to the scowling man. "Aunt Nell, Mom and Dad probably didn't invite him to our party."

It could have been funny if meeting his eyes wasn't comparable to staring down the barrel of a gun.

Whenever I'd been given the lecture on strangers, he'd easily fit what I envisioned as a "bad guy."

"Hurry up, Nell," the man grumbled, his voice made of quiet thunder.

We both shrank back at his glare and glanced at each other. I hated seeing my own fear reflected back at me.

Neive reached out and plucked her favorite stuffed toy, Damien, from the edge of the sandbox and hugged it tight. It had been a gift from our aunt as an apology. A scary movie we watched with her while she was babysitting had scared Neive so badly she threatened to tell our parents.

"It's okay, girls," Aunt Nell cooed, meaning to tenderize our unease. "We're going to the zoo like I promised, remember?" She held out her hands for us to grab. I noticed the new jean-jacket she was wearing. On the breast, a peculiar symbol was sewn in black thread. It was a dramatic swirl with an angled line through it. I had almost forgotten about the jacket. Looking over my shoulder at Blondie, I recognized the same symbol stitched into his leather vest.

Wiggling her fingers in front of my face, Aunt Nell sang, "The longer you wait, the less time we get to spend with the kangaroos."

Neive snatched Aunt Nell's hand without hesitation. Neive's side of the room was stuffed with wombats and kangaroos. Mom used to joke that the instant we were old enough, Neive would be hopping off to Australia, ironically with a stuffed bear named Damien.

I glanced back at the man in the gate. We couldn't go with her, though as much as I tried to protest, I realized I was holding out my own hand.

"We shouldn't go," I told Neive. She blinked at me as she was pulled to her feet. "You'll die today if we do."

The instant I felt the small give of control to tell her what was going on, the scene changed.

* * *

Aidan was sitting at our usual table in the college cafeteria. The group was together again, including five-year-old Neive and Nora.

Little Neive and Nora could barely poke their heads over the table across from me, but they managed to eat their sandwiches all the same.

Aidan stretched his lips in his signature polite smile. Damien stood behind him; his eyes caught mine, and I stiffened. Leaning forward, he cupped his hand around Aidan's ear and began to whisper. Aidan didn't flinch, continuing to smile until it looked plastic. Read, who sat beside Aidan, didn't seem to notice the demon to his right.

Glancing up and down the table, I realized they all were oblivious to Damien. Cody and Robin were talking, but I couldn't make out what was said. It was like the volume had been turned down.

Phoebe nudged me. Her magazine was laid out in front of her with the spread of food that took up half the table. She said something, but I couldn't hear. Her face contorted in confusion as she repeated herself, waiting for my response.

I shook my head and tapped my ear. "I can't hear you."

Phoebe breathed out, exasperated, and asked the

little Nora squished beside Neive.

Aidan's plastic smile faltered.

Little Nora shook her head and looked at me with large blue eyes. Her voice rang in the quiet, echoing. "No, she's not good at being a sacrifice. In the end, she'll stay."

Neive nodded her agreement, pulling the mayo-greased lettuce out of her sandwich.

"Say something," I whispered to the dark-haired little girl.

She didn't look up when she said:
From the lightning in the sky
As it passed me flying by,
From the thunder and the storm,
And the cloud that took the form
When the rest of Heaven was blue
Of a demon in my view.

Blinking, I glanced up at Damien, his black eyes locked onto mine as he whispered in Aidan's ear.

The demon in my view. I realized I knew that poem, from class. I should know it.

Neive jumped down from her seat, dark hair swaying in its ponytail. Her childish laughter pierced my ears like firecrackers.

Then she turned and ran.

The tables behind ours had evaporated into shadows, and Neive ran into them before I could stand.

Struggling out of my chair, I shouted at her to stop when a beefy hand latched onto my shoulder and shoved me back down. Nearly toppling into Phoebe, I looked up to see the half scarred and half burnt face.

Charred skin flaked away as Jordan spoke, peppering my shoulder with ash. "Think I should make her as pretty as me, sweetie?"

* * *

"*Stop*!" I bolted upright in a cold sweat.

I rubbed my shoulders; it almost felt like the hand was still there. I scrubbed away the horrible sensation and realized with a start that I was back in the tower room—alone.

Grabbing the nearest chair, I staggered to my feet.

Every bruise and scrape flared. The side of my face where Jordan hit me made my jaw feel stiff. I scanned the room. Aidan wasn't here, and neither was the door.

Just a dream, I told myself. *Just-a-dream.*

Taking a deep breath, I heard the rattle in my lungs. "Guys?" I called.

Shoving away from the chair, I stood up on my own and blinked.

All at once, there was light.

* * *

Gasping, I shouldered someone, and they caught me. Before I could scream or panic, Aidan interrupted me. "Wake up!"

My fists were pressed to my eyes, and I slowly lowered them to see his electric blue eyes staring down at me.

Blood had crusted to the side of his face, making him somewhat ghoulish. Aidan wobbled on his bum leg to hold me up, and I reached out to the grey wall for support. My muscles weren't nearly as weak as before. I could stand without feeling like I was going to fall over.

The small, gloomy room with grey walls and green carpet held a black door.

"Where'd you come from?" Aidan asked, stepping back. "When I woke up, you weren't here." An inky shadow passed through his gaze. "Were you with him?"

I shook my head. "I was dreaming." I remembered the tower room; Damien had said I could hop. Was I really just in our world? It had felt so real.

"I was sleeping too, but I didn't disappear." Aidan's eyes narrowed on my jaw. "I don't even remember getting out of that Challenge." He rubbed the crusted blood on his temple. It fell off in crisp pieces, revealing Aidan's reddened skin and reminding me of Jordan's half-charred face meeting the white scars.

Shuddering, I asked, "What is the last thing you remember?"

Shaking his head, he winced when he found the cut near his hairline. "Jordan had pulled me out from under the bed and held me upside down. Then you said something, I can't remember what, but you ran from the room.

"Jordan had pulled out a knife and said that this was going to be the last thing that I would ever see. But instead of cutting my throat, he dropped me and then slammed my head into the bedpost. The rest is hazy."

"Is that all you remember?" I asked after a pause.

"Just remember little things like a fire and a lot of smoke," Aidan said. "And you, screaming." His eyes narrowed on my jaw again. "Did he do that to you?"

Touching the tender swelling on the side of my face, I wondered how bad it looked. It didn't hurt so much to talk anymore. "Yeah, he was a bit of a bully."

Aidan's face flushed.

Licking my lips, I remembered Jordan asking me why of all the places in the world Aidan would pick Leland to go to college. "So did you move to Leland? Because of your grandpa's house?"

"Kind of," Aidan said.

I gestured for him to continue.

"Oh, is this the part where we share?"

I swallowed that one back and took a deep breath before saying, "I told you about my sister."

Aidan looked away, still looking bitter, but at least I saw a smidgen of remorse. "There was a family dispute over the will. My cousin Adam, the one who owned the Maserati, was supposed to inherit it, but he died six months after grandpa. The next in line was me. My uncle seemed to think it should belong to him instead."

"So you own that house?" I breathed, feeling the shock sway me a little.

Aidan hesitated, still not looking at me when he muttered, "According to the lawyers, I will on my twenty-fifth birthday."

The thought hit my brain and shot out my mouth before I could stop myself. "I wonder if your cousin knew about the darkness between worlds."

My hand jerked up as if to cover my mouth, though it was too late. I disguised the move by tucking loose hair behind my ear and clearing my throat.

"I'll have to ask him one day," Aidan said.

"I thought you said he was dead."

"He is."

I got the picture. "Don't think like that. We're close to the end."

Aidan rubbed more dried blood from his face and winced. "Yeah," he said, unconvinced.

"We're going to be fine," I cajoled, knowing they were weak words.

This was it, our final, sixth run, and we'd be free. We could figure out what was going on with our friends, finally. The dream with the mists had seemed so real that I wondered if I'd really seen them. If that were true, it meant they were together and alive, though Cody was still a mystery.

"Nora?" Aidan's shoulders had tightened, and I followed his gaze down to see the button on my shorts was missing and the zipper halfway down, revealing my favorite purple underwear.

"Oh," I said, startled.

The shame struck like a tidal wave. I knew I shouldn't feel like I'd done something wrong, but somehow I felt tainted, infected. If he'd gotten around to raping me, I didn't want to imagine what I'd be feeling then.

Doing up the zipper with shaky fingers, I heard Aidan breathe, "Is that why you were screaming? Did he…?"

"No," I answered too quickly.

Aidan's pale eyes rolled up to meet mine. "*Did* he?"

"No, Aidan," I snapped, feeling my face warm in embarrassment. "We have better things to talk about than that asshole. He's dead. *Burned* alive and gone."

And showing up in dreams instead.

"What did you say about dreams?" Aidan asked.

Did I say that out loud? "It's stupid," I said.

Aidan glanced at the black door behind him. "What do you remember?"

"About the dream?"

Aidan nodded and shuffled in one place. "Since

we're being so open and honest."

"A, uh, poem by Edgar Allen Poe." I shook my head to unclog the memory. "But only part of it."

"Can you remember it?" Aidan raised his eyebrows, still looking down.

I nodded, the memory sticking to the inside of my skull like honey.

From the lightning in the sky
As it passed me flying by,
From the thunder and the storm,
And the cloud that took the form
(When the rest of Heaven was blue)
Of a demon in my view.

We stared at each other for several seconds before Aidan sighed. "I don't understand."

"Neither do I," I confessed.

"Aren't you an English major?" Aidan asked.

I sneered at him.

"Was Damien in the dream?"

Raising my eyebrows at him, I frowned.

"Did he say anything to you?" Aidan ignored me and looked up.

I shook my head and motioned to him. "He was talking to you, actually."

Aidan's eyes grew round, and I felt time begin to slow. *Whoa, whoa, whoa*, I'd hit a land mine, and I could see the realization playing on his face. "Did—did he talk to you in your dream?" I asked, caution slowing my speech.

Aidan hesitated before asking incredulously, "In the cafeteria?"

I leaned back against the wall of our small box-like room. *He's invading our dreams; but then how did I end up in the tower room again*? The cube being my test, the threats about cheating...where was all this coming from? I remembered the knife rattling on the floor and the hot pinpricks that raced under my skin. I'd moved that knife just by wanting it.

"What does this mean?" Aidan asked.

"I don't know. What did he say?" I countered, lowering my hands to my camisole, clutching it in my fists.

Aidan shook his head. "It was just a dream."

"I don't think it was, Aidan." I pointed to the door. "That's our last Challenge, and that poem makes no sense to me. If you have something to add..."

Scratching more of the crusted blood from the side of his face, Aidan shrugged. "I don't think it has anything to do with the poem."

At my glare, he stopped rubbing and sighed. "He said I should give you up, sacrifice you in the next Challenge. Then he'd release our friends."

Little Nora had said to Phoebe, *"No, she's not good at being a sacrifice."*

"And what..." I swallowed hard. "What did you say?"

"Nothing!" Aidan protested, holding up his hands as if I'd aimed a baseball bat at his head. "I didn't say anything. I couldn't! I was frozen there in that seat and watched you talking to two little kids. Then I woke up and you weren't here."

"Are you sure that's all he said?"

Aidan glared at me. I could see his hands curl into fists, trying to hide them in his crossed arms. "Where were you, Nora? Where'd you disappear to?"

Frowning, I glanced over my shoulder at the door.

"It's hard to explain."

"Try."

The hardness in his voice gave me pause. Should I tell him about bouncing back and forth between here and the tower room? If I did, it wouldn't mean anything. I couldn't take people with me, and I barely understood how I managed to do it myself. It wasn't cheating if I came back, right?

"I think I've been bouncing back and forth between here and the tower room."

There. It was out. I saw Aidan glance at the black door.

He wouldn't look at me when he asked, "Is that why he asked you about jumping?"

Nodding, I said, "I didn't really get it then, but I keep waking up sometimes in that room, alone, and then I'm suddenly back here. Damien seemed to think I had some connection to this place, but I think you do too."

"Because of the house." Aidan rolled his eyes. "You got the messages, remember?"

"Yeah, but when Cody said your name, Damien got this look on his face and then told me not to tell you about my family. Now, he's whispering to you in dreams. I think your grandpa knew about the Demon's Grave," I said. "What if Damien knew your grandpa?"

What if Nell knew his grandpa? Or worse, maybe Aidan knew who she was.

Aidan shook his head after a pause. "But you did tell me about your family. Or was there more?"

"There's more," I said and instantly regretted it.

Aidan raised his eyebrows, saying nothing, waiting for me to continue. When I didn't, he took a deep breath, looking away. "And you can't tell me now because it would be cheating or something?"

I swallowed. "He said he'd kill people."

This made him pause, his shoulders relaxing a little. His pale eyes darted to the black door, and his mouth pinched as if he'd eaten something sour. I wished I could have asked him what he was thinking but didn't dare.

Aidan brushed past me and without a backwards glance opened our final Challenge and stepped through.

CHAPTER THIRTY-FIVE

Behind us, the final door slammed shut, frightening ebony birds.

Glancing over my shoulder, I watched the black door fade at the edge of the swamp. Vines as thick as my legs wound their way around ancient trees. Lush wide-leafed plants came up to our waists, blocking our feet from view.

I breathed in the pungent, stale air, testing to see if the swamp were truly real. This was it. This was what the doppelgängers warned us about.

I looked to Aidan, but he kept his face turned away.

The river in front of us was mostly still water, littered with algae and glistening driftwood.

Aidan pointed across the river. It was as lush with vegetation as our own.

Not seeing anything, I whispered, "What is it?"

He waved at me to keep quiet. I noticed the movement on the opposite riverbank. If it hadn't moved, I'd have never seen it there. The crocodile, or maybe it was an alligator—I'd never know—slid on its belly through the muck and into the dark water. As its tail submerged, the beast barely cast a ripple before disappearing under the glassy surface.

Even with the reptile under water, I had the unnerving sensation that we were being watched.

Worry wrinkled Aidan's eyebrows. "Nora, we're in a swamp."

"He's just trying to psych us out." I tried to sound brave, though one glance at Aidan proved I was unconvincing.

Licking his lips, Aidan said, "This is our last chance to be honest with each other, you know."

The words stopped me cold and left me blinking at him. "I've told you everything I can," I said, waiting for the anger.

Instead, he crossed his arms. "Have you?"

"Yeah, have *you*?"

Snorting, Aidan dropped his arms to his sides and stepped by me, making a point not to look at me. The mud sloshed around his sneakers, and he grimaced. "What do you think about the poem?" he asked softly.

"I don't know yet," I said. To prove my bravado, I stepped up beside him. My sneakers disappeared beneath squishy, dense mud. I could feel the cool slop against my ankles. Waving my arms for balance, I took my next step and my next until I reached semi-solid ground where the plants didn't hide my feet. Mud caked my shoes and socks, and I wiggled my toes; they were still dry but not for long. The humidity was enough to stick my clothes to my body even standing still.

Getting ahead of Aidan, I tried to shake off the

excess mud from my shoes. Mostly, it just made a bigger mess, splattering mud up my bare legs.

Aidan took two large steps and came up beside me, touching one of the twisted trees for support as he wavered in the slippery mud.

Trying to watch my feet and the marsh at the same time, I noticed an eerie dark cloud creeping in on the other side of the river.

Aidan must have noticed it at the same time. "I don't think we want to be caught in that when we cross."

"Why are we crossing the river?" I asked, taking another sloppy step.

He pointed to something dark just ahead of us along our shoreline.

Frozen in the eerily calm waters, a dead log had been pushed onto the bank.

Squinting, I realized it wasn't just a log; it had been hollowed out, like a man-made boat. How had he seen it right away? From here, I'd have never picked it out of the swamp. "Might as well check it out," I agreed, keeping my voice low.

Aidan glanced at me and held out his hand. I paused, unsure if it was sincere or not. He had made a point of avoiding me most of the game, though to be fair, he hadn't once left me behind. I thought of how he saved me from the witch's house and ran with me through the museum. It was just the two of us now.

With a small smile, I grabbed his hand, and together we stumbled along the river bank.

The mud slid under our feet, threatening to sling our legs out from under us.

The water slapped against the shore, and Aidan hissed for me to stop, his body stiffening in mid-step.

Struggling to stay upright, I almost slipped. Leaning forward, I had to keep my hands straight out, still clutching to Aidan for support. Wobbling on shaky legs, I froze as best as I could, my body shaped in an L just to keep from falling.

Searching the swamp for whatever could have spooked Aidan, I eased my spine straight.

The waters had calmed since my lurching stop, leaving the eerie silence.

I squeezed Aidan's hand to get his attention and raised my eyebrows in a question.

He hesitated, opening his mouth as if to explain, but cast one last look around the swamp before mouthing, "*Sorry.*"

Releasing my hand, he trudged toward the shore, staying just within the jungle's canopy.

I started to follow when he turned back around and motioned me to stop, eyes wide with warning.

I started to shake my head when he motioned me to stay put with both hands. Narrowing my eyes at him, I frowned, and he rolled his eyes before motioning me to stay again. He paused, waiting for me to protest, and when I didn't, he eased toward the shoreline and out into the open.

He might think he was hiding me, but I didn't want to separate. With us this close to a success, Damien was sure to have a surprise pop out somewhere, and I wasn't about to let Aidan out of my sight, even if he thought it best.

Facing his back, I shuffled forward, keeping a safe distance. Stopping just outside the thick brush, I could see my feet. Mud had given an extra sole to my shoes, and my legs noticed the additional weight.

The little boat was just a few feet out in the water. The problem was, it was in the water, away from the shore.

Aidan hobbled into the shallow water, testing each step and taking his time.

Drawing in air, I prepared myself to scream a warning if I saw anything. The sickening feeling of being watched hadn't lifted, and I didn't doubt that something was hiding just beyond our sight.

Aidan was up to his mid-calf when he was able to reach the hollowed-out log. Fingers curling around the edge, he strained to grab it, pulling it closer. It didn't sink as it skidded across the smooth surface toward Aidan.

A small break at least.

Glancing over his shoulder, Aidan saw me at the tree line and frowned. He pointed at me as if it were an adequate threat.

I wiggled my fingers in a sarcastic wave until he turned to drag the wooden boat closer to the muddy shore. Aidan's efforts cast ripples outward, slopping the green and brown debris onto the shoreline.

The boat scraped bottom, sounding volcanic compared to the swamp's eerie silence.

Standing when it was done, Aidan allowed himself a smile that was genuine.

Smiling back, I lifted one foot, hearing the mud's suction against the ground. Looking down, I noticed a movement behind me and jerked my head up. Aidan had noticed it too, and his smile wiped clean.

"*Move!*" he mouthed, pale eyes wide.

I picked up my foot to step closer, ducking instinctively when I realized it was lodged in the mud.

Looking down, I tried to move again, but my left foot was stuck. Twisting, I attempted to reach for a branch or vine above but found nothing in my reach. Stepping forward, I pulled, feeling my swollen knee twinge.

Desperate, I stretched fingers to Aidan and whispered shrilly, "Pull."

Aidan pointed behind me, though he inched closer, careful not to get stuck in the mucky shore.

I leaned as far forward as I dared. I could feel the heat of those eyes. As I dared to look over my shoulder, every hair on my body bristled.

Three pairs of deep red, glowing eyes peered from the brush, and they were focused on me. One of them blinked slowly, seeming lethargic and bored, as if it had all the time in the world.

Fighting the urge to scream, I snapped my gaze back to Aidan warning him.

"Can you slip out of your shoe?" Aidan asked in a whisper. His arms stretched out to catch me, but he was a foot out of my reach.

And run without a shoe? In the middle of the jungle? I hated the idea and wiggled a little more. I was altogether stuck.

Waving him closer, I hissed, "Just pull on me first."

Glancing at the eyes behind me, Aidan licked his lips.

The hesitation stopped my heart.

I watched his eyes harden, and he took a step back, looking over his shoulder at the boat then across the still river. I saw it at the same time.

Nestled just within the trees was the shiny black door. The top wasn't hidden, though vegetation crowded near the base, like a protective barrier.

It had never appeared so early before, but then it hadn't been offered anything before either. It was our way home, and Aidan had the boat. He could leave me behind if he wanted.

My arms started to ache, and I lowered them, feeling the balance of his decision thicken the air.

Twisting my foot, I could tell I could slip out of my shoe, but something stopped me. I wanted to see what he would do. Sacrifice me, like Damien suggested, or help me across the river?

Standing straight, I tried to look confident though I felt like a fish out of water. I wondered if he'd look back before walking to the boat.

I looked over at the red eyes; they were still there, waiting.

Would the sacrifice be like Neive's? A quick death? Or did Damien have other plans? I thought of his obsidian eyes watching me over Aidan's shoulder in the dream. *She was never good at being a sacrifice.*

Without warning, Aidan turned and jumped at me.

Startled, I strangled a yelp and almost moved to fend him off when he grabbed both my wrists and jerked back.

Catching his eyes, I felt relief flooding me all at once, and I grabbed his wrists in return.

Wriggling my foot to free it from the sneaker, I felt my heel inch free.

Aidan's shout shattered the silence. He was looking past me.

Ducking, I felt a wind rush past my head as if something had swung at me. With one final yank, my foot was free.

Aidan grabbed my arm and propelled both of us into the shallow water beside the boat.

Staggering with him, I looked over my shoulder, but nothing was there.

The brush was silent; not a single leaf had been disturbed. Whatever Aidan saw had vanished, though I doubted it was gone. I still felt those weighty eyes.

Despite the stillness, we scrambled for the boat. Sweat bubbled Aidan's brow, wetting the blood and making it appear slick. It must have stung.

The boat, having been carved and gutted from a large tree, was dark, maybe rotting. Holding onto the vessel with cramped fingers, I heard Aidan whisper to *jump in*.

Without waiting, I awkwardly lifted a leg and rolled into the small log, nearly tipping it over when a stick jabbed into my back. Sitting up, I noticed the twisted deadwood paddles on the bottom. Struggling for balance, I snatched one. The dry, grey wood dug slivers into my palms as I shoved it into the muddy shore at the same time that Aidan pushed.

The boat scraped the bottom for what felt like forever. I kept my eyes on the brush, shoving the paddle deep into the muck.

Aidan dug his heels into the shoreline, his face strained and red, until the boat broke free of the bottom and floated.

With one final push, Aidan leapt into the boat with me. The entire wooden vessel rocked, water sloshing over the edges. Biting back a yelp, I gripped the edge with my free hand.

Rustling from the brush alerted us to movement, but neither of us stopped what we were doing. I tossed

Aidan a paddle when I felt confident in my balance.

Together, we began to push through the brown water as fast and as hard as we could. Farther down the shoreline, past a fallen tree, I heard the distinct splashes. Something was joining us.

Halfway out into the river, Aidan dropped his paddle across his lap, heaving. Twisting his neck to see the shore, he asked, "Any of them follow?"

I stopped paddling, allowing the boat to drift in the still waters. "I think they jumped in over there." I pointed toward the fallen log where I heard the splashes. "What were they anyway?"

Aidan shook his head. "I have no idea. I just saw a figure. It almost seemed human, but it was dark."

Catching my breath, I muttered, "Thanks for not leaving me."

Aidan tried to smile, then without looking at me nodded.

I wanted to ask him why he didn't but decided against it. Together, we searched the mire for any signs of what might be hunting us. The brush behind us was silent; not even crickets or frogs graced the swamp.

Aidan let his breath out in a *whoosh*. "Let's get out of here."

I gripped my paddle, the splinters prickling my palm as I dug through the water. Pushing off in long, smooth strokes, I felt the muscles in my shoulders ache. Aidan quickly followed my lead, making the motion easier.

On my fifth stroke, the paddle abruptly stuck on something. The bottom already? Automatically, I jerked at it, but it stayed in place. Nothing scraped the bottom of the boat, and I shook the paddle with both hands, rocking the boat beyond Aidan's comfort, and he hissed at me.

Holding the upright deadwood, I eased the boat's sway. The paddle was really stuck, but on what?

Leaning forward, I decided to give it one last yank. As if expecting it, the paddle ripped from my hands in a blur, stabbing slivers into my skin and disappearing beneath the water.

Gasping, I cradled my flaming hands to my chest.

I didn't want to look at them.

Aidan had stopped paddling, his eyes round. We watched where my paddle had been, waiting for it to resurface. The ripple of water was the only evidence it had ever been there.

Looking to the opposite shore, I could see we were almost there. The black clouds overhead had grown thicker, creeping along the riverbank, edging over the water.

Bubbling water had me following Aidan's gaze to the disturbed surface next to our boat. Ripples swirled out as if something had surfaced before I had a chance to look, but Aidan had seen. Tilting up my chin, I started to ask when something on his face stopped me cold.

Aidan swallowed hard, his electric eyes snapping to me. "Nora, I think I should tell you something."

"I don't think this is the best time, Aidan." My gaze swept the surface of the murky waters, feeling apprehensive about what he may have seen.

Something slapped against the side of the boat. The force rocked us back and forth. Snatching the sides, I tried to stay centered and balanced, gritting my teeth.

Aidan's paddle was half-in and half-out of the boat,

the handle on the floor and the paddle dripping on glassy water.

"No, I think I should tell you now." Aidan gulped as the boat settled again. "It's about what Damien said."

"What?" I snapped.

Out of the corner of my vision, there was movement. As if electrocuted, I shouted, "Paddle, Aidan!"

Before the words left my lips, a hand broke the swampy surface and latched onto the edge of the boat.

Skeletal fingers flexed and tightened their grip, revealing tendons and stark, white bone. It was a human hand once. But now it was grey with green algae.

Terror tore through my throat, and I screamed.

A second hand breached the surface and slapped the side of our wooden craft. The boat rocked dangerously. Each swing was harder and stronger than the last. We could hear the *thuds* beneath our feet, mocking us with rapping knuckles.

I held on, intensifying the fiery pain of the cuts in my hands. If this kept up, we were going to flip. I didn't want to imagine what was waiting for us in the caliginous water below.

Aidan started to paddle, trying to veer us closer to the shore. His electric blue eyes shone, hardly blinking with each paddle slap that sprayed water in all directions.

Another rotted hand curled around my fingers and gripped the edge of the boat.

I screamed, nauseated by the slimy thing, and jerked back. I kept both hands close, trying to balance by locking my knees together and pressing my feet to either side of the shallow log.

A thump from below lifted the boat out of the water. I felt it rise and drop with my stomach and tried to lean the opposite way so not to flip us.

Before the boat landed, Aidan's startled shout was cut off by a *splash*.

Chapter Thirty-Six

The boat slapped back into the water, jostling my insides.

I shifted my weight to prevent myself from pitching overboard, all the while staring at the empty spot at the head of the boat.

The decaying hand had disappeared, and all the knocking below ceased, which scared me more. Splashing to my right made my heart stop, and I almost didn't turn my head.

Peeking over the edge of the boat, I felt a jolt of relief, which flooded into a smile.

Aidan was still above the surface, treading water. He was several feet away, but he wasn't gone. I gestured wildly until he met my eye.

Sputtering swamp water, he nodded, scanning the surface.

"Hurry," I hissed, craning my neck to look for whatever haunted us below the surface.

For a few clumsy minutes, Aidan's sloppy breast strokes didn't seem to getting him anywhere. Each second that ticked by was an invitation, and I sat up taller in the boat, readying myself to pull him in. *Don't separate, don't separate*, I repeated in my head until the breast strokes evened out, growing longer and smoother. He didn't dare duck his head under the muddy surface.

I held out my hand, ushering him closer, afraid to speak and disturb the quiet.

Aidan hesitated in mid-stroke, sinking in his panic. Spitting out swampy water, he gagged. "Something touched my leg."

Shaking my head, I waved my hands for him to hurry. I couldn't swing the boat around without a paddle, and I didn't dare put my hand in the murky water.

Swimming again, Aidan drew closer when his breath sharpened, and he stopped swimming again.

I gritted my teeth in irritation. Pressing my chest to the edge of the craft, I strained for him. He was almost in arm's reach, just a few more strokes and…

Aidan jerked beneath the surface so fast it took me a second to realize he was gone.

The water rippled where he'd been. Bubbles surfaced as the water began to smooth as if it were never disturbed, just like the paddle.

"Aidan?" I dared to ask, hearing the squeak in my voice.

A loud *thunk* against the bottom of the boat made me jerk my extended arm back to my chest.

Struggling to decide what to do, I heard a sharp scraping, like something was scratching the side of the wood. Clamping my hands over my mouth to prevent a noise, I glanced at where Aidan disappeared.

Without warning, the raft lifted again. Teetering, I tried to center my balance, but it was too late. I was going over. In my panic, I jumped. I didn't want to be any closer to whatever hid below than I had to be.

The hollowed log rolled as I met the water in a horrendous belly-flop.

The cold water sparked a shock straight through to my bones.

At first I sank, feeling the chill itch its way into my core. Bubbles escaped my lips, reminding me to swim.

Wriggling in a panic, I struggled for the surface, kicking hard to circulate my sluggish blood. At least I hoped I was aiming for the surface. The water was so gloomy and dark I could barely see my own hands in front of me.

Kicking as hard as I could, I broke the surface and breathed in deep.

Aidan. I spun in a circle, searching for him, but he was still missing. The boat was upside down, several feet away, and the foggy shore was even farther.

Ready to shout for him, I heard water dash against the other side of the boat, inconveniently out of my line of sight.

Overhead thunder boomed through the silence of the swamp, jarring every sense.

Swallowing the scream, I started for the boat. I needed a higher vantage to find Aidan. If he was still under the water, I had no idea how I'd find him in the gloom. The little light that was left had me squinting, straining for any sign of him. What if he'd left? He couldn't sacrifice me when looking me in the face, but if we're separated now…

Shuddering, I concentrated on swimming for the overturned boat, careful not to splash and draw unwanted attention. There were crocodiles, after all.

With each kick, my legs became hypersensitive to anything that might touch me or, worse, drag me under. The anticipation was almost worse than an attack.

I almost forgot to breathe until my fingers touched the side of the overturned boat.

I listened, but I couldn't hear splashes or the knocking. Reaching up, I slapped a hand on the top of the rounded log to pull myself higher. Still, nothing touched my ankles as I dragged my soaked body up the side.

My hands throbbed and my body shivered from the cold.

I eased my way to the top, straddling the overturned boat with my legs curled up on either side and out of the water.

I was secure in my perch when the water burst only a few feet ahead of me.

Shrieking, I slapped myself down onto the boat, clinging to it as if it could hide me in open water.

In a spitting, splashing, thrashing display, Aidan emerged for a second time.

Aidan bobbed in the water beside the boat. He was struggling, hitting something in the water, and gasping noisily for air.

I stretched out my hand, bracing myself against the boat, and shouted, "Grab it!"

His wide, pale eyes caught mine, and our fingertips grazed. Something unseen stole him under the water again. His arms flailed over his head to grab at air. I tried to catch his hand but missed.

Staring at the empty space in shock, I wasn't sure what to do. Should I dive in after him and hope to find him in the shadowy ridges of the swamp? The coward in me wanted to wait, but the voices from the first Challenge echoed in my mind. *"We died because of each other."*

I thought about Jordan's attack, how scared and embarrassed I was. I'd wanted Aidan's help then, though he couldn't. But right now, Aidan needed me.

Shaking away the crusty fear, I crouched on top of the boat, preparing to dive. This could be it. It could be all over in just a few minutes, and despite my efforts we could die because of each other anyway.

I dove off the boat. The icy water scorched my limbs all over again.

I waved my arms as hard as they'd allow in the frigid surroundings, forcing each kick to find him. He couldn't have been taken far, *could he*?

Descending deeper, I was no longer sure if I was following him down or if I had arched somewhere in the process and was slowly floating up toward the surface.

My heart hammered in my head as I felt my lungs aching a warning. Arching my back, I twisted and changed directions until I broke the surface.

Spinning in a circle, I couldn't see him above the water. The thunder overhead vibrated, and I took a deep breath before ducking back beneath.

Squinting through the algae and debris, I realized I couldn't see really anything more than a foot ahead.

I focused my rhythm through the water, knowing it was slowing.

This was useless. I needed something to see by. Otherwise, it was trying to catch a minnow in the desert. It was only a matter of time before whatever had Aidan would come for me.

As if hearing my thoughts, thrashing bubbles erupted to my right. If it was Aidan, I knew I had to follow it. But what if it wasn't him? I ignored the fearful thought, foolishly.

My lungs began to tighten, and the water became shallower. I could see a little more than before. A silhouetted figure was grabbing his own leg. It certainly was the shape of Aidan.

I swam closer, hoping it was him. When I caught one of the flailing arms, it felt solid, not slimy or slick like a corpse.

Looking to me, hair floating around his shadowed face, he grabbed my wrist and I kicked back to pull. He twisted and kicked at whatever had him.

Straining to see what held his leg, I couldn't make it out. It was in the muddy earth of the river, shrouded in darkness.

Tugging at the resistance, I used my arms and legs to try to breach us, almost hitting the man in my grip in the process.

I felt the pressure begin to accumulate in my chest, warming my insides. Would he let me go if I needed to get to the surface, or would we both drown?

The familiar warmth roiled up my limbs, coating the chill of the water. I could almost imagine steam lifting off my bones.

The electricity snapped from my fingertips, the fire ants marching up and down my arms at a feverish pace.

Aidan's hands tightened, and I felt my electricity

shoot into him. I could almost follow the pattern of charges as they rocketed through at breakneck speed into his body and through his legs.

Bubbles escaped Aidan's lips, and he twitched as the energy cracked into whatever was at his feet.

Without warning, whatever held him let go.

Aiden released my wrist, and we shot for the surface. Both of us were careful not to touch, careful not to pull the other under until we could breathe.

Choking on freedom, Aidan touched my shoulder with his fist and motioned to the boat.

Between wet coughs, he said, "We can't—stay in the—water."

The thunder roiled, almost drowning out his words, and we both looked up. The dark clouds were thickening, grumbling like an overstuffed belly, before lightning shot from cloud to cloud, blinding me.

Gargling on grimy, coppery-tasting water, I was stunned to hear the echo of the thunder still ringing in my head.

Moving jerkily, we turned to the overturned craft. A bony arm slapped onto the side of the boat.

We stopped, our teeth chattering. The emancipated arm hung over the boat from the other side. Tendons and muscles were visible, clenching and tightening as the thing dragged itself up.

I glanced to the black door near the shore. It was close, but would it be close enough to swim to?

Aidan's choke jerked my attention back to our boat. A once-human face peeked over the side. Bony fingers clawed into the wood, marking it as it bellied its way to the top.

Skin hung loose off yellowed bone, sagging like an

oversized suit. The eyes were depressed in their sockets, and the lips had completely deteriorated, leaving a crude, toothy grin of black and yellow teeth. Long, thin orange and white hair streamed from its skull, dripping with swamp water.

The creature focused paled eyes on us and emitted a hissing groan that rocked fear up my spine harder than the thunder.

"Nora, the dream before we woke up..." Aidan began, his eyes straining to tear away from the creature.

"Aidan, I really wish you'd save this for later. You didn't sacrifice me. It's okay." I began to kick back, pushing myself away from the boat. Maybe we could get a head start to the shore. To Aidan, I whispered, "Should we make a break for it?"

"Nora!" Aidan snapped, catching my attention.

I glowered at him.

"It was my grandpa, and he passed me a note that said: *She met him before*." His electric gaze drifted to the creature on the boat when he added, "I had thought that maybe it was Damien, and since you weren't there when I woke up..." He shook his head and pointed to the creature on the boat. "Didn't you say that one of the guys with your aunt had a leather jacket with his initials in the sleeve?"

My eyes snapped back to the living corpse. The jacket was tattered and nearly falling off the bones, but the initials were stitched on the shoulder partially covered in mud: "JWD."

My memory flared, picturing the tall, skinny man with long, orange hair.

"They never found them," I said, spitting water. Every muscle in my body demanded to move. The five-year-old Nora in me didn't want to stay and see what type of fear he could subject her to again.

Aidan glanced between JWD and me. "Let's swim to the shore."

"We won't make it," I whispered. It was hopeless; we might as well have drowned.

This couldn't entirely be possible though, could it? Was that really JWD? I stared at the foreign corpse-like creature. I couldn't let it catch me, not like before. My shoulder ached with a phantom pain, and I nudged Aidan.

"Yeah, to the shore," I sputtered.

Every muscle quivering, but now it wasn't from the cold water. I'd almost drowned today; I didn't want to risk it again.

"There's more than one," Aidan warned.

A second peal of thunder pained my ears, and lightning brightened the mire, making the rotting thing on the boat shine.

At the boat's tip, a face peered just above the smooth surface. Bubbles rippled out of a hole where a nose once was. A mess of blonde hair strung over his face, and one eye had been eaten clean from its socket, but I recognized the hateful stare. It was the same man who'd stepped into our backyard to help Nell take us away.

The shock of being watched shot through me as sharp as the lightning, and I shoved at Aidan to move.

"Don't get caught, don't get caught," I repeated as we struggled through the water. The mantra followed each stroke, and I focused on the shore, unwilling to look behind me. I could feel Aidan beside me. His elbows and knees knocked into mine.

The shore was slowly getting closer. Too slowly and I gargled the words.

Kicking down, I'd hoped to find something to run on. On my third attempt, I found the ground.

"Aidan, there's the bo…" The stony fingers wrapped around my ankle, digging into the bone.

Before I could scream, I was yanked under.

CHAPTER THIRTY-SEVEN

Yanked under, I felt the dirty water spear my sinuses.

Twisting violently, I kicked with my free leg. *Don't get caught.* With each flail, I didn't hit anything. It was either at a clever angle or was able to dodge my foot. I couldn't see it in the dark.

I was being dragged down, but I wouldn't stop fighting—I couldn't. The last thing I wanted was to let these guys win again. They took away my sister! They wouldn't have me too.

Swinging blindly, I hit something with my socked foot. The impact crinkled my toes in a hot flash of pain.

The hand released me, and I swam to the surface, arms flailing, then splashed for the shore. Another hand grabbed my forearm but didn't pull me under; it pulled me closer.

Wiping the hair out my eyes, I stopped struggling when I saw it was Aidan who had me.

The rain began to fall, pelting my cold skin as if the

drops were ice chips. The clouds gurgled above before belching another bolt of lightning. The light shone on the black surface of the door, inviting us closer.

Aidan pulled me up until my foot touched the soft mud.

Staggering with him, I choked on the stagnant water and wanted to gag. The shore wasn't nearly as sludgy as the other side. Pausing, I tried to catch my breath and looked behind us. The water was disturbed by the rain, but I couldn't see the two men.

Aidan's electric eyes met mine. "Was it them?" he asked, wiping his mouth.

As an answer to his question, a moan resounded from the river, and the two corpses began to emerge. Water spurted out of rib cages and holes in their flesh like from a leaky garden hose.

The one with the yellow hair uttered what could have been a cackle from the good side of his face. The other side was missing half the lower jaw.

"Come on." Aidan grabbed my hand.

I held onto him, grateful that he was there. If I'd lost him, the doppelgängers would've been right.

Together, we stumbled into the trees.

The door wasn't far.

Reaching for it, I prayed for it to come closer. My hand brushed the doorknob, the solid, cool surface a relief beneath my fingertips. I didn't get a chance to curl my hand around it and twist before it disappeared.

Fingers collapsing together, I almost fell forward. If Aidan hadn't been holding my hand to tug me back, I would have run face first into a tree. "What the hell happened?" I demanded.

Aidan heaved a frustrated growl and glanced over

his shoulder. "I don't know, but *they're* almost here."

Don't get caught, not like before. I didn't need any more encouragement than that.

With Aidan taking lead, we loped through the jungle, hopping and tripping through the thick brush.

Our feet were completely hidden by the thick vegetation, making it easy to falter over vines and exposed roots. The rain thickened until not even the canopy of trees could shelter us from the storm.

Branches clawed for our eyes as we ducked, dodged, and swatted at them. The dead men were doing a much better job at avoiding the pitfalls. They didn't trip or stumble behind us, slowly advancing.

Knocking through the leaves and trees, the zombies seemed louder than us, unless it was my imagination.

Distracted by what was behind me, I didn't see the clearing until we blundered into it.

Aidan threw up an arm, crossing it over my stomach and halting me in my tracks.

Catching my balance, I saw the reason. Inches from the tip of my toe was a sharp drop. The crevice in the earth was clouded several feet down. There was no telling how far we'd fall. If I had kept running, I would have run right into the rocky gorge.

Shakily, I took a step back, feeling the vertigo that often came with heights.

Aidan snatched my arm and pulled me off to the side. I twisted to see the swinging bridge. It crossed over the cut in the earth, striking hope.

Across the bridge was a tall, black door, just within the tree line. I swallowed hard, pondering whether this one would disappear on us too. Were we following a bread crumb trail to a trap?

Hearing the harsh gnashing of teeth behind us, I didn't peek. It was eventually drowned out by the reverberated roll of thunder. I could feel it through my ribs.

As we neared the bridge, I couldn't mask my suspicion. "I don't think it's safe." I eyed the gnarled, frayed rope. Moss clung to the cracked, grey planks that still remained, though not all of them were there.

Stepping onto the decaying bridge, Aidan shouted back, "Better than the alternative."

I looked back to see the two men reach the clearing.

Turning back, I saw Aidan was already shuffling along the planks, gripping the ropes on either side as he tested each new plank before stepping on it. The boards creaked and groaned between thunderclaps but held together. "Do as I do!" he shouted back.

Lightning shot from the sky, but instead of reaching for another cloud, it rocketed into the gorge. The thunder reverberated through the skies like an angry god.

Following Aidan, I mimicked his steps and didn't look back. Clinging to the ropes, I braced myself as the bridge swayed under our shifting weight.

I tried to convince myself not to look down and concentrate on each new step, but my eyes betrayed me. They caught sight of the abyss below. If I fell, I'd be falling forever. The idea prompted me to lift my chin.

Behind us, a horrible raspy moan could be heard, sounding closer than before.

I glanced over my shoulder to see the dead men step stiffly onto the bridge. Their weight didn't affect the crippled boards the way ours did. They walked on the planks as if they didn't notice the dangerous plunge below.

Aidan and I kept going at a steady pace and made sure that each new board was safe while our pursuers were both unhindered and unafraid.

They were gaining on us without much effort. I warned Aidan, and he started to skip the testing phase and just eased into each new plank, lengthening each stride.

Mirroring his every move, my heartbeat raced as we edged forward like sloths. I would have given anything for a fast-forward button.

The weather-smoothed boards were becoming slick with the extra rain.

A wind brushed my back, and I looked behind me and screamed.

The tall, decaying creature wearing the tattered JWD jacket swung an arm at me again, whistling past my shirt.

My scream launched Aidan forward into a run. I raced after him, abandoning caution for fear.

Slipping on the planks, I tried to ignore my inflamed palms. The fraying rope grew hot as I slid along it to keep from falling. The bridge swung hard with each leaping step, threatening to pitch us both over. Lightning snaked from the heavens, and there was nothing but a brilliant white light.

For a split second, I thought I was dead.

Blinded, I stumbled, unable to run. It wasn't until the thunder bellowed that I knew I was still alive. My ears ached.

I nearly ran into Aidan's back when my mud-soaked foot slapped on solid ground. My clattering nerves didn't ease as much as I would have liked.

Shouldering past Aidan, I realized why he'd stopped.

Short flames licking at the jungle's bed ahead of us, crackling and hissing in the moisture. It wasn't large, but it wasn't small enough for the rain to extinguish either. Seeing the fire, I was reminded of the poem.

"From the lightning in the sky..."

I looked to my companion to tell him when he dropped to his hands and knees, facing the bridge.

I stopped to see what he was doing. The men were moving with steady certainty. There wasn't much time.

Aidan's muddy fingers fumbled to unravel the rope that held the bridge at the base.

"No," I whispered. "The door is right there. We can make it." I grabbed his arm to tug him along with me. The smell of smoke was thicker; it seemed the heavy rainfall wasn't putting out the flames.

To my surprise, Aidan jerked away from my grip. "If they're not dead, I bet that door won't stay when we reach it."

It was a good theory, but after a quick inspection of the knots, I knew the impossibility of his mission. Years of weather had drawn the ropes so taut it would take a knife to cut them lose.

Digging into my pocket, I pulled the glass key free. "Here!"

Aidan snatched it from me and tried to shatter it on the wood, but it remained intact.

Staggering to my feet, I ran into a tree veined with ivy. One of its broken branches dipped into the fire that was starting to spread just within the tree line where it was still dry.

Darting for it, I pulled on it, cracking it free of the

tree and dragged it from the brush. It was roughly the length of a baseball bat and twice as thick.

Nervous, I turned the awkward thing in my throbbing hands, trying to find the right grip. The dead men and their permanent grins were getting closer.

Aidan had flung the skeleton key aside and persisted at the knot with an agonizing stubbornness.

I ran for the black door, which was a few feet from the fires. Wanting to prove Aidan wrong, I grabbed for the doorknob.

To my surprise, the door didn't disappear, but the golden doorknob faded the instant my hand drew closer. My hand swept straight through as if it were a mirage.

My heart skipped a beat. Aidan was right.

The door appeared solid. Reaching to touch it, I saw it begin to fade, the vegetation behind it becoming visible. I drew back quickly, before it could disappear, and the door appeared solid again. The last one must have disappeared because I'd thrown myself into it.

Spinning around, I saw the fire had grown twice its size. The smoke snaked up the trees and over the edge of the gorge.

We had to figure this out, and there wasn't much time.

"Aidan!" My voice vanished in the thunder.

He didn't look up, the enemy shambling just a few feet from him.

Inching away from the trees, I remembered all those safety posters and videos from grade school announcing not to stand beneath a tree during a lightning storm.

Avoiding the majority of the heat from the fire, I danced along its outer edge, narrowly avoiding the deadly drop to sidestep the fire. The heat stung my cold skin and my numbed fingers as they struggled to keep hold of the newfound club.

The men shambled within arm's reach.

I grabbed Aidan's shoulder and pulled. He didn't resist me this time and stood up, his expression dripping with disappointment. Backing away from the bridge, we stopped when the heat behind us grew too intense.

It had consumed the dry tall grass beneath the canopy of jungle, blocking access to the black door.

CHAPTER THIRTY-EIGHT

"Nora," Aidan warned.

Scraping my brain for options—too few that were useful—I felt fear seize me by the throat and froze mid-idea.

"What do we do?" Aidan demanded, shaking my shoulder.

An excellent question. Just seeing the two men, despite their frail frames, made my knees weak and my blood pump acid.

The only way to win was running. It worked before and they disappeared. Glancing back at the fire, I tried to think about that night only to find fear.

I gripped Aidan's arm for support. The muscles in my legs were twitching as if ready to collapse. He should have sacrificed me when he had the chance.

"We have to fight," I wheezed.

Aidan shook my arm again. "How do you kill a zombie?" he asked.

Taking a deep breath, I focused on Aidan's pale eyes. There was something in his gaze that steadied me. I straightened my posture, and my wobbly legs gained some stability. They weren't the same men who'd kidnapped me; they were walking corpses—zombies.

Something in my face must have startled him, because he let me go and glanced at our pursuers.

As I lifted my club, the lightning flashed, brightening the decayed faces as they stepped on solid ground. The lip-less grins twitched with what flesh was left around their mouths.

The Edgar Allen Poe poem had been the clue. The lightning from the sky, the demon in my view. Aidan had said it himself; his grandpa had told him that I'd met him before. I thought about my sister. They threw her into that fire, and it was only right to do the same.

"Cutting off their heads won't be enough," I said. "They have to burn."

Still gripping me, Aidan paused, looking between me and the zombies before saying, "Fair enough."

As if it were a cue, I thrust my club into the flames that warmed our backs.

The zombies lunged forward, but the flames hadn't caught the drenched club quickly enough.

Aidan swung, stepping in front of me, and knocked a hard fist into the jaw of the one-eyed zombie, Blondie. The other half of its jaw crumpled under the blow and spun to the wet grass.

The two staggered to regain their balance, and Blondie was quick to fling an arm and shove Aidan to the ground.

I checked on my club to see the smoke as the fire licked down to the dry center, blackening and sizzling the tip.

JWD snagged Aidan's loose shirt, dragging him to his feet. Time had run out.

My wild swing with my sizzling club missed JWD, though it hit Blondie in the chest before he could launch himself again.

Adjusting my grip, I shoved the amber tip of the club forward like a lance. The tip jabbed between two ribs, and I pressed my weight into the thrust. The one good eye focused on me and sharpened. Bony fingers reached out, scratching deep into the wood.

Baring my teeth, I shoved at him again. The sound of one of the ribs shattering echoed between thunder cracks.

As I stumbled forward, the club penetrated deeply, throwing us both off balance. The flames from the club flourished, finding something dry within the zombie and devouring what it found. All I could imagine were dried innards roasting, and I almost let go.

Blondie produced an unearthly shriek, reeling away from me.

This close, the fetid stench of rotting meat and stagnant water prevented me from breathing.

I ripped the club free, but he didn't collapse as I'd hoped, though the fire feasted on him. Light glared from the empty eye socket and created a perverse Jack O' Lantern grin.

I swung again, missing by inches as he stumbled back toward the bridge. There was only two ways to go: through me or across the bridge.

Batting at his chest, Blondie spun into the rain, distracted.

Raising my elbows, I held the club like a baseball

bat, ready for another attack.

Out of the corner of my eye, I saw Aidan fall near the edge of the gorge. His arms flew out for balance before rising to protect his face. JWD's back was to me as he towered over my friend.

Aidan eyes met mine as I switched targets.

Striking down, I hoped I wouldn't aim false and used every available muscle. I didn't just want to hurt JWD; I wanted to kill him.

Aidan ducked as the club collapsed the corpse's brittle shoulder.

The aim wasn't perfect, but the impact injected a jolt up my elbows.

* * *

The worst moment had been when the car stopped. It meant they weren't going to leave us alone anymore. Neive and I had ducked off the backseats and huddled on the floor. The blood at the edge of Neive's lip, where Blondie had hit her, had stopped.

I had glanced up at our aunt, who peered out the window, eyes narrow and intent. She had smiled at me whenever I'd looked up, as if it were all part of the game, but this time she didn't look at me.

The two men got out first, rocking the little car as they did, and Neive and I pressed ourselves to the seat, attempting to blend in with the upholstery.

Aunt Nell opened the side door, allowing us a view of our destination. I could make out the coniferous trees and untrimmed grass. No campers, no noise outside the forest—it was just us. The sun was going down in the distance, and it would be dark soon.

I whimpered as I turned to my sister. I was grateful to have her with me. In our short lives, there had rarely been a moment I'd done anything without her.

Sliding out of the car, Nell moved so Blondie could reach in. He snatched Neive's arm, yanking her from me as easily as if he were picking berries.

Shrieking a protest, Neive kicked, almost hitting me in her frenzy.

The door behind me swung open, and the redhead caught my arm. I pulled back and tried to wrestle my way to the other side. Two hands grabbed my arm, stinging my skin. Then he tugged hard. A sharp, wrenching pain shot up my shoulder. I'd never felt pain like that before. It wasn't like scraping a knee on the pavement; it was dizzying, scalding, and unyielding.

Screaming, I was wrapped up in one arm and lifted out of the car. JWD's free hand slapped over my mouth to muffle the agonized shrieks. "Shut up or I'll pluck out your eyes," he growled in my ear. The scorching in my shoulder hurt at every move. To this day, I can't compare it to any pain I've endured as an adult.

I couldn't stop crying but managed to stop screaming to hear Neive shouting for help so loud and shrill her voice cracked.

Calmly, Aunt Nell walked up to me and the redhead. Her eyes met mine then latched onto my arm. "What did you do?" she asked, though I barely heard her over Neive's screaming.

"What?" the redhead snapped.

Her arm shot out like a snake and cracked my head. The strike stunned my vision. The world tipped a little farther, and the pain in my shoulder was now coupled with a fire in my cheek.

Neive went still, her breath hard and short. Blondie had one arm around her stomach, carrying her at his waist like a sack. Dark eyes round and frightened, Neive looked to our aunt.

"That's better," Aunt Nell said and asked again, "Her arm is broken?"

"No, it's not," JWD scoffed. "Dislocated, see..."

I shrieked before he could touch my arm, and he stopped.

Aunt Nell took a deep breath. "Just tie them up. We have work to do." As she turned her back to me, the coldness was almost as harsh as the slap. Aunt Nell had always been warm. Her visits were always fun. This wasn't the aunt I'd known. She couldn't be the same woman who brought us presents and let us watch grown-up movies. This was an impostor, a stranger.

In the clearing, sticks, hay, and logs had been piled to a peak. Dirt had been dug all around the monstrous mound, leaving barren ground for several feet. Nell walked toward it and produced matches and a little black book from her pocket.

* * *

As I raised the club again, the scared little girl fell inward, and the fury burst free.

The flames on my club caught tattered strings on JWD's jacket, singeing the edges and burning the side of his neck. The zombie shrieked, turning its haunted eyes to me.

It discarded Aidan, and its talon-like fingers reached for my neck.

Behind it, Aidan rolled out of the way. His hand

slipped, and he caught the long wet grass before he could fall right over the edge.

I jumped away from the outstretched hand and spun, falling straight into Blondie. The battle cry tore from my throat, melding with the thundering clouds.

As I swung the club, Blondie caught my wrist. His other hand snagged my free arm. *Trapped.* The idea seized my stomach.

The little flesh that was left slid off his bone and stuck to my skin. The fire within his chest had been pinched out, leaving his innards sizzling and red but not flaming.

Twisting, I tried to yank free. JWD ripped the club from my hand, flinging it away.

I watched in horror as it landed several feet away in the tangled wet grass.

"Aidan!"

JWD hissed, his foul breath choking off my shouts. Raising cruelly tipped fingers, he aimed them at my eyes.

Blinking, I turned my head and felt JWD's bony hand grab my chin. Hard fingers pressed against my jaw, threatening to break my neck.

Turning my face, I felt the sharpened fingertips were inches from my eyes.

Squeezing my eyes shut, I anticipated the pain. He was going to have to tear through my eyelids to get to my eyes. The thought set me trembling with the same disabling terror as when he had yanked me from the dandelion-colored car.

The jerky grunt caused me to open my eyes.

The pointed fingers at my throat scratched as JWD twisted to the side, releasing me.

Aidan was there, balled up fists, swinging at the zombie as a distraction.

Seeing my opportunity, I twisted in Blondie's grip, dropping to the ground. The force of my fall jerked me from his grip.

Frantic, I crawled past JWD, feeling something snag the back of my shirt. I heard the fabric tear, but he didn't stop me. Aidan kicked JWD's shin, and I heard the crunch as I fumbled in the tall grass for the club.

The fire was drawing closer, rising higher and hotter. The rain didn't seem to be able to put it out. A mile away, lightning shot down into the gorge.

My fingers curled around the stump. I wanted to shove it into the flames, but there wasn't time. On my knees, I swung back blindly.

Missing, I used the momentum to stand and gripped the club in both my hands to keep swinging. JWD leaned back, avoiding one as it collided hard into Blondie's fractured chest.

"Into the fire!" I shouted at Aidan, and he charged.

Together, we caught Blondie under the arms and pushed him toward the wall of flames. His one eye watched me, and his hand snaked around my wrist. The merciless heat burned my face, but Blondie was a lot lighter than I anticipated.

The hand snapped, cracking the wrist in half as he flew toward the flaming wall. It took me a second to realize the hand still clung to my arm. A shriek pierced the night, high pitched and grating, as Blondie disappeared into the fire.

Turning, the club in my free hand, I saw Aidan had reached JWD first. A swift kick had left the corpse without a working leg, and Aidan had his ankle. He was dragging JWD toward the fire.

The zombie grabbed Aidan's arm, fingers curled as if to strike for his eyes, and he pulled at my friend to bring him down.

Warmth roiled my insides, building just likes the flames, and the scalding ants reminded me of the peculiar savior I held within. My test with Damien must have been positive, and there was no time to think if that was a bad or not.

Thrown off balance, Aidan was forced to release JWD and fall to the grass.

Raising my club, I swung without aiming. I didn't worry about accuracy this time. With all my weight, I threw the heat from my warming stomach, up into my limbs, and into that single strike.

I wasn't a little girl anymore; he couldn't hurt me.

CHAPTER THIRTY-NINE

Neive had to be tied-up and gagged. They hadn't bothered with me because of my arm. As we sat next to the car, they busied themselves with the bonfire.

I held my injured arm, wishing over and over for the pain to go away. Tears weren't working, and I thought I'd used them all up.

I was shaking from the shock. It only made my shoulder hurt more.

Neive wanted me to run, but I didn't. Fear and uncertainty kept me sitting next to my sister. I couldn't leave her, either.

With all eyes averted, I picked at Neive's knots instead. It was extremely hard to do with only one good hand.

I'd run but not without her.

The flames of their bonfire strained to reach the darkening skies. Mom and Dad would be worrying about us. They'd come and save us, wouldn't they?

We were far enough away from the fire to be denied its warmth. Goosebumps raced up and down my arms and bare legs.

In front of the warm fire, Aunt Nell raised her left arm up to the sky. She eased opened the worn spine of her black book. Words that I didn't recognize began to roll off her tongue. At the end, she finished with, "...Dismal is the Demon's Grave. Dismal and dark to what I crave. With one soul of blackened sin. One with power..." *The rest was muddled in the back of my mind.*

The next thing I knew, the sky rumbled with dark, swirling clouds. Lightning streaked, followed closely by a ground-shaking thunder clap.

It was enough to make us both jump. Piercing pain ripped through my arm, and I cried out. Luckily, my voice was disguised by the noise above.

My fingertips were scraped raw against the rough fibers of the rope. Having to sit next to my sister prevented me from taking more than a fleeting glance at the knot at a time. Our captors weren't completely dumb. They'd check us from time to time to make sure we were silent and complacent.

The knot had loosened a little, though it wasn't enough. When the redhead stalked toward us. I was quick to drop my hand, trying to seem fidgety. He came for me anyway, cold eyes focused and unwelcoming.

He picked me up under the arms, and I began to cry. The pain rolled through my shoulder, preventing me from struggling.

I heard Neive's frantic screams below as she wriggled on the ground to stand.

Aunt Nell's haunting words rippled through the air, seeming to affect everything. The darkened sky began to leak rain, and the fire grew stronger. A breeze flowed through the surrounding trees, shaking the branches above.

JWD walked me past my aunt, and I pleaded with her, hoping that maybe whatever evil possessed her would snap at my voice.

JWD lifted me high over his head, above the flames.

The fire prickled my skin. My throat was raw, and I kicked, trying not to twist. My arm felt as if it were about to fall off. The white-hot pain was making my head swoon.

"Remember to toss her in the center," Blondie grumbled.

I looked to the fire and gasped. The pain no longer mattered. I didn't care if I had to carry the pain for hours. I didn't want to die in that heat! I twisted, and JWD almost lost his grip as he held me high.

"Wait!" my aunt bellowed, stopping both of the men.

"Not yet. If you put her in too soon, he won't come." The anger in her voice was hypnotizing. "If I hadn't opened my eyes, you two would have botched it!" She sounded furious; I had never heard my aunt like this before.

Blondie grabbed me from JWD, holding me at arm's length, and I swallowed bile. Grinding his teeth together, JWD turned his furious gaze back to my sister. With excellent timing, Neive wriggled from her bonds and stood up, free. She took off at a run.

I howled for Neive to keep running, to find our parents.

Winding a foot back, I kicked with the heel of my bare foot and caught something soft between Blondie's legs.

He shouted, dropping me.

I fell, stunned. It was Neive's voice that launched me forward. Gripping my arm, I ran after JWD, but my aunt grabbed the back of my t-shirt, dragging me back. "Now!" she shouted. "We cannot open the portal without her! Now!"

I twisted in her grip and swung my good arm for her face. As I clawed at her eyes, a nail caught her eyelid, and she let me go. Warm blood smeared my fingertips as I raced into the trees, high-pitched screams following.

I turned just in time to see JWD, with Neive in his arms, swinging her around like a doll and smiling. The bleeding had started around her mouth again.

Ducking into the trees, I was momentarily forgotten and kept still, afraid to move or breathe.

Neive shouted words that I only heard our father use when he was extremely mad.

"Just have this one!" JWD told Nell. Blondie was still on the ground clutching his groin.

"Then use her. But now!" Aunt Nell commanded.

My eyes caught Neive's dark ones from the brush. I ducked down to avoid being seen, fear holding me in place. I wanted to save her, but I didn't know how.

JWD didn't hesitate. There wasn't any dramatic suspense. He just threw her into the air as if she weighed as much as a puppy.

She never screamed, but I did, tears streaking my face.

I couldn't see her through my tears. The flames had completely engulfed her body.

The flames shot high, several feet higher than the woods. Blue sparks crackled upward, twisting as if caught in a vortex.

My voice had alerted JWD, and I turned and ran deeper into the trees. My helpless panic propelled me through the forest, ducking and weaving.

Clutching my arm tight to my chest, I never looked back.

* * *

The club slammed into the back of JWD's head.

The crunch was sickeningly powerful. A spiderweb of cracks split down the center of his skull but didn't cave it in. I felt the heated anger in my stomach burst, leaving me weaker when I raised the club to swing again. The club felt as if it had gained fifty pounds.

JWD gargled a shout, his jaw opened unnaturally wide. Raising an arm for protection, I gloated in satisfaction even when JWD began to form words, his tongue thin and loose, but I heard little before the thunder cut him off. "Jus' lie…"

The zombie staggered into Aidan, who rolled out of the way. The corpse caught a tree before it could collapse. Spinning its irregular head towards us, it emitted a growling hiss and repeated in a powerful voice, "Jus' lie 'im!" I wouldn't have thought a corpse could have a voice. Wouldn't his voice box have shriveled by now?

I looked to Aidan for help.

Aidan's eyes were round as he repeated, "Just like him?"

That's when JWD dove at me.

CHAPTER FORTY

My club punched JWD in the jaw.

His fingers were inches from my face. JWD's skull snapped backwards, and a sour, rotten smell gagged me.

Aidan picked up JWD's leg. With a violent tug and bared teeth, Aidan hauled the creature toward the forest fire.

Before JWD could sit up and attack, I slammed the club down onto his head, chest, legs—whatever I could to keep him down. Each blow crumpled the living corpse, twisting it at impossible angles.

The righteous violence no longer coursed through each swing. I was numbed, like I was watching someone else drive each hardened blow. Someone else could do something like that without emotions, not me.

It was like I was on auto. I wasn't going to give him a moment of hope.

I remembered that crude smirk when he stalked out

of the trees with Neive under his arm.

My next strike burst the zombie JWD's left eye like jelly. I should have felt sick, I should have stopped, but I couldn't. As I lifted the club again and again, it seemed to gain weight with each swing. Gravity dealt half of the blows as I followed Aidan to the scorching fire.

It wasn't until Aidan dropped JWD's leg that I swung the club away from me and into the brush.

Reaching down, I swatted at the flailing arms. I curled my fist around the tattered jacket, the letters on the sleeve hidden by my palm. With a jerk, I sat him up and peered into the shattered, smiling face. The infamy of his memory seemed silly, almost exaggerated.

Broken and helpless, he resembled what I should have empathized with.

I wish I could tell you that I felt a little remorseful for that final shove, that a part of me regretted it later, but that would be lying. Forgiveness was the furthest thing from my mind. He might have been human once, but he wasn't much of one any more.

With Aidan's help, we flung JWD's corpse into the flames.

Blue sparks snapped and roared to the sky. They were the same hues I'd seen with Neive.

JWD's final shriek was cut off.

Somehow I'd thought there'd be more satisfaction, but I felt nothing. *Dismal is the Demon's Grave.*

The clouds overhead rumbled, and I realized Aidan was staring at me. Panting, he reached up and curled his fingers around the clinging severed hand on my arm, Blondie's hand.

I had to pull away before the fingers snapped loose.

Bone scraped skin but didn't cut.

Lifting the hand with missing fingers up for me to see, Aidan tossed it into the flames. The flesh flared in repulsive sizzles.

"The door," I croaked, seeing the black surface shimmer just over the lower flames near the gorge. The fire was approximately four feet, which was small compared to the rest. The grass could only sustain it for so long, and sitting out in the rain, it wasn't nearly as protected as the body of flames in the trees. There wasn't a tree, and from where I stood, there was only one option.

Aidan ran his grimy hands through his hair, slicking it back against his scalp. "Maybe we should walk down 'til we find where it hasn't reached."

"Or," I offered, "we can run through it."

Aidan's face pinched. "You're joking."

I shook my head and saw the disbelief on his face. "It's not at its hottest yet. It's a new fire, right?"

"Well, yes…"

"And we're not exactly dry," I said, facing him. The flames reflected off his electric eyes, making them appear almost white.

I pointed to the trees. "Do you really think Damien will make it easy for us if we walk down the forest line?" I knew I should be scared of those flames. They had devoured JWD and Blondie like tinder. The fact that we had made it this far, survived most of the swamp, made me feel invincible somehow. The scrapes, bruises, and gashes were all worth it. Never in my life had I felt like I conquered something so great. I wasn't about to let fire stop me.

Reaching over, I took Aidan's hand, gripping his

chilled fingers. I didn't want him to hesitate. "On the count of three." I watched his face change until his grip tighten, reassured.

He tried to smile, failing. "Ready," he rumbled in a voice that had been inhaling smoke.

"One."

We readied our stances.

"Two."

Aidan raised his free hand to his head, against his hair, and I did the same.

"Three!"

Together, we took off. Right foot, left foot. Long strides fought every ache we'd endured.

The fire intensified the closer we drew.

Scalding heat ready to peel flesh grew insanely hot, and I felt my stride falter. This could be a bad idea.

Aidan tugged my hand, and I jumped.

Steam hissed, and I breathed out as the feverish heat burned my lungs. I smelled burnt hair before we landed on solid, untouched soil within the trees.

We staggered together, and I spun to snag Aidan's shirt, gripping him to make sure he was real. My heart pounded so hard it made me dizzy. Blinking, I could see the ash tipping my eyelashes. I gave myself a once over to make sure I wasn't on fire.

After a long pause, Aidan broke out into delirious laughter. He wrapped me up in his arms with a ferocious, "*Whooooo*!"

Stunned, it took me a second to realize why we were celebrating. We had just walked through *fire*.

Laughter bubbled up before I even knew I was laughing. I returned the hug, clinging to him as if he might let me go. "The door! Before it disappears!"

Aidan didn't let me go like I had expected, one arm wrapped around my waist, holding me tight to him. He brushed a hand down my head to the back of my neck as if he couldn't quite believe I was real.

My mouth pressed to his shoulder, and I felt myself smiling. He leaned his head against the side of mine. He smelled like sweat and smoke and life. He smelled like safety.

We stood like that for several seconds, the fire crackling and the rain pattering the leaves. It almost felt as if we were in our own world.

I think he whispered, "Thank God," but I couldn't be sure when he pulled away.

His limp seemed to have worsened. Keeping one hand around his waist, I ducked under his arm, hoping to support him. He grimaced but didn't protest. Easing up to the door, I half expected it to fade from view, but it remained solid, just as Aidan thought it would.

No symbol etched itself in the wood; instead, it was a smooth, dark surface reflecting the flames behind us.

Reaching out with one hand, Aidan grabbed the doorknob. It was solid in his grasp, and he twisted, swinging it inward for us to see a lush, green meadow.

It was sparkling from a recent rainfall. The clouds above were heavy globs but broke enough to allow strips of moonlight through.

As we stepped through the threshold, we were forced to release each other. We'd traded buckets of chilling rain and adrenaline for a peaceful meadow. I felt relief slowly begin to relax my shoulders.

Aidan nudged me and pointed to our right. A tall, square structure made of crumbling pieces of stone sat entirely out of place.

Pillars stretched to the sky, displaying large stone-carvings that I had never seen in history books. They were odd creatures. One looked similar to a sphinx, except it had a bear-like body and a horse's head. The pillars rolled down the meadow along an overgrown pathway, beckoning us in.

Statues of people stood between the pillared walkway. Most had fallen over, though some were only missing chunks or limbs. Everything had been marred by weather and time. The place looked ancient.

"Should we go check it out?" Aidan asked huskily.

I nodded, unsure what to think. Wasn't this the end? Shouldn't we be given some options for our friends? A doorway home? Damien, even?

Cautious, we approached the intimidating structure, taking our time. The bright full moon proved to be an excellent guide. Very few shadows were hidden, though in the meadow, nothing could jump out without giving us a very long head start. The only place something could hide would be the temple ahead, which naturally was where we were headed.

As I kicked through the tall grass, it tickled my calves and ankles. My already soaked sock and shoe weren't fazed by the dewy droplets.

"What do you think?" Aidan's breath tickled my ear.

I shook my head, undecided.

The walls were vertical, unlike a pyramid, though it was as tall as a five-story building with no windows.

"You think it's a trap?" I asked.

Aidan's wonderment melted, the smile twitching, and he squeezed my hand without answering.

My sock landed on something hard and smooth, unlike the soft earth. Looking down, I saw cracked white pavement, much like the building's walls. Weeds sprang up between the walkway's splits. Slowing our step, we focused on the only opening available. The archway was dimly lit, but I couldn't see much from the edge of the grounds.

"We finished the Challenges," Aidan said after a pause. "This can't be a trap."

I thought, *Depending on those rules Damien clings to.*

As we followed the pillared walkway, I could make out the claustrophobic hallway and the torches lining the walls within.

"Looks like we've been expected," Aidan observed in a hushed tone.

I nodded stiffly. Questions began to plague my good mood as we slipped beneath the stone archway and into the narrow hallway. It was cramped within, easily a trap. Our footsteps announced our presence. The farther we ventured, the more I expected something to go wrong. The flickering torchlight flung our shadows around like baited fish.

After what felt like fifteen minutes—though it was probably much shorter—we could make out a shimmering black door. It was crudely out of place in the ancient ruins.

Reaching the door, I glanced over my shoulder to ensure we were alone. Aidan followed my stare before reaching out to grab the brass knob. Before his fingertips could graze it, the door voluntarily creaked inward.

Freezing, we watched as the circular room ignited with the same wall torches as the hallway. An ominous stone table lay in the center of the empty space.

Aidan took the lead, his hand not leaving mine as we slipped inside. The table was the only piece of furniture. On the stone slab was a beautiful jagged crystal that glowed with a pale pink light. I stopped within a foot of the doorway, ready to run back the way we'd come. Aidan stretched our arms as if my hand was a leash, and we both watched the glow of the crystal flicker and fade like a struggling light bulb.

"What now?" Aidan's whisper bounced off the walls.

"I think that this is it." I tilted my head back, looking up at the domed ceiling above.

"What do you mean?" Aidan asked. "Shouldn't there be a door leading us to everyone else?"

"I mean that we might have to do something else to get home."

"Correct." The voice was low. It resonated a vibration, nailing my feet to the floor. "I think it's time we all had a chat."

Chapter Forty-One

Damien was uncomfortably close.

My shoulder brushed against his chest, and I stepped back, colliding with Aidan.

Damien's lean figure lounged against the doorframe, barring our escape.

Aidan pulled me closer, centering us between the door and the stone table.

Damien's obsidian gaze narrowed as he stepped inside and slammed the black door shut with a jerk of his arm, never removing his gaze.

The ear-splitting slam made me jump.

Wearing only black, Damien crossed his arms over a well-defined chest. His clothes clung in all the right places. In our world, women would be tripping all over themselves. Hell, so would I, which made me wonder if this was what he really looked like or if it was another illusion.

Aidan broke the uncomfortable silence first. "So

then talk. We've won and are ready to take our friends and go home." His voice didn't waver, and I was glad he decided to confront the demon.

Damien leaned against the closed door as if we were casual friends, and his predatory eyes glistened. I couldn't decide whether it was amusement, excitement, or anger. "You disappoint me, Birket." He said the name as if it were poisoned. "You had a golden opportunity."

I glanced at Aidan, but his pale gaze was combating Damien's, unafraid. I had to give him points for that; I could barely hold the demon's gaze without wanting to fidget.

With a dismissive wave of his hand, Damien said, "Find the doorway and you can go home."

I swallowed hard before venturing the one question I dreaded to ask. "What about the rest?"

Damien tilted his head. "The rest?"

"Yes." My free hand twisted at my camisole, and I kept my expression from twitching, while inside, bombs were going off.

"Our friends. We won the Challenge, didn't we?"

I could have been mistaken, but I could have sworn the muscles in his arms twitched and his body stiffened, though his expression remained neutral. "You certainly did, and you can go home. They didn't. They're mine now."

Anger seeped between Aidan's teeth. "You told me that I could have them back if I won." It wasn't posed as a question. We both knew what Damien meant.

"Yes, if you stood up to our agreement and handed her over." Damien arched a straight eyebrow as if daring Aidan to Challenge him. "Then you would have." I opened my mouth to argue, but Aidan beat me to the punch.

"That isn't fair! I won, so it should stand either way." Aidan stepped in front of me.

Damien sighed, exasperated, and rolled his eyes heavenward before answering. "*Nothing* is fair." Despite his apathetic answer, he looked to me pointedly, and something heated flashed in those dark eyes.

I couldn't help but think of our friends trapped here with him. I licked my lips; my voice was softer than I would have liked. "Were those men real? The ones who kidnapped me?"

"Yes."

"Did they lose a Challenge?" I asked.

Damien nodded once.

"Are they dead?"

"You didn't notice? They've been dead for a long time."

I thought of Phoebe as a zombie. Would they suffer the same? "But it was them. How did they get here and…" I almost said her name and tried not to look over my shoulder at Aidan.

Damien's smirk held no pleasure.

I thought of the faceless people of Aidan's nightmare, of the witch Cody killed. Could they all have been real people playing a Challenge to stop others? Those evil men had lived here for years and suffered. Their souls—if such things existed—hadn't been allowed to leave.

Aidan readjusted his fingers in mine. It was a small comfort that meant a lot more than I think he realized. It meant someone was on my side. Someone had been through Hell with me.

Unable to look at Damien, I asked the wall beside his head, "How did Nell get out?" I waited for lightning to strike me down for mentioning her name in front of Aidan, but the demon didn't flinch.

"She never entered the Demon's Grave."

Aidan thankfully remained quiet.

I cleared my throat and heard the nervous laugh. "After all that, she never stepped foot in here?"

Damien didn't answer, just stared.

I shook my head. "That doesn't make any sense. Why kill a little girl?" I remember she wanted him to come to the flames. "Was it you she wanted or something else?"

Pushing himself away from the door, his arms still crossed, Damien tilted his head. "It was me she wanted."

"Why?" I demanded, hoping I'd get something out of him, a hint to his rules. I'd mentioned Nell in front of Aidan, but I hadn't told Aidan specifically. It was the only reason I could think as to why he didn't head off to kill Phoebe the instant I asked.

Aidan's fingers had tightened in mine, and in the demon's silence, he asked, "Why not take the portal at my grandpa's house?"

Damien smiled. "Why not, indeed?"

I glanced back at Aidan, lips parting as the pieces began to click into place. "Your grandpa wouldn't let her in."

"Keepers are good for that." Damien's voice echoed off the domed ceiling.

I could see the wheels turning in Aidan's head. "So she found an alternative route." He looked past me at

Damien. "There has to be an alternative way to get our friends back too. Always a loophole, right?"

Turning my head too fast, I felt dizzy. Aidan was right; there had to be a way. Nell found a way to contact the Demon's Grave. She sacrificed a little girl and sent two of her own accomplices into the Challenge.

Damien said, "Finally, an interesting request. You wish to negotiate?"

Between a rock and a hard place. I suddenly became very aware of that cliché. Clenching my jaw, it hurt with the rising bruise, but I needed the pain to ground me. Our answer could trap us into something, couldn't it? Negotiating with a demon couldn't come out pretty.

Aidan cleared his throat. "Just tell us how to get them back."

"Aw." Damien didn't mask his disappointment. "Re-entering the darkness between worlds could grant you such a request, if you survived, that is."

"You mean we'd have to go through another Challenge?" Aidan asked.

If Damien were aware of Aidan's disgust, he didn't respond physically. "Yes."

Aidan glanced between Damien and me. "There is no way that we can save them now?"

I couldn't stop the shaking that rippled through me like water. I could feel my chest heave at the idea of losing my friends. The distinctly strange warmth in my stomach began to build. Gritting my teeth, I glared at Damien. "We fought to get them back and we're getting them back."

Damien's eyes rolled down my body in a way that made me feel naked. Not in a sexual way, but the way a scientist might stare at a specimen. So detached and cold it was disturbing. I was exposed to so much emotion at once while he seemed oblivious. Out of the corner of my eye, I saw a flash of light.

The crystal in the center of the slab had changed colors from the light pink to a red. I was reminded of the little bomb from the museum.

Damien said, "Did you wonder how it's possible to influence the Challenges around you? You think that heated sensation you feel in your gut is purely coincidence?"

Aidan beat me to the punch. "What do you mean? Influencing the Challenge?"

Damien nodded toward me, watching Aidan. "She has sway. and she's catching on. Go too far and it's cheating," His dark gaze shifted to me, the threat lingering. "You came very, very close."

Behind me, the crystal faded to a pink, and I felt a lump in my throat.

Damien watched, fascinated, but otherwise held his mask of tolerance. I glanced at Aidan to see he'd paled a little.

He caught my eyes and mumbled, "How can that happen?"

"You're the Keeper. You should know," Damien shot back.

Aidan and I glanced at each other again, our confusion reflecting back and forth.

"Well," Aidan looked away first, "I don't, so help me out here."

"I don't train Keepers," Damien said sourly, "only Neophytes to the grave."

His grandpa, I thought. Aidan had said that his

cousin was supposed to inherit the house until he died shortly after their grandfather, leaving the Demon's Grave open to anyone. The guardian or Keeper must have been there to keep people like Nell out—to keep us out.

"Well, what if there technically wasn't a Keeper?" I tore my eyes from Aidan. "There must be a way we can leave with our friends. I mean, you just stole them from us."

"Did I?" Damien raised his eyebrows, the smile twitching. "Or were they victims of their own mistakes?" He gestured to the door behind him. "Opening doors without keys, succumbing to fear, wandering off the path, or just not being quick enough—these are all reasons for their failures. I'm afraid the only way to get them back is to replace them. Two for two."

Aidan growled, his hand crushing mine.

"How?" I asked.

Aidan jolted, and he shot me a glare, letting go of my hand. Stepping back, he looked at me as if I were an impostor. "What are you doing? This won't solve anything. Who would you even choose? There are four people stuck here."

"What about me?" I asked Aidan, lowering my voice. "He offered it to you before." The words were surreal; I wasn't sure I meant them. Trapped here forever? Me? *Don't think about it*, a voice snapped, *not now*.

Shaking his head, Aidan glanced at Damien before whispering to me, "Are you nuts? Come on, Nora, think about it. We can do this again. We can."

"You mean get out of here and come straight back

in?" I twisted the bottom of my shirt in my fist. Once out, would I be able to come back? Would Aidan? We'd be safe at home, no thoughts of survival or demons and nightmares.

"I'll give myself up," I said loudly, for Damien to hear.

Aidan shook his head at me, eyebrows pinched. "No, she doesn't."

"I could be a," my eyes darted to the stone slab, "sacrifice, couldn't I?" It took all I had not to cringe at the word. "Like you said before? Isn't that what Nell did to those two men?"

The smile tugged at the corners of Damien's mouth. "Clever conclusion." His eyes darkened as he stalked toward me, his pace smooth and unnerving, like a hunter.

"Nora, don't," Aidan hissed in my ear. "That won't help anything. He said it before. We can do another Challenge."

"What will it be, Nora?" Damien demanded, his lithe form advancing, taking his time.

I dreaded and welcomed every step. It was maddening.

Aidan stepped in front of me. "She's not going."

"I believe that decision is not yours." Damien's obsidian gaze never lost its focus.

Aidan turned to me. "Listen, Nora, you can't go."

"What if I can save everyone?" I whispered to him. "What if everyone could go home?"

He shook his head. "There is a better way than just giving yourself up. You think Phoebe would let you stay behind?"

"She'd have no choice." I crossed my arms. I didn't

want him to see that I was trembling inside, that every fear wanted me to stop what I was doing. *This was crazy*. My sister died as a sacrifice, and here I was offering myself over on a platter.

"Aidan, I lost someone to this place. I really don't want to lose everyone to it," I begged. I didn't expect him to understand. "Let me go."

He shook his head. "You're being selfish."

I stared at him in shock.

"You can't stay here and leave me to do this alone. If you stay, I'm still coming back."

I jerked as if someone threw a bucket of cold water over my head. "I…" I hadn't considered that. If Aidan were sacrificing himself for everyone, I wouldn't want to go home. That fact would hover over me for the rest of my life. After seeing what I had seen, knowing what those two men turned out to be. They deserved it, but like Damien said, *nothing was fair*.

"Nora, we've made it, and this doesn't have to be the end," Aidan whispered, his eyes pleading with me. "We'll figure something out. I won't give up on them, but I need you with me."

Swallowing back fierce pride I felt in my chest, I tried to speak but couldn't find the words. Over Aidan's shoulder, I saw Damien roll his eyes.

"That's very noble of you," Aidan said dismissively, "but Damien can't keep them forever."

"Yes, I can."

Aidan's eyes were wide, but he didn't look back at the demon. "Let me take her home this time."

"I can't let you. She has to allow it." Damien stepped around Aidan, circling us with the slow, methodical steps.

The pressure of their gazes was a physical weight, and I weakened a little. To give up everything so that these people I grew up with, these people who didn't deserve this, could go free. Or should I try and save them another way? With Aidan, I was sure we could try it, but there was always the idea that we'd fail.

I opened my mouth then closed it, taking what air I could. Fumbling for Aidan's hand, I said to Damien, not looking at him, "We'll be coming back."

Damien's hand snaked out in a blur, hard fingers gripping my arm, forcing me look into the demon's stony face. Everything in me went cold.

Aidan bristled like a mad-dog, but he paused just long enough for Damien to say, "Exchange yourself." Damien's lips hardly moved, eyes never blinking. "When you realize you can't find the way, the guilt will be far worse."

It took several seconds to find my voice. "Why won't we find the way?"

Aidan tugged at my other arm, but I resisted.

Damien held my eyes, something seething just beneath the ebony shine. "You'll regret it," he said so softly I almost didn't hear.

Would I? Somehow, I wasn't sure if he was speaking to me or to himself.

Aidan pulled on me harder. "Nora," he insisted.

"Then I guess in the end, I didn't stay." I couldn't stop the bitterness from seeping in. I was wet, cold, covered in mud, dirt, and who knew what else. My mood wasn't the best.

Damien's biting into my bicep loosened. "This isn't the end," he said.

Something stung with those words, something real.

Fear scored a hole in my chest, and I looked away, breaking the spell. Aidan pulled on me; I stumbled into Aidan but couldn't take my eyes away from Damien. I half expected the demon to tighten his grip once more. Instead, his fingertips trailed down my arm, leaving goosebumps in their wake. The fire in my stomach erupted, and I winced. Hot, white pain was so fleeting I had to wonder if I felt it at all.

"Why won't we find a way?" I repeated, shocked.

I glanced back at him as he stood alone in the center of the room. In that instant, he looked painfully lonely, and unable to help myself, I felt a tug of remorse. I hated myself for it, and it was brief, but I knew that I'd remember this.

"Damien? What aren't you telling me?" I asked, jerking free of Aidan's hand as he tugged me farther away.

"He's trying to trick you," Aidan whispered, though I wasn't entirely sure I believed him. As he pulled me around the table, I saw the crystal a hot red, fading once more to pink. It had flared when my back was turned. Warily, I kept my distance, remembering the blast that obliterated the mummy.

I started to shake my head, trying to focus. "Damien? Is there a way back?"

"It won't be like before," he answered, the threat lingering.

"Over here," Aidan said and turned my attention to the wall behind the slab. I followed his finger to where he pointed. A short, blue marble door appeared; it had been hidden behind the stone all this time.

Stepping before it, Aidan patted the large brass knob experimentally as if he expected it to burn.

I glanced over my shoulder one last time.

Damien was gone.

Doubt itched at the back of my mind, but I turned around in time to see Aidan open the tiny, familiar door, revealing the inky black.

He glanced up at me. "We're doing the right thing," he said, meeting my gaze.

I tried to nod, smile, anything to let him know that I understood. But I didn't understand. I was already feeling the strings of hesitation.

What if we couldn't find our way back?

Within the doorway, the tiny streaks of multi-colored lights flashed in their hollowed hole. It had never occurred to me until now that it might lead us nowhere. What if it just sucked us in and we were just as lost as our friends? Could that be what Damien meant? I checked over my shoulder one last time, wondering if perhaps he'd come back, but he didn't. Only the pink crystal glowed against the torchlight.

Turning back to Aidan, I croaked, "Let's go." There was only one way to find out.

"Don't worry, Nora. We'll get them back." The way he said it, the confidence, almost had me convinced. His hand was warm against my cold fingers. Our eyes locked, and I nodded. Better now than never.

He ducked into the door first, pulling me with him as he disappeared in the inky black. Crouching, I looked back just in time.

The cool, pale hands slid on either side of my face. I took one quick breath before Damien pressed the same cool, soft lips to mine.

Stunned, I was motionless at first.

My blue eyes were reflected in his dark ones. A

question erupted with a fierce heat, at least until I kissed him back. I felt Aidan's hand dissolve in the darkness; mine was still within the doorway. The darkness tugged, drawing me away from the Grave.

Pushing toward Damien, I couldn't say I was thinking. I just played off the queer emotions and the shock that somehow honeyed the fire ants. The smooth, rippling sensation was like warm water. It made me not feel like a dirty rag of a human being. I felt powerful, and the charge gained momentum with each kiss.

I could kick ass, I realized. I could take my friends back. The idea was delicious, even if impossible. Tongue grazing his, I tasted the dirt from my own mouth.

In that instant, I realized what I was doing.

Breaking the kiss, I jerked back, mouth still red and body still aching to grab him. "I…"

The half knowing smirk tugged at the corner of his mouth.

With that, he raised one hand and shoved me.

I lost my balance, and the darkness swallowed me whole. Damien and the Demon's Grave disappeared, and everything was numbed.

Chapter Forty-Two

Somewhere down a tunnel, far, far away, a garbled voice echoed. "She's…re…con…ness."

My legs and arms tingled, but I could feel them.

"She's been breathing on her own for the last twelve hours," a closer voice said.

I tried to feel for Aidan's hand, but instead there was something soft, like fabric. My body pained me from head to toe, and for an instant, I thought I was going to wake up in another nightmare.

Drifting closer to the surface of consciousness, I tried to force myself to wake up.

"Her eyes. Did you see? Nora?" It was Mom.

My eyelids were held down by sandbags, and I had to strain to peel them open into slits. It was bright at first, but eventually I could make out the white, tiled ceiling.

Turning my head, I saw Mom and then a nurse playing with a machine beside my bed. Everything was so damn white. No black, no darkness.

I breathed in, hearing the rattle. My throat was sore, and I reached up to touch it.

"It might be a bit tender," the nurse said warmly. "We had to put tubes down your throat. They're gone now, so don't you worry. We're just glad to see you back."

"It's okay, Nora," a voice said to my left.

I turned my head slowly; it felt as if my brain were coated in layers of cobwebs. A doctor, a petite African-American woman who I recognized, was smiling at me. "You're at the Leland Hospital," Dr. Clark explained.

I croaked, "Aidan?" It hurt to talk. Swallowing, I winced and was handed a flimsy paper cup half filled with water.

Dr. Clark said, "He's just fine. The two of you are really lucky."

Sipping my water, I shook my head before forcing myself to swallow over the flames in my throat. "Where's everyone?"

Mom's eyebrows furrowed, and her lips scrunched the way they had when she told me grandma had died. She was on the verge of tears, fighting, but dangerously close.

Reaching out to pat the top of my fingers—because my hand was shoved with needles—she said softly, "The police are looking for them." Mom's eyes darted to the doctor and nurse.

Dr. Clark nodded and motioned to the nurse. "We're going to be out in the hallway if you need anything, Mrs. Fuller." The two left the room, their clipboards in hand.

Mom looked at me with eyes brimming with tears.

"Oh, Nora, I thought I lost you."

"What happened?"

She wiped the corner of her eye with a tissue. "I was about to ask you the same thing. The police will want to talk to you."

I took another sip of my water and lied. "I don't…remember."

Mom's shoulders collapsed, and she muttered, "Aidan said the same thing."

Good.

"How long was I gone?" I asked. I knew I should probably stop talking, but the fierce curiosity wouldn't allow it.

"Three days," she said. "What's the last thing you remember, sweetie?"

I closed my eyes briefly then looked back at my Mom, contemplating what to reveal. I wasn't sure what Aidan had already said, and our stories had to be very similar to avoid the wrong questions.

"We went to sleep at that old house on Aidan's property," I ventured.

Frowning deeply, she pursed her lips. "Mr. and Mrs. Birket found you both on third floor of that old farm house. Apparently the two of you weren't waking up. So they called the ambulance. What were you all doing?" Mom was beginning to lose her composure. Anger swelled in her voice. "Was it drugs? Did anyone else show that you didn't tell us about?"

I patted her hand. "No, it was just us. No drugs."

She tried to smile but faltered. I could see she didn't believe me. "I'm not angry with you, honey. It's just…"

Suddenly, a glimmer caught the corner of my eye. Looking to the bedside table, I recognized the glass skeleton key. *From the Challenge!* Aidan had thrown it away. Why was it here?

Holding my breath, I averted my eyes quickly to avoid questions. "Where's the family?" I asked, referring to Dad and my two sisters.

She'd already followed my gaze to the key. "Home. We've been taking turns coming here." She picked up the glass. "Do you remember this?"

Timidly, I shook my head.

As she twirled it in her fingers, I could have sworn it glowed a pale pink before fading to clear. Eyes narrowing, Mom muttered, "They found this key in your pocket when they picked you up."

I stared at it and frowned. "Shouldn't the police have it?"

My mother's eyes glazed a bit. "They didn't want it. Said it was part of the house." As if snapping awake from a trance, she reached over and hugged me. IVs that were pinned inside my arms stretched with a twinge. "At least you're all right," she cooed and sniffled. "This amnesia is probably only temporary."

"Mom," I protested, feeling a buzz radiating the air and knowing instantly what it meant: Aidan was close. Just like before the Challenge, I could feel him coming.

Mom instantly released me and apologized several times before looking back over her shoulder and waving at someone to come in. "Whoever did this is going to pay," she said seriously.

Leaning on crutches in the doorway, Aidan smiled weakly at us. "Mrs. Fuller," he said politely. He was in regular clothes again, clean clothes with clean bandages on his forehead. His knee was covered in sweat pants.

That familiar buzz still electrified the air. My

stomach twisted, and my insides squirmed at the warning. Suppressing it with a smile, I tried to shove it aside. After everything that'd happened, I wanted it to go away; it didn't belong here with him. "How are you?" I asked.

He glanced at my mother. "A little shaken up," he said.

"Me too." I chuckled nervously.

Mom glanced between us before standing awkwardly and smoothing her clothes. "I should call your father. He'll want to know you're awake. He'll probably bring the girls." She cast Aidan a suspicious backwards glance as she passed him, but he didn't seem to notice.

Once she left, Aidan hobbled closer and sat in the empty chair by my bed. "Said anything?"

"Temporary amnesia. You?"

Aidan adjusted his leg while sitting and shook his head. "Let's just keep this Demon's Grave thing to ourselves," he said.

"Yeah," I sighed, and we smiled at the same time. It was a bitter, secretive one, but mutual in its understanding.

Aidan's leaned closer, and before I could move, he kissed my forehead. His warm lips stayed there for several seconds, tickling with the buzzing sensation that vibrated through my scalp. He jerked back and bit his lips together.

"Now tell me you don't feel that," I said huskily.

His eyes trailed to my lips before taking a deep, slow breath. "It's not like that—usually."

"I don't feel like I don't belong anymore?"

Aidan blushed and looked away.

The joke fell sour, and I glanced at the key that was left on the bedside table. "Guess it wasn't all in my head," I muttered.

Aidan's cheeks still flamed, he said, reluctantly looking at me, "No, but Damien was trying to manipulate us both into thinking we were enemies."

I didn't want to say that I thought it was Aidan who'd done most of that. "He never told me you were my enemy," I said instead.

Aidan stiffened. "Oh."

"What did he say to you?" I raised my eyebrows.

He shook his head.

Seeing the broken trust fragments, I said, "My aunt killed my sister. Her name was Nell, if you hadn't already guessed."

He finally looked at me. "She was with those two zombies?"

"They were men at the time, but yeah. I guess she sacrificed them to the Demon's Grave, but I don't know why."

"Where's she?"

"A high security mental hospital. She was the only one caught." I told him about the bonfire and how I was supposed to be thrown in first. I told him everything. We weren't in the darkness anymore. My promise to Damien seemed moot without me there. I only hoped that he couldn't hear us out here in our world.

When I finished, Aidan pinched the bridge of his nose and breathed in deep. "Christ."

Falling silent, I wasn't sure how I should react.

"The dream," Aidan released his nose and sniffled, "when Damien was talking to me. He said I should sacrifice you because you belonged to him, not me."

I raised my eyebrows, hoping he'd elaborate, but he said instead, "We have a lot to do." Aidan had trouble meeting my gaze. "The, uh, marble door is missing."

I wanted to twist at my shirt. I didn't move my hand and tried to absorb everything he'd said. I didn't belong here. That's what Aidan had said he felt about me, and Damien had played on that. He must have when he kissed me.

Swallowing loud enough to hear, I listened to the beeping instruments and murmurs from the hallway. Not a single noise could distract me from feeling his mouth, and I concentrated on blocking it out.

I squeezed my eyes shut.

There wasn't a doorway anymore. The Keeper had failed.

I reached back and plucked the key from the bedside table to show Aidan. Gripping the tip so the glass handle shone in the florescent lights, I turned it around in my fingers, much the way my mother had. The glass key flashed a color, but it was so quick it could have been a trick of the light.

Aidan grimaced. "How are we going to do this, Nora?"

Dismal is the Demon's Grave. Dismal and dark to what I crave...

Tilting my eyes to him over the shining key, I said reluctantly, "I have an aunt who knows how to make a portal."

MIDNIGHT RULING

Book Two

E.M. MacCallum

They weren't supposed to go back, and they weren't supposed to take innocent people with them. Damien is getting closer to the truth, and Nora realizes she has more enemies than friends.

Out Now!

ABOUT THE AUTHOR

E.M. MacCallum grew up in Southern Alberta surrounded by harsh winds, prairies, and wonderful people. She's an avid reader, writer, and random hobbyist.

You can find out more about her on her website: emmaccallum.com

Or follow/like on Twitter @EMMacCallum & Facebook: facebook.com/AuthorE.M.MacCallum